# NATURAL DUAL-MAGE

# Also by K.F. Breene

**DDVN WORLD:**

**FIRE AND ICE TRILOGY**
Born in Fire
Raised in Fire
Fused in Fire

**MAGICAL MAYHEM SERIES**
Natural Witch
Natural Mage
Natural Dual-Mage

---

**FINDING PARADISE SERIES**
Fate of Perfection
Fate of Devotion

**DARKNESS SERIES**
Into the Darkness, Novella 1
Braving the Elements, Novella 2
On a Razor's Edge, Novella 3
Demons, Novella 4
The Council, Novella 5
Shadow Watcher, Novella 6
Jonas, Novella 7
Charles, Novella 8
Jameson, Novella 9
Darkness Series Boxed Set, Books 1-4

**WARRIOR CHRONICLES**
Chosen, Book 1
Hunted, Book 2
Shadow Lands, Book 3
Invasion, Book 4
Siege, Book 5
Overtaken, Book 6

# NATURAL DUAL-MAGE

K.F. BREENE

# CHAPTER 1

"WHY DO I keep getting myself into these messes?" I ducked under a reaching branch and jumped over a fallen log. My feet pounded on the moist leaves as I sprinted down a wide pathway, zipping past the little painted doors and carefully written signs attached to the tree trunks. Soft afternoon light filtered through the heavy cloud cover overhead, lighting the deserted walking area.

Breathing heavily, I rounded a smooth trunk and paused, my hands out.

Somewhere on the other side of the narrow stream to my right, heavy boots crashed through the brush.

Reagan.

Somehow, she always got to patrol the safe areas, and I always ended up with a vicious creature chasing me through unfamiliar terrain. At least she wasn't laughing or calling me a coward for running away this time. That was something.

"Did you see it?" she called out.

"Shhh!" I batted my hand through the air, not car-ing if she could see the gesture or not. My heart rattled against my ribcage.

Yeah, I had seen it. Sitting up on a branch and looking down at me. At first it had looked like a grumpy old man with a serious case of the uglies, but it had transformed into something vile—a goblin with red eyes, protruding teeth, and a clumpy rust-red hat. I'd felt its magic weave through the beautiful natural elements around me as it raised its eagle-like talons and prepared to jump down and rip me apart.

I'd seen it and done the logical thing: run like hell.

Sure, I had experience now. In the two months since Reagan, Emery, and I had defeated the Guild and their hired goons, I'd trained like a madwoman, taking almost everything Reagan and Emery could throw at me. I'd also let Reagan talk me into five bounty hunter gigs that Darius deemed *safe enough*.

Safe enough if your partner wasn't a homicidal maniac.

Each time, she somehow managed to shove me into the line of fire. Then she'd take off, leaving me to essentially catch or kill the creature on my own. And each case had been harder than the last, with creatures the local Magical Law Enforcement (MLE) office either didn't want to handle, or couldn't.

I should've known better than to take this gig. Especially after the last one, where Reagan had led me into a dead-end alleyway, sprinted up a ladder, and proceeded to pull the ladder up and leave me for dead.

She'd thought it would build character. And while it had forced me to come up with pretty amazing spells so I wouldn't die, it had also dropped her onto my *people I should immediately cast out of my life* list.

There was exactly one person on that list.

So why was I in the middle of Ireland, in the freezing cold, being chased through a children's fairy village by a nasty goblin that killed people and then dipped its hat into their blood?

Because Ireland, that was why. Because I'd gotten a free trip to Ireland. Darius had even arranged a meeting of powerful potential allies around it, opting to meet in Northern Ireland rather than back in the States.

I was no longer sure any of it was worth it.

Palming my chest didn't slow my rampaging heart.

"I quit!" I yelled, chancing a glance around the tree again.

"It can't understand English," Reagan called out, moving around to look through the brush lining the stream.

"Yeah, right. And brownies make good house helpers. Sure."

"How was I supposed to know you'd piss off that brownie? I'd heard nothing but good things from the vampires."

"Consider the source." I looked up just in case the goblin had somehow hopped from branch to branch and now dangled above me, ready to pounce, rip a hole in my chest, and renew the crimson gloss on its disgusting hat. "I thought you said these things hang out near rocks."

"They usually do. They like ruins and castles best, especially the ones with a history of mass bloodshed. They feed on the negative energy."

"Then what's it doing in a toy fairy village?" Seeing nothing above me but a lovely pink fairy door—about six inches tall, wooden, and decorated with little wooden flowers and beads—nailed into the tree's trunk, I looked back again. A petite play well (I couldn't think of any other term for it) partially blocked my view. Instead of water, fake gold poured from the bucket suspended from the roof by wire, and the mini-slanting roof, head height, was covered in fake grass they were pretending was moss.

It was very cute. In fact, the whole place was adorable. Colorful little fake fairy doors were clustered on the trunks or at the bases of stumps. Tiny little wooden mushrooms and clotheslines decorated stoops or fake patches of grass near the doors, trying to convince children that the fabled creatures lived there. They didn't, of course. According to Reagan, real fairies were a few feet taller, lived in burrows like varmints, and liked to cause havoc.

I rubbed my hands together and blew. The hot air from my mouth cooled by the time it got through my half-numb fingers.

That was something I hadn't counted on—doing magic with numb fingers. It wasn't easy. Easier than trying it with gloves, though, so I had no choice but to risk frostbite.

"I have no idea," Reagan said, looking around. "I mean, besides the obvious. Killing tourists and such."

"I knew what you meant," I murmured. The pictures of people with parts of their bodies torn out, faces ripped off, and limbs shredded flashed through my mind, turning my stomach. I'd gotten a little better about not upchucking when I saw (or created) carnage, but the truly gory stuff would always be hard to handle.

Freaking Ireland and its majesty. I blamed it for seducing me into coming and taking this God-awful job.

"It's too still," Reagan said in a low hum, shifting again. The rustle from her feet reached me from a hundred feet away.

Which meant the Redcap goblin wasn't moving. Or else…

"These things don't fly, right?" I whispered, looking upward again.

"What?" she shouted way too loudly.

"*Shhhh!*" I spun around, just in case it was sneaking

up on me. A large stump bolstered a house made out of a tree limb, surrounded by little mushrooms, fountains, and seats, behind a sign that said "Queen Erica's Weekend Retreat" in sparkly purple letters. Beyond, a string draped between two trees, the festive papers attached to it flapping in the light, though horribly cold breeze.

"How in Fairy Godmother's underpants am I supposed to focus when there is so much cute going on around me?" I asked through clenched teeth, feeling a putrid sort of magic snake through the air.

"That's *exactly* what I was thinking. Why do you think I took this side?" Reagan said, her hearing annoyingly great. I was pretty sure that was a side effect of bonding her elder vampire boyfriend.

"Cute, as in, I want to go around looking at all of it. Not try to battle a bloodsucking monster intent on killing me." I brushed my hand against the trunk, collecting natural elements in an organized mass above me, ready to form them into a spell.

"These things don't suck blood, they just coat their hat with it and walk around looking stupid." The volume of her voice suggested that the goblin *could* understand English, and also that she was taunting it.

I blew out a breath, trying for calm, and thought about changing locations. It could hear me. It knew where I was. If it *could* somehow move without making a sound, it must be zeroing in on my location, choosing the weaker of the two magical workers in the area.

I was a powerful natural mage, a rarity in the magical world, and yet I was still more mundane than the other magical worker trying to look through the bushes like a goof. If I didn't have bad luck, I'd have no luck at all.

"You gotta go find it, or it'll stalk you and take you out from behind," Reagan yelled over.

"I know, I know." I took a deep breath, steeled my courage for the shock of a nasty goblin jumping out at me, which would happen in some shape or form (it always did), and carefully stepped away from the shelter of the tree. The thing's vile magic twisted around me, cringing from the elements gathered above my head.

With extreme effort, I boosted the wholesomeness and positivity of my mood, the effect drifting into the flowing, swirling energy in my magical bubble. Immediately, the goblin's magic pulled back even more, its corrosive effects diminished.

"You're a nasty little creature, aren't you?" I asked as I carefully placed my next step, slowly drifting into the clearing. I eyed the nearest tree trunk, carpeted with moss, sprigs jutting out of it like a twisted porcupine. Dead leaves caught in those tiny branches nearly obscured a little hole at the bottom.

Breathing heavily, I stalked closer, scanning the area

before narrowing my focus back to that hole. Prickles of warning rolled over my skin. Something had its focus on me—I could feel it. If it wasn't the goblin; it was something else just as dangerous.

"Does it change size?" I called out as quietly as I could, bracing for something to run out at me. I chanced a glance up, just in case. It had been in the tree a few moments ago, after all. After seeing me, it had transformed to its goblin form and scampered down so fast that I'd nearly peed myself.

"I've heard the really powerful ones can, to a certain degree."

"I saw it change shape from an old man to a hunched…goblin-like creature."

"Wow, you nailed that description. You should be a report writer for the MLE office."

I ignored her teasing. "It doesn't shift into anything else, does it?"

"Not that I know of."

"Why an old man?" I asked myself softly, scanning the area. Reagan shifted, and brush crackled under her heavy boots. "Would you find a way over here? It's here, not there. A little help would be nice."

"Nah. It's more fun when the mark chases you around."

My positive and upbeat mood withered. "How you have any friends, I do not know."

"Me neither. It's a mystery."

The vile magic continued to pulse in the air around me, filling my mind with images of ancient ruins, battles waged and lost, and dusty, wind-swept plains.

The last didn't make sense to me unless it was in a world other than this one, of which there were apparently two. The Realm, for magical folk, and the Underworld, for demons and the like. I hadn't been to either.

A slow exhale, and I was inching closer to that hole, pulling elements out of the mass above me and winding them into a loose weave. It was an attack spell starter weave—ready to be hurled at the enemy after I stuffed in another component or two. I'd devised this approach when training with Reagan so I could get closer to matching Emery's speed in creating rapid-fire spells.

"Don't jump out at me," I whispered, drawing closer to the hole as a furious tingling overcame my body. My legs started to tremble, and my Temperamental Third Eye insisted I brandish a sword and go on a killing rampage.

My Temperamental Third Eye, something much like intuition but a lot more persistent, had saved my life more than once. Even so, it had always been wonky, and after our huge battle with the Guild's hired thugs, it was downright screwy. The thing wanted me to be like Reagan, unhinged and ready to charge into a battle at any moment.

I now actively ignored it, lest I lose my grip on reality.

"Are you hiding in there?" I whispered, feeling the expectation around me rise. Feeling danger draw closer.

I dashed forward and kicked into the hole to clear the way before blasting magic in it.

Rustling sounded behind me.

I spun and threw another spell, green flying through the empty air. A single branch waved. Neither an old man nor a goblin was perched on it.

Dancing backward, I bent to look at the hole at the base of the tree. It gaped emptily up at me.

"Why'd you pick such a small hole to accost?" Reagan called over in a voice suggesting she badly wanted a seat and some popcorn with which to watch the show.

"Because things always seem to jump out at me, and to do that around here, it would have to be in that hole. I figured I'd beat it to the punch."

"Umhm." This would be when she put a few more popcorn kernels into her mouth.

I pushed her from my mind and crouched, turning in a circle. The branch above me waved to a slow stop. The wind worried the leaves on the ground, creating a tiny amount of movement. Everything else was still.

"That thing might not be silent, but it is very, very

quiet." Forcing myself to remember to breathe, I scanned the mossy trunks until my eyes landed on the messy branches reaching overhead. If that thing dropped down on me, I'd lose it. I would absolutely lose it. The only thing worse than the unknown jumping out at you like a bloody jack-in-the-box was it thunking down onto your head like bird poop.

"How many groups have tried to catch this thing, did you say?" I asked, getting another starter spell ready, knowing it could see me from its hidden location. I felt its eyes digging into my back. Its magic festering within mine.

*Kill. Soak. Ruin.*

Soak. It wanted to dip its hat in my blood.

"Your attachment to messed-up fashion is freaking cracked, did you know that, you miserable, buck-toothed donkey?"

Much to Reagan's dismay, I hadn't gotten any better at swearing. I couldn't, not with my mother around. She'd stayed in New Orleans after that last battle. Every time I *thought* of swearing, there she was, ready to lecture me. It wasn't worth the hassle for an f-bomb. It really wasn't.

I closed my eyes for a moment, trying to follow its magic back to the source. But it hung in the air around me, floating like fog, listless and lazy. I couldn't get a reading.

"Two groups," Reagan answered. "The first group was just assessing the situation. One of them lost an arm and bled out."

"Bled out…like bled to death?"

"Yeah. Died." She paused, probably to see if I'd ask another rush of questions, like why she hadn't shared that chestnut before I accepted the gig. "The next group was supposedly Ireland's best. Two guys and a girl. Tough as nails, I heard. As experienced as they come, and boasting a near-perfect capture record."

"They couldn't find it, or…?"

"Oh no, *they* didn't find *it*. The Redcap found them. That's what usually happens. People don't see it, they go wandering by, and it springs out at them and goes to work. A couple seconds is all it needs. Or so I was told by the local MLE office." I could imagine her waving a hand dismissively. "Stories always get bigger, and the enemy more extravagant, when someone fails." She paused for a second, and branches creaked overhead, gently swaying in the breeze that had kicked up. Freezing air slid across my cheeks, and my nose started to run from the intense cold. "Of course, one of the bounty hunters from the last team did get torn up pretty badly…"

Her voice trailed away and I stiffened. "Did he or she die?"

"Yeah. He didn't even get a chance to bleed out.

They dragged him out as the creature scampered away with its bloody hat. The other two wouldn't go back in. They were rattled. Said this Redcap is much more powerful than the rest of its kind." She huffed. "But like I said, stories always get bigger to justify a failure."

I clenched my teeth as I worked my way back toward more of the fairy stuff, the vibrant pops of color distracting among the muted greens and browns. The magic seemed thicker over here, pumping into the air in waves. The smooth trunks and bare branches didn't harvest any ugly old men, though. No large red eyes blinked at me from the soft shadows in the overcast day. Everything looked peaceful. Serene.

"It should be here," I whispered, frowning. I turned in a circle, my senses screaming at me. The source of the corrosive magic was in my vicinity. I could *feel* it.

But where was it?

"People just go wandering by, huh?" I asked quietly, my footfalls soft, my hands held out and ready. I couldn't feel my fingers. Magic twisted and boiled above me. My upbeat mood was long gone.

"Yeah. The MLE office says no one knows how the hell they missed it. One second it was all clear, and the next they were ambushed. But there didn't seem to be anywhere for the creature to hide."

"Hidden in plain sight," I said softly, trying to work out this problem.

A birdhouse on a stick, unpainted and constructed of faded wood, rose to my left, not nearly as fresh and cheery as the rest of the fairy village. Possibly it was a relic from the time before the village had been created as an attraction for the local children.

Next to it sat a little stone gargoyle-looking thing with a dopey smile, moss covering its head and shoulders, and a cheery red scarf wrapped around its neck in an effort to make it fit in with the surroundings. About ten feet beyond it, I could see another stump with a tiny door and little round stones leading to it. Off to the side, a miniature stone leprechaun lay back in its buckled hat and green coat.

I continued on, my teeth clenched and my spell ready. Shivers crept up my spine. The wind moaned.

The goblin's magic intensified. Came pulsing toward me in strong waves.

Confused, I stopped and then back-pedaled, feeling for the source of the magic. I stopped five feet from that gargoyle-looking thing with the dopey smile. And the deep red scarf. The color of blood.

*Hiding in plain sight.*

"You're positive it can't shift into other forms?" I asked in a hush, staring at the stone gargoyle. Feeling the potent, vile magic pumping into the air.

Stone eyes moved. Changed. Colorized.

Turned as red as the scarf.

My mouth went dry.

I worked a few final elements into my spell, preparing to blast the thing. I just needed to get distance between us before it launched at me.

Too late.

Stone crumbled away, revealing crusty, deep gray skin. Long, curved claws at the end of knobby, knuckled hands flew up. It pushed out of its crouch and jumped at me faster than I could flinch.

I didn't even have time to scream.

# CHAPTER 2

I KNEW ONE moment of blind terror before something body-slammed the creature from the side. Reagan. Her sword came up and flashed downward as they tumbled onto the ground.

She'd been across the freaking river! I hadn't heard any water splashing.

Stupid me. For a second I'd forgotten she could fly-hover with her nutso-powerful magic. Thoughts were slow in getting through my head.

The creature screeched and twisted, swiping a claw toward her face. She jerked back, her faster-than-human speed saving her.

"Fast fucker, aren't you?" I heard her say in a series of grunts. She hacked at its limbs with her sword, but the creature was on the move, twisting out from under her weight and springing up.

I shot out a stream of white survival magic. After that scare, it was on hand and ready to be used. The creature morphed into stone, one moment an organic, living thing, and the next a bristling stone creature that looked way more like a gargoyle than the dopey thing from a moment ago.

"Oh yeah, it can change shape, all right." My magic hit its stone surface and bounced off at an angle, catching a tree and burning a hole through its trunk.

"Oh-kay. That's a helluva trick," Reagan said as she thrust her sword at its middle. The blade clanged off the creature's belly and the Redcap morphed back into an organic being, launching at her with a growl. "Bugger!"

She jumped and kicked, her boot hitting it in the face and sending it staggering backward. I shot out another stream of magic, but the creature shifted back into stone as it tumbled across the ground, once again deflecting my efforts.

"Shizlefritz banana hammock," I ground out, weaving a more intense, highly powerful spell that should twist its head right off. It would be gross, but that thing and its crusty red hat had to go. "How the heck can it make its hat change into a scarf and back?" For some reason, that struck me more than the whole changing-into-stone thing.

I flung my hands forward as Reagan took a running leap at the creature, my spell getting to it just before she did. The spell splatted against the stone but wouldn't wrap around its neck. Unrealized, it fizzled back into the nature around us.

"Did you do that?" I asked her, frustrated and possibly suffering from cardiac arrest.

"You'll need to think outside of the box for this one," Reagan said before ramming into it with her shoulder and rolling across the ground. "Come back to normal, you filthy creature, so I can kill you!"

"Oh yeah, that approach will work, definitely."

And yet the creature bounded up, bucking her off. Its hiss emitted a putrid smell that made her hesitate for a moment, her eyes going hazy.

"Oh no!" I shot a trapping spell at it before following with a kill spell.

The creature stopped its lunge for her and snapped back into stone right before my second spell could make contact.

"Dang it, Penny, I would've had it." Reagan kicked the now-inanimate statue, catching it in the head and sending it cartwheeling end over end across the ground.

"How was I supposed to know? I thought you'd been stunned."

"Magic from creatures of the Underworld doesn't work on me." Her tone carried an implied *duh*. She ran after the creature, which had come to life again and was scampering up a tree.

"I didn't even know vampires existed a year ago." I sprinted after her. "How in Mary's cookie jar am I supposed to keep track of the magic of random creatures and how it reacts with yours *if you never explain anything?"*

"I just did." She caught up to it as it tried to scurry up a tree. She grabbed it by the ankle and swung her sword around.

As she should've expected, the sword clanged off stone. It dropped to the ground. Once there, it changed again, clearly not taxed by the constant shifting like a vampire or shifter would be. It slashed at her with its sharp claws.

She dodged and countered, just as fast, twice as vicious.

Her fist met stone. "Damn it. Stop with that stone crap."

This wasn't working. At this rate, it would wear us down until we were tired and making mistakes. We needed a Plan B.

I stilled, closing my eyes for a moment and racking my brain. The name of the game was to stop it from changing to stone. Which meant I had to somehow block it from using its magic.

The nature around me whispered its song, centering me in the moment. Fanning my magic higher. I let it balloon out then blossom, confident that Reagan would keep the creature occupied.

I felt what I was looking for, hidden within the natural elements. A strange sort of magic wove through it, turning certain wisps brittle. The differences between these rogue strands and the heavy fog I'd been feeling were minute, barely discernible, and the magic was slippery when I tried to tap into it. Evasive.

Like the creature. It refused to heed me.

This was a puzzle and I wasn't totally sure how to put it all together.

"Taking a wee nap, are you?" Reagan asked, then grunted.

Peeling up an eyelid, I realized she was talking to me. I also realized she had met her match when it came to speed and cunning. The creature dodged her attempt to sweep its legs out from under it before ducking under her left hook with a feral grin. She jabbed with her sword, only to hit off stone. She surged in to grab it, but when she made contact, it was once again an organic creature, and its claws swung up seemingly out of nowhere.

Air wrapped around the creature, her ice magic (I could never remember the Latin name) lifting it and then crashing it to the dirt. But stone was more durable than the rain-softened ground, and the battering did nothing more than dirty the creature.

It turned back into itself before striking out. She dodged and blasted it with fire. The flame washed across stone.

"That is the fastest shift I have ever seen," she said through clenched teeth. "I can't even burn it. What a crock."

Stone turned back to gray skin. "I will dip my hat in your blood yet." Its voice was deep and scratchy, like the words were scraped with sandpaper.

"You'll have to pull it out of your ass, first," she replied, facing it with her hand and sword out. "Because that's where I'm going to shove it."

"How does it withstand your magic?" I asked her, trying to figure out the riddle.

"It hits off the stone and just…slides away. I have never, ever seen a creature withstand my magic. Never. I can't feel any spells or anything. I can't fathom how it's doing it."

"I was given special gifts by the gods," the Redcap said as it tried to circle Reagan, looking for an in. This thing thought it could win. It was not worried. And if I knew Reagan, she shared its sentiment. "I am not like the rest of my kind."

"Well, aren't you suddenly Mr. Chatty. How'd you get up to see the gods? A great big ladder?" She dashed forward, faster than lightning. But not faster than the goblin. Her sword tip scraped stone.

"Try to rush it with your magic, not the sword," I said in exasperation. "And there are gods?" Something else no one had bothered to tell me.

"Killing it with a sword will be so much more gratifying." She hacked down onto the stone. "This. Thing."

She hit it with each word, putting all her strength into it. Venting. "Is. Pissing. Me. Off!"

Panting, she stepped back, staring down at its dopey smile. "Change back, bastard. I want another go."

It did as she said, and I caught a little pulse of power, like a subtle spark way down in the depths of the thing's magic. This was different from everything I'd felt before—this was what allowed the goblin to change.

"Got it," I whispered, letting my eyes drift closed and focusing.

"Allegedly, there are gods, yeah. Though some people call them angels. The hearsay is vague on that topic," Reagan said in a series of grunts ending in sword clangs. "Allegedly, I have strands of their lineage. Allegedly, you can only get to their kingdom of paradise through the dreamscape. Which you can only do if you are a Dream Walker, or guided by a Dream Walker."

"Why do you keep saying allegedly?" I monitored that little pulse of the creature's magic, feeling how it interacted with mine. I needed to coax it in so I could use it in a spell, but it was still evasive. Slippery. I couldn't get a proper grip on it.

"Because I have neither met a Dream Walker—they are *incredibly* rare—nor heard of anyone who has seen, screwed, or gotten rewards from a god. It's all a little far-fetched."

"All the crazy in your life, and you think that is a

little far-fetched?" I shook my head. "Think, Penny, *think*." I squeezed my eyes shut while struggling to open myself to the magic. Invite it in.

"Don't think…just do," Reagan said with strained words.

I just *did* earlier, and that hadn't helped.

My temperament was too even-keeled for this creature, that had to be it. This would work better if I shared Emery's personality—wild and unruly, reflective of the harsher sides of nature.

I could work with that.

"Fine." I rolled up my sleeves and immediately regretted it as the cold bit down on my skin. I yanked my sleeves back down. "You want it, you got it."

I thought of Emery. Of his strength and power. The force he could wield with his broad, powerful frame. I thought of his occasional mood swings, the death and sorrow he'd experienced in his life plunging him into the depths of torment. Of his rough hands moving over my body as he entered me with a forceful and deeply passionate thrust.

My face heated and I quickly yanked my line of thought in a different direction. I wasn't after X-rated memories just now, no matter how pleasant.

My magic boiled, turning and rolling above me. My mood blackened at the thought of what the Mages' Guild had taken from Emery. At what they had taken from me. My father, his brother, our freedom.

Anger surged, soon burning into rage. Despair seeped in on its heels. I had no idea how we would beat the Guild at their own game, on their home turf, something we'd soon need to plan and get underway. Fear rushed in last, the fear that our second break-in wouldn't go well. That I'd lose all that I held dear. All that I loved.

I let anxiety come crashing into me, blackening my mood.

Sure enough, a heavy dose of the goblin's magic came rushing in too, feeding on my turmoil. Delighting in my strife.

Nasty little door knocker!

I picked through all the elements, focusing on those rogue strands. Feeling out how to best hijack and manipulate them.

A pattern emerged in the shape of a series of feelings, pushes, and prods more than anything concrete. An ebb and flow of sorts.

"Got you!"

"Penny, look lively!" Reagan shouted.

I snapped my eyes open as the creature lunged for me, its eyes glinting in malice.

It had felt me messing with its magic. Connecting us.

"I got you, you little creep!" I pushed out my hands

as a surge of vicious magic dumped out of me. The weave nearly created itself, using some of Reagan's magic and a lot of the goblin's.

An invisible wall spread out in front of me, shimmering with magic that would zap the creature full of electricity when it hit. I waited for the goblin's spark, knowing the creature would sense the spell and turn to stone. I latched on to the spark as soon as I felt it, engaging in more careful analysis of what happened when the Redcap shifted to stone.

"I'll get it." Reagan rushed over and gave it a kick, making it skitter across the ground and slam into a little fairy door attached to a stump. The toy door cracked and fell off. "Huh. That was strangely gratifying."

"Don't break kids' fairy doors," I admonished her. "That isn't right."

"I'll just burn the stump. They'll never know."

"That is not the right answer to this problem!"

Reagan ran after the goblin as it turned back into its gross self. It blinked at me with those large red eyes twice before Reagan shot a stream of fire at it. I felt her complex weave, so perfect and tight that it barely made sense. Then came the goblin's little spark again.

"Ah ha," I whispered as the goblin's magic, in stone form, split Reagan's stream. In my mind's eye, I could see how Reagan's magic was being picked apart before the whole weave blinked and died. "Amazing."

"Not. Amazing." Reagan was battering the stone goblin with her sword again. "Really. Damn. Annoying!"

"Leave it. Try again," I said, still crouching, eyes closed. "Don't let it kill me."

"Hear that, you little stone bastard?" The clanging stopped. Reagan's footfalls indicated she was backing away. "Come out. I'm about to kill you."

"I am invincible," I heard in that scratchy sandpaper voice.

"You're a turd," came the reply, and the sounds indicated she'd launched at it again.

This time, I pounced the moment I felt the spark. I twisted the thing's magic and shoved it into mine, counteracting the dank, dark flow with pure joy and light. Dousing the spark with it. Foreign magic flowered inside me, strong and potent and powerful, unlike anything I had ever experienced. It crawled through my body, forcing the air from my lungs. Adrenaline dumped into my bloodstream as I gasped for air, but it was nothing compared to the ancient feeling super-charging my power and winding through my body. I stilled, feeling the lightness of it, the effulgence, as my power pulsed and surged, begging to be used in some grand fashion.

A victory shout went up somewhere in the distance. Light flared all around me. Magic and energy danced. I felt majestic. Invincible.

And suddenly it all dimmed.

"Penny?" I heard, a small sound at the end of a long tunnel. "Penny!"

Something slapped my face. Energy blossomed, and a weave somersaulted from me, attacking my attacker.

"Holy crap, what—"

My lungs burned, no air coming in. Feathers stuffed my head.

I felt so alive with this magic. The feeling was indescribable.

All the while, I was dying from asphyxiation.

A spear of white-hot magic punched through my center before expanding outward, turning colder with each passing moment. It mingled with mine—icy cold heat and light warring with the combination of my magic and the Redcap's—before fusing with it, rising through my middle.

A shock of magic roared through me. I convulsed, sucking in a huge breath of fresh, delicious air. I choked and gasped, sucking in another while blinking my eyes open.

Reagan was straddling me, a knee on either side of my body. Somewhere along the way I'd collapsed, sprawled out on the cold, wet ground. I could see the abject terror in the lines marring her pretty face. Her velvety brown eyes darted between my eyes, lips, and chest.

"I think I have a girl crush," I said hoarsely, my head still dizzy and my throat feeling scratchy and sore.

"I think I am going to bash your head in for scaring me. I don't like being scared. It's an annoying feeling."

"What happened?" I twisted to roll over so that I could get up—the moisture was seeping into my jeans—but she put a hand on the center of my chest, keeping me put.

"That's my question. What happened? Are you okay? Do we need to go to the hospital? I swear, Darius will absolutely kill me if I kill you, and I don't even want to get started on Emery. I'm confident I could take him, but it would be a wild ride."

"Since when do you babble?" I tried to slap her hand away.

"You're as weak as a kitten. Crap. I broke you. But how did I break you? *What happened?*"

I tried to gauge her with my gaze. She slowly pushed up to standing, stepped over me, and squatted again, hovering.

"Cut the apron strings, Mable, I'm fine," I said, rolling to my side and continuing to suck in lungfuls of air.

"I don't even know who you are right now. I mean, I like the change, because that's funny, but I'm worried you have brain damage. Do you have brain damage? Seriously, what is going on? You clearly solved the riddle of how to keep that nasty little creature from changing. I got my sword through it, *finally*, but then I turned around and you were lying flat on your back, not breathing. Did it somehow have the power to make you stop breathing? I didn't notice my air drying up, and usually I do."

I waved my hand in front of my face to stop the bombardment of words. "I don't like when you fret. It's unnatural. Fretting is my job."

"Yeah, I know. How do you think I feel? I didn't know I had it in me to fret. I hate it."

I huffed out a laugh before sitting up painfully and rubbing the back of my head. I'd clearly fallen on it first, somehow. Thinking back, I relayed everything I'd felt, including her magic surging in and balancing every-thing out.

"I'm pretty sure you saved my life," I finished, slow-ly getting to my feet.

She grabbed my arm and helped me up. "I felt mag-ic warring within you somehow. I panicked. Don't tell anyone."

"I'm in no position to judge—I panic all the time."

"It's funny when you do it."

"Great," I mumbled, my mood souring.

The Redcap goblin lay in a pile about thirty feet away, a sword through its middle and a pool of red around its body. A charred speck sat off to the side, still smoking.

"What happened there?" I pointed.

"That was its hat."

"Ah." I twisted to each side, trying to stretch my back. It felt like I'd run back-to-back marathons. "It had some extremely powerful magic." I put up my hands. I could still feel the power surging through my blood. "And it isn't dissipating. Usually when I latch on to someone else's magic, it's only while they're near me. And alive, obviously. This magic should be long gone." I widened my eyes. "Did you make sure it was dead?"

"Of course I did! I hacked the hell out of it. Vicious, yes, but warranted. It was a nasty little—Anyway, maybe it wasn't lying." Reagan's brow furrowed. "Maybe gods are legit and it…somehow…got a gift of power…from one of them?" She scoffed and shook her head. "That just sounds absurd. It's a goblin. Why would a god give a nasty little creature like that a gift of any kind? It was more deserving of a kick. Right to the head."

"Maybe the goblin killed whoever had the power first, and it somehow managed to ingest the magic." I ran my hand down my chest, feeling a strange tingling and lightness, like nervousness and butterflies and excitement, all mixed up. It didn't feel like it belonged. "I can't think how else this would be possible. Then again, I know next to nothing about the magical community, so…"

"This is a question for Darius. Regardless, you're alive, not still dying…" She lifted an eyebrow at me. I shook my head. The danger had passed; I could feel it. Whatever was going on with the magic wouldn't kill me. Not yet, anyway. "And next time, when a creature says something about power from the gods, we'll know how to handle it."

"No." I shook my head and about-faced. "No way. This was the last time. No more. I am done with these bounty hunter gigs. Absolutely done." I waggled my finger behind me. "You can call the cleanup people or whatever. I'm out."

"You don't have a car," she yelled after me.

I didn't even care. I'd walk in the cold. Anything to get away from her inevitable effort to talk me into another hunt. I really was done. Totally finished.

# CHAPTER 3

E MERY SAT IN a chair at the edge of a green field
dotted with occasional white specks, the last of the
snow from yesterday finally melting away. The temperature was still down near freezing, but the cold
couldn't permeate the blackness of his mood.

He sighed deeply and a cloud of white left his lips.
He'd jumped at the chance to go back to Ireland with
Penny. He'd follow her to the ends of the Earth if she
asked. His feelings for her had only gotten stronger.
And *would* only get stronger as they continued to weave
into each other's lives.

But he'd been assailed by bad memories of the time
he'd spent here alone. Of his life after his brother,
having to kill liberally to stay alive. Emery couldn't help
but wonder how different things would have been if his
brother had lived and *he* had died. Would Conrad have
been able to turn things around? Emery only knew how
to maim and kill, not save. He was a rogue, a recluse,
and he'd never be as easily liked as his brother had been.

He shook his head and reached for the glass of

whiskey resting in the grass next to the sinking leg of his chair. Not for the first time, a thread of guilt wormed through him. Penny deserved better than a guy like him. And he felt guilty for praying to God she never realized it, because he didn't know what he'd do if she left. She'd put the color back into his life. The depth. She was his anchor.

And if she were here right now, she'd tell him to stop dwelling.

He grinned and looked at his feet. She'd be right, too. Life felt better when you enjoyed the positive instead of lingering on the negative.

Soft footfalls reached his ears, somewhat quicker than a human would naturally walk. A moment later, he could pick out the rhythm of the gait and the careful steps. He was well versed on all things dangerous, and the approaching individual was one of the more dangerous things in the world.

Darius. A cunning elder vampire who was *way* too deeply involved in Emery's affairs.

Judging from the overcast sky and short days, he guessed it to be about four or four thirty in the afternoon. Evening had replaced the day.

Penny and Reagan would be finishing up with paperwork about now, Penny sour about whatever had happened, and Reagan likely filled with pride that her training buddy had come up with unique and airtight spells. The two of them were as effective as they were hilariously predictable. He got endless enjoyment out of listening to their squabbles.

"Black thoughts?" Darius asked quietly, setting down the chair he'd grabbed from their rental house across the road. Emery sat on one just like it.

"Just reflecting on my life choices." Emery took a sip of his whiskey and leaned back.

"Dwelling, as Penny would call it?"

Emery huffed out a laugh. The vampire couldn't actually pick thoughts from his head, but he was so good at reading body language, mood, and situational cues that it practically came to the same thing. "It's easy to blame myself for what the Guild has become. For years they were merely festering, but I resurfaced, raised havoc, and suddenly they're spreading like a virus. In just a few months they've claimed a couple dozen new cities around the world and a host of new talent. The mages who vocally oppose their methods are being slaughtered. If I'd left the whole thing alone, the darker magic wouldn't be spreading, and innocent mages wouldn't be in jeopardy. Penny would be so much safer. It's a lot to feel accountable for."

"Pardon me for a moment." Darius stood up and zipped off so fast that Emery had woven together a spell before realizing he'd been startled. Usually when an elder vampire moved that fast, he was two seconds from ripping out a throat. A moment later, though, Darius was sitting down again with a snifter filled with a deep brown liquid.

Apparently they were about to have a man-to-man chat. No doubt Darius would use it as an opportunity to glean information. You could never trust a vampire, and elder vampires were the worst kind.

Yet…Emery found himself leaning back a little more into his chair, interested in what the vampire had to say. Whatever else he might be, he was also incredibly intelligent and knowledgeable.

"Let's go over the facts, shall we?" Darius asked, crossing an argyle sock over his designer jeans. The vampire did nothing by halves, including dressing casually. "Before your brother's death, the Guild already had a firm hold over Seattle, and they had started increasing their scope."

"But they haven't done much in the three and a half years since my brother was killed…until now."

"This is true. Of course, organizations largely operate in fits and starts as their leaders change over. It was bound to happen sooner or later. You—and I—have ensured that it happened sooner."

"Dangling an untrained, naive natural in front of them really helped speed things up, yes," Emery said dryly, trying (and failing) to push away the surge of guilt. "It's their desire to obtain her that has driven this sudden focus, I have no doubt. I've put Penny in extreme danger."

"Ah." Darius swirled the brown liquid in his glass. "I think that is the root of the problem, is it not? The issue of Penny has been weighing on you."

Emery leaned his forearms onto his knees. He didn't comment. Darius had been subtle about it, but Emery knew the elder had been watching him. Cataloguing his actions and noticing his mood slips. The vampire filed away everything he saw into that incredible computer of a brain, puzzling out the patterns and working out how he could manipulate the present situation into what he planned for the future. Emery shouldn't give him any more fodder for his plans, but…

Well, when it came down to it, he wanted to know what the vampire had to say. Wondered if Darius had any wisdom to impart.

Emery desperately wanted to make this situation with Penny right. He wanted to dig himself out of this hole. If he had to temporarily get chummy with a vampire to do it, he would.

Darius paused for a moment, looking out over the field.

"We must remember, she had already stumbled onto magic when you first met her," he said slowly.

Emery huffed out a laugh. Penny's version of *stumbling onto magic* had involved turning a coven of witches into zombies. That woman could really unravel a situation. Like him.

"She was a ticking time bomb," Darius went on. He paused again, and it almost seemed like the words were being dragged from him. "Being an elder, I've largely shrugged off many things. The idea of each of us having one true mate, for example. Fate as a whole, actually. However…" He took a sip of his drink. "I've looked into what it means to be a natural pairing."

Ja, an extremely old vampire whose interest in Penny had forced her out of the bored stupor many vampires fall into if he or she gets old enough, had said Penny and Emery were a natural pairing, something Emery had heard was even rarer than natural mages. It meant Penny was the yin to his yang, and together they formed a balanced whole. That sort of natural affinity was different than the kind that could be achieved magically—something he'd shared with his brother.

Emery absently wiped at his chest, the familiar pang of loss cutting him deeply. He remembered what it had felt like when the dual-mage connection had been ripped out of him by his brother's untimely demise. Like someone had punched a hole in his chest, yanked out his ribs one by one, then used a dull knife to extract his heart. The feeling had spread throughout his body, flash-boiling his blood, crunching each bone, and twisting his guts. If the Guild hadn't tried to kill him that very night, he might've succumbed to the mental anguish. He might've let it take him.

His rage had saved him in the end.

Darius cut into Emery's dark reverie. "Further research has revealed that a natural pairing is actually not rare at all. It is widely believed that everyone has one. The rarity is that each member of the pairing should find each other. Some magical creatures can only love their natural pair, and in extreme cases, they can only produce offspring with that person or creature. In a huge population, it stands to reason that you would never meet the one 'destined' for you. This goes double for you, since you've spent so little time living amongst the human population over the last three years. The chances that you would meet your pair were so slim, they might well be classified as miraculous."

"Except…" Emery scratched his nose. "I'd have to think that a natural's pairing would be another natural. Which means there would only be so many options for me."

"Interesting assessment." Darius's thumb tapped his glass. "Meaning…instead of being a human with magic, you are reduced down to your own subset of species, a natural." He shifted and his brow furrowed. "Be that as it may, and we cannot know if there's any truth to it until I look more thoroughly into the matter…"

Emery grimaced. Any entanglement with an elder

was bad, but long-term entanglement was parallel to entrapment. And here he was, giving the elder new information to digest. That would just give the vampire more ideas.

"Anyway," Darius went on, "even if it was because you were naturals, there are a few other naturals scattered around the world, and you never planned to have a connection with any of them. Yet you were brought face to face with your natural pairing when you took an unplanned day trip into a medieval village to waste time."

"Except I left with nothing but her name that day."

"Only to have her miraculously find you in the middle of a magical battle. And the only way she knew to go to that magical battle was because her curiosity had been piqued by her foray to New Orleans the month before."

Emery shook his head. He was losing the thread of the conversation. "And... So what's your point?"

"Despite my personal beliefs about fate, an unbelievable series of coincidences have led you and Penny to this exact moment. From one stop on the journey to the next, even a nonbeliever like me would shake his head at all the connections that brought you here. She came out of her shell at just the right time. She was primed to meet you when you showed up."

"Sounds far-fetched."

"Yes. But if it hadn't been for you grabbing her when you did, she would've done something to out herself. Of that we can be sure. Without proper magical protection, she would have been picked up by the Guild. If we go a step further, the Guild would've trained her the way they train everyone. How *you* were trained. They would've squashed her truly unique way of doing magic, and thereby diminished her ability. If not for you, she would be a shell of herself."

Emery blinked as the words rambled to a stop. "So…you think I actually saved her, instead of dragging her into this mess?"

"I think that is evident." Darius's tone wasn't just confident, it was full of the kind of certainty of a scientist who's just proved a theory. "As I said, fate is largely preposterous, in my opinion, but in this one situation, I can't help but…" An uncomfortable expression crossed his face.

People who valued knowledge and strategy didn't much like the idea that things were out of their control. Emery wasn't a control freak to nearly the same degree as Darius, but he understood—and felt—his discomfort.

"Only fools believe in coincidences," Emery mumbled. "I think Ms. Bristol said that once."

"In this case, I would have to agree."

"Still seems far-fetched."

"Even if they were coincidences, it has to be

acknowledged that her magical journey was already underway when you met her. She ran from what happened in New Orleans, but that wouldn't have kept her away from magic for long. She would've sought out knowledge in her area, which would eventually have led her to the Guild. You know what would've happened next."

"The Guild would've pieced her parentage together, just like they did after she showed up at my magical battle."

"Without you and your connections to shelter her, she would not have stood a chance. Either way you look at it—fate or logic—you crashed into that girl's life in the nick of time. Had you come earlier or later, you would've missed your opportunity, and her future would've been bleak."

Emery blew out a breath, something warm infusing his chest. He'd gotten there in a roundabout sort of way, but in the end, Darius had known exactly what to say. How to view the events that had unfolded. Looking at it that way, he could hardly deny the vampire was right. And Emery's guilt wasn't such a constant pressure on his shoulders.

"So you see, Mr. Westbrook," Darius said softly, back to swirling his drink, "you are actually that girl's knight in shining armor."

Emery laughed and sat back. "You had me, and then

you lost me."

A small grin lit Darius's face. "Be that as it may, we're here now. However it happened, this is where we are. Rather than dwelling on the past, we must look forward to the future."

Shivers spread over Emery's skin, and it wasn't from the cold.

"You are already a natural pairing," Darius said conversationally, "and have a deep connection you tried to run from and could not." Emery swallowed into the pause, dreading what he knew would come next. "Have you thought of becoming a dual-mage pair?"

# CHAPTER 4

A LL THE BREATH left Emery's lungs. Yes, he'd thought about it. All he'd done was think about it. Every time Penny curled up in his arms, the idea ran through his mind. Every time she defended him to her mother. When she gave him her sleepy smile. When she whispered that she loved him. When he looked at her beautiful face. When he laughed at her hilarious antics…

He wanted to offer her forever. He wanted to give himself to her, in his entirety, to do with as she would.

But each time the words surfaced on his tongue, the memories would resurface: throwing up from the pain. Blacking out. Wishing for death.

"I can't do that to her," he said, emotion choking him. "I can't, in good conscience, tie her to something that could possibly deaden her inside. I can't protect her if I form a dual-mage pair with her."

"But you've told us that, should the worst happen, we should save her over you," Darius said. "Very few would make that sort of pact, especially with a vampire.

Correct me if I am wrong, but haven't you already decided you'd give the ultimate sacrifice to protect her, whether she's your dual-mage or not?"

"I know what it's like to lose a magical partner. If we become dual-mages, my death would give her incomprehensible pain. If she survived, which you'd likely ensure, she could very well go insane. It has happened in the mage world more times than you can count. And if she didn't, she would walk through life with a hollowness I can't even begin to describe." Emery rubbed at his chest before downing the rest of his whiskey. Heat prickled his eyes as he imagined the most precious person in his world having to go through what he'd endured. He shook his head. "No. I can't do that to her."

"Ah." Darius sipped his drink. "And this is what you are really thinking about, out here in the cold, stark emptiness."

Emery frowned down at the ground. This was getting a little poetic for a man-to-man talk. And he didn't even want to think about what it meant that he'd chosen to bare his soul to the soulless.

He needed to reassess the choices he made in life.

"It is common to think our beloved needs a better man than we are capable of being," Darius said, looking out over the fields. "I am not a man at all, not anymore, and I have felt that same way. But the truly courageous look past their fear."

"Looking past my fear won't help Penny."

"I wasn't speaking of you. It is Penny who needs to decide. Who needs to weigh the risks. Just as Reagan did in bonding a creature that history has deemed the very worst sort. We can but pose the question. They must choose their path."

"Penny would go for it in a heartbeat."

"Then trust her."

"She doesn't understand the risks. She has no information to pull from. She'd make the decision solely based on her feelings."

"She has always gone on feelings, and it has made her great. How would this be any different?" Darius was back to swirling his drink. "I will tell you what I told Reagan, because it will be just as true in your situation. I trust you will keep it to yourself." His tone, deceptively light, hinted at a very real and dangerous warning. Shivers coated Emery's body. "The dual-mage connection would only enhance what you already share. Your love wouldn't deepen, but you would have another way to explore each other." He turned and looked Emery dead in the eyes, which was extremely awkward, given the intense conversation they were having. "What if she died today? What effect would that have on you?"

A shock of pain bled through Emery, followed by helplessness. He knew exactly how he'd feel. In his down periods, he often had nightmares of losing her. He knew that would emotionally be the end for him, and it horrified him to think of what sort of person would rise from those ashes.

"She has loved you from the beginning. She waited for you even when it seemed hopeless, even when she had available suitors eager for her attention," Darius went on, clearly seeing the answer on Emery's face. "Do you honestly, in your heart, believe denying her a dual-mage connection would save her from completely unraveling should you die?"

He was talking about hearts now. Guys didn't talk about hearts in these things.

Emery shifted uncomfortably, but the vampire didn't back off. He continued to stare with that intense gaze, making things even more uncomfortable. For a creature that was excellent at reading body language, he was sure missing the mark on this one.

"Think about this, as well," Darius said. "If you refuse the connection, you will prevent her from reaching the next level of magic. A level you will certainly need if you take on the Mages' Guild. In trying to protect her, you are placing her in graver danger. You fear for her, and that is commendable, but it is still *your* fear, not hers—and in your fear, you are taking the decision away from her."

Emery stood from his chair and gripped the back.

He knew Darius was manipulating him. That was what elders did, after all: they moved people around like pawns. Darius had an ulterior motive for wanting Emery and Penny to become dual-mages, and he was going to try and work Emery around until it happened. But he was also right. Emery *could* give Penny that next level of power. And he could prove, in a magical way, that he wanted her forever.

An image flashed through his mine: Penny drooling, her head cocked to the side and her eyes staring at nothing. His gut twisted and his heart wrenched. He knew someone who'd looked like that after losing his dual-mage partner. It had been a love pairing, too. And it had broken the surviving mage. Broken him beyond repair.

"The ladies are back," Darius said softly, collecting his chair and heading back to the house. "And by the sound of it, they had an adventure."

"What else is new?" Emery's throat was tight and uncomfortable. Even he could hear the effect it had on his voice.

He stared out at the field in front of him, knowing he should probably hang out until he managed to shake off the pallor. But the desire to see Penny's blue, sparkling eyes and beautiful smile called to him.

Filling his lungs with sweet yet biting air, he hefted his chair and followed Darius back to the humble farmhouse nestled between the green fields.

"If you'd told me five years ago that I'd be getting love advice from a vampire one day, I would've laughed in your face," Emery said, hearing shouts coming from inside the house.

Darius stopped at the closed door. At least Reagan hadn't angrily kicked it in. That meant they'd gotten their mark. "There are stranger things, I can assure you," Darius said somberly. "Much stranger. I am living them."

Emery didn't have time to wonder what that meant, because Darius opened the door and the yelling rushed out.

"You're lucky you're in the inner circle, or I'd be forced to kill you," Reagan said, standing by the worn kitchen cabinets with Emery's bottle of whiskey in hand.

"How are you going to kill me? I know how to stonewall your magic." Penny's face was red and laced with wary anger. She stood next to a pulled-out chair at the four-person kitchen table.

"By strangling you with these bad boys, that's how." Reagan lifted her hands, the whiskey bottle still in one of them, with a dead-serious expression on her face. "Besides, you can only stonewall me half the time."

Penny's eyebrows lowered slowly. Magic started collecting in an organized mass above her head.

"Don't even think about it," Reagan said in a low tone. "Don't even think about trying to blast me with something."

The magic continued to collect.

His dark mood evaporating like water on the baking cement, Emery felt a cockeyed smile drift up his face as he leaned against the doorframe. Penny and Reagan were each capable of wreaking havoc in their own right, but get them together and they were a wild display of fireworks. He loved watching it.

Reagan peeled a finger away from the whiskey bottle. "Don't."

"You always say practice makes perfect." Penny started a weave, the magic crackling strangely. Emery couldn't make out the spell's purpose.

"Do you really want to go there?" Reagan asked, setting the whiskey bottle down slowly.

"Ladies, this is not the right place for this," Darius said in a melodic voice.

"That is very pleasant," Penny whispered, and sparkling new magical threads wrapped into those already established, the weave tight and graceful. The effects would be vicious. Emery knew how Penny worked. The nastier the spell, the more pleasant the counterweight she used to balance it.

"Do not help her, Darius," Reagan said between clenched teeth.

Penny flung the spell forward. Immediately, Reagan's magic started to dissolve it away, unseen to Emery's magical eye. Except...

Reagan gritted her teeth and furrowed her brow as Penny's spell regenerated. Slower, but still moving, it drifted toward Reagan.

Emery pushed off the doorframe and centered his weight, unsure of what had just happened, and why Reagan was standing there as a vicious spell drifted toward her.

"What's happening?" Darius said, his voice taking on a rough edge. His frame tightened, and Emery could tell the vampire was wondering if he should engage, too. This was clearly a standoff of some kind, and an extremely dangerous one. It wasn't like their usual disagreements, which never had any teeth.

"You better move, or that spell is going to burn off your face," Penny said with a smug smile. She leaned back on her heels.

Reagan's brows lowered. Without warning, she rushed forward, charging through the spell. Heat flared, and then fire exploded in her face and ignited her hair. Not slowing, she grabbed at Penny.

"Fizzing blackjack sand dogs!" Penny jerked right, just missing Reagan's grabbing fingers. She sprinted for the door. But Emery was standing in the middle of it, and couldn't get out of the way in time.

"I still have my hands," Reagan yelled, in hot pursuit. She must've launched through the air and hit Penny square in the back, because Penny barreled into Emery, knocking him out of the door.

He grabbed Penny and maneuvered her so his body would cushion her fall.

"Crispy donuts, Emery, you're harder than the ground," Penny said in grunts as she struggled to get away from him and Reagan, who'd piled on top of them.

Reagan rolled to the right, ripping Penny with her.

"Now do you see?" Reagan said, locking her long legs around Penny's middle and her arm around Penny's neck. "I don't even need magic. Now what?"

Penny struggled, trying to get her elbow around to do damage, but she was well and truly stuck. Magic collected again, but before it could shift into a weave, Reagan squeezed her legs and arm, squishing Penny's middle and cutting off her air.

"I could crack your neck right now, Ms. Natural Mage," Reagan said, shaking Penny a little. "Crack it in two. Say uncle."

"No! Reagan—" Penny tried to get an elbow around, but couldn't find any body parts to hit. She scratched at Reagan's arms. "Uncle. Uncle! You don't need magic!"

"All right, then." Reagan released her, letting Penny

tumble to the side.

Darius stood in the doorway with a straight face and keen eyes. "What is this about Penny's magic nulling yours, Reagan?"

# CHAPTER 5

E MERY STEPPED IN front of me, blocking me from Reagan and Darius. He was giving me time to get back onto my feet. Magic rolled over and through his body, wild and unruly. His tall, broad body flexed, exuding raw power and strength. Electricity surged between us as our magic mingled and ignited, unfurling around us in fits and starts.

I sighed in contentment, feeling my tight muscles relax. A graceful feeling of complete balance poured through me. I loved how it felt when our magic mingled.

"Penny ingested a Redcap's unheard-of ability to shift into stone," Reagan said, getting to her feet agilely. "That ability somehow protected the Redcap from my magic. When Penny took it, I was able to kill the Redcap. Unfortunately, for some reason, the magic then tried to kill Penny." She put her hand up, staring at Emery. "It's fine. I sorted it out...somehow. But it appears the magic has stayed with her, and she can sometimes nullify my magic."

Darius shifted, the slight movement drawing Reagan's notice.

She shrugged. "I don't know how, either. The filthy goblin said the magic came from the gods, but who can trust goblins?" Reagan palmed her bald head, then felt down to her eyebrow-less forehead. "Kind of a dick move, making me go to the big meeting tomorrow with no hair. I'll be a laughingstock."

"You're the one that rushed through the spell," I said in a scratchy voice. I put my hand to my throat, wondering if it was all the yelling that had affected my vocal cords, and let Emery help me up.

"Excuse me…" Darius paused, looking between Reagan and me. It wasn't like him to be at a loss for words. "What is this?"

"Let's move this inside," Reagan said, heading for the door. "I'm hungry. Darius, are you cooking?"

"Are you okay?" Emery asked me, sliding his hand along the small of my back.

"She's not great at breaking news to people." I closed my eyes and exhaled, savoring the warm tingles that spread through my body at Emery's touch. Heat infused my middle. "I'm fine, really."

Reagan and I gave the guys details while Darius cooked up some Irish staples—sausages, beans, rashers of bacon, and some delicious potato pancake things. Midway through the story, we moved to the table and finished it up while we ate the feast, though, by silent agreement, Reagan and I skipped the part where she'd freaked out over my refusal to do another bounty hunting gig. Darius and Emery both stared at me, Darius with a blank face and Emery in confusion.

"Since when does a goblin shape shift into stone?" Emery asked, pausing in eating a piece of sausage.

"Good question," Reagan said with a full mouth.

Darius's head shake was slight, but he didn't comment.

Reagan caught it, stopped eating, and narrowed her eyes. "Do not keep us in the dark on this, or Penny and I won't give you any other details…about anything."

It was a bluff. I was terrible at keeping secrets, and even worse at lying.

"I have never heard of a Redcap with that ability," Darius said, his eyes rooted to mine. I could practically see the wheels turning in the velvety depths. "In times of great strife, I have heard of select individuals being blessed with a gift of magic or power from the gods, entities that are basically equivalent to humans' stories about angels. The blessed individual is usually exemplary in some way, working toward the betterment of all. Working to end the strife, whatever the strife may be." Darius turned his gaze to his hands, clasped on the table. I could just barely see the crease form between his brows. "It is a rare occurrence…" His voice drifted away.

"He's going through that giant memory of his," Reagan said, leaning back and putting a hand on her stomach. "That was good. I like the food in this country. *Meat!*"

"Yes." Darius nodded slowly, still looking at his hands. "The gods' magic is transferable in some respects. The power diminishes somewhat, but it is possible to take the magic into oneself by force, or for it to be given as a gift."

"There's no way that Redcap received a gift. No way," Reagan said with raised eyebrows. "It was a nasty little creature."

"By force, then." The crease in Darius's brow deepened. "I have not heard of someone being blessed in…years. Years upon years—"

"That means, like…five hundred or more," Reagan said, and finished her cup of tea. "He's over a grand old."

"As soon as it was learned that the magic could be transferred," Darius went on, locked in a recital of information and ignoring her, "those who received the boon were quickly found and destroyed for what they possessed so as to gain the magic. Anyone rumored to have the magic became a target. For this reason, the gods withdrew their generous hand, including the gift of Dream Walking, which allowed magical folk access to them. They closed their gates to outsiders, as it were. Now, as far as I know, the Dream Walker ability can only be passed down genetically. That is why it is so incredibly rare."

He blinked a few times, looking up at me. Studying me.

Emery bristled and laid a warm and reassuring hand on mine.

Darius's smile was slight. "Have no fear, Mr. Westbrook. The godless do not have the ability to harness the magic of the gods. She is safe from me."

"Can I harness it?" Reagan asked, raising her hand. She looked at me. "I'm not saying I'm going to kill you for the magic. But in the event I kill you for some other reason, I want to know if I can reap the rewards of your magical, goblin-stolen gift."

"I didn't steal it," I muttered, uncomfortable about this whole conversation. About what it might mean.

Reagan must've seen it. "We have no idea if this is true," she said, leaning toward me. "Darius has been known to pick up information from books and pass it off as though he lived it. When it comes to things that happened that long ago, I honestly think he gets confused. And we all know people who write books just want to spout off. It's not all true."

Darius studied Reagan for a moment, his eyes dulling, indicating he was back to sifting through his memories. If he'd heard her dig, he didn't show it.

"No, I shouldn't think you could use the magic, Reagan," he said. "The human myths on angels have such a strong likeness to the gods that it is almost as if the gods walked among the humans. I'm not sure why magical creatures shifted to thinking about them as gods—"

"Stick to the topic at hand, please," Reagan said, rubbing her temples.

Darius's eyes fluttered, as though he were coming out of a trance. "Yes, of course. As I said, the human myths on angels are pretty accurate, and one of those is that angels are at odds with Lucifer's realm. That would mean you are forfeit."

"Okay, sure, but my mother's lineage stems, in part, from a god." She held up two hands. "Don't get me wrong, I think this is all a little far-fetched"—she pointed at me—"I told Penny that earlier. But just for shits and giggles, wouldn't I get to play with the godly power since I am…some part god?"

Emery cocked his head at her. "How were you able to keep your pedigree a secret this long?"

"I was kept apart from society at an early age by a woman much better at staying hidden than I ever will be."

Darius glanced between Reagan and me before shaking his head. "I don't know. I'd have to research further. I was a young vampire when I came upon this knowledge, in the middle of some tumultuous times. The memories are not clear."

Reagan tightened her lips as she gave her knowing nod. "So we really have no idea what crazy power Penny stole from the goblin."

"I didn't steal it, I just…cut the goblin off from it for a moment. I think." Something occurred to me. "But it stands to reason that godly—or angelic, I guess—magic would null the magic of the Underworld, right? As its opposite?"

"For every spell, there is a counter-spell," Emery said as though reciting it.

Darius was staring at me, and his eyes sparkled in a way I did not love. I could tell he was eager to learn more about this new facet of an already prized asset (me).

Thin strands of anxiety crawled up my spine. I wasn't just in danger from the Mages' Guild, I was in danger of my world being controlled by an extremely intelligent, strategic vampire who was always *way* ahead of me. I needed to deal with the Mages' Guild and get out from under his thumb.

If only it were that easy.

Emery pushed back his chair and took our plates to the sink. "What happened today might not have anything to do with godly power," he said. "As Reagan said, it seems far-fetched. If the gods stopped giving gifts of power many generations ago—which they must've, because I've never heard of this—then it is hard to believe the power would be found in a goblin, of all things. Regardless, this changes nothing. We need to focus on what comes next with the Guild."

Darius cocked his head, and a small smile played across his lips. "I wouldn't say it changes nothing. For one, if she does possess a magical gift from the gods, she will have an incredible asset with which to take on the Guild. Secondly, the target on her back right now will be *nothing* compared to the price on her head if this were to get out." Darius's eyes glimmered. "Third..." His smile grew. "She would be the key to unraveling the Underworld."

Emery bustled me out of that room so fast that my head spun. "We need an exit plan," he said when he got me upstairs to our shared bedroom.

Only the four of us were staying at the modest farmhouse in the middle of Ireland, located about an hour away from the recent bounty hunter gig. Darius had thought it best that we keep a low profile, which meant not including his super-pretty, well-dressed, and fast-moving entourage.

Moss, Marie, and the rest of his usual group awaited us up north in a place called Derry. That was the set location for the high-powered gathering the next day.

"There is no point in leaving now," I said as Emery shut the door. He didn't bother locking it, since vampires could magically pick locks. Instead, he slapped a ward across the wood that would alert us if anyone came through. "We'd be hunted down. Besides, we need him to confront the Guild."

Once the shades were pulled, Emery turned to me, his deep blue eyes lost to the shadows in the room. He moved toward me slowly, deliberately, not bothering to switch on the light.

The fire of expectation sizzled up my skin as I took in his handsome face, with his sharp cheekbones and full lips. His touch whispered across my body.

"I'm not sold on the godly power idea, but one thing is certain... you were able to null Reagan's magic," he whispered, running his palms up my arms and stopping at my neck. He ran a thumb along my jaw. "That makes you even more important to Darius. He's mentioned some wall in the Underworld that keeps non-demonic creatures out. He thought maybe you and I could crack it. That was before this new situation." His hot breath dusted my face. I saw his smile in the dim light. "How do you get yourself into these messes?"

His teasing tone loosened my shoulders, and the sensation of his hands sliding over my shoulders and onto my chest set my heart to thumping.

"It's a gift," I said with an answering smile and a

sigh, knowing by now that he didn't hold my constant weirdness and abnormal…everything against me. Often he relished in my unique way of doing things. I exhaled and dropped my head back. He yielded to my silent demand and skimmed his lips along my neck. "I was just trying to solve the problem of how we could stop that creature from constantly shifting to stone." My eyes fluttered shut as he lightly sucked in my fevered skin.

His palms slid down my hips before drifting inward, toward my pants buttons. "You had a close call. Hearing about it scared me. Reagan had assured me you were never in any real danger on those bounty hunter gigs."

I huffed. "I'm *always* in danger. She thinks it's hilarious."

"I saw her expression." He swallowed hard and his hands stilled. He leaned his forehead against mine. "She didn't think it was funny this time."

"When she worries, she works miracles. Honestly, it was fine. I'm sure I could've figured it out before the end. She just got there first."

He shook his head, making quick work of the rest of our clothes before backing me toward the bed. "I'm overbearing, I know that. I just—"

I laughed. "Have you forgotten what I grew up with?"

His kiss curled my toes, deep and intoxicating. "I don't want to lose you, Turdswallop," he said softly.

I used a made-up swear word *one* time, and suddenly it was the joke of the century.

"What if I did accidentally steal the godly gift or whatever?" I asked in a small voice, wrapping my legs around him as he lowered me to the bed. "I mean, I don't mind gifting it away if it's going to cause a problem, assuming someone can tell me how to do that, but won't the gods be pissed?"

He pulled one of my knees higher on his hip before settling low. His next movement pushed away all of my thoughts and worries, stilling me in the moment.

"We'll figure it out, Penny," he said, confident and sure. When he wanted to, he could handle anything, I was sure of it. "Whatever happens, we'll figure it out. I won't let anything happen to you."

I relished in the feeling of him, winding me higher until I arched and panted his name. But the escape would be short-lived, and I knew it. Tomorrow, we would meet a couple of huge powers in the supernatural world, and soon thereafter, we'd declare war on the Mages' Guild and their secret vampire allies.

The time for learning my craft was over. Now it was time to use it.

# CHAPTER 6

"WHAT'S UP, GODLY One?" Reagan said the next day with a smirk. She had on a new pair of leather pants without one scuff, ending in heavy black boots that had been used to kick in more than one person's teeth. A fanny pack encircled her waist, filled with empty casings that she pretended contained spells so as to hide her magic. On top of it all, she wore a lovely green silk blouse that looked absolutely ridiculous with everything else, especially since she'd lost her hair and eyebrows to my spell last night. She was an odd specimen, but she couldn't care less.

"Not appropriate," I said through mostly closed lips, looking around to make sure no one was within earshot. I adjusted my tailored suit jacket for the hundredth time and smoothed my black slacks down my trembling legs. Marie still bought my clothes for me, and she had such great fashion sense that I didn't protest.

We'd walked into the beautifully renovated stone building like we belonged there, and now we were leaning against the wall, watching as human office workers in suits or business casual attire strolled by on their way home or elsewhere. We had time to scope it out while we waited for Emery and the vampire crew to park the car.

"You stole from a god." She snickered. "And I thought I had a dim future."

"You'll have no future if you—" I pressed my lips together. Smack talk wasn't my thing. I couldn't sell it. Especially not to Reagan, who would take those words as a green light to beat me over the head with her shoe, or whatever else she had handy. "Does Darius own this building?"

Reagan's brow furrowed as she looked around the leafy plant next to her. On my side there was an entrance to a small cafe, still open to catch those needing a boost before they started their commute home. Beyond it, a large man stood at a larger desk, watching everyone with acute focus.

"No," she said. "He hasn't said who does, but I can feel when he owns something, and not just because of his owner's pride. He knows the person who owns it, though. He was checking everything out with serious interest."

"He didn't say who?"

"No. Which means I won't like whoever it is. I have a few ideas."

Their relationship was exhausting, but there was no

denying they were made for each other. Nobody else would have them.

"Too bad, though," she said softly, looking around the spacious lobby. "This is a cool building in a freaking awesome city. That old stone face on the outside was fantastic. And the huge wall around here, with the cannons? It's my kind of city. I'd love to spend more time here."

I completely agreed. Located in Northern Ireland, which was actually part of the United Kingdom and not the Republic of Ireland, Derry was famously surrounded by a giant wall, two people high and over ten feet across. Cars entering the city had to go through old gates, some of the openings so small that people entering and leaving had to take turns going through. Back in the days when the walls were used to keep attacking enemies at bay, the city had never been breached.

"Roger brought someone," she said, eyeing the front doors. Roger was the Alpha of the North American shifter pack, which oversaw all the other packs in that territory. I knew that he and Reagan had suffered some…differences of opinion in the past, but I'd never actually met him before. "I didn't get a name, but Darius accidentally dropped a few hints. I think it's the Alpha of the European pack. An American who's as hated as he is feared. He couldn't rip away Roger's mantle, but he was able to kill the European Alpha and assume his position with brute force." Reagan shook her head slowly. "If only it wouldn't make me enemy number one to kill him…"

"Why wouldn't Darius just tell you who's going to be here? And why would shifters stand for someone like that taking power?" I fluffed my hair, wondering how long it actually took to park a car. And how many people needed to be a part of it.

"A real Alpha is a leader. Someone you would trust with your life. Someone you might fear, yes, but someone who holds your loyalty through respect. Don't tell him I said this, but Roger is a true Alpha. He's strong, smart, and sure. His people are in good hands. But sometimes a shifter is so strong that he gets to be Alpha because of brute force. He leads through fear alone. He doesn't garner loyalty—he cages people in by threat of death. Or, sometimes, by threatening loved ones. I have no proof, but this other guy seems like that type. And why doesn't Darius fill me in? Because he knows what it'll do to my aggression. I'll walk in, see the ass in question, and cause a problem. That's not what we need right now. We need subtlety and manipulation. This is his game. I'm just a player."

"But why would we want to work with that kind of Alpha?"

"Because we need shifter help, and if there is one thing this guy excels at, it is killing. He's a blunt instrument, and Darius is a pro at using any instrument, blunt or otherwise."

I blew out a breath, shifting my weight from side to side. Darius might be a problem down the road, but boy was I happy that he was on our side now.

Reagan glanced up at the organized mass of magic hovering above me, something that always happened when I was in pressurized situations. She couldn't see it, but she could feel its presence. "Does your magic feel any different today?"

"No. Not at all."

"Nothing different about the power or anything?"

"Nope. I did some magic with Emery, and he didn't feel a difference."

"I heard." She waggled her bald eyebrows at me.

"Ew. Something is wrong with you."

"Yes." She stared down a passerby who'd made the mistake of looking at her fanny pack. The lady started when she realized a crazy person was giving her the stink-eye. "It doesn't make sense that the goblin turned to stone, yet you don't seem any different."

"I null your magic. That's different."

"Yeah, but…I would expect something else. That goblin shifted *and* nulled my magic. We're missing something."

"The magic probably reduced in strength when it transferred. Or maybe it didn't transfer at all and I finally figured out how to null your magic. Actually, that last possibility sounds more plausible. It's like I can finally feel my way through your magic, and kind of do a counter-spell."

Reagan nodded slowly, eyeballing someone else. "Take a picture while you're at it." The man ripped his gaze away from her bald head. "It could be that you figured it out. I knew you were bound to. Seriously, what is up with these people? Their staring is riling me up."

"Being around people riles you up."

"Yes, but staring people rile me up more. They aren't staring at you."

"I don't look…eccentric."

Reagan turned to me with a hairless frown before looking down at herself. "What? I'm business casual."

I just shook my head. Clearly she didn't see the difference between bounty hunter business casual and office business casual. But Darius hadn't commented one way or another, so what did I know?

"Here we go," Reagan said, and I followed her gaze.

Darius and Emery strolled through the foyer of the building like two *GQ* models heading for the runway. Darius moved like a lethal dancer, his over-the-top handsomeness and elegant grace drawing eyes from across the foyer. Those eyes then moved on to Emery, topping Darius's height by two inches and swinging a broader set of shoulders. His gait was powerfully confident and his bearing screamed rough and tumble. Both were decked out in tailored suits that fit them like gloves, shiny watches, and hair styled and gelled *just so*. Moss and Marie strutted along behind, dressed to impress and owning their apparel.

"I look as good as they do, right?" I asked, straightening my jacket again and smoothing my pants.

"If you would stop slouching, fidgeting, and looking around like you are about to be attacked, yes, you would look as good as they do."

"So…no, then."

"No. Not on your life, no. You look like an out-of-place nerd in an uncomfortable suit."

"At least I'm not wearing a blouse with leather pants and army boots," I muttered, trying to straighten up.

"I don't think it would matter if you did. You'd still blend into the surroundings."

That was a good thing. That was *my* thing, actually, and it worked for me. I'd just stick with that.

"Ready, ladies?" Darius said, stopping near us with hard eyes. His gaze cut right through me, predatory and ruthless. He looked like he was going into a battle zone.

"How are you doing?" Emery asked me, his stance exuding confidence and power. Despite the presence of the elder vampire rocking his designer apparel, Emery owned the room. Or lobby, as it were.

"Good. Great." I threw them a thumbs-up. "Feeling like I should flee the scene, but hanging in there."

Emery chuckled and rubbed my back, apparently thinking that was a joke. "We have the best in the business on our side." Emery flicked his gaze at Darius as we headed beyond the burly desk jockey without checking in. "He has done his homework."

"I've been in a situation where he was supposed to have done his homework," I said as we neared the elevators, "and that didn't turn out so well." I'd nearly died back in New Orleans after accidentally setting off Darius's houseguest Ja.

Darius pushed the up button and stepped back, his hand slipping into his pants pocket. At the same time, Emery pulled his hand out of his pocket and checked his watch. They both shifted, their shoulders leaning in opposite directions but the movements still strangely synchronized, followed by Moss half turning and Marie basically striking a pose like a super model. It was like a dance of *cool*.

Reagan and I stood out. Badly.

"This time…" Emery scratched his cleanly shaven chin, his brow furrowing. No one helped him find the words.

The slim ray of hope I'd held that this team of powerhouses would prevent me (or Reagan) from creating "a situation" dimmed.

No one spoke in the elevator, and when we stepped out onto the shiny wooden floor, a strange feeling rolled over me. Like soft kisses slithering along my skin.

"Do you feel that?" I asked Emery.

"No. What is it?" he said, his eyes darting around and his face hard. He was ready for trouble.

I shook my head, unable to really describe it.

Darius led us to the right, gliding through the hall in a loose way that spoke of attack readiness. He wasn't going into this meeting with closed eyes. That was good.

Interesting modern paintings hung on the cream walls, and white crown molding ran along the edges of the ceiling. Slowly, little by little, the feeling of my surroundings changed. The air condensed, thickening until I could almost hold it with two hands. A feeling slithered along my skin, curious yet watchful.

*He's guarding his territory.*

Confused, I slowed, looking for a security device or someone watching in the corridor. Feeling the intent of magic was a gift I had, but I didn't feel or see any actual magic, and I had never assigned a sex to intent before.

Perfectly synchronized in a way I didn't understand, the others slowed with me, each glancing in a different direction, covering all bases.

A single thread of power curled within my awareness, twisting and turning, flirting with my senses and begging to be noticed. And still the presence in the air bore down on me.

The spiciness marked it as a vampire, and it had the dustiness of an elder, but it had another dimension to it. One thing was in our favor: the vampire wasn't hostile, and he didn't want us to turn around.

He just wanted us to know we were in his domain. His territory.

"A vampire owns this floor," I said, my legs locked and not wanting to go any farther. "It's not Ja, and I don't feel any actual magic, but I would really rather not accidentally wake up an extreme elder again." I looked hard at Darius, because his lack of preparedness had already put me in one uncomfortable situation. I'd hoped the partial destruction of his house would teach him his lesson, but who was to say?

Darius turned to me slowly. "An elder owns this building. What are you feeling?"

"Like…this place…belongs to someone…" I shook my head because I didn't quite know how to explain it.

"Like someone peed on the walls to mark his territory?" Reagan nodded, staring down the hall. "Vampires like other creatures to know who owns what." Reagan glanced back at me before walking forward. "I could only sense that after I bonded Darius. Is this the first time you've noticed it?"

I swallowed around a dry throat. "Yes. It's incredibly…"

"Disconcerting. You'll learn to deal with it." Reagan glanced at Darius, paused for a moment, and lightly nodded. "Interesting, indeed."

I didn't get a chance to ask what she was talking about. Before I knew it, we were all walking again, Emery's hand on my back keeping me from running off toward the double doors at the end of the hall.

Reagan tried one of the artful handles, which lacked a keyhole of any kind, only to find it locked. The walls beside the doors were smooth, no pad for a keycard.

"Knock, enter, or bust our way in?" Reagan asked Darius.

"This is a meeting of minds. We want to make a positive impression," Darius said, knocking softly.

"Right."

One of the doors opened in a swirl of air and fragrance, revealing a gorgeous woman in a leather duster, her cleavage popping out of her tight corset. She stood in incredible high-heeled boots in a balanced sort of way that didn't hint at the discomfort she had to feel. The overall *look* was as dazzling as it was sexy, but it had to be ten times more painful. I wasn't sure beauty was worth such a steep price, even for a vampire.

Reagan barked out a laugh, Darius turned to me slowly, and Emery bent to hide a chuckle. It was then I realized that, in my nervousness, I'd muttered my thoughts out loud.

"Sorry," I said, my face heating. "I was thinking about something else."

"Just stop while you're…where you are, Turdswallop," Emery murmured, a laugh riding his words.

"Off to a great start," Reagan said with a giant smile.

"Mr. Durant, we've been expecting you," the female vampire said in a lush, smooth voice so dense it practically worked at my pants buttons.

"Awkward," I whispered, desperately trying not to do the heebie-jeebie dance.

"Yes, of course." Darius stepped forward at an angle, cutting Reagan off from following. He bent his head toward Reagan.

She nodded, like he'd said something, and he disappeared through the doors. Moss and Marie followed him without a word, both on edge. Reagan didn't take a step, and instead waited until they'd closed the doors behind them, locking us in the hall.

"Well…that was unexpected," I said, staring at the doors.

"He thinks you need a moment to collect your thoughts. He doesn't realize that this *is* you with collected thoughts." Reagan leaned her back against the door and pulled her phone out of her fanny pack. She lit it up, then dropped it back in. "We'll give him five minutes to get everyone comfortable before we head in. What do you guys think? Should we go in on offense, defense, or just stir the shit?"

"Some of the most powerful people in the magical world are in there, right?" I yanked at my suit jacket. She nodded. "Okay, so let's go in normally. Just walk in."

Reagan sighed. "Fine. But tell me this: how hard should I kick in the door?"

"Would you—" I ran my hand over my face. There was no talking sense to her. To my dismay, Emery was chuckling again. He clearly didn't realize she was serious. That she wanted to rile everyone up so she could gauge their weaknesses. She was awesome at winning a fight, but subtlety was completely lost on her. Completely lost. "Go in meekly," I said through clenched teeth. "Just go in meekly."

"Ah." She wiggled her finger at me, as though we were sharing an inside joke. "I'm hearing you."

*Oh no…*

In one perfectly practiced, smooth movement, she turned, balanced, and kicked, all while I yelled, "*Noooo!*"

Both doors burst open, swinging hard before slamming against the walls. As Reagan strutted in, loudly saying, "Ah crap—really, Darius? *Him?*" Emery stepped over to me quickly, pushing me a little to the side before bending to whisper in my ear.

"I wasn't supposed to say anything, but Darius went

in first to set the stage. He wants us to each go in how we feel most comfortable. Okay? You'll be great."

"Wait, you mean there was an actual plan for once, and no one thought to—"

He was gone, strutting through the door after Reagan, holding his head high and his shoulders straight like he owned the whole room.

"—tell me," I finished, suddenly standing on my own in a pressurized situation. More times than I could count, it was in this exact type of situation that things went painfully, horribly wrong for me.

Darius had clearly not learned his lesson.

# CHAPTER 7

M Y SPINE COLLAPSED immediately and my confidence totally deflated. I hated being the center of attention and worried I'd accidentally do something crazy, like blast one of the shifters, or start a war with a vampire. I drifted to the doorframe, getting a quick look in before anyone noticed me.

A large conference room greeted me, with an oval table in the middle surrounded by plush chairs. Moss and Marie each stood in a corner, standing tall with their eyes directed straight ahead. In another corner, a block of a man took up residence, clearly a vampire on the same detail as Moss and Marie.

Darius sat on the side facing the door in the windowless room, his elbows on the table and his fingers steepled up near his face. Opposite him sat a burly guy with tree-trunk arms and dirty blond hair, his broad back to me. The seat to his right was open, but the one beyond it was filled with another stack of muscle with dark brown hair, wearing a suit that pulled at the seams, fighting to stay in one piece over his large expanse of shoulders. Shifters, both of them.

Reagan sauntered around the end of the table toward Darius, exchanging words with the muscular blond guy. Emery walked behind her, drawing the attention of everyone in the room. He pulled out the chair at the head of the table and sat down like the room should praise him for showing up.

It was clear he could really strap on the ego when he thought it fitting.

A slight shifting drew my notice to the left, and a little lean-in revealed two more people, a woman and man, each with a certain pose and balanced stance that yelled *fighter*. Another couple shifters. The woman in the corset was out of sight, which meant others might be, too.

Knowing I couldn't, on my best day, strut in like I owned the place, I figured I'd take Darius at his word. Hoping to stay hidden, I skulked into the room, veering right, and slipped toward the corner, where I was happy to notice a big, bushy office plant. It would do swimmingly to hide me from these extremely intense individuals who really didn't seem like they should be cooped up together in a confined space.

Having achieved my partial hiding spot, I put my back to the wall and finally took a glimpse at the other end of the table. I sucked in a quiet breath, which I then held.

The most unbelievably gorgeous man I had seen in my entire life, on the big screen or otherwise, sat in the high-backed chair at the foot of the table, his posture perfect and his manicured hands on the table. With cheekbones and straight nose seemingly etched out of marble, he looked like one of those pictures in a history book depicting nobles. Lean body exuding power, he was refined grace and infallible charisma wrapped up in a perfect package.

Like…almost too perfect. He didn't even look real, he was so incredibly attractive.

I wiped drool from my chin with the back of my hand. He was so hot he literally made me drool. That was a first.

"Now, since we are all here…" the stupidly attractive man said, his voice so perfectly pitched and smooth that I caught myself leaning forward a little bit, anxious to get it to my ears just a little more quickly.

*Son of a marmalade maker, Penny, get a hold of yourself!*

"Sabrine, please, if you would?" the man said, and I forced myself to lean back again.

Ms. Corset—Sabrine—strutted toward the doors, her hips bobbing and swaying so much that I almost got queasy watching them. She passed the shifters a little too closely, skimming their comfort bubbles and smirking when each of them stiffened, before fitting the doors into the frame as best she could. She didn't so much as glance my way.

Vampires and shifters didn't like each other, I remembered. No, that wasn't right. They *hated* each other. And hating, in the magical world, often resulted in death.

And here we all were, in the same room. Spacious or not, the room was still much too small.

"I am overjoyed I could host such a group of people. What luck that this location was agreeable to you," Unnaturally Handsome said with a smile that tightened my body in worrying ways: arousal and fear and excitement.

The brown-haired shifter at the table moved in his seat, clearly not as overjoyed. He leaned forward, resting his large arms on the table. His biceps strained his suit jacket to the point of absurdity.

"You didn't introduce anyone around. Is that the other mage?" He pointed at Reagan.

"Nope," she said, leaning back in her seat. The low light glinted off her bald head. "I was only invited because I'm banging this guy." She hooked a thumb Darius's way. Cleary this group didn't know what she really was.

"She was the first to thwart the Mages' Guild in Seattle," the blond-haired shifter said, his voice deep and rough and his posture tense and ready.

"But she's not a mage?" Bursting Jacket asked.

"Not a mage, no. But rest assured, gentlemen," Darius said. His voice, once smooth as silk, now sounded a bit gravelly. Unnaturally Handsome was doing a number on me. "She will be an infallible asset. Now, if we could move on…"

"Wait." Bursting Jacket leaned forward then back, practically buzzing with pent-up energy. He glanced at the blond shifter. "Am I remembering this wrong? Weren't there two mages that battled the Guild in Seattle? I was told they'd both be here."

"And so they are," Unnaturally Handsome said.

The blond shifter clasped his hands, and I could tell it was in confusion. It occurred to me that neither of them had noticed me enter. They didn't know I was in the room.

Reagan clucked her tongue and shook her head, the light moving around her shiny skin scalp like a disco ball. "Roger, I'm surprised at you. I mean, your nitwit friend I get—lots of brawn, no brain—but *you*? That's a big miss…"

Ah, so that was Roger. I sank a little closer to the bush, because Reagan's joy of riling up shifters was not in the best interest of this overall meeting, and also because the shifters were on my side of the table.

As expected, Bursting Jacket puffed up, putting that jacket under even more strain. Shifter magic exploded through the room, jagged and hot, smacking into me and putting my energy on boil.

*Attack. Kill.*

A weave sprang through my fingers, unbidden, ready to slice Bursting Jacket in two if he so much as flinched in Reagan's direction. I clenched my teeth and squeezed my eyes shut, focusing on keeping calm. In this room of power players, I was not needed for defense. I needed to mind my own business so Darius could talk everyone around.

"Oops. Now look what you've done," I heard—Reagan, as calm as a spring day. "You went and got the *other* mage all riled up. That's okay; I like your beta better anyway. It would probably do everyone a favor if she took over."

That intensely powerful shifter magic continued to pump into the room, burning my eyes and making me grind my teeth.

*Shred. Rip.*

I felt the energy building, the shifter close to changing shape. I wondered if it would have a spark like that goblin, and if it did, if I could just reach in…and quell it. Stop the change.

"Calm yourself," came Emery's voice, a whip crack of command. Rough and masculine, it flowed over my skin like a caress, *so* much better than Unnaturally Handsome's voice. "Get it under control, or things are going to get violent."

Another wave of shifter magic vibrated toward me, more potent than the first, whispering of trees, cold mornings, and the thrill of the hunt. It must've been Roger's magic, and I savored the natural feel of it. How it sang through my bones and seamlessly blended into my surroundings.

The power soaked into my body, and my already raging energy flared. Elements flowed through my fingers again without my consent, weaves half realized before I could force them to dissipate.

I shouldn't have come. This was a huge mistake.

"Darius, calm it down, *now*," Emery said.

A warning sounded somewhere in the back of my head. The train was a little too wobbly on the tracks. And while this might've happened a lot when I was first learning to use my magic, I knew better now. And, on the flip side, I also knew a lot more deadly spells.

"Gentlemen," Darius said, an edge to his voice, "may I present Penelope Bristol?"

Fabric groaned, and I wondered if Bursting Jacket would tear out his seams when he looked around.

"You see," Unnaturally Handsome said, "vampires have a tendency to keep track of the most dangerous person in the room, even when he or she is disguised in such a perplexing way."

Like the tide going out, the magic receded slowly,

leaving me shaky and trembling in its wake. I peeled an eye open in time to see Bursting Jacket smirking at me through a big, square face and small, beady brown eyes. He turned back around and his magic diminished to the point of a whiff. The other shifter's magic followed suit. I sighed in gratitude.

"Most dangerous person in the room?" He chuckled. "She looks terrified. She's not even trained, right?"

"Precisely," Unnaturally Handsome said, his finger firmly on the pulse of the situation.

Bursting Jacket shook his head, still chuckling, clearly thinking this was a farce. I bet I could still reach in and flick off—

"Nope." Reagan stood. "This might not work, boys. I can control my dislike of that meathead because I mostly dislike everyone. I've had practice. But she hasn't, and she is planning horrible things. I can feel it."

Emery nodded and shifted so he could look back at me, his eyes sparkling with confidence. He wasn't passing judgment. He was ready to fight with me, if it came to that. I could see it in his posture, feel it in his magical chemistry as it connected with mine.

His chemistry? What the hell was going on with me?

"Let's start again, shall we?" Darius stood and gestured me over.

"I must admit, Darius, you have come a long way,"

Unnaturally Handsome said, his perfectly smooth voice filled with delight. "That was a fabulous demonstration. If only we'd had the resources to let it continue."

As I drifted toward Emery, trying to straighten up but wary of what a little confidence would do to the energy still surging around me, I realized the blond shifter, Roger, hadn't stopped assessing me, staring with one brown eye and one blue. He hadn't written me off as the other one had.

His magic simmered on low heat, pleasant and wholesome, and I knew, without a doubt, that he was someone I could trust. I felt it so deeply that I didn't think to wonder how I knew. To have any shot of winning, we needed him on our side.

# CHAPTER 8

"NO BIG DEAL, and it's totally fine," I said quietly to Emery as I grabbed the back of a seat near the end of the table and rolled it closer to him. I didn't want to sit too close to Bursting Jacket, for fear he'd set me off again, and nor did I want to be on the other side so Roger could continue to stare at me. While I didn't question his trustworthiness, he had a crazy kind of intensity that liquefied my bones and turned my stomach to mush. I could see why he was Alpha. "But I'm cracking up a little. Just a little, and it'll probably pass, but I don't feel entirely normal."

Emery glanced at me, his gaze guarded. "Can you make it through this?"

I sure hoped so.

"Did you not smell her?" Reagan asked Roger.

"No," he said, his gaze pounding into the side of my head. "Not even a whiff. I didn't hear her, either."

"She was encased in a spell, of sorts." Emery scooted over a little and dragged my chair even closer to share the space at the end of the table. "We have what's called survival magic, and Penny uses it in ways…I've never seen. This time she was blending hers with mine to create a sort of…shield, I would call it."

Oh. That made sense, but it was my first indication I'd done any such thing.

"Yes," Unnaturally Handsome said, delicately clasping his long fingers on the tabletop. "Her person was obscured from view. My eye wanted to move along, but in a way I haven't experienced with similar spells. I just…didn't want to notice her. I wanted to forget her presence."

"Penny has an innate ability to feel out the perfect spell for any given situation. Unfortunately, in dire circumstances, she does it unconsciously," Darius said, drawing everyone's attention my way. "We're working to change that, of course. In Emery she has found someone who can train her exactly how she needs to learn, and in Reagan she has found safe chaos in which to practice to her full potential. She is progressing rapidly."

"Rapidly enough for what lies ahead?" Unnaturally Handsome asked.

Darius pulled his gaze away from me and met Unnaturally Handsome's. "Whether she has or not, we've run out of time." He swept his gaze around the table. "Let's officially start, shall we? Why don't we go around the table and introduce ourselves. Everyone knows

Reagan and me, so we won't bore you with redundancy. Penny, why don't you start?"

"I'm Penny." I cleared my throat as the intense gazes of the shifters and the velvety gazes of the vampires pinned on me, all disconcerting. "Penny Bristol. And"—Emery chuckled, though I had no idea why—"I'm the untrained natural witch we were just talking about."

"Did you say witch?" Bursting Jacket's haughty tone indicated he was less than impressed.

"Mage," I amended quickly.

"No." Emery dropped his warm hand to my knee. "Witch was true enough. She wasn't trained in the typical mage style. She has largely felt out her magic, like witches do. She's stronger for it. I learn from her as often as I teach."

"But…she has the power of a mage?" Roger asked, and there was no condescension in his tone. He was simply trying to clarify, unlike the other Alpha.

"She has the power of a natural," Emery said. "She easily rivals me. I have more experience and world knowledge, but she has more creativity. Together, we are the perfect team."

"I can validate his assessment. They work exceptionally well together," Darius said. "The best I have ever seen, and they are not yet dual-mages." Emery stiffened slightly. "This is often the case, of course…with a natural pairing."

Unnaturally Handsome leaned forward just a little, his body language showing the interest his face didn't express.

"I'm Emery Westbrook." Emery took his hand from my knee and leaned his forearms on the table in a position of power. "The Rogue Natural. I'm sure you've heard of me."

"I heard you and your brother were a natural dual-mage pair until the Guild killed him," Bursting Jacket said, about as subtle as a steel mace.

"One of their barons ordered it, and an underling carried it out," Emery said in a monotone.

"So this is something of a Hail Mary to you, huh?" Bursting Jacket swiveled in his chair, bringing his massively broad chest to face Emery. "You want revenge, and you knew the vampires would be all too happy to stick their hands in the Mages' Guild's pot. Probably get to nibble on a few necks while they're at it." He huffed out a patronizing laugh and shook his head. "Why are you wasting our time? Didn't anyone tell you that we don't support vampire agendas? And we sure as hell don't help them take control of organizations they have no business messing with, all so some spoiled kid with an ego can get revenge."

Emery silently held Bursting Jacket's stare, and shifter magic leaked into the air again, prodding at me. Bursting Jacket might've looked confident on the outside, but he was feeling the pressure of a natural staring him down. Neither the vampires nor the other Alpha interrupted the silence. A bead of sweat dribbled down my back. Magic started boiling above me again. A grin spread across Reagan's face.

"If it were up to me," Emery said finally, his voice low and dangerous, "I'd be long gone. The Mages' Guild could choke the life out of the magical world in the Brink, and it wouldn't bother me in the slightest. I only returned from the wilds because Penny was in danger. Being that I had a hand in placing her there, I felt it was my duty to see it through. You have Penny to thank for my willingness to help save your ass. Because while your packs might not be directly affected now, it's only a matter of time before the Guild crates you…and walks away."

The pressure in the air coated me like a blanket. Bursting Jacket pushed back and crossed his arms over his chest, his jacket practically moaning with the effort to stay in one piece. "That right? Crate me?" The threat was plain in his voice. When Emery didn't respond, and didn't look away, a small crease wormed in between the big shifter's brows. "And how about you, little witch?" His eyes slid to me. "Why are you here?"

I took a deep, steadying breath, trying to ignore the constant thump of his magic on my chest, like someone repeatedly poking me. "First, because the Mages' Guild is trying to hunt me down and capture me. My pre-ferred style of fighting is usually defense turned offense. They made the first move. I'm retaliating.

"Second, and most importantly, because they are a corrupt organization that is flouting the laws with abandon because no one is strong enough to stand up to them. Not the vampires, and not the shifters. That's why you guys are here. This isn't just a mage problem anymore—it's become a magical people problem. And like Emery said, it might not affect you now…much…but at the rate they're growing, it won't be long until they do. Since your job is to ensure humans don't find out about magical people, the Guild flouting the laws falls under your jurisdiction. It's *your* problem more than the vampires'."

"She is correct. I have seen their power grow incred-ibly quickly," Unnaturally Handsome said. "They have infiltrated magical communities in the Brink to an unprecedented degree, promising things that"—his gaze fell on Emery—"*most* mages covet. Power. Money. Acclaim. Penny is right. This is a universal problem that must be taken out by the root. But please, let's continue with the introductions before we go into more detail. Rex, since you are only seeing the very tip of this, you'll certainly want some proof of what is inevitably headed your way."

Bursting Jacket was named Rex.

"Wait, do you turn into a T-Rex?" I blurted out. I waved it away. "Never mind. Sorry. Not important. I mean, it would be incredibly cool if you did…" I waited for some sign that he did. Nothing came. "And it would explain the stronger-than-thou vibe you're hellbent on pushing in everyone's face…" His face remained stoic. "Right." I nodded. It was probably taboo to ask a shifter which animal they changed into, much like it was to talk about how swampy vampires were in what Reagan called their "monster" form. "This isn't the time. I get it."

"She's bad at people," Reagan said, and Emery coughed into his fist, trying to hide his chuckles.

"I turn into a Kodiak," Rex said in a growl.

"Right. Standard animal, then," I said softly.

"That is Rex Keel," Unnaturally Handsome said, trying to restore a sense of decorum in the meeting. "He is the Alpha of the European Union." His gaze shifted to Roger, clearly trying to keep things moving.

The shifter didn't skip a beat. "For those who don't know me"—I got a glance—"I'm Roger Nevin." Another glance. "A wolf. I've been following the situation in Seattle closely. My people are in a tight spot there, but we don't have the resources to combat the issue. While it is no secret that I would rather not work with vampires, I can see no alternative in this *one* instance. That is, *if* we have enough manpower to settle this. I do not intend to send my people to their deaths."

Roger shifted his intense stare to me. "I've heard a lot about you, Penny," he said. His stare softened my bones and scrambled my stomach in nervousness. A song of wolves drifted into my mind's eye, and the smell of evergreen trees on the night air infused my senses. It was lovely, don't get me wrong, but the guy was intense. There were no two ways about it.

"And, Miss Bristol, my name is Vlad. It is lovely to make your acquaintance." Unnaturally Handsome's velvety gaze stroked across my skin.

Vlad. That name rang a bell, but I couldn't place it.

Before I could give it more thought, Rex had pushed forward and banged down his forearms on the table. "Time's a-wasting. What's in this for us?"

# CHAPTER 9

A N HOUR LATER, Rex hadn't gotten any more likable. The opposite, in fact, if that were possible. What he had gotten was more intense. With each perceived (or outright) slight toward him, he magically flew off the handle, slamming the room with his aggressive magic while staring hostilely at whoever had set him off.

He wasn't the only one misbehaving. The room was like a swamp of prickly egos, and they were all barely trying to get along. Since the Redcap goblin, I seemed to be able to feel the magic of others more strongly, and surges of it kept rolling over me from all directions. Everyone seemed to want something for helping. It wasn't enough that they were ending a very real, very terrible threat—they wanted a say in how things got remade. And, in the vampires' case, they wanted to actually be in the Guild. To make decisions.

*Over my dead body.*

I blew out a breath as yet another wall of magic smashed into me, this time from Vlad. He gazed at Rex, and the look was entered onto my *never ignore* list, under the subset of *when you should run like hell.*

"Wait, wait, wait." Reagan held out her hands, just as worked up as everyone else. "Do we even know which elder is siding with the Guild? And the size of his or her faction?"

She was talking about the revelation, some months ago, that the Guild was no longer working alone. Their vampire allies had infiltrated Darius's group and blocked an SOS call from me when Emery and I were cornered by mages in New Orleans. Darius had been blindsided, and shifters had saved Emery and me.

Darius steepled his fingers. "No. We don't know who is giving the orders. I've extracted two vampires from my faction that I had thought were loyal to me. Sadly, they went to their eternal grave before I could get sufficient information. I know only that it *is* an elder pulling the strings."

Vlad's hard stare beat into Darius. "You had a breach of loyalty?"

I cocked my head to the side. Was it just me, or was Vlad a little too anxious about Darius's breach of loyalty?

"Yes," Darius said. A new wave of ferocious vampire magic swirled through the room, the first time Darius had come close to losing his cool. "I would look into your people, Vlad, if I were you. The breach was…wholly unexpected."

For a moment, the unnaturally handsome mask peeled away from Vlad's face, and I knew that no matter how lovely he looked, he was a ruthless killer. A predator of predators. Shivers coated my body.

"So let me get this straight," Rex said. He braced a huge hand on his knee. Sweat beaded his brow. "You'd be going up against a host of some four hundred mages or more, at least one natural, and an unknown number of vampires, one of whom is an elder?" He paused to look around the room. "And you'd do this with only one more *untrained* natural, a bald bounty hunter, and one more elder, who I wouldn't trust with my worst enemy's life?" He laughed, shaking the table. Roger watched him silently. Angry, potent magic from everyone else slashed at my senses. "No wonder you are desperate for our help. They got numbers and the home field advantage, and you've got a losing battle. I mean, look…" He tapped his finger on the table, his grin implying we were all idiots. "It's pretty obvious they'd wipe us out. I get the issue, but—"

"Do you?" Reagan leaned forward against the table and speared him with a hard stare. A challenging stare.

Rex's magic blasted me again, slicing into my body and jabbing at my energy.

*Rip. Kill. Tear.*

"How in holy hand grenades are you in charge of

anybody?" Struggling to breathe, already on edge and barely holding it together, I squeezed my eyes shut and clasped my hands together, the desire to jump to Reagan's defense so strong I could barely think.

"What did you say?" He swiveled toward me slowly, his eyes on fire. Emery stiffened next to me.

I rubbed my temples, my mind hazy from the constant battering of powerful magic. My filter was long gone. "When someone argues with you, your first inclination is to rip them apart. It's so second nature that it seems like it must usually work for you. You've learned brute force ends arguments. But you haven't stepped up once tonight. I can only surmise that it is because you are, at heart, a coward. Here, among these powerful people, you know you'll lose. You are the worst kind of leader. The worst kind of person to have power at your disposal." I squeezed the bridge of my nose, his new blast of magic suffocating me. The desire to lash out at him boiled my blood.

"We have but a small collection of mages," Darius said, somehow unruffled by the fuss and clearly ignoring me, "but their power and experience is vastly superior to anything that will be thrown at us. And I can't imagine I have to tell you the power Vlad and I can summon. We each have vast resources at our disposal. More so than any other elder."

"Their natural is nothing," Reagan said, tag-teaming

with Darius (while also ignoring me). "Emery is indisputably the best mage in the world. He is above everyone else…save Penny. Together, they are better still, as we've said. The Guild's natural might be as powerful as each of them individually, but she will not stand a chance when confronted with Penny and Emery together. Not a chance."

"Says the bounty hunter?" Rex pushed.

"Yeah," Reagan said, her eyes glittering menace, her magic flirting with mine. "Says the bounty hunter. Don't play dumb. I know you've heard of me. Your shifters give me a wide berth. Why do you think that is? Because I smell weird?"

Rex scoffed and turned. "Look, Roger, I get why you'd want to bring me in on this. Two elders and two naturals? It sounds great on paper. But this"—he gestured around the table—"doesn't add up. Not compared to what they're up against. It isn't our fight, but it would be our deaths. And for what? We'd be pushed out of the end prize."

"You are only this flippant because you have no idea what the Mages' Guild is doing," Reagan said, frustration ringing clearly in her voice. "You said you had some bad mages filtering into your area. Just a couple, you said, right? Well, that couple has run you ragged. What do you think a host would do, and you powerless to stop them?"

"We're stopping it before it starts," Rex bit back. "They won't get a host in. We'll kill them before they do."

A wave of dizziness overcame me. "He's the wrong sort." I shook my head, power pumping through my middle. I exhaled and wiped my eyes, but it didn't help dislodge the strange feeling of disembodiment. "We don't need *all* the help; we need the right help. And he is not it. If there is anyone in the world I wouldn't want to go into battle with, it is that man right there. Oh good, there's another blast of magic. I was worried he'd suddenly learned to control himself."

"You okay?" Emery asked quietly.

"No. I don't know. I don't feel right. But one thing is certain—he won't step down from leadership. He craves the power. We can all see that. And clearly, none of the shifters can, or will, tear him down. How many people is he squashing with his rage? How many people have been killed because of his ego and small-mindedness?" I shook my head, and a wave of vertigo had me leaning forward. "Wow, I need a breather. But before that...I can help. We want the shifters to help us, so we should help them. It's only fair. I can help...and I should. Right?"

Confused silence descended, and I struggled to piece together coherent thoughts. I couldn't think past what I *knew*, in my heart of hearts, needed to be done—

the right thing, which only I could accomplish. But I couldn't stop to analyze my own thoughts. Shifter magic was shoving me. Rolling me. Yanking me. It was like I was trapped in the rolling, surging tide, no idea what direction was up.

"Please stop," I begged. "I'm losing control."

"Do it."

Darius's words on the breeze. Barely loud enough for me to hear, but plenty loud for me to feel.

Because I could feel words now, apparently.

Rex leaned forward just a little, and the power shoving me thickened. He was pushing his advantage, I could feel it. Bullying me with his brawn and, perhaps unknowingly, also bullying me with his magic. He didn't think I had the might to take him.

"Rush him," Reagan said softly.

Without warning, all four vampire guards from around the room charged forward, right toward Rex. Roger surged up, his magic erupting. The shifter sentries launched into action.

Reagan's magic pumped out and then through me, wonderfully complex. A solid wall of air cut the rest of the shifters, including Roger, off from Rex. The Alpha roared, something unbalanced and vile about the sound. He braced and ripped his arms forward into a flex, his jacket finally giving way. It ripped at the seams and across his back.

I reached through Rex's magic with a kung fu fist, battering away all the wires and spindly parts and strange things that I didn't understand, until I found the root. The spark. The thing that made magical creatures change. It had been in that goblin, it was in Rex…and it was also in the vampires. Pulsing way down deep, far below the surface of their magic.

Rex's spark flared…and I twisted it, snuffing it out, just like I'd done with that goblin. Magic ballooned in the room, but his animal didn't emerge.

The vampires reached him, and I felt their sparks erupt before their claws and fangs extended.

Roger slammed into the wall he couldn't see, his magic whirling around him, ready to change.

"Don't hurt him," I yelled at the vampires, now hustling Rex out of the room. He howled like a beast, and his magic choked me, but he didn't change. Couldn't. I'd blown out his spark. "Do not hurt him! It's no longer a fair fight."

Clothes tore as the other shifters in the room, save Roger, erupted into clouds of fur. A snarling weretiger and werewolf fell down on all fours, but the wall of air held them. They had nowhere to go.

All the magic swirling in the room sucked me up in a tornado, dragging me under.

"Easy, Penny," Emery said, his hand on my arm.

Roger stilled as Rex disappeared and the vampires

followed him out. The North American Alpha clearly realized he was trapped, and instead of raging or losing control, he switched gears. His calculating gaze surveyed the empty air in front of him. In turn, he studied those left in the room, his eyes lingering on me the longest. I had no doubt his animal form was incredibly dangerous, or he wouldn't keep his position, but he was ten times as cunning as a man. He wasn't a person you'd ever trust to be confined to a cage.

We needed him on our side.

"What just happened?" he asked.

"Why, we proved a point, did we not?" Vlad put out his hand, inviting Roger back to his seat. "Do not be alarmed. Rex will not be hurt. He will be thrown outside, that is all. He will then be free to go about his day."

"What just happened?" Roger asked again, the warm edge of anger riding his words.

"We proved that Penny and Emery are every bit as powerful as we said," Reagan said, also breathing quickly. She sat down slowly, and without knowing why, I was thankful she included Emery in what had just happened. "And they made sure Rex will not shift again. I've heard stories, and now I've seen him in action. There's no way he was equipped to be an Alpha. You should've stepped in, but since you didn't, the naturals did it for you. You're welcome."

Roger's jaw clenched.

"We have a lot of power at our disposal," Darius said, his eyes on me. "We will not lose. We can't. But we need the shifters."

He was reading my mind. Or else I was muttering out loud again. Anything was possible at that point. The haze still covered me like a thick fog and my body felt strung out. Magic pinged through me, but I couldn't handle it anymore. I was shutting down—I could feel it.

"I will commit to this venture," Vlad said, his words coming slowly. "We can discuss the resources we will need, and we will also discuss my level of involvement in the restructuring of the Guild, but I will mark this as—"

"No." I pointed at him, battling through the haze to make this very important point. "No. You will help us take down the Guild, and you will *have input* in its resurrection. But that is where your influence will end. Abruptly end. That goes for all of us." I swung my finger at each of us in turn, ending with Emery and me. "The Guild will be rebuilt as a democracy, with rules. With morals. Mages will decide its fate, not other creatures."

Silence descended again, and the remaining vampires in the room clenched their jaws.

"Are you a woman who sticks to her guns, Penny Bristol?" Roger asked, and I realized he hadn't said too much for the whole meeting. He'd been listening.

"I don't usually have any guns. I've always gotten pushed around." I wiped my clammy forehead and leaned against Emery's arm. "But in this, yes. I will not bend. And if the rest of the people in this room won't agree, then I'll tear down the Guild some other way. I will not go through all this trouble just to end up in the same situation again later, with only the players changed. And if you let a vampire in to run anything, you can bet they'll end up owning you in one way or another."

Vlad put his elegant hand to his chest. "That's hurtful."

Laughter bubbled up through me, because I doubted even a stake through the heart would hurt that vampire. He wasn't like Darius—he had no emotion to speak of. It made him unpredictable and ten times more dangerous. I had one thing going for me. Judging by his sparkling eyes and dazzling smile, he was teasing. We were on the same page.

"I'm in," Roger said flatly, but I could see the tightness in his eyes. The tension in his shoulders. What had just happened with Rex had deeply shaken him. That didn't prevent him from thinking rationally, though. "We'll need to talk more specifics, but as long as Penny has a major hand in rebuilding, I'll join this endeavor. But let it be known..." He leaned forward and his intensity kicked up a notch. "This does not mean I trust vampires any more than I ever have. When this is over, things go back to the way they were. Is that clear?"

"I already miss our newfound connection." Vlad's tone was light, still teasing, but it felt like a blade resting on billowing silk. They were also on the same page.

"This alliance, however temporary, will be one for the record books." Reagan shook her head. Her magic pumped into the room. "Then it'll get thrown out, because no one will believe it."

"The enemy of my enemy, as they say." I gripped the table ledge as another wave of vertigo hit me. I tried to wave the magic off, but my hand felt like lead. My heart rushed through my ears and my stomach churned. Blackness rushed in, clouding my vision.

# CHAPTER 10

"THIS WILL NEED to be solidly planned," Roger said with reservations. "Rex had a point. We're up against incredible odds." His jaw clenched as he said the other Alpha's name, and Emery could tell he wanted to ask more about what had happened to Rex. In truth, Emery wondered the same thing, but delving into the Rex situation might mean upsetting the fragile alliance they'd just formed.

"Ugh." Penny put the heel of her hand against her head.

"You okay?" Emery leaned forward to try and glimpse her face. This was another situation he badly wanted to get more information about. She'd been periodically acting strangely throughout the whole meeting. With tension running high, some outbursts were expected, but even so...

"I don't feel the best..." She pitched forward suddenly, her head thunking on the table.

He shot up and leaned over her, resting his hand on her back. Heat blazed into his palm; her body was on fire. Her forehead felt the same.

"What's wrong?" Reagan said, standing. Her chair sailed back and hit the wall.

Roger stood too, pushing the chairs away so he could lean in and see Penny's face. He felt her forehead. "That'd be a bad fever by shifter standards…"

Shifters ran hotter than normal or magical humans. Penny was burning up.

Without another word, Emery scooped her up into his arms and swung her away from the table. Reagan was by his side a moment later, looking anxious.

She put two fingers to Penny's neck. "Is she breathing?"

Emery felt the shallow rise and fall of her chest as he hurried for the double doors. "Yes."

Penny was probably fine. It was probably just a fever, inflamed by the intensity of the meeting. She'd likely just fainted.

But as he headed for the door, a warning blared at the back of his head. Penny hadn't been acting normal, even for her. She'd had a scare yesterday. She could suddenly null Reagan's powerful and complex magic. She'd done something to Rex to prevent him from changing, a feat Emery had never imagined possible before yesterday.

*Only fools believe in coincidences.*

If she *had* ingested some form of magic from that

goblin, which also hadn't acted as normal goblins should, she might have a magical parasite in her body. Judging from what Reagan had said, that parasite had tried to shut her down yesterday, and it could easily be trying the same thing today.

So many *ifs*. Too many. He was flying blind when it came to the most important person in his life.

"Hurry up," he yelled at Reagan, wanting to get out of that room. Hoping that as soon as they got some fresh air, away from all the powerful magic, Penny might revive.

"Get her out of here," Darius barked, and it was the first time Emery remembered seeing the vampire visibly lose his cool.

Vlad's gaze turned keen as Reagan ripped one door out of the way, and Roger broke down the other. The Alpha had enormous strength, so it wasn't much of a surprise.

"Go, go!" Reagan urged, not that Emery needed the encouragement—he was already on his way out of the door with Penny in his arms. Reagan came jogging after them a moment later, sparing a backward glance at the shifters trapped in the air walls. "Come on. I'll let them out when we get farther away."

At the elevator, Reagan jabbed the down button, then hit it two more times. "All we need is for freaking Vlad to figure out what's up."

"And what is that?" Emery rocked from side to side, his cheek resting on Penny's terrifyingly hot head.

"What do you think? Something is up with Penny, and Vlad's old enough to take a guess at what it is."

The elevator chimed and they rushed forward. Reagan stepped in front and center and turned toward the doors, the first line of defense if someone followed them in.

"If that godly stuff was legit, I would've heard about it," Emery said, his hands shaking as he pressed the button for the lobby. "I've traveled all over the Brink and the Realm. I've talked to all sorts of creatures. I've heard secrets beyond secrets. Stories about dragons, unicorns, you name it, I've heard of it—"

Reagan's head whipped around. "If I were you, I would never, *ever* say that last creature again. Not ever. Not even to me. And don't speak to the person or creature who was talking tall tales. They'll end up dead, and so will you."

"Right. So now I believe those stories. Regardless, I've never heard of godly magic. Never heard of anything Darius told us last night. If godly magic existed on our plane, it's long since disappeared."

"Then what is going on?"

"I don't know, but whatever it is, it isn't good."

"Can you sense any difference in her…bubble, or whatever? Her energy?" Reagan asked.

The elevator bumped down. A chime announced the doors opening.

Emery pulled his head back to look down at Penny's face as he hurried her out of the elevator. A blast of fresh, chilled air hit them. Her eyes didn't even flutter.

Four vampires waited in the hall, stock-still.

"What are you clowns doing down here?" Reagan gracefully put herself between him and them.

"Helping keep the peace," Sabrine said in a bored voice.

"With the bigger shifter gone, it will be more comfortable for Roger if we weren't in the room," Moss said. "It will help our cause."

"Right. Fine," Reagan said. "Moss, I need to take the car. Get—Stop shaking your head. It'll be fine. I won't crash it."

"I'll take you," Moss said, his face closed down. "Marie, tell Mr. Durant that I will send another car around to him."

"I've figured out how to drive on the wrong side of the road," Reagan said as Moss stalked ahead. She waved Emery forward. "It'll be fine—Well, he's not listening. How annoying."

"What happened to the witch?" Sabrine's gaze tracked Penny.

"She passed out. Too many charming personalities in one place." Reagan winked. Sabrine gave her a blank stare. "You should go into theater. So expressive."

"Come on," Emery said.

"As I was saying," Reagan said quietly, out near the security desk now. Another large man had taken the place of the first. "Do you feel anything different with her magic?"

"Nothing. Not all night. Her energy rolled and surged, but it was always timed with someone getting pissed. That's to be expected. With all the power in that room, and with her special gift to sense and use other people's magic, she must've felt their hostility."

"And that was a lot of hostility." Reagan hurried to reach the door first and pull it open. "What about her emotions? Anything odd there? Do you feel any new traits?"

Emery stepped out into the cold night. "I forgot our jackets."

"It's fine. Here's Moss. Crap, he's speeding. He knows something's wrong. It must be obvious." Reagan rushed forward and opened the door.

"I'm carrying a limp woman. Of course something's wrong." Emery delicately put Penny into the car before running around to the other side and getting in with her. "Darius is great at damage control."

"Sure, for Roger. But Vlad is the most cunning crea-ture you'll ever meet. Ever. He already knows a ton. Darius is going to need all his wits to keep Vlad in the dark."

"Luckily"—Moss's dark eyes flashed in the rearview mirror—"he has brought all his wits today."

"Yes, thank you, peanut gallery." Reagan sat in the front passenger seat. "So?" she asked Emery. The car pulled away from the curb quickly. "Can you feel anything?"

"I don't have a bond to her other than our energy. When she works magic, everything feels exactly the same. I have no idea what's going on right now."

"The natural pairing doesn't let you feel her emotions?"

"No. We'd have to be a dual-mage pair for that, and then it is only a magical connection. It isn't like a vampire bond."

"Well, a magical connection is at least *something*. Why haven't you gone down that road yet?"

"Because he is a coward." Moss flashed accusatory eyes into the rearview mirror.

Reagan pointed at Moss. "There it is."

Emery gritted his teeth.

"She was not acting herself tonight," Moss said.

"She did get weird there toward the end," Reagan said. "And for her, that's saying something."

"Could just be the flu..." Emery pulled her head down onto his lap and smoothed her hair away from her burning forehead. "We need to get a temperature gauge."

"Thermometer, genius." Reagan tapped the window. "Can't you go faster, Moss?"

"You are usually unbearable, but when you worry, you are even more so," Moss said in his deadpan monotone.

Despite the situation, Emery couldn't help but laugh.

After a quick stop at a corner store, Moss brought them to a swanky hotel. Emery barely noticed the furnishings as they vaulted up the stairs to the third floor. Moss unlocked the door to their suite with the wave of his hand, pushed it open, then stepped aside so Emery could enter. Cradling Penny in his arms, he ran through the sitting area to the room at the back, the blackout curtains open, revealing the cloudy night.

Once he got Penny on the bed, Emery sat beside her, laying his hand on her forehead. Still burning. "Grab the thermometer."

Moss ripped open the package, not sparing any time.

"Here's the thing…" Reagan paced in the space between the bedroom area and the sitting room. She put her hands to her hips. "You're worried for Penny. If you guys bond, and then you die, you think she'd go nuts, right?"

"Do we have to have this conversation now?" Emery

took the device from Moss, a wand of sorts with a bead of glass at one end, a screen in the middle, and a button below the screen. "What is this?"

"A thermometer." Moss tapped it.

"How..." Emery pushed the button. It clicked electronically then beeped, and the screen glowed to life. A number flashed within the green light. "I just hold it to her head? What happened to the kind that you put under the tongue?"

"Technology has advanced." Moss unfolded the instructions.

"She could be dying," Reagan continued, "and you have no idea, because you won't bond her. Or whatever the dual-mage spell thing is called. She could have some seriously crazy magic fighting her right now, and you're forcing her to fight it alone. All because you're scared she might...one day get hurt...down the road...maybe."

"Put that end on her head"—Moss tapped the curved end—"and move it back and forth across her forehead while pushing the button."

Emery shoved Reagan's voice out of his head and did as Moss said, hearing the little electronic clicks as he did so.

"Don't you think, in hindsight, your reasoning is stupid?" Reagan stalked closer, leaning over to peer at the thermometer gliding across Penny's forehead. "I mean, I would really like to know what the fuck is going on right now. I do not like the thought of crazy goblin magic running rampant in my friend. But I can't fight what I can't see, do you see what I mean? Maybe my magic could help, like before, but I can't possibly know, because we don't have a guy on the inside. That guy is too much of a coward to do what he needs to do."

Emery gritted his teeth again, just barely stopping himself from throwing a spell. The only reason he didn't was because Penny would object. Reagan was worried, and she was acting out because of it. Still, the woman was fraying his last nerve.

He released the button and pulled the thermometer away. The light flashed orange and the number came up. One-oh-two.

"That's high, but it's not hospital high," Emery said softly, putting his fingers to her cheek. He shook his head, Reagan's words replaying over and over in his head. "I've never heard of magic causing a fever."

Reagan dug out her phone and tapped the screen. "I've never heard of half the crazy things she gets in to. Doesn't mean they aren't legit." The light from the screen was reflected in her eyes. "You're right. At one-oh-three we need to call the doctor." She let out a breath, but her brow was still furrowed. "But she's unconscious. Or is she sleeping? Shake her to see if she is sleeping."

Moss strolled into the room with a white towel. Emery hadn't even noticed him leaving.

"Here"—Moss handed the cool towel over—"put this on her forehead."

"She's been in a lot of high-pressure situations, and she's never fainted before. That woman isn't a fainter." Reagan bit her lip, worry still in her eyes. She started to pace again. "Damn it, Emery, I don't mean to give you a hard time, but had you bonded her, we'd know what was going on. At the very least, we'd be able to rule out magic as the cause. A fever is fine. We can work with a fever. Shitty little goblin residue, however…"

"Or maybe Emery would be unconscious as well." Moss moved to the corner of the room and stilled. "Maybe it is a blessing they have not formed the dual-mage connection."

"Thanks, Moss, but I have more experience," Emery said softly, looking down at Penny's angelic face. "I'd have a better idea of what to do." Emery leaned over her, propping himself on one hand. "I can't seem to make the right decision when it comes to her."

"Or maybe," Reagan said, pacing closer, "you're thinking about it too much. Maybe you're using your head and not your heart. Or intuition, if saying heart makes you freeze up in man-fear."

"Man-fear?"

"Yeah. You know. The fear of being too touchy-feely. I get it." She waved it away. "Did you shake her?

She hates waking up. She might be sleeping."

"I'm not going to—"

Reagan dashed in, as fast as an elder, and gave Penny a good shove.

Without thinking, Emery called up elements, wove together a spell, and thrust it at Reagan. Her reactions were quick, but he'd acted so fast that no one would've been able to get out from under that spell.

It concussed against her, rocketing her into the air. She hit the wall with a *thwack* before sliding down onto her butt, her mouth forming a silent *oh*. A moment later, her lips curled into a smile. "Good one. I didn't see that coming."

"What?" Penny inhaled deeply before frowning and fluttering her eyes open. All that blue hit Emery full force, and he barely stopped himself from smothering her with a hug. "What…" She glanced around in confusion. "Where am I?"

"In our hotel room. You…fainted at the meeting." Emery stroked her chin with his thumb. "How do you feel?"

She fingered the towel on her forehead. "Did I whack my head? Am I bleeding?"

"Jump to disaster, that's our girl." Reagan hefted herself up and scooted closer. "What's going on with you? Does your magic feel weird?"

Penny patted herself on the chest before looking

over at the corner where Moss stood. "I thought I felt a vampire. No, my magic is fine. I mean, I feel like everyone else's magic is battering me all the time, but other than that, it's fine."

"A good battered or a bad battered?" Reagan asked.

"When would being battered feel good?" Penny blinked up at Reagan. Her face colored in the dim light. "Oh. Right. No, the bad kind. Not horrible, but…present. Like I always know what creatures are hanging around. And oftentimes, I'd rather not. No offense, Moss."

Moss sniffed.

"Maybe that's what happened at the meeting," Reagan said, chewing on her lip. "With all that power constantly beating into you, it makes sense you'd either crack up or shut down. Cracking up might've started World War III, so you shut down."

"Is that your expert diagnosis, doctor?" Moss said dryly.

Reagan narrowed her eyes at him. "Seems you've outed yourself, Moss. You like Penny after all. I didn't realize vampires could get worried."

"She is an important asset in Mr. Durant's arsenal, that is all."

"You're lying. Admit it, you like her."

"I don't know why that is your means of taunting someone…" Penny sighed and closed her eyes. "I still don't feel great, but I feel…different. If I still have the ability to douse a magical creature's shifting ability, I can't feel it with Moss. Earlier, with that shifter, his spark almost called to me, asking to be doused. That sounds crazy, but…" She shook her head and winced before touching the towel again. "I don't know what is happening with my magic, I really don't. But my body aches and my head hurts. I feel like I have the flu."

"You might." Reagan was chewing her lip, trying to figure this out. "That might be all there is to it. You learned a new trick with that goblin, taxed your body with its magic, and it is all catching up to you."

After a moment, Penny nodded. "That's probably about right. Otherwise I'd feel differently."

"I'd imagine so."

But when Reagan's worried gaze swung back to rest on Emery, he knew she didn't entirely believe what she'd said. Or maybe she'd just said it for Penny's benefit.

Taking a deep breath, he stood, Reagan's words still weighing on him. His own self-judgment ringing loudly in his ears. Penny didn't know enough to know if something was wrong. And without a man on the inside, no one else would, either.

He'd need to talk to her. Tell her all the risks with the dual-mage connection.

And then he'd need to let her choose.

"Roger agreed to help, right?" Penny asked, as Emery checked the closets. Sure enough, their stuff was already put away. A guy could get used to Darius's people always taking care of things.

"Yes," Emery said, pausing in the doorway to the bathroom and scanning for his toothbrush. "There are some details to work out, but he's in. The fainting witch didn't scare him into backing out."

Penny's lips curled in a slight smile. "So what happens now?"

Reagan sniffed. "With two extremely experienced, resourceful, strategic, and grabby elder vampires?" She shook her head. "We keep our wits about us and try not to let them derail this whole thing so they each come out with fifty percent ownership of the new Mages' Guild."

"You're getting ahead of yourself," Moss said as she passed him. "Again."

"Right." She stopped between the bedroom and sitting room. "First we go to Seattle...and prepare for battle."

# CHAPTER 11

TWO DAYS LATER, with a dull ache throbbing through the back of my cranium that I couldn't seem to shake, I took Emery's hand and let him help me out of the nondescript black Town Car. A large house greeted us, situated comfortably amidst lush green trees. Lights shone across the front and highlighted the walkway leading to the door, flanked by artful stone columns.

It was Darius's house just outside of Seattle—the same one we'd used for shelter after busting into the Mages' Guild compound the first time. Judging by the number of vampires stationed off to either side, hanging out in the darkness and watching us enter, this place was meant to be our home base until we had our plans sorted.

A wave of nervousness washed over me. This was it. This was the first leg of our rebuttal against the Guild. They'd come for Emery and me, and now we were going to them. The battle would decide the future of mages. My future. If there was one.

"How's your head?" Emery asked me as Darius stalked toward us, followed by Moss and Reagan.

"Good. Hardly hurts anymore." I flicked my hair, trying to look blasé about the lie.

His lingering gaze said he didn't believe me. He'd been peppering me with questions about the goblin's magic—how I'd dealt with it, what it had felt like, and how it had felt when Reagan helped me. They all ended the same way—his confused brow furrow and silence.

But honestly, except for the stupid perpetual headache and the heightened sense of other creatures' magic, nothing had changed. I really, truly believed that I'd just figured some different things out about my magic. Maybe now that we were settling in at our battle headquarters, I'd have time to show Emery what was what. Then we'd both have constant headaches. Yippee!

Darius had a stern face and hard eyes, his movements as graceful as ever but now with an added edge of viciousness. Magic rolled and boiled around him. He was in the battle zone, and it showed.

"What's the situation here?" Emery asked with an air of command. Electricity kissed my skin and warmth expanded through my middle.

I sucked in a sweet breath, savoring his natural scent. A pleasant dizziness rolled over me. For a moment, my headache cleared, and I felt utterly at peace. Balanced and whole, as if my being had reached across the universe, dug deeply into the ground, and spread out through the air. Whole.

So sure, I was still cracking up a little, but this one aspect of the weirdness felt too good for me to want to fix it. It was best not to mention it.

"We've got our core team set up," Darius said, falling in beside Emery. The two of them strutting toward the house like they were on a rough-and-tumble style runway. "We're the last pieces. Vlad has secured his own locations for himself and his people. He did not want to stay in any of my properties—"

"Because of the territory-marking thing, right?" I asked. I now felt that marking situation every time I went into a shifter or vampire establishment. Thankfully, mages and humans didn't do it. It really was disconcerting.

Emery studied me again.

Darius hesitated for a beat before saying, "Yes." The word rode a release of breath; he seemed slightly derailed by my question. That, or he wasn't being entirely truthful on why Vlad was choosing to stay removed. He recovered quickly. "Roger is bringing in the shifters who are best suited for this situation. He has an estate in the hills that he has fortified. He says the location is locked down. We'll see."

"I've heard he is extremely capable." Emery stopped near the mouth of the walkway to the front door.

"He is, I'm loath to admit. He has cut down the number of our children who survive adolescence by half. He's a remarkable leader, which will benefit us greatly in this endeavor..."

A grin slowly spread across Emery's face. "But any other time, he makes your life hell, is that it?"

Darius spared Emery a glance. "Just so. That is easily remedied, of course. Or was..." I took a step back when Darius unintentionally blasted me with a wave of his spicy magic. "Rex is useless. His people were always in complete disarray. I often took my business into his territory. They never noticed my presence. I have a feeling that territory will soon change, forcing me to change with it."

"Not my problem you're breaking the rules," I said, standing my ground. "Rex was a gobbleturd. He shouldn't have been in charge of people."

"A *gobbleturd*?" Reagan moved up next to me, her spiky eyebrow hairs looking like two mini porcupines crawling across her forehead. Her hair didn't grow as fast as it needed to, given her skin's ability to withstand the effects of fire. Emery and I had tried to fix it, but Callie's healing magic was a gift. One Emery and I didn't possess.

"You can use it. I don't mind." I gave her a thumbs-up as Emery started chuckling.

"We're at least a few days out from any real strategizing," Darius said, and I wondered why we were standing around in the chill outside the house. Yesterday had been my first fever-free day, and I wanted to keep it that way. "We need more information. Updated numbers."

Emery and Reagan both nodded, businesslike, each facing a different direction.

"I want to talk to a few people," Emery said, squinting in the darkness. A form stood sentry within the branches of the tree, mostly masked by the night. The movement had been so slight—barely a flicker—that I wouldn't have noticed it if I hadn't been watching Emery. "And see a few things for myself. Tomorrow we'll go in town around twilight and feel things out."

"That's not wise," Darius said. "You're easily recognizable."

Emery's smile said Darius was missing something.

"Of course," Darius said, his tone implying he was rolling his eyes at himself. A vampire would never stoop to actually rolling his eyes. "Then be wary of other mages hunting for those using magic."

"This isn't my first rodeo." Emery's voice was low and rough. "This has been my life for the last three and a half years. I know where I stand."

"I suppose I don't have to tell you to watch her." I got another flick of Darius's eyes.

"He means you." Reagan nudged me.

"Yes, I gathered." I pulled my sweater tighter around me.

Emery didn't answer. Instead, he waited quietly for something.

Darius nodded and started for the door. "I'll leave you to it. My people know to heed your word. I expect to be updated in all matters. No detail is too small."

"We'll see," Reagan muttered.

"I'll be grilling you especially, *mon ange.* Privately." I didn't miss the sudden warmth in Darius's voice. His magic changed, too, a floral sweetness riding the vampire spice, reminding me of the flowers draped from the banister in his French Quarter house. Beautiful and elegant. Freshness among the death.

"I guess we're stuck with you, huh?" Emery barely turned, but it was clear he meant Reagan.

"Are you kidding? He's letting me out to cause havoc. I'm not passing that up!" She shook her head, looking at the sentry Emery and I had noticed earlier. "He's too young for such a prominent spot. He twitches too much. He'll have to be moved."

"I agree." Emery took a few steps toward the house, his gaze taking in the structure.

I raised my hand. "We're not going to be causing havoc. Just FYI. We're still lying low, at least until Darius has a plan."

Emery chuckled softly. "Who are you fooling,

Turdswallop? You cause havoc as a normal course of your day."

"No. Not anymore. I've turned over a new leaf." I lurched forward when Emery started walking again, cutting across the decorative mulch.

"We'll need to tear down whatever ward is here and put up another."

I nodded, not able to see the magic of the ward, which was normal with a lesser, run-of-the-mill variety spell. I could feel the pulse of it, though. *Keep out.*

I rolled up my sleeves, the cold around Seattle milder than in Ireland. I didn't immediately have to pull them back down again. It took another few seconds.

"Reagan, take a tour around the property." Emery pointed to the side. "Check for any magical tripwires or traps. If you find any, don't take them down—I want to analyze them. Look for any trails around the area. Anything that looks out of whack."

"On it." She took off at a faster-than-human walk.

"We'll need to set some new magical tripwires," Emery continued, turning to look at the driveway. "If someone knows about this place, and they probably do, since Darius had a breach of loyalty, then I want to know who's visiting. I want to know which species. The age of any vampires. The type of shifters." He looked down at me. "Do you think you can work that? I can't do the details of age and type."

"Oh." I glanced back at the house. Clearly he didn't mean to do all of this now. We hadn't even gone inside yet. "Yeah, sure. Probably. I don't know. We'll see."

His eyes softened and he ran his thumb across my cheek. My body heat flared as his skin touched mine. A sensual hum settled low in my body and the universe opened up like it had a few minutes before, welcoming us in, whole and happy and perfect.

I did like cracking up when it felt like this. I really did.

"Focus, Penny Bristol, or we'll both be lost," he said, sliding his hand along my forearm before grabbing my hand. He kissed the tips of my fingers. "Though I don't know how much more lost to you I could be."

I smiled like a lunatic and fluttered my eyes as he leaned down to me. I savored the feeling of his soft lips and hard body. All too soon, he pulled away, letting his touch linger as he exhaled forcefully. "We need to secure this house before we…sleep."

I felt feverish again, but in a good way. Hot and achy and desperate.

"Focus, love," he said, and while he said it to me, I knew he really meant it for himself. I'd need to lead the way so he could get his mind back on track.

I totally didn't want to, but I forced the delicious heat pulsing in my core to the back of my mind, where the headache had hung out lately. Except in these moments of oneness between Emery and me.

"Right," I said, back to business with a husky, wispy sort of voice. "What's next? Wait, should I be writing all this down?"

His smile didn't help my newfound sense of clear-headedness. "Let's head indoors and wait for Reagan. Whatever she sees will probably affect the ward and tripwires we set."

He held the door open for me, and the first thing I heard was "I've seen better security at the local grocery store."

"Ah nuts." I back-pedaled into Emery. "Who thought it was a good idea to bring my mother?"

# CHAPTER 12

"**W**AIT—" I HELD up a hand, my back against his front. He wasn't letting me escape. I rounded on him. "She isn't one of the core people, is she? Because working with her through text is probably *the* best strategy. You know this. Everyone knows this. I shouldn't have to tell you."

He slid his hands down my back, his touch annoyingly soothing.

"No." I flared my elbows, shrugging off his hands. "Seriously, she has to go. She'll harass me constantly about you sleeping in my room. You want me to check out the city with you? Good luck convincing her."

"Come on, Penny Bristol, let's say hi to the older half of the crew," he teased.

I shook my head with my mouth downturned. "Don't want to." He turned me around and walked me forward. I was still shaking my head. "Don't want to. I was really enjoying my freedom."

The interior of the spacious house was as I remembered it—elegant, rustic, and perfectly decorated for the area. In the living room, Dizzy and Callie were sitting on the couch, their satchels at their feet. Across from them in the leather recliner, her fingers wrapped around the barrel of her shotgun, rocked my overbearing mother.

"Really? You have the shotgun out here?" I slouched as her eyes came around to me. The vampire she'd been berating about security scooted back to the wall, probably relieved to be spared the abuse.

"Have you seen what they have posing for security around here?" She scoured the vampire with another hard look. "Of *course* I have the shotgun handy." Her gaze zipped over my shoulder. Reagan was as silent as an elder vampire, but I could feel her magic coming closer. Had she always been this stealthy, or was it another benefit from her bond? "What in the devil happened to your hair?"

"Reagan, now, I thought you were past losing your hair." Dizzy clasped his hands over his pot belly and clucked his tongue. "You were clearly being too reckless. You're lucky Callie brought the right supplies to fix you up."

"It wasn't me." Reagan pointed at me. "Her fault."

"Penny is very good, yes," Dizzy said, "but she shouldn't be surprising you with spells. You've had much more experience than she has."

"She didn't surprise me." Reagan leaned against the

doorframe. "She let it float toward me, nice and slow." Dizzy and Callie's expressions closed down into confusion. "She stole some magic from a goblin, and now she can nullify my magic. I couldn't very well let her threaten me, could I? No, I could not. So I choked her to show her I wasn't helpless."

"Come again?" my mother said, inching forward in her seat to look around me and see Reagan.

"She picked up a new trick on a bounty hunting gig. She can now nullify my magic." Reagan pushed away from the wall. "Or…she could. We haven't had the chance to try it in the last twenty-four hours. The second the new trick fails, though, it is *on*." She moved her finger through the air. "Anyone want a whiskey?"

Callie raised her hand. "How did she—Did you say goblin?" Callie shook her head. "I might need a couple shots to make sense of this."

"I'll have a whiskey as well." My mother raised her hand.

"I see the double standards are in full effect," I said as my mother adjusted the shotgun so she had a better hold on it. "Suddenly you're a whiskey drinker, and I suppose you'll harass me if I partake…"

"Nothing has changed, I'm just not hiding it from you anymore." My mother waved me on. "Now, go help Reagan get drinks."

My mouth dropped open, because I'd started walking without meaning to.

"No, no, Emery. You stay here," my mother said as I left the room. Her tone was ominous.

I should've gone back and saved him, but…well, he was a big boy.

"My mother and Callie in the same house is going to be hell," I said to Reagan as I entered the kitchen. "They fight as often as they get along. And *when* they get along, they won't rest until everyone does what they say."

Reagan chuckled and looked up from pouring the whiskey. "Nah, they'll be fine. They can bitch to each other when we ignore their express desire that we stay here and out of trouble."

I slipped onto a chair at the L-shaped island. "What are you planning?"

She took a deep breath and leaned a hand against the counter as Emery entered the kitchen behind me. With a flat expression, he tapped one of the empty glasses and slipped into the seat beside me.

"There's beer in there." Reagan jerked her head toward the fridge. "Or wine."

"I need something stronger," he said.

"That's what's great about dating a vampire." Reagan went to the freezer and got out an ice cube tray with giant cubes. "All the in-laws are long since dead. He didn't get so lucky, of course. You think Ms. Bristol is bad? Just think what it must be like when your girlfriend's dad runs hell." Reagan pushed a glass of whiskey at me.

I pushed it away again. Spiting my mother wasn't worth the foul taste. "I thought the Underworld wasn't hell?"

"Come on; this will help with the headache." She pushed the glass back.

Emery's head whipped around, his eyes now studying my face.

"Big mouth," I mumbled. "But it's fine."

"Yeah, sure. Here. Maybe it'll go down easier with ice." She dropped one of the large cubes into my glass. Whiskey splashed. "I know how to tell when you're hurt. I have to, or I might kick you too hard. Although…" She tilted her head. "No headache right now, huh?"

"No. It's good." The whiskey smell wafted toward my nose. I grimaced and pushed the glass to the side for Emery. "I'll have wine or beer. Or water. Water would be a nice option once in a while. You know, so we don't turn into alcoholics."

"Says the sheltered girl with the mother who has secretly been drinking her whole life." Reagan stilled, clearly thinking over what she'd said. "Yeah, good call. You're probably right to be worried. Beer it is."

"That's not…" I let it go. A beer actually sounded

good. Traveling in luxury with Darius was definitely awesome, but it still wore on a girl.

"What'd you find out?" Emery asked, dropping his hand to my thigh.

Reagan finished pouring the drinks and pushed the bottle aside. "I found four tripwires that seem to be more of a watch-and-report situation. That definitely sounds like the Guild to me."

"They'd have to be within…a certain distance for the spells to alert them." Emery took a sip of his drink and his face tightened up.

"Exactly," I said. "It's not good. I don't know why you bother."

He squeezed my thigh softly, his eyes twinkling. "How strong were they?" he asked Reagan.

She lounged against the island as Darius came in, dressed "down" in a button-up shirt and designer jeans. If he owned sweats, I'd never seen them. "Upper-middle tier, I'd say."

"We're not talking about vampires." Emery huffed out a laugh.

"Did you know what I meant?"

"Yup."

"Okay, then." She glanced at Darius before turning to the cabinets behind her and pulling out another bottle and a snifter. "We've also got vampires patrolling. Not ours. They clearly knew where the tripwires were, and avoided them. Middle to lower tier. Minions. They got close enough to the house to make me nervous, but they didn't mess with the ward."

"How do you know they were vampires?" I asked.

She spread her hands, the cap still in one of them. "I'm awesome."

"Riiight…"

"Any shifters?" Emery asked.

She shrugged. "Not in animal form. I didn't see any tracks. Just boots, shoes, and feet with vampire claws."

"Is there a way to track those who come onto the property?" Darius asked, joining Reagan at the island. He took his snifter before switching it to the other hand and wrapping his arm around the top of Reagan's hips. He looked…almost human. "To find out where they go?"

"Yes…" A line formed between Emery's eyebrows and he turned to look at me, his gaze hazy. "We can track them, but the problem is distance. If they're far enough away, the magic trail will fade. And it'll dissipate with time. Which is why I was asking about their power level. They'd have to stay somewhat close to feel anything from the tripwires. A couple miles, maybe, given the power level of the spells. Maybe a touch more."

"This house isn't as secluded as it seems," Darius said. "There is a town not far away. Houses between here and there." He swirled his cognac, staring down at it. "Tracking them would be answer enough."

"Tomorrow night, then," Reagan said.

Darius met her eyes, and silence fell between them.

I lifted my eyebrows. They usually weren't so lovey-dovey among other people. When my lifted eyebrows didn't do the trick, I cleared my throat.

"Patience, Turdswallop," Emery said with a laugh.

"They can do this later." I motioned between them, and Darius noticed. He moved his gaze to mine. Reagan looked away. Still no one spoke. "This is getting awkward."

Reagan laughed and shook her head. She grabbed two of the drinks. "Penny, you are not one for details, I'll say that."

"Why?" I frowned at her. "What did I miss?"

"Their conversation," Emery said.

I rubbed my head. "I feel like I'm going crazy."

"Yes, about that," Darius said. I perked up. "I do not have much time to research your condition. I can't spare the time, if we hope to have any chance with the Guild." His gaze settled on Emery. "The research, as it were, needs to come from another source if we hope to know what is going on."

Emery nodded, but didn't comment.

"Okay, look, I don't read subtle. What is going on?" I asked, annoyed. I pushed off the stool to get that beer before glancing over my shoulder to make sure my mother wasn't walking down the hall toward me. This was why I didn't want her hanging around. I couldn't be myself. Or normal.

"Darius and Reagan can communicate silently," Emery said, "and Darius has been hounding me about something for months. We're all on the same page."

"Well, I mean…" I raised my hand. "Not all of us, obviously. They can communicate silently?"

"Emery, since you know this area a little better than Reagan, it might be wise if you took the lead tomorrow," Darius said, ignoring me. As usual. "She's been instructed to keep a low profile. All you should do is get a feel for what's going on. Keep your magic up and your heads down. I'll work out the particulars with Vlad and Roger. We have a map layout of the Guild. We'll be starting there."

Emery blew out a breath as he watched me come back to the island. He absently took the bottle and twisted the cap off before handing it back. "Reagan trying to lie low, and Penny being Penny. It's a recipe for disaster."

# CHAPTER 13

"OH HEY, I remember this bar," Reagan said the next evening as we sat in a rental car in the heart of Seattle. Down the street was our destination, as determined by Emery—the bar owned by his friend Joe, a wolf shifter with a gruff attitude and kind heart. His bar had been a gathering place for Guild mages, or at least wannabe members. "I'm not sure the bartender likes me much."

"That doesn't really surprise me, given that you chase the shifters in New Orleans around with bread sticks." I checked the compartments of my utility belt, feeling the pulse of a few of my power stones. Mr. Happy-Go-Lucky, a brown rock with various colors slashed through it, was desperate to get out and get into some danger.

"That was *one time*," she said. "They all knew I was joking. I was pretending the bread stick was a sword, for fuck's sake. *Clearly* I was joking."

"They thought you were going to bust their heads in. They did not know you were joking."

"Well…if I caught them…I would've. But all in good fun! They're shifters. They're used to fighting for their position. What's a little scuffle among friends?"

"Definitely a recipe for disaster," Emery said quietly before flicking up the flaps on his utility belt, which was exactly the same as mine.

"It'll be fine. So far I don't see anyone suspicious." Reagan turned in her seat to look behind. "No one followed us."

Emery nodded, scanning the street. "Since our new wards didn't go off at Darius's, I'd suspect no one wandered by last night or early today. More sentries have been posted, so that makes sense." He looked over at me. "You have your phone?"

I patted the first compartment of my belt. "Got it. My mom is on standby."

He glanced in the rearview at Reagan. "You're positive the dual-mages are staying put?"

Reagan grimaced, a much nicer look now that Callie had regrown her hair. "No. But they probably are. They aren't used to staying at home, but they seemed to see the sense in keeping the scouting group small. Hopefully that means they'll stay put. It's never a given, though."

"Sorry," I said softly, offering him a little smile. I felt bad for him. He could've had a quiet life in the wilds. Sleeping in the dirt had to be better than dealing with my crazy mother, a couple crazy mages, Reagan, and a bunch of meddling vampires.

His eyes softened and he took my hand. "Worth it."

"Ew. Get a room—"

"Really?" I shot Reagan a glare. "Did I say anything last night when you were staring into vampire dearest's lovely brown eyes?"

"They're hazel. With green specks—"

"No, I did not. So you can just wait."

"Yes, you did, and I was talking to him with my brain. Why aren't you this lippy with your mother?"

I huffed and turned to face forward, ignoring Emery's silent chuckles. "I'm practicing on you. I'm working up to my mother."

"Joy," Reagan said dryly, and Emery laughed harder.

"Is this what your bounty hunter gigs are like?" he asked. "The two of you bickering the whole time?"

"Nah." Reagan adjusted her fanny pack. She didn't want to get a utility belt, fearing it would be easier for people to realize that she wasn't really using the casings she carried to do magic. She was a headcase. "Half the time she is running away screaming from the mark. We only bicker the other half of the time. Come on; let's go. We're losing the daylight."

"Why are we doing this during the day, again?" I asked, stepping out of the car as I ballooned a concealment spell around myself. It made me uneasy to think that Darius and his people couldn't serve as backup.

Emery exited the other side of the car and put up the same spell, but with little embellishments and intricacies that would make it more durable.

"You always seem to show me up," I grumbled, moving so Reagan could get out of the car and climb right into my spell. "Don't touch anything, Reagan, remember."

"I know, I know—Crap." The spell started to dissolve when a flare of her magic zipped through her fingers as she stepped into it. "My bad. Can you nullify my magic as we go?"

"Doing that takes a lot of concentration and energy. I don't think I could do that and maintain a spell at the same time."

"Good to know." She clasped her hands low and kept her elbows close to her body. I increased the size of the spell.

"Let's merge these spells and get going," Emery said, coming around to us.

"You can merge spells?" Reagan put out her hands, her elbows still held in close, so she could feel what we were doing. "I didn't think that was possible once the spells had been realized."

"It is," he said with glimmering eyes, "if you have a clever little turdswallop to accidentally do it when she's mad that your spell is taking up too much room."

"That's a bad word, just so you know." I tried to hide my threatening smile. "When you call me turdswallop, you're calling me a bad word."

"In British," he said, his smile growing.

I rolled my eyes, letting my smile break free. "We're venturing out while it's still sunny…why?"

"Because they have vampires too," Reagan said. "But they don't have shifters."

"Then why didn't we leave earlier?"

"Because they have a lot more mages than we have shifters, and we might need the vampires to save our asses. I could get us out of a bind, but that might get me into a bigger bind."

"And me," I said, grabbing Emery's bicep like it was a walking stick. "The size of this freaking thing…" I moved my hand down to his forearm so I could actually grab on. "And if your father found out about you, it would get me into a bind, too. Because if I can null your magic, I can probably null his. Right? Didn't you get your weird from him?"

"Like you can talk."

"I think I got my weird from both parents, actually. They didn't hand over any normal to go with it." I tuned in to the various magical vibes of the area flowing around me like the breeze. "Well, even if I couldn't null his magic, I could figure out something. We beat a bunch of mages and mercenaries in dumb hats; we can take on your dad."

"We probably wouldn't be enough," she said in a strangely thick voice. "But I've noted it for the files."

"Two naturals and a nut case?" Emery's voice was a low hum. He was probably worried about sound leaking out of the spell. "We'd dominate."

Reagan huffed. She didn't comment, but her magic surged. I grinned, ready to tease her about her squishy heart, when a foreign feeling wound around my leg. Just my leg, and nothing else.

"Slow," I said quietly. The feeling tingled as it worked up my leg, lightly tapping. "Something is…touching me." I opened my eyes and looked down. Nothing was there. No magical strands or weaves. "Reagan, do you feel anything?"

"Not magically." She put her hand on my shoulder and turned, scanning. "Something is here, though, watching us. I feel…danger. You can't tell what kind of magic it is?"

"No. I've never felt it before. It's…" I tilted my head, then flinched at a sharp pain, like a pinch, on my hip. My magic welled up in response. Emery's Plain Jane power stone, which I carried around because I was the designated power stone jockey, throbbed in its compartment in my belt. "Ow."

"What?" Emery asked. He tensed and stopped before turning slowly.

"Something pinched me." I rubbed the offending spot, feeling a light breath of intent.

*Observe.*

"It's watching us," I said in a hush, my eyes widening as I looked around for something hiding in the shadows.

"I literally just said it was watching us," Reagan whispered.

A few people ambled along the sidewalk on the other side of the street, by themselves or chatting in groups of two. One person wandered toward us, thankfully stopping at a car up the way. Everyone seemed loose and normal—no one else seemed to have a clue something dangerous, or several dangerous things if you counted us, lurked in their presence.

I shook my head, frowning. My intuition, which usually picked up odd lurkers, didn't even stir. Without that magical touch, I would've had no clue someone was in the area, spying on us.

"Sun is out, so it can't be a vampire." Reagan, her hand still on my shoulder, turned so as to better see behind us. "We should be invisible, so it is something that can see through magic, or at least feel it."

"Druid," Emery said, sounding as close to afraid as I'd ever heard him. He rolled his shoulders. "It's a druid."

Reagan swore quietly and a burst of her magic shook my bones. I barely patched up the spell before it dissipated entirely.

"What's a druid?" I asked quietly, sweat beading on my brow from Emery and Reagan's reactions. They wouldn't react this way to a mage or vampire, so whatever this was, it had to be ten times worse.

"Any druid in the Brink would be of the warrior class. They're usually used as assassins." Reagan pushed me to get me moving. "I've heard they can hide in plain daylight. Right next to you, and you wouldn't know it until the druid's knife was in your neck. I've never seen one. I don't even know what they look like."

"Like large men or lithe women," Emery said quietly.

"Are you positive that's what it is?" Reagan asked. "Do you see it?"

We moved slowly down the sidewalk, my magic rolling and boiling above me, ready to be used in a hastily created spell.

"I didn't see it, no." Emery's hands were in front of him, prepared for battle. "I was hunted by one of them. After I escaped the Guild the first time, they sent one. I know exactly the effect a warrior druid has on my senses. Exactly."

"You aren't dead, so you clearly escaped. That's a good sign," Reagan said, her magic coming in thick waves, pounding into me. Twisting through my energy and seeping into my body, ready to be used should I need it.

"I am very dangerous right now," I whispered, just so everyone was on the same page.

"That's a good thing," Reagan replied, just as quietly.

"When that druid was after me, I'd never had so many forewarnings come in the space of two days," Emery said. His gaze stayed pointed in one direction, not locking on anything. He clearly knew the general area the creature was hiding, but the fact that he couldn't pick it out, when he could spot vampires, was…disconcerting.

"I don't like this. Let's get out of here," I said, ready to sprint. Fighting against a shadow didn't appeal to me. I hated the unknown.

"Did you get him in the end?" Reagan's fingers tightened their grip on my shoulder.

"I did get *her* in the end," Emery said. "When you can see them, it's like battling any other extremely fast, extremely capable magical fighter. Their power is in their ability to hide in plain sight, as you said."

"Yeah, there is some serious danger nearby." Reagan's fingers jerked on my shoulder as she turned and looked the other way. "I used to feel like this before I could see through the vampires' invisible sheets."

"You can see through those?" Emery asked, his voice calm and breathing even. He was readying for battle. "That must make things easier."

"Much."

"Cool, yeah," I said, picking up the pace. "Invisible sheets, yeah. Is it following us, do you think?" That foreign magic swirled in front of me before moving on to Emery, still exploratory. "It's sussing us out. Trying to get a read on us, I think. I don't get vicious intent from it."

"That doesn't mean it doesn't plan to kill us," Reagan murmured. "Most of them are healers and nature lovers. Peaceful folk. Only a select few get the warrior strand of magic. They don't go into battle with rage or aggression; they do it with a sense of business economy. And even when they're on the attack, they keep their finger on the pulse of peace. Or so I have always heard."

"That doesn't even make sense." I licked my lips and realized Reagan had been right in that the slow buildup to trouble was the absolute worst. It was better when it came at you quickly, like ripping off a Band-Aid. "We need a plan."

"The bar is just up ahead. Let's go in," Reagan said. "Let's see if it follows."

"Christopher Walken's yoga pants," I muttered with a tight jaw. I could feel shifter magic pulsing from the bar, claiming it and warning off those looking for trouble. It was probably something that had always been there and I just hadn't noticed it before, but right now it was not helping keep me calm.

"Christopher Walken's…yoga pants," Emery said, pulling the terms apart slowly, like he was examining them.

"Just have Penny swear at our watcher," Reagan said drolly. "He'll get annoyed and take off."

At the door to the bar, I took a deep breath, feeling that pulse of power. Knowing I was bringing in all sorts of trouble, and not wanting an attack from both sides.

"Why did we stop?" Reagan asked, watching the street.

I sucked in a breath and walked in. The layout was the same as it had been on my last visit—tables along the right and a large square bar to the left with an open area in the middle—but everything looked way fresher. New paint, redone bar, and the far side, the gathering area beyond the bar, looked totally new.

"Did he renovate?" I asked, choosing the right side of the bar instead of the more popular and busier area beside the bar.

"Is there a hole in the far side?" Reagan asked as we crossed the threshold as a group.

"No…"

"Then yeah, he renovated." Her body braced as we

eased farther into the bar, probably a preparation in case the watcher would surge in after us.

"Penny, can you feel any magic?" Emery took his forearm out of my grasp and grabbed me instead. He clearly expected some sort of attack, too.

"No," I said. "Nothing out of the ordinary. Though maybe the potent shifter magic is overpowering it."

"How about mages?" Reagan asked, glancing at Emery before looking to the far side of the bar.

"I only feel shifter magic." I sorted through all of the various waves of magic meandering around the room. "A bunch of it."

"As Roger calls in more people, they'll head toward the shifter bars." Reagan relaxed slightly, her hand loosening on my shoulder. "This will be a dead giveaway to the Mages' Guild. Darius better hurry up with that plan, or we'll have to go in without one."

I shook my head, but there was no point in arguing with her. She wasn't the one in charge. Not until she forcefully took over, anyway.

She ran her hand through the air and dissipated the concealment spell around us. Emery tugged on my arm, his eyes on the door, but he headed for the bar counter. "Watch those shadows," he said, resting his forearm on the wood.

I backed into his body, letting my attention wander and muting most of my senses so I could focus on the magic around me. The strands and playful twists drifting and lingering in the air. It was the way I could help the best.

"Oh hey, I didn't know you were back in town."

I recognized that deep, gruff voice. Joe, the shifter bar owner who had given Emery and me shelter when we'd needed it the most. We'd been a danger to him, and he'd done it anyway. He wasn't the sort to cast aside friends in need.

"No way. Get her out of here," he yelled.

Unless Reagan was involved…

Peeling an eye open, I found yet more proof of my theory: Reagan and shifters typically did not get along. And now we were going to be thrown out of relative safety, directly into the path of whatever waited for us outside.

# CHAPTER 14

"**G**ET HER OUT." Joe flung his finger toward the door as he stalked toward us, thunder clouds on his face as he stared at Reagan. He was a wolf, I remembered, and I felt the call of the forest and the thrill of the hunt as he neared. Similar to Roger, but slightly different from the feel of Red the dog. Huh. I could decipher the differences in shifter animal. I wondered if that mattered.

"Emery, what are you doing messing around with her?" Joe stopped in front of us, and I could see people on the other side of the bar turning and trying to look through the island of liquor bottles to watch the show.

"I'm trying to keep a low profile, bro," Emery said quietly, his eyes still on the door.

"Then you shouldn't have brought this chick in here with you." Joe braced his large hands on the bar. His big arms bulged with muscle, leading up to a wide girth of shoulders and down to a brick of a body. Most shifters were impressively muscled, but Joe was a solid boulder.

"That is highly unfair," Reagan said, spreading her

hands in front of her. "I wasn't the one that blew up your bar. Guild flunkies picked a fight with me."

"You blew up the bar?" I asked her.

"Did she blow up the bar..." Joe's voice rose an octave. People ducked out of the concealment of the back portion of the place and drifted toward the clear area at the end of the bar, emerging to catch the drama. "Yes, she blew up this bar! I *just* got it fixed up last month. And you want to come back and wreak havoc again?"

"Darius footed you the money while you waited for the insurance to kick in, didn't he?" Reagan asked. "We took care of it."

"You okay, Joe?" someone called from the far corner.

"Don't know. I might need help tossing out some riffraff," he said. "No offense, Emery, but you should've seen this place. She blew the whole side and back half off. That room you use sometimes—oh hi, Penny—well, that was gone. Blown to shit—"

"Yes, but..." Reagan put up a finger, "I would like to take this opportunity to remind you, once again, that a *mage* blew up your bar. Not me. I was an innocent bystander, like everyone else."

"An innocent bystander?" Joe's magic flared. "You pushed those mages to do it. You practically egged them on!"

She crinkled her nose. "I think we're remembering

different events."

His magic pulsed harder. "You think we're—"

"Look, look, look, hey, hey—" Emery leaned in and put his hand out between them. Without missing a beat, Reagan took a step back and turned her gaze to the door. There was something to be said for two survivors working together. And then there was me, the square peg. "Ordinarily, I'd get her out of here. You know I would, Joe. But you must know why we're here."

Joe took a deep breath, staring at Reagan with anger-heated eyes. "Why is she staring at the door? Who has she got following her this time?"

"Oh, nobody," she said, her attention not wavering. "Just a druid with an interest in us. No big deal."

Joe's face bleached of color. His gaze sought Emery's. "Is she for real?"

"We didn't get a glimpse, but I'd bet my life on it," Emery said, leaning over the bar. "We're just looking for information. I thought I would check in. Do you have any mages stopping through here anymore?"

Joe shifted, his eyes heading toward the door as well. "If you got a druid out there, you don't want to be staying in one place. You'd best get behind a ward."

"Wards don't keep them out," Reagan said. She shrugged. "Assuming the rumors are true. That's why they make the best magical assassins."

"We're better off in one location without a lot of

shadows." Emery shifted a little closer to Joe, trying to catch his focus again. "Joe, the mages?"

Joe shook himself a little, fear lingering in his eyes. "Yeah, right, uh…" A line formed between his eyebrows as he tried to snap back to reality. He'd been blindsided by our ragtag crew of mayhem. "Mages—a few. I've had a few wander through, eyeballing everyone. They didn't start any trouble, though. And my people left well enough alone. But the bar is filling up, what with Roger bringing in more people." Joe paused, as though making sure Emery was in the know. "If any mages wander in now, they aren't long in leaving."

"Yeah." The word rode Reagan's sigh. "Not good. We should've accounted for that."

"What?" Joe asked, his gaze drifting back toward the door.

"We gonna get service over here, Joe?" someone shouted across the bar.

"He's talking," Reagan called back. "Mind your manners, or I will mind them for you."

"Don't you start." Joe leveled a finger at her. "Do not start a fight in my bar. Roger might have a soft spot for you, but he does not own this bar."

Reagan huffed and glanced at Joe. Her smile grew as she took in the serious look on his face. "If that hard mug is Roger with a soft spot," she said, returning her gaze to the door, "I'd hate to see what he's like with an enemy."

"Yes, you most certainly would," Joe said.

"Do you have any information on how the Guild is preparing?" Emery asked, his voice still low.

Joe glanced behind him, looking suddenly uncomfortable. He held up a finger to the crowd that had gathered across the bar. "Just hang on a sec, will ya? Let me sort them out, and I'll be back." On his way around the bar, he pointed at Reagan again. "Don't mess with anything. I'm watching you."

"You are very jumpy, Joe. Very jumpy." Reagan rolled her neck. "I'm getting a bad feeling."

Emery's eyes hazed over for a moment, and I knew it was a premonition that warned him when someone or something was about to deliver him—or me—a death blow. He frowned and wrapped his arm around my waist. "We've got trouble."

Magic cocooned us, ready to rip out the second an attack struck. But nothing happened.

"What'd you see?" I asked, noticing shifters still peering at us with interest through the island of bottles. Joe must've told them who we were. Basically, the crew many of them would be working with soon.

"A…warning, of sorts." He shook his head and turned to face the door before shifting to look at the wall behind us, loosely draped in shadow. "I've seen one like it before, but that last one was a vision of *you*. Back in New Orleans. They're not like the usual premonitions…they're just warnings. I can't describe it. I don't know how to get out from under them."

"Easy, take down the Guild," Reagan said, bristling. She glanced behind at the wall. "Something's not right."

"No." Emery let out a slow breath. He rolled his shoulders. "It isn't. We gotta go."

"I agree. Dang. Joe looked like he was going to spill something juicy. And if I know his type, he won't want to tell Roger. He's got a wife and kids; he doesn't want to endanger them by getting wrapped up in danger."

"How…do you know all this?" Emery asked in confusion.

"What kind of woman do you take me for— someone who *doesn't* learn about people before I instigate their bars getting blown up?" She stepped toward the door, looking behind her again. "Come on. Get away from that wall. I feel like something is going to bust through it."

"I have absolutely no danger warnings," I mumbled, closing my eyes and feeling the magic. "Did that goblin kill my Temperamental Third Eye? Because that is going to be a problem."

"God you're weird." Reagan's boots clunked on the floor as she stepped farther away.

It hit me like a shot, making my body tingle and my legs shake. My flight reflex roared to life, insisting I get the hell out of that bar.

"Never mind. In good working order. Let's go, no time to lose." I blinked my eyes open and lunged after Reagan, but put on the brakes a moment later, making Emery slam into my back.

Magic surged up from outside, blackened and putrid and awful. Twisted elements rolled and surged, vile intent dripping from them and infecting everything in the vicinity.

*Slice. Maim. Destroy.*

"Mages, and they know we're here. That, or they are after the shifters." I clutched Emery's arm. "Back door. Or do we fight?"

A loud *bang* sounded from the other side of the bar, followed by an explosion. The building shook and people shouted. Shifter magic exploded and the sound of ripping clothes filled the air as several people changed form.

Reagan ripped her sword off her back. "We're in it to win it, folks. Prepare for battle."

# CHAPTER 15

"**D**ON'T FREAK OUT, don't freak out." I yanked open the compartments of my utility belt and drifted off to the side of the others, the three of us making a loose triangle. The power stones throbbed in my belt, and I lifted a couple of them out and placed them on the bar. If we had to run, I wanted to snatch them as quickly as possible.

Mr. Happy-Go-Lucky sent out a pulse of power. Emery's Plain Jane throbbed.

"Here we go," I said, sucking in a breath as adrenaline flooded me.

Magic tumbled through the door, hot and sticky and oh so vile. It felt wrong, worked in a way contrary to nature and fused with only the most evil of intentions.

That made it weak. Unbalanced.

I started a weave to counter it, but Reagan was already there, zipping open her fanny pack, smashing an empty casing against her sword and mumbling, "Fuckity-fuck-shitty-fart."

"What is she doing?" Emery said, glancing at the back of the bar. More shifters were transforming on the other side as magic rolled in from the front like a barbed wheel. People or animals darted this way or that, chaos reigning with the surprise.

"She's pretending to cast a spell, remember?" I said, reaching forward to join our half-formed spells. "You've seen her do it before."

"Not with the swearing. *Get back*," Emery yelled, pushing the counter-spell toward the jagged, destructive thing attempting to mow down the shifters.

"We were in the wrong place at the right time," I said, jogging a little closer to the door and turning so I had the best angle. "They were after the shifters."

"Seems so."

"Boy will they get a nasty surprise," Reagan said in a singsong voice. She was in her element.

More magic flashed through the front door. Reagan pounced, hacking through the spell with her sword. The fragments of it withered away, not drifting into nature as they should've.

"This magic isn't right," I yelled over the din. "It leaves a bad taste in my mouth."

A concussion of air blew through the other side of the bar, a silent explosion. Debris from the back area slapped the walls and tumbled across the floor. The mages were clearly trying to pose a double-pronged attack on the front and back.

"Do you feel a difference between the magic coming at the front and the back?" Emery asked, zipping off another spell across the room. "Because I don't. Middle power level, no creativity. If they'd show themselves, I could take them down easily."

"I'm on it!" Reagan darted out of the front entrance, clearly forgetting the freaking warrior creature that was loitering out there somewhere.

"Hurry," I said to Emery, rushing forward with her.

Before I could make it outside, a body flew in at me. I jumped back just in time, the man windmilling his arms before tumbling into the barstools at the bar and landing on his face. Reagan's words rolled in after him. "There's one."

"She's nuts," Emery said, spreading a spell over the struggling body. I weaved in a little of Reagan's magic, hardening the air and making the guy lie still.

"Got more out here," Reagan yelled from some-where outside the door. She grunted. "I'm not so easy to sneak up on, you fecking turdswallop!" Another body tumbled through the door.

"It sounds like a really bad word when she says it." As I helped Emery secure the newest mage, I felt Reagan's magic drift away, too far for me to use it. She was probably chasing someone. "Right, she's got this entrance covered. Let's close down the back."

Emery ran across the front of the bar, weaving between two small wolves with tails low and hackles raised. I followed until I felt the intent of a spell coming.

*EXPLODE.*

Spinning, I saw magic billow through the front entrance of a building on the other side of the street, clearly created from multiple people with different grasps on spell work. It was both clumsy and powerful enough to do the job.

Letting Emery handle the back door, I surged toward the front, pulling elements fast. Though I would *not* admit it to Reagan, the bounty hunting gigs had sharpened my reflexes. I concocted a spell that would both counter the mess surging toward me and take out the casters behind it.

That sent off, I caught movement to my right.

"Penny!" Emery screamed.

He'd had a premonition. I was already on it.

The enemy mage got off his spell, but I was ready. My counter-spell cut through it and blasted into him, knocking him off his feet and onto his back. He didn't even get a chance to scream.

A quick glance at Emery revealed he'd already turned around. He knew I had it handled.

The mages across the street screamed as my spell homed in on them. More screaming came from the side. Three mages were sprinting down the center of the street in my direction.

I braced myself to fire a spell at them when I saw why they were running.

Reagan ran behind them with a grin and an outstretched sword. "Do not pick on my friends!" she yelled.

A horn honked as she shoved them to the ground, cackling manically.

I looked both ways but didn't see or feel any more magical enemies. The humans that had their phones out, aimed at the woman chasing people through the streets with a sword, would have to be dealt with later.

The cops would be here shortly. We needed to get out of Dodge.

"Hurry up," I yelled at Reagan. I spun around to check on Emery in time to see one of his spells shooting toward the back door. A huge wolf followed, snarling. A scream died almost as soon as it erupted, but another started up, turning hoarse with terror. More shifters launched toward the back door.

Something tingled my awareness, coming from the right. The wall directly behind the bar was empty, which indicated no one had made it over the bar. That didn't mean they weren't using it to hide.

I spread a mini-ward across the door that would alert me if anything came through. That done, I ran forward and peered over the counter, seeing a black mat pocked with holes spread across the brown floor. Something clinked and I caught sight of the heel of a foot.

Thinking of Joe, I hefted myself onto the bar.

Not Joe at all. A skinny man with an open satchel and herbs spilling out. It was a mage, and he was hiding from the opposition.

"You slimy little coward," I seethed, having fired off a spell to keep him put without even thinking about it. I didn't have the help of Reagan's magic, but I had plenty of my own power. I slammed him with it, hearing his surprised yelp before the force of my magic knocked him out.

*That was cool.*

I pushed back onto my feet, hearing a distant blast echoing from the other side of the bar. Emery was still mid-battle and could probably use my help.

I jumped back from the bar, away from the barstools, and turned, the heels of my shoes squeaking against the bar floor. Before I could move forward, a hand came out of literally nowhere and curled around my neck.

"Holy dump truck ping-pong!" I gasped, immediately surrendering to the surprise and terror. As expected, my survival magic kicked into high gear, electrifying my body and blasting the hand touching my neck.

A *zzzzzz* sound preceded the hand flinching away. Shadows moved and coalesced as a massive man stepped away from the wall. At least six-four in height, heavily muscled yet graceful, he slipped around me to block off the exit.

Black clothes covered his body from neck to ankle. Clear blue eyes wrapped in thick lashes the color of midnight surveyed me without emotion. His face was startlingly handsome, but the planes and angles of its bone structure, along with the way his thin nose ended in a slight hook, gave him an almost harsh look, enhanced by the throbbing aura of competence.

His intelligent eyes surveyed me, cool and analytical. Sizing me up.

"I can see you," I said, as though that were some kind of threat. Magic rolled through my fingers, a weave even a vampire couldn't outrun.

"I have two contracts outstanding," he said, his voice like a lullaby, something people wouldn't mind hearing as they slipped into their grave. "One is to kill you."

"That's my cue." I shot out a line of red, the vermin zapper.

Shadows moved and spun, confusing my eyes. I heard a grunt, three feet farther to the right than I'd anticipated. I turned to blast him again, but an arm suddenly wrapped around my waist before pure brawn sent me into the air.

"Good gravy, that's confusing." I shot off a wide spell, guaranteed to wrap him up. Crashing against the wall didn't even faze me. Practice made perfect, as they said, and I'd been thrown around a lot in my training.

The spell sliced across the collection of shadows, the way he masked himself, and slammed against the wall behind him.

"You can dodge spells?" I hit the ground, not stopping. "Luckily, I am a problem solver." I zapped off another spell just to keep him at bay, but that dang hand came out of nowhere again, snatching me off the ground and pinning me to the wall.

Survival magic tore through my body and smacked into his torso, flinging him back. He rammed the edge of the bar and knocked all the chairs down around his feet.

Shadows started to collect, pulling around him as he fought the barstool legs to keep from falling. I felt the whisper of his magic against my skin. It connected him to the world around us in such a hypnotic way that I could but stand there for a moment, eyes closed, drifting on his magical breeze.

"Please," he said, the lullaby wrapping around me. "I did not mean to startle you. The second contract is to protect you. One to kill, and the other to protect."

Reality seeped in through the dreamlike effect of his

magic, waking me up. I blinked my eyes open, meeting that glacial gaze, strangely not cold, just beautiful.

"I'm not sure what's going on," I said. "Are you hypnotizing me with magic, or is this another sign I'm cracking up?"

He didn't respond, and no reaction bled through his expression. "I can name my price in either contract. I have never been in this situation before. I wanted to meet the target and decide for myself if she should live or die."

"I hate to be the bearer of bad news..." Reagan's voice cut in from just inside the door, my mini-ward having been dissipated without my knowledge. Her sneaking prowess was so good that not even the stranger heard or felt her coming.

Shadows pulled from around the room and flew at the stranger, confusing my eyes. I was magically onto him, though. I could feel the center of that dizzying storm, softly flowing from one place to the next, moving so fast, zigging and zagging, it was hard to keep track of it.

A solid wall of air formed in front of him and slapped him back. His body flew out of the shadows and hit the back wall horizontally. He crashed down to the floor.

"If you choose the wrong side, *you* will be the one dying. Not her." Reagan sauntered forward with her sword in hand and magic swirling around her in a complex harmony not even this stranger could match.

His eyes widened as he slowly rose to his full height. He wiped a drop of blood from his lip with the back of his hand. Then looked at it. When his gaze came back up, his eyes gleamed.

"I wondered when I might see another of your kind." The pitch of his voice changed slightly, dropping just a bit. Putting on a little gravel.

He changed his voice to best affect whomever he was talking to. Strange.

"There is no *my kind*. I'm just a bounty hunter. It's her you feel." Reagan gestured at me, and I realized she'd put herself on the line in my defense. She might hold back her magic when defending herself, but she didn't hold back when it concerned me.

My heart swelled. She was sometimes the worst friend imaginable, but underneath her love of torturing me, she was loyal and pure of heart.

"I can feel her magic," the man said. "Its essence. She has been touched, but at her core she's still just a mage. You…are not a mage. You…are the Heir. I have met two of you. I have known one. All the other Heirs have expired. But you have the right current through your blood. I feel it. You are true. He will know, soon enough."

Reagan jutted out a hip, studying the stranger. "My,

my, you're old, aren't you?"

He didn't answer, and his expression didn't change.

"And you're a druid?" she asked.

He stared.

"Not much of a talker, huh?" She nodded as jogging footsteps sounded from the other side of the bar. Emery came into view, looking around wildly. He caught sight of what was going on and slid to a stop. His eyes pinned to the stranger, and the vibe around him turned brutal and savage. He thought I was in danger, and it didn't take a genius to know that he would lay down his life to protect me.

My heart swelled even larger. Electricity sizzled through the room, kissing my skin and infusing my core. Even from the distance, our magical energies joined and hummed. My current cracked-up serenity balanced his fire-spitting wildness.

"You," the stranger said, his voice raspy now. His features did alter this time, anger, pain, and fear rolling across them so quickly that I almost missed it.

"Yes," Emery responded, magic weaving through his fingers. "I know how to circumvent your magic. If you make a move toward her, you will not see tomor-row."

"You killed one of my kind," the stranger said, no inflection in his voice.

"Yes," Emery replied. "It was self-defense."

The stranger nodded, his head jerking up once, then back down. "We are banned from taking contracts on you. You are too much of a liability." Emery didn't react. The stranger turned his attention to Reagan. "We are also banned from taking contracts on any of the Heirs, through our respect of Lucifer."

"That doesn't make me like you better," she said. "What's your move here, bub? The cops are nearly here. We haven't got all day."

It wasn't until then that I heard the wails of the police sirens. Yet the bar still *felt* quiet. No one had entered to check things out. Joe hadn't come back in to assess the damage or throw insults at Reagan.

It was as if a veil had dropped around our small gathering.

The druid's clear blue eyes were trained on me. "But my decision had already been made. You are pure of heart, which has earned you the loyalty of those around you. It is commendable. They judged wisely, touching you. I will take the contract to protect you." He stared at the air in front of him before his eyes flashed, as though illuminated by a light bulb. He pushed the invisible wall Reagan's magic had created, and I felt a shift in the magic. It didn't falter, as far as I could tell, but he'd moved it.

Reagan took a step back, as though startled, and her eyebrows dipped. She was a lot more impressed with his moves than I was. "Can you do that with all Underworld magic, or is mine just underdeveloped?"

"Yes," he said as Reagan released her wall. He stalked forward. "Yours is fully developed but not fully utilized. You still have much to learn."

"Yeah. Story of my life," she said, and in that moment, she sounded like I did most of the time. It was nice to know I wasn't alone.

"When does the contract start?" I called as he neared the door. "And does it protect me from my mother?"

# CHAPTER 16

E MERY LET OUT a shaky breath as he let the weave he'd finished drift back into his surroundings. His legs shook and a bead of sweat dribbled down his temple. That druid was more powerful than the one he'd fought. Older, too, judging from the fact that he'd talked about knowing the other Heirs of Lucifer, people who hadn't been around for hundreds of years. Emery hadn't realized druids lived that long.

"That was a trip." Reagan nervously chuckled and smoothed her hair along her head. Sirens wailed close by. Blue and red pulsed in the frame of the doorway. "That guy's power was intense. It nearly made my eyes water. Did you see him push my magic back? No one has ever done that before, not even demons."

"Yeah." Emery shook his head as footsteps approached from the back of the building. He remembered the feeling that had nearly kept him from re-entering this front section of the bar a few moments before. If not for the knowledge that Penny was still inside, he probably would've found somewhere else to be. To go back to her, though, he'd fought the odd feeling.

He'd had no idea druids could do *that*, either.

"I must've gone up against a younger druid," he said, spanning the space still separating him from Penny and Reagan. "I don't think I would've gotten out from under that one."

Reagan let out a shaky breath, and Emery could see that she was equally gobsmacked. Penny, on the other hand, dusted herself off as though nothing had happened. She didn't seem to be affected at all.

"You okay?" he asked as he reached her. She gave him a confused look.

"How did I know I'd come back into my ruined bar and find *you* standing around?" Joe said as he walked in, sports sweats swishing with each step and his chest bare.

"Your bar is…" Reagan looked around with raised eyebrows. "Mostly fine. Just a few scratches."

Piercing sirens stopped just outside the bar. More shifters in human form filed into the bar, all hurrying to get some clothes on after their shift.

"They were coming for you, not her," Emery said, motioning for Penny to get moving. "The battle has begun. Tell Roger. His people need to get out of sight."

Joe's eyes narrowed, but he nodded slowly. "I'll pass it on, though it'll probably be faster for your people to contact him. I'll be dealing with a bunch of police tape"—he shot Reagan a scowl—"again."

"I'm starting to get the idea you are holding a grudge…" Reagan said.

"You might not be fighting, but you're still a target, Joe," Emery said as Penny weaved together a concealment spell. "You all need to lie low. Keep your family safe."

Joe nodded and heaved a sigh. He rubbed the back of his neck, looking around at the bodies littering the ground, the various holes and burns, and the debris from whichever mage had blown in the back area. "I must have bad luck," he murmured.

"Come on," Emery said, helping Penny finish the spell before draping it over them. Reagan ducked in, keeping her hands low.

"This is way easier than taking off running," Reagan said as they stepped out the door. Policemen were blocking off the surrounding streets and surveying the damage.

They wouldn't be able to get the rental car out of there. They'd be stopped immediately.

"We need to hoof it." Emery led them to the right, where the cops were just putting up a barricade to keep people off the street. The sun had disappeared into murky darkness, only splotches of magenta and tangerine splashing the sky. "Maybe we should call Darius.

Vampires will be out shortly."

"The mages weren't expecting us in that bar," Reagan said as they neared the corner. Another police car pulled in. She pushed Penny to turn the corner and put distance between them and the human authority figures. "Did you leave any of the mages alive to report back to the Guild?"

"No, but that doesn't mean there wasn't someone monitoring the attack from a safe distance. They could've called for reinforcements." Emery took Penny by the upper arm, confused by her non-reaction to the events. She wasn't fired up or freaking out. She didn't even seem to care that they were still in danger without a plan.

*She has been touched, but at her core she's still just a mage.*

The druid had said that. *Touched.* What did that mean? Had Darius been right about the whole godly power thing?

"Penny, are you okay?" he asked, giving her a small shake in case she was fighting a daze.

"Yes," she said, and there was a sigh riding her words, pleasant and serene.

Fear wormed through his gut. What had that druid done to her? Had he cocooned her with some type of magic that kept her from properly responding to her surroundings?

He hated all these questions. All these riddles locked up inside of her. If even one of them was dangerous…

"We're invisible. The vampires aren't going to be able to find us," Reagan said. "Let's either keep moving until it's dark enough to call Darius or grab a cab. There is no sense fighting anymore tonight."

"You're shying away from a fight? That has to be a first. Someone should write that down," Emery said, picking up the pace. They'd find a cab. It would be faster. He needed to know what was going on with Penny, as soon as possible.

"No, no. You've got me all wrong." Reagan pointed at a cross street with more traffic. She clearly agreed on the need for speed. "I just want to wait for the bigger fight when we have that giant druid shadowing us. I want to see how those suckers move."

"Quickly," Penny said, her voice somewhat sing-song. "Expertly."

Reagan finally clued in, pushing up so she could see Penny's face. "What's your deal? You fought him for a second, didn't you? Are you in shock or something?"

"My premonition never went off," Emery said, remembering his utter shock that Penny had been standing with walking death, and he'd never felt a ping of warning.

"There was something about him." Penny tucked a loose strand of hair behind her ear as they neared the busier street. "Something calming. Alluring. I can't put my finger on it, but it's…pleasant. I hate to let go of it."

"Crap," Reagan said. She reached around Penny and punched Emery in the arm. "She's not right in the head, and I blame you."

Emery massaged the spot. The woman could throw a punch. "You're the one that forced her into that bounty hunter gig."

"Well, only an asshole blames herself, so it's your fault," Reagan shot back, her attempted flippancy ruined by the worry tinging her words.

"Don't you always tell people you're an asshole?" he said as a car engine revved behind them.

"Touché." Reagan peeled off to the side, grabbing Penny and pulling her along. Emery kept pace on Penny's other side. "What have we got here?"

A Lexus SUV, so new it didn't have a license plate, slowed dramatically and swerved toward the parked cars next to them. Reagan braced herself. Penny groaned.

"There goes my good mood," Penny whispered, and in the next moment, Emery learned why.

The car stopped, still running, and the hazards glared to life. The driver's door opened and Ms. Bristol climbed out in a flowery top and loose pants. Her expression was surly, and when the front passenger-side window slid down, Callie stuck her head out and revealed a matching frown. The window behind rolled down as well, and Dizzy's head filled the space as he looked up and down the street.

"Are you sure this is the spot?" Dizzy asked.

Ms. Bristol turned sideways to squeeze through two parked cars and stopped just down the sidewalk from them. She glanced down the street, then shifted her gaze to a corner alarmingly close to them. She brought up the old, worn watch on her wrist.

"You come out this instant, Penelope Bristol!" Ms. Bristol demanded, lowering her watch. "I told you going to that bar was a terrible idea, and now look. You're wandering around in a busy city with enemies every-where, just hoping to *out* yourself to humans and possibly get caught up in something to do with mages and shadows."

"She can't see us, right?" Reagan whispered.

Emery eyed the spell the Bankses were talking to life. "For now, no."

"Then how the hell does she know we're here?"

"Do you now see how hard it was to keep any se-crets from her growing up?" Penny asked, not making a move to take down their spell. None of them did. "She probably saw this location in her crystal ball, a device I thought was fake until half a year ago, when she pulled out a real one and used it. For years I've looked like a dummy squinting into a fake white ball and making up predictions. Did she ever help me out? No, she did not." She shook her head.

Emery felt a grin work up his face. This was the old Penny, and something tight and painful inside of him loosened just a bit.

"Come out this instant," Ms. Bristol demanded.

A passerby on the other side of the street glanced over in confusion. A car coming up behind the Lexus slowed before going around it.

"*If* you were right," Callie said, "we'll flush them out. Ready, Dizzy?"

"I have one premonition go wrong, about something not at all important, and suddenly I'm a two-dollar hack that hangs around on street corners?" Ms. Bristol jammed her fists into her hips. "It was just pizza, for crying out loud, and I was barely trying. I really don't think that should be held against me."

The Bankses' spell twisted into existence, bold and straightforward, spraying the sidewalk with magic before expanding out to the sides, rolling over the three of them and setting their spell ablaze in color.

"They are a perfect example of mage training going right," Emery said as Ms. Bristol turned their way with a scowl. "Their execution is spot-on."

"And you could counter it with minimal effort," Reagan said in a hush as Ms. Bristol stared them down. "What do we do? Do we run?"

"I vote run," Penny said.

"Get out of there." Ms. Bristol stalked forward, and both Penny and Reagan flinched, as though barely keeping themselves put. Chuckles rose through Emery's middle. All the danger they'd faced without flinching, and they were contemplating running away from an older, out-of-shape woman. What a trip.

"Drag them out," Callie called out of her open window.

"I think Emery is too big to drag anywhere," Dizzy said.

"The jig is up," Penny said as she slumped. Their spell winked out.

"Karen does have a gift, hon," Dizzy said to Callie, delight on his face. "She knew almost exactly the time and location all three of them would show up. That is a rare gift."

Callie sniffed. "But when you try to find out where the pizza got to, suddenly it's a great mystery."

Ms. Bristol stiffened for a moment before she started dragging Penny and Emery toward the car by the elbows. "Come on. In a few more minutes there will be vampires roaming all around this city. If I were a betting woman, I'd say the vampires are trying to get their fingers into the Guild's pockets, and the coming battle will be an excellent way to do so. They are choosing sides."

"We have Vlad and Darius. They've chosen the wrong side," Reagan said as she crawled into the third row of the car, a tight space for an adult.

"Let's hope so." Ms. Bristol made sure Emery helped Penny in before returning to the driver's seat. Someone honked behind them. "Hold your horses!" she bellowed. "Can't you see I'm picking up my daughter?" She put the car in drive, and they surged forward. "They seem to think we're all in a hurry."

"Careful…Mother." Penny clutched Emery. "Who let you drive this car?"

"Moss will never know I borrowed it," she replied.

"If he didn't want people taking his car, he wouldn't have left the keys on the key hook near the door," Callie said.

"Yes, exactly," Ms. Bristol responded.

"Pairing them together was a terrible idea." Penny leaned her head against Emery's shoulder.

"What was with the fuzzy, moving shadows in the bar?" Ms. Bristol asked as they jerked to a standstill before the stop sign. "Touchy brakes."

"A druid," Reagan said, and any mirth Emery had felt immediately dried up.

Dizzy half turned to look back at Reagan with wide eyes. Callie did the same, looking at Emery. Ms. Bristol stared out through the windshield, her eyes tight in the rearview mirror.

"And did he or she make a decision that was favorable to our side?" Ms. Bristol's voice was thick with worry.

"We are in no danger from him," Penny said, and her voice was wispy again. "He is goodness. Justified power."

"Goodness? He kills people for a living, and he doesn't care who it is as long as he's paid enough." Reagan leaned forward against the seat. "Emery, slap her. Snap her out of this."

"And Emery," Ms. Bristol said, her voice even thicker. Resolve hung heavy in her tone. "How about you? Have you made a decision?"

Emery met Ms. Bristol's eyes in the rearview mirror, and in her look, he could tell she knew he'd been contemplating the idea of forever. Soon, it would no longer be in his hands. It would be in her daughter's.

# CHAPTER 17

"CAN I SPEAK to you, Penny?" Emery asked as we backed into the parking space at Darius's house.

Full night had fallen, wiping away all the little details the sun had highlighted in the house's beautiful surroundings. I'd missed Seattle and its green, lush beauty. I was happy to be back, even though the circumstances were less than ideal.

I snorted. Understatement of the year.

"Sure," I said as the last of the pleasant haze left my mind and body. I'd figured out how to latch on to the druid's magic, and, in so doing, had found a treasure trove of delight for my senses. He had his finger on the pulse of the natural world, his roots going down through the bedrock, and a natural essence pumped through his blood. My magic had practically vibrated around him, connecting me more solidly to my environment.

He'd followed us for a spell, though at a distance. Close enough that I could still feel his magic pulsing through my veins. Far enough away that neither Reagan nor Emery had sensed his presence. It was as though he knew I could feel his magic, and was letting me bask in the experience.

But the sensation had started to fade once we got into the car, and now it was just a memory.

"Penny?" Emery asked again, helping me out of the car.

Moss waited off to the side, staring at my mother as she stepped out of the driver's seat.

"It has a lot of power." She tossed him the keys. "Thanks for letting me use it."

"There are automobiles set aside for community usage," Moss said with a flat voice.

"Yes, but those are all five-seaters. I needed that third row." My mother patted Moss on the shoulder. "Thanks."

His glare followed her to the house.

"What's up?" I asked Emery, getting a weird little flutter in my stomach from his intense gaze. Something was bothering him. "No headache, I swear. I feel good." His expression didn't clear. "That druid wasn't there to hurt me. After the initial tumble, I mean. I held my own, though. I would've figured him out. But then he stopped, so everything was fine. Honestly, I was only in danger for, like…one minute. Tops."

"Can I have a few minutes of your time?" he asked,

and his voice quavered. It was like he hadn't heard me at all.

My stomach flipped, dread spreading through my body. Flashes of how our last visit to this house had ended took up prime real estate in my head. He'd told me he had to go. When I'd awoken, he'd been gone.

Barely able to breathe, I followed him silently through the house, holding his hand in a death grip. I wouldn't let him go this time. I was stronger when I was with him. He brought out the best in me, leveling me out perfectly, and vice versa. He was the teammate I craved, the partner I loved, and the missing piece in my life.

I'd always thought that missing piece was magic, but I'd been doing magic my whole life, largely without realizing it. Magic was inside of me. It had always been a part of the whole.

The thing I'd always been missing had been him.

"Okay, look," I said as we walked past a straight-faced Darius. His eyes were knowing, but his expression didn't give anything away. Oh God, this was going to be bad news. "I know I've been acting weird. But I'm trying to get a handle on it."

We walked down the hallway toward the bedroom we shared despite my mother's wishes.

"I just have to grab something really quickly," he said, leaving me just outside the doorway. He pushed the door nearly closed so I couldn't see inside.

Heart in my throat, unshed tears stinging my eyes, I gulped and looked down the hallway. My eyes landed on a sign on one of the doors. *Shhh, editor hard at work.*

Happiness fought for space amidst the dread. Veronica had come. She was surely in danger here, but given her track record as my friend, she was probably in danger everywhere. I was happy to have her around.

Emery opened the door, misery lining his face, and all thoughts of Veronica fled.

I knew that look. He was about to do something that he thought was the best possible thing for me. It was exactly how he'd looked the last time. Before he'd left.

"Life will calm down soon," I said as he took my hand again and led me down the hall. "It'll calm down. I know the odds are stacked against us, given the sheer number of mages we're facing on their home turf, and their vampire helpers, but we've stood against impossible odds before. Actually, we're always against impossible odds. That's how we roll. So this is just another day, know what I mean?"

Dizzy gave us a thumbs-up as we passed the living room. In contrast, when we walked through the kitchen, Reagan gave me a solemn look, standing next to a straight-faced Marie.

My breath came out in fast, shallow pants, fear eating at me.

When we reached the door leading into the garage, Emery finally stalled, his hand on the knob. The fear I felt was reflected on his expression. He probably thought I would fly off the handle and try to kill him.

I might.

"You don't have to do this," I said, trying to talk past the tightness in my throat. "This probably isn't best for me. Whatever it is you are going to do, it's probably not the thing I really need. What we have right now is perfect. I'm happy just as we are."

He studied me for a long moment, indecision eating through his eyes.

"We're good," I pushed, seeing an opening. "We're fine. Let's just stay this way."

His fingers loosened on the knob. He shifted a little away from the door.

I sighed with relief and tugged on his other hand. "We're good. We'll sort through this weird goblin situation, and we'll be good."

Worry clouded his vision again, and I knew I'd said the wrong thing. He turned the handle and pulled the door open. This time, he was the one tugging. Getting me to follow him.

"No," I whispered, my feet turning to lead.

He flicked on a switch in the two-car garage. It was empty of vehicles, but light showered down on a large desk supporting two monitors and some basic office supplies. The surface was spacious and immaculate, and I knew this was where Darius must have toiled over the files we'd stolen from the Guild's record room on our last break in. His lackeys had scanned them all.

On the other side, in the corner, sat a rickety card table with one folding chair on either side. A fake crystal ball with a permanent white cloud hunkered in the center of the table with a pile of colorful rocks beside it. A deck of tarot cards sat next to that, and a colorful sash lined the side of the table.

I stumbled to a stop, utterly confused. It was my setup from my old job as a fake fortune teller at the Renaissance village near my old house.

"What..." The word trailed away as Emery tugged me forward again, leading me to the chair behind the table. The metal frame groaned under my weight. He settled in the chair facing me, his eyes liquid pools of blue.

"I'm sorry I couldn't do this with more detail," he said softly. "I didn't have a lot of time. Just imagine we're back in that village, with electricity surging through the air between us."

"But..." I looked over the power stones, seeing many familiar ones that I'd used back then. Their power was minuscule compared to the ones I'd collected since, but they still had their quirky personalities. "How did you get all this?"

"I had Darius's people grab it out of your mom's storage…just in case."

I shook my head, running my finger over the tarot cards. In my hands, they were just paper with pictures on them. In my mother's hands, they were the future unfolding.

I'd understood so little back in the day. So many things going on beneath the surface of my world without my knowledge.

"I don't understand. Just in case…what?" I asked, sentimentality swelling in my heart. I remembered when he'd first sat down in that rickety chair, facing me as he was doing now. He'd given me advice that had forever changed my life.

*You don't need more than what exists in the wild. You just need the strength of your will to make it so.*

"I need to tell you what happened to me when my brother died," he started.

I listened in rapture and with a sinking heart as he opened up about the horror he'd faced. It had wounded him deeply—I'd already known that, but I hadn't quite understood the extent of it. Callie had explained what a dual-mage connection was, and the risks if your partner were to die, but she hadn't explained it like this.

Hearing that the man I loved had gone through such torture tore me apart. Brought tears to my eyes. All that pain. All that misery. And on top of it, he still blamed himself for not being there. He still blamed himself for not being able to warn his brother, and not going with him, and not fighting beside him.

I sat quietly, not moving, as tears rolled down my cheeks. Pain clouded his gaze as he finished his story, willing me to understand what he'd told me.

"We don't need to form that connection," I said into the following silence. "I don't need it. I'm happy just as we are."

He shook his head, his gaze connected to mine, his body too far away. "You're only saying that because you think I'm afraid to feel that pain again."

I clasped my hands, because he was right, and clearly I was not picking up what he was putting down.

"I won't let you die, Penny Bristol. That might mean I will go before you. And I cannot…" He paused, shook himself slightly, and started again. "I *do not* want to put you through what I went through."

"I'll be in pain regardless. But like I said, we don't have to do this. We already work perfectly together. That's plenty for me. As long as you don't take off again, I'm good." I wiped a hot tear off my cheek.

He sat very still. "I'm worried. You are the genius that creates mischief as you discover your magic. I am the experienced mage that sorts everything out. But this time…" His chest inflated with his deep inhale. "I don't know what's happening inside of you. I can't help you. In trying to do what I think is best for you, I could be hurting you more than we know."

I leaned my forearms onto the rickety card table before remembering it was a bad idea. It groaned as I leaned back again, threatening to collapse. "So...I'm confused. What now?"

"A dual-mage pair...shares magic, in a way. No, that's not right..." He furrowed his brow as he scratched his nose. "It's like...it boosts both of the mages' magic and, in so doing, merges them and their magic in a way. Kind of creates a level plane on which they can both work."

"Okay..." I didn't get it.

"And through that connection, I'll be able to look under the hood, so to speak. I'll be able to see what that goblin magic is really doing to you, and hopefully help sort it out. Because it'll affect me in the same way."

"Right." I went to lean forward again before stopping myself. "So where does this leave us?"

He took a deep breath, and for reasons I couldn't explain, I got a surge of butterflies in my belly. He dug into his pocket and pulled out a little blue velvet box before setting it on the table.

Nervousness and love dripped from his eyes. "Penelope Bristol, you've affected me from the first touch. You've been on my mind, haunting my thoughts in the best possible ways, from that moment until this one. I've loved you from the beginning, but for a while I got in my own way. I respect you. I cherish you. I am so very, very—" His voice hitched. He clasped his hands on his lap and looked down at them for a moment, trying to choke back the emotion. "I'm so very proud of you. Of your courage to be unapologetically different. Of your willingness to try anything. Of your steadfastness and loyalty. The druid read you perfectly. You are pure of heart, and you always have been. You are the shining light in my life. How I find my way home. I love you more than I can express."

I could barely breathe. New tears made a trail down my cheeks.

He reached forward and unclasped the box. It creaked as it opened. Within sat a ring with a glimmering purple stone, pumping with a deep power that soaked down through my middle and warmed up my body.

"I went through every power stone Darius could collect for me," Emery said, and now his voice shook. His smile was faint. "That vampire will go out of his way to get what he wants." His smile slipped and nervousness took over his expression. "This stone made me think of you. Beautiful, pure, and deep. Will you…"

He swallowed, and I waited with bated breath for what would come next.

# CHAPTER 18

H E PULLED HIS hands away from the box. "Penny Bristol, will you be my forever? Will you share your life with me? You can choose how—if you're willing, that is." His smile didn't break through his nervousness. But I couldn't put him at ease. My heart had taken over the whole of my chest and I'd stopped breathing. I could scarcely think through the flurries in my stomach. "I offer myself to you however you will take me. As my wife, as my dual-mage, as my life partner, or as that creepy guy who lives next door and waits outside to say hello every morning and goodnight every evening." His smile amplified his handsomeness. "Well. Maybe not that last one. You'd probably sic Reagan on me."

I huffed out a laugh, and I was crying again. Huge, joyous tears rolled down my face. "But your past?"

He shrugged, and for once, he was hunching like I usually did. "It wouldn't be fair of me to make that decision for you, Penny. You have all the information now, so you should choose your own destiny. Either way, whatever you choose, I…" He shrugged again. "I hope to be a part of it."

My hand shook as it reached out for the ring, but veered at the last minute and rested on the fake crystal ball instead. "Does my mother know this is happening?" I vaguely remembered what she'd said in the car. "She does."

"She knows," he said. "She didn't threaten me away from you this time, so I figured that was a good sign."

I laughed, looking at the ring. I couldn't bring myself to touch it. To see if it fit. It was hard to believe I could be so lucky. Or so happy. It felt like a dream, and I worried that if I touched the ring, I'd wake up. "The others?"

"Darius and Reagan have been pushing for this. Darius for his own reasons, and Reagan because she wants me to fix you." His smile was soft. "Like you have already fixed me."

I took a deep breath. One of many. I had to risk waking up.

Steeling my courage, I gingerly slid my fingers across the smooth surface of the small power stone, about the size of a two-carat diamond. A pleasant vibration welled up inside of me. It felt like love. Emery's love. He'd chosen perfectly.

I wiped a tear away with the back of my hand. "I don't want us to become dual-mages if you have reservations. I meant what I said. I'm happy to stay like we are if that's where you'd rather be."

He sat forward in his chair. The chair wobbled with the weight shift. "I'd rather be on a beach with you somewhere, safe and sound," he said. "If our lives weren't so dangerous, I would've already asked you about becoming dual-mages. We're perfect together. There is only one true pairing for me, and that's you. Nature has made it that way. Please believe me, Penny, the only reason I've held off is because I'm afraid for you. But that fear has shifted, and I worry that I might be doing you harm. There's just…" He shrugged. "I can't strategize like Darius. It seems I'm doomed to blindness when it comes to what's actually best for you."

"You are best for me," I said softly, resting my fingers on the edge of the box. "You're best. I will be your dual-mage, and as soon as we've dated for another couple years and my mother has stopped harassing us, I'll be your wife. And your life partner, in case you didn't realize that was the same thing."

Relief washed over his face before a smile lit him up, sparkling in his gorgeous blue eyes, like the Milky Way on a clear night. He stood slowly, and I held my breath as he walked around the card table and knelt by my side. He lifted the ring box gently before extracting the beautiful power stone ring and reaching for my hand.

I shoved it at him eagerly, my heart full to bursting. The feeling of connection, both with Emery and the universe, was taking over, softening the headache that had been throbbing the moment before.

"I can't believe I've gotten this lucky," he said under his breath, gently encircling my ring finger with the metal. He shook his head slightly. "I feel like I'm going to wake up at any moment."

I ran my free hand down his cheek. He looked up, his eyes glassy.

"I was thinking the same thing just a moment ago," I said, laughing through the tears.

He chuckled as well, holding my gaze as he slipped the ring down my finger. "Penelope Bristol... Turdswallop"—we both laughed a little harder—"will you join with me in a dual-mage partnership that will connect us magically for the rest of our lives?"

"Yes," I said softly, resting my hand on his shoulder.

He paused with the ring almost all the way down my finger. "Wait...should I hold off on the ring until we're ready for it? Just because of your mother and her—"

"Yes," I said, laughing harder. "If I'd had any doubts that you were the perfect guy for me, that just cemented it. Can you imagine? She'd go between anger that I was promising myself to you so soon, and anger that we were waiting so long to actually have a ceremony. We'd end up just eloping for some peace."

He was still frozen with the ring nearly on my finger. His eyes dipped down, and I could tell he wanted to slide it on the rest of the way. That he worried this was his one chance, and if he didn't seal the deal now, he might not get another opportunity.

"It'll be more special if I've never actually worn it before," I whispered. "And just think, you'll have more time and freedom to come up with a nicer table and a couple chairs that don't want to break when they're sat in."

His smile stretched and he looked up, hopefully getting the assurance he needed. He nodded before pulling the ring away with obvious regret.

"It's perfect, though," I said, feeling my own regret. "I like the feel of it. And the color."

"It's unique." He fitted the ring in the box but left the lid open. "And more powerful for it. Just like you."

I fell into his kiss then, soaking in the passion and emotion we both felt, roaming my hands over his hard body. I was desperate for us to explore these feelings further in our room. But he backed off and glanced at the far corner of the garage by the door, where a moveable Asian-style divider was set up.

"Shall we?" He stood, his eyes so deep that I could see all the way to his overflowing soul.

In perfect trust, I let him help me up and then followed him to the corner, where he folded the divider and set it aside. A wave of nervousness washed through me upon seeing a black cauldron. Next to it sat a stack of marked and labeled containers.

"Wow. Prepared." I rubbed at my butterfly-infested stomach, remembering the last time I'd done a potion. As Reagan and the Bankses would never let me forget, I'd accidentally turned a bunch of witches into zombies. "We're sure we have the right spell, and all the ingredients are fresh...and everything?"

"Darius is the prepared one. More so since the goblin incident. This station has been kept in a constant state of readiness. As for the spell..." He moved around the side, looking for something. Not finding it, he turned in a circle, scanning the storage shelves and Darius's desk across the way. Looking around the cauldron area again, he clucked his tongue and stepped toward a black binder that sat propped up on the shelf. "Right in front of my face."

Flipping the binder open, he read the first page before his brow furrowed. He moved on to the second page, then the third, running his finger down and across the lines, taking it all in.

"It's that long, huh?" I asked, wanting to step closer and get a look—and also wanting to keep my distance.

"No...these are...other spells." Emery flicked the pages, pausing a moment on each. When he reached the spell he was looking for, he tapped it once and then went back to look at a few others. "These are…advanced spells. Extremely complex. They'd need a crap-load of power to complete."

"Which he assumes we'll have after we become dual-mages?" I finally moved closer. As I scanned the page, magic sifted and twisted around me, ruffling my hair and caressing my skin. Whispered words seeped out of the darkness in my mind, and various words lifted off the page in sparkling color.

I'd read a good few spells in the last year, the ones from Reagan more complex than most, and voices had never whispered in my mind before.

I took a step back. "Something is wrong with those spells."

"Why?" Emery flicked a page before looking at me. Whatever he saw erased the good or analytical mood he'd been in. "Let's get working."

With smooth economy, he took the lid off a large container marked *distilled water*. After sloshing that into the cauldron, he set up the binder on a spell stand a couple feet from the cauldron, leaving it open to the dual-mage potion directions. That done, he read them over, then checked the ingredients again. He was no novice when it came to creating potions.

"Okay," he said, motioning me closer to the binder. "At first, this will be a potion like any other. Feel the intent and follow the steps accordingly. About three-quarters of the way in, you'll start to feel a tug…about here." He put his palm to the bottom of his ribcage, the place where I'd often felt a tug while doing magic.

I nodded to show I was following.

"That's the start of the actual connection. That tug will seem to be connected…" His hand drifted out, and stopped at the same place on me, prompting a gush of warmth. It moved back to him. "You'll feel the first connection to me."

It was hard to breathe with all the heart swelling and belly flutters and excitement, not to mention the fear I'd severely screw up and turn him into something awful, so I just nodded again.

"The feeling will increase as we move on. With…" Sorrow moved in his eyes and he cleared his throat. "With my brother, it was an exciting feeling, like collaborating on an intense new project. But I've heard dual-mages feel different things. I've never heard of it being a negative experience."

I licked my lips, knowing nothing I dabbled in ever came out normally. "Let's hope we're not the first."

A smile tickled his lips. He must've read my mind, because he bent and ran his lips across mine. "We'll be fine."

His thumb slid a trail of fire across my chin before he went back to the binder.

"Toward the end, the intensity will dramatically increase. That's when our magic will fuse, as it were. We'll both feel an increase in our normal power level, as well as little details and variances from the other person. Good and bad, I'll share what I've got going on, and you'll share what you're working with." His hand moved back and forth between us.

"Will you be able to siphon magic from other people, like I do?"

He studied me for a moment. "That's a question I've wondered myself. My brother didn't get my premonition ability, and I didn't get his ability to easily decipher truth from lie, so possibly not."

"He could tell truth from lie? Like…just know when people were lying to him?"

Emery nodded, organizing the containers now, probably into what would be used and when. "To a degree, yes. It really helped him in the Guild. Clearly, it didn't save his life. I have a theory that mages have extra little individual gifts in addition to their magic. The higher the power level, the more apparent the gifts are. It's a recent theory…" He gave me a sheepish smile. "In the past, I just thought my brother and I were prodigies."

"Well…you were. Two naturals coming out of the same family is kind of a big deal."

"Right, but I let myself think there was more to it

than that." He shrugged, and I could see a boyish delight shine through. "Think superheroes."

"Ah." I glanced at the opened binder, curiosity pulling at me. Fear holding me back.

"But in seeing your pretty extreme gift, I can't help but wonder if other mages have them to a lesser degree, or maybe just naturals get a little something extra…"

"We already have so much. That doesn't seem fair."

He chuckled as he straightened up. "There's that pure heart. Here I was thinking about being a superhero, and you're debating the fairness of it all."

"Your brother did a lot of the intense decision-making, didn't he?" I asked, angling my face up as he ran his fingers along the underside of my jaw.

He smiled again before he brushed his lips against mine. Not satisfied, he deepened the contact, opening my lips with his and probing with his tongue.

My body turned molten and I moaned into his taste. The wildness of his magic throbbing around us. The feel of his body against mine.

"Focus, Penny Bristol," he murmured against my lips, his breath fast, his smile gone. His palms spread up my stomach and cupped my breasts.

"I'm not the one copping a feel." I closed my eyes and leaned my head back, lost in his touch.

His hot lips trailed down my exposed throat and his hands kneaded. I sucked in a breath as his thumbs moved across my nipples. "Focus," I heard again, wispy. He kissed my collarbone but straightened up. Slowly. His hands moved down to my hips, gripping tightly. "We have all night for that. We need to do this spell."

He stole one more kiss before stepping back and running his fingers through his hair. He blew out a breath and a boyish grin worked up his face. "I am certainly approaching this spell differently the second time around." He shook his head and picked up a large wooden spoon before handing it over. "Don't turn me into a zombie."

All the air went out of me. Scowling sullenly, I took the spoon. "Low blow."

"Yes, my brother did make all of the intense decisions. Most of the decisions, big and small. He was the oldest, after all. I'd been trained to do as he said or get the snot beat out of me. Even when I got older and could hold my own, I still remembered those early lessons."

"I know something of that." I edged up to the binder. "Because of Reagan."

"It helps, though. In the long run. Makes you tough."

"I'm certainly blasé when I'm thrown against the wall by an enemy. Which is not something I ever thought I would say." Magic danced around me as I neared the spell stand. My energy fizzed and spurted.

Words jumped off the page in bright, sparkly colors, vying for attention, pointing out the most important part of the spell, and what could go wrong.

Wind kicked up, brushing against my face and tossing my hair. But when I put my hand up to pat down my flyaways, they hadn't been disturbed.

"This spell doesn't look overly complex," I said, confused as to what was causing this reaction in me.

"It's not." Emery picked up the second ingredient, a jug of orange juice. Knowing Darius, it was hand-squeezed. "You have to have enough power to do it, but I've seen mages barely more powerful than witches form a dual-mage pair."

But as my gaze moved over the lines of instructions, the environment in the garage changed. The ghost of a wind fought the stagnant, still air. A floral whiff drifted past my nose, replaced by the lingering scent of paper from books mixed with grease left over from when a car had been stored in the space. Leaves brushed against the roof or rain gutters outside, longing to come in and be a part of this. Even the very words of the spell seemed to beg for more natural elements to play with.

Emery stilled with the jug held out, waiting for me to read the first line.

"This potion was meant to be performed outside." I looked down at the cauldron. "We need to move. To the trees."

He just looked at me, the jug still held out. I shook my head at him, suddenly frustrated beyond a rational amount. "And you need to get your head in the game. You're slipping back into how you used to do magic. That's not the right way. It won't bring out the true essence of this spell."

A line formed between his brow and he tilted his head, surveying me. The glimmer of boyish excitement seeped away, and a part of me felt really crappy because of it. But the part that was in control didn't back down. I pointed at the cauldron, and the stack of containers next to it, before grabbing the binder and fitting it under my arm. "Come on. This spell seems simple, but if you look below the surface, and do it right, it is actually quite complex. I can feel it. It can also go badly wrong. I intend to do it right, and we need to move so we don't get steamrolled by the effects."

# CHAPTER 19

T HE GREAT THING about vampires was they were very strong, and could move a cast iron cauldron filled with water with minimal strain and no spillage. The great thing about Darius and Reagan was they took my spell work as it came, and never batted an eye at my crazy demands.

Callie, Dizzy, and my mother, on the other hand…

"I have personally done this spell, and it doesn't need to be executed in the freezing cold rain," Callie said an hour after I'd initiated the move, tromping behind me through the trees to a little clearing down the way. Vampires had been called in to set up a tight perimeter so we wouldn't be disrupted by any enemies deciding tonight was a good night to attack. It was a necessary precaution after the bar battle earlier that day.

Our timing wasn't great.

"The garage would've been fine. I know a dual-mage pair with half the power of Dizzy and me, and they did it in their living room without a problem." Callie hurried to my side, pulling the hood of a black raincoat over her head. Her bright yellow velvet sweat-suit pants peeked out the bottom. "You'll catch pneumonia out here."

"It'll be okay." I pulled up the hood of my own raincoat, squinting up at the dark sky. Drops shimmered in the battery-powered lamp I held, sparkling as they fell. "A moon would've been helpful."

"Did you tell her, hon?" Dizzy called out as we neared the new cauldron site. A party tent sprawled across the top, held up on metal poles and draping down a little on the sides. If the wind kicked up any more, raindrops would be blown in through the sides, drenching our bottom halves.

Emery waited by the cauldron, still toting the orange juice jug, though he'd taken his raincoat off. Despite his long-sleeved shirt, he didn't seem to feel the chill. He was probably too busy wondering how he got himself into this mess—or how he could best get himself out of it.

"Sorry," I said as I ducked under the tent and took my place at his side. "It's just—"

"Because you really could just stay indoors," Dizzy said as Callie trudged into the tent after me. "That's what Callie and I did. And look, it worked."

"I'm not about to start questioning you now," Emery whispered, and tucked a strand of hair behind my ear.

"Penelope Bristol, dancing in the rain is one thing, but you've dragged us all out here for something the Bankses say isn't necessary." My mother stalked up with her shotgun. She was ready for a battle.

"Mother, Darius's people will take care of guard duty," I said. "You can stay in the house."

"I most certainly will not. With my daughter standing out here in the rain, unprotected from anyone wandering in? No. Someone needs to oversee security." She stalked off into the trees.

"Let her help in her own way," Emery said quietly, touching my arm.

"Well...we'd better put up a ward, hon." Dizzy sighed. "Kids these days just have to be different. We were the same, I suppose, we just did it with circles and demons."

I'd opened my mouth to say a ward wasn't needed, but his words made me change gears. "Huh?"

"Go, Callie, Dizzy." Reagan stalked through two bushes without rain gear, Darius following close behind. "I'll watch them. Go join Ms. Bristol."

"Actually, if you all could clear away." I waved my hand in an arc. "We'll set up a concealment spell. We'll be fine out here."

"Also a good plan." Reagan stopped with her hands on her hips. "Right. I'll just meander, then, will I? Unless you guys are cool with me coming in to watch?"

I shook my head, feeling the wrongness of that suggestion. Usually it wouldn't matter, but for this…

"Let's go," Darius said. "We should do a perimeter check anyway."

When they were all gone, some of them grumbling as they went, Emery unscrewed the cap of the orange juice. "Are you okay reading out the spell? I didn't really think about it earlier."

"It's probably better," I replied. "Last time a spell was read, I just took over. I'd hate for that to happen again."

"And you also turned everyone into zombies. I'd hate for that to happen again, too."

"I don't know why you think that's so funny. It was a really terrible thing."

"I'll bet. Zombies are gross."

Laughter bubbled up through me, easing a little tension. "Okay. Be serious. Time to focus."

"We are." He pointed around the cauldron at the swirling wisps and threads of magic—a natural occurrence whenever Emery and I shared space. Electricity rolled over my skin and infused my core. He stepped nearer and his voice softened. "We don't need to practice at focusing, Turdswallop. We just need to keep our hands off each other. The rest comes naturally."

I smiled and bumped my shoulder against his. "Okay. Here we go."

Just as before, the words jumped off the page, color-ful and vibrant. This time, though, a real wind kicked up, fluttering the tent. Rain fell heavier, pattering on the overhead tarp. Nature moved and swayed around us, heard through the rustling of the leaves and creak of the branches. A soft song drifted on the wind, curling and turning, playing with my senses and lending a buoyancy to the spell.

"This is new," I said under my breath, the fates thumping around us, trying to sweep us up and take us away. "And that is new. Maybe I just shouldn't do potions."

"You'll be fine, love. You're a natural. It's in your blood."

"Tell that to the zombies."

"I can't. Reagan killed them all. But rest assured, if you turn me into something heinous, I'm sure she'll help you kill me, too."

"That isn't funny."

"Then why are you laughing?"

I tried to wipe away my smile, but I couldn't. His mood was infectious, and the moment just felt so right.

"Hold on to your butt." I took a deep breath and read the first line, emphasizing the word *pour*, since it was glittering and waving around on the page, and feeling a deep *thrum* when the directions told me to choose who would stir first. I held out the spoon for

Emery.

He set down the empty container of orange juice and took the spoon without a word, about to put it in the liquid. But something felt off, like a thread drifting into the breeze, unraveling the fabric of the spell as it did so. Before I could say anything, he'd stopped and stilled, closing his eyes.

"I'm on autopilot a little bit," he said, and took a deep breath. "When I did this with my brother, I don't think either of us was really concentrating. It's such an easy spell that a natural can do it in his sleep. We certainly didn't check in with the environment around us. That's not something mages are ever taught or told to do. But..." He put out one of his hands and his fingers wiggled through the air. Magic rose around him and flirted with his moving digits. "I can feel the difference. When you say the words, I can feel the expectation of the spell. I can feel your utter conviction. It's another lesson, one among many. It's why I'm learning right alongside you, Penny. Even the most basic spells can have a profound effect."

He put the spoon into the liquid, and this time the magic didn't drift away. It rose, swirling in the air as he moved the spoon. After two times around, he pulled the spoon up just how I said, stepped back, and held it out to me.

I took it without a word, but didn't immediately

cross to the cauldron. Instead, I took my time and leaned my back against his front, relishing in the energy around us and the electricity zinging through me.

"I love you," he said as his arms came around my middle.

"I love you." I bent my head back so I could get a languid kiss before stepping up to the cauldron.

This time he read off the instructions, and I felt the magic tug at my middle as I moved the spoon.

"Did you feel the—"

"Tug," he finished. "It happened so early this time. Who knows if it will matter."

"It'll matter."

He continued to read, and I added the next ingredient. After that, we switched turns reading and adding ingredients, sometimes after one of us used the spoon, and sometimes in the middle of a line. We didn't discuss it, and we never faltered. Completely immersed in our magical bubble, we worked off each other as we'd learned to do. Working this spell felt like working all the others, second nature.

Natural.

Three-quarters of the way down, the tug on my middle was so extreme that I had a hard time breathing. I gripped Emery's forearm with one hand and the spoon with the other. The cauldron bubbled, though there was no heat. Magic spun and twisted from within, pouring over the cast iron lip and spewing onto the ground.

Emery connected gazes with me, but he didn't ask if we should keep going. He took the spoon and stepped up, waiting until I took his place and called out the next line of instructions.

A hard yank on my ribs preceded heat seeping out and down through my stomach. A new feeling washed over me: closeness. Intense intimacy. Support.

Snippets of the most fear-filled moments in my life played through my head, starting as early as I could remember. In every single one, a new presence was felt.

Emery's.

He was backfilling all the little holes in my life, adding support and comfort to each terrible memory still rattling around in my head. Even in sixth grade, when stupid Billy Timmons, the bully nemesis of my youth, pointed out to everyone that I was wearing a bra for the first time, Emery was right there beside me, changing my horror and embarrassment to straight-backed courage and purposeful indifference. At my father's funeral, my mother stood on one side of me and Emery stood on the other, holding my hand and coaxing me through the pain. He was helping me take on all the little beasties of life, going back to the beginning.

Tears came to my eyes as I felt Emery's arms wrap around me, his body heaving. His pain was like a suffocating blanket, his loss so deep that I was sucked into the well of it. In a moment he stilled, shuddering. His chest rose with a deep breath.

"Don't tell anyone I cried," he said with a shaking voice. "It'll make me seem less manly."

I laughed through my tears. "You can tell people I did. People already think chicks are weak, so crying is expected."

He backed off and looked into my eyes. "Let them. That way, it's easier to blindside them with your strength."

"Or with a well-timed headbutt."

Laughter shook him. "Yes. Exactly." A crease formed between his brows as his smile disappeared. "It wasn't this intense with my brother. This is… We didn't have this."

"That's probably because you didn't do the spell right. I bet nobody does the spell right. Saying words isn't enough. You have to feel it. Put emphasis on the sparkly parts."

His eyebrows lowered. "The sparkly parts?"

"Turtle turds, that's not normal, is it?" I blew out a breath. I explained what I saw when I looked at the directions, knowing the spell would wait. The cauldron still bubbled away, no explanation as to why. And it would keep bubbling, I knew, until we tore down the magical bubble we were working in.

"And when you changed those witches into zombies?" he asked, not teasing this time.

"I felt the pull to do the potion, but there weren't any sparkly or emphasized words. But I didn't have an Emery and a magical bubble when I was in that church."

"Hmm." He turned back to the spell, and we started again, effortlessly working through it with a depth and complexity I doubted most mages knew was possible. The warmth inside me increased, and the tug was back, building until it ended in a stronger yanking sensation.

More magic gushed out, and memories flitted through me again, this time the good ones. Emery's presence filled in holes there, too, and he shared in all my accomplishments, rooting for me.

Buffeted by his own memories, he found my hips with his hands and leaned against me, his lips grazing my bare neck. I closed my eyes and lost myself in him, knowing we were buffered from the outside world. Wanting to ride the feeling. It felt right. We probably could've skipped it and the spell would've been fine, but...well...

I turned in a rush of passion, unbuttoning his pants and shoving them down. He didn't waste any time, crashing his lips onto mine and sliding my jeans down my thighs. His warm skin and bumpy muscles delighted me as I lowered to the ground, knowing he'd get there first. I straddled his hips, nothing in the way, and my eyes fluttered as I sank down onto him.

"I love you," he murmured against my lips, his fingers twisted in my hair.

I rose and fell with abandon, my desire surging as the cauldron bubbled behind me, echoed in the magic bubbling inside of me. Magic swirled and danced around us, no longer contained within our energy bubble. Not even contained in the concealment spell. It poured out into the world and flitted around, prancing and soaring among the trees like a live creature.

The yanking sensation peaked as I did, and my whole world blasted apart, the universe opening up and swallowing me whole. Pleasure filled every part of my body and I vibrated in ecstasy. Emery shuddered under me, crushing me to him tightly, his arms circled around me.

We panted for a moment in the aftermath, catching our breath.

"I'm going to need more of that," he said, running his lips across mine.

"After," I said with a smile, pushing myself up and pulling him up after me. "Later."

"It was a good idea to be outside. The garage would've been no place for this."

"Making love?" I stepped into my pants, bringing a few leaves with me.

He chuckled. "This spell. You were right, as you often are when it comes to natural things. This spell was made to be outside. Also, I like how I can point out you were right about something, and you don't gloat."

"Reagan gloats enough for the whole world."

He laughed harder, clearly because he knew I was also right about that.

Both of us turned to look at the spell. There were three lines left. I read the first, expectation overcoming me. He stepped up behind me and, holding me tightly, read the second. As a pair, we picked up the lavender, the last ingredient save our blood, and put it in the cauldron together, the whole thing rocking in place.

"That can't be normal," I heard Emery mutter, but he wrapped his hands around mine on the spoon and helped me mix it all together.

Like a dam bursting, a rush of magic blasted through me, sucking me under. I sputtered as I tried to make sense of it, rolling on the huge waves at high seas. It felt like the storm of the century. Like tornados whipping around within me, battering me from the inside out.

Emery's magic was nuts. It was crazy. It whipped and tore at me, punching and pulling me before turning me end over end and throwing me against a rock. All of this happened internally, and I reached out to find something to hold on to, some way to get my bearings.

No wonder the guy was wild and unruly, with this

volatile magic roaring through him.

My hand hit empty air and I turned, seeking him out.

He lay flat on his back, his hands around his throat, gasping for air.

# CHAPTER 20

"OH NO—EMERY?" I fell to my knees beside him, shoving the effects of his magic to the back of my consciousness. My temples throbbed with the effort, but I pushed past it, my gaze roaming his face.

He pounded on his chest. Held his throat.

He couldn't get any air.

The goblin's magic. It had to be.

"Reagan." I jumped up and ran for the edge of the concealment spell before realizing I was an idiot and tearing it down. "Reagan!" I screamed into the night. "Reagan, help!"

Would she be in the house, or out in the trees?

Trees. She wouldn't sit idle if there was even a remote possibility someone might ambush us.

But where in the trees?

"Reagan!" I screamed, moving elements through my fingers into a harried weave. Putting the magic to my mouth, I shouted, "Reagan!"

Sound amplified, blasting out like a loudspeaker. The neighbors a mile away probably heard that. She would come running, I knew she would.

No time to lose, I spun around. Someone zoomed out of the trees—a vampire and, given that he didn't try to kill me, one of ours.

"Go find Reagan," I yelled, falling to my knees next to Emery. "Hurry!"

Emery's feet kicked and he scratched at his throat. Panic welled up inside me.

We shared magic. It was fused.

Wasn't that what he'd said? Maybe I could fix this from my side.

I closed my eyes, yanking his magic back to the forefront. Raw power pushed and shoved at me. I'd need to come to grips with this, then mix it with mine.

*I hope that's right.*

Half falling, I straddled Emery, knowing I was running out of time. I dropped my head to his chest, opened up, and let our combined power consume me, leveling out as I did so. The electricity I'd always felt around him vibrated through my body and tingled my hair follicles. It stretched my skin and made my heart thump, but it wasn't the right magic. It wasn't what was causing this!

Sifting through our combined magic, I focused on how it flowed, on its balance, its life, and tried to isolate the new element. The eternal power trying to find a home within his body. Within mine.

Time pressing on me, panic barely kept at bay, I was still searching for the foreign power when a familiar magic came into my scope. Awesomely complex in a way I barely understood, light and dark and fire and ice, the universe stretched out before me.

Reagan was here.

Before I could borrow her power to help Emery, he gasped, sucking in a breath, before coughing and bucking, throwing me off.

"What happened?" Reagan asked anxiously.

"Didn't…assimilate…magic," Emery choked out between lungfuls of air.

"Come again?" Reagan bent and put her ear closer to him. "You sound like you're dying. I can't understand you."

I tuned them out. Flares lit up the dark night, putting a rainbow glare on everything. Time and space seemed to stretch around me. When I put a hand up, it felt like I could reach through the clouds, past the stars, and to eternity beyond.

The soft patter of rain took on a different tone in my brain, combining with the subtle movement of branches and the wind worrying the leaves. It became a symphony, living in my blood and expressed through my magic.

Wide-eyed, I glanced up at Reagan, leaning down over us. A pitch-black halo surrounded her, the exact opposite of the bleach-white light pulsing from me. Emery had a mix hovering around his body, his black survival magic muddying the white of this new magic, blending the two anti-colors together and bringing out the rainbow hidden therein.

"There, see?" I said, and my voice seemed muffled, as though I were speaking through fabric or fog. "No more black survival magic for you—now you're colorful, like a unicorn."

Emery stood slowly as this crazy magic flitted in and around us. Pumped through us. Set me on edge.

"No." Emery held out his hand, and a wave of support and comfort welled up through me. Emery, filling in all the holes with his presence. "Don't hide from it, Penny. Accept it. It feels foreign, just like my magic does, but it won't hurt you."

"Will someone tell me what's happening?" Reagan asked, and I could tell she was on edge.

I could also see a thin strand of gold connecting her and I, floating through the air, though not taut. Another strand connected Emery and I, and this one was as thick as my arm and glittering gold. Then another hung between Reagan and Emery, basically flapping in the breeze.

"Uh-oh." I pointed it out. "There's the triangle my mother was talking about. Seems like my mother was right. But where's the kingdom?" I squeezed my eyes shut and grabbed my head. "I really, really hate hallucinating. I didn't like when Reagan made us do it, and I don't like that this magic is making me do it."

"I know." Emery put his arm around me and walked me out from under the canopy. "But you can't keep resisting it. That has been your problem in the past. You've pushed it away."

"What the hell is going on?" Reagan demanded again, following us.

Vampire magic throbbed from two points close to us—one was unmistakably Darius, and the other was a mid-level vamp hiding in the trees.

"Huh," Emery said under his breath. "That's helpful."

"What is?" Reagan asked, by our side.

"Penny has shared her rare ability to feel other creatures' magic." He gave me a squeeze. "It's…helpful."

"It's stronger than usual." I wiped my face of sweat before realizing it was rain. "I feel like I'm cracking up. Worse than before. I hate this."

"I know. *Shhh.* I know." Emery rubbed my arm before marching me into the trees. There he stopped and turned me, positioning my body opposite his. "You haven't totally assimilated my magic with yours, and you're resisting what I can only assume is the goblin's magic. I can feel it tearing you up. Messing with your mind. It'll drive you crazy eventually, Penny. You have to open up and let it all mix together. To fuse. Otherwise you'll never totally be at peace with magic again. You'll always feel like you're cracking up."

"Can I help?" Reagan asked, peering in my face.

"She needs to do this herself." Emery's thumbs stroked my arms. Rain trickled through the trees and splatted on the top of my head in fat drops. "Go back out to the clearing. Keep her mother and the other dual-mages there. Keep them away from her. And get rid of that vampire that's hanging around. He's distracting me."

"So it worked?" Reagan asked. "Did the dual-mage spell work?"

"Not yet. First she has to accept the magic. Then we need to finish the spell with a blood oath." Emery wiped the increasingly wet hair away from my face. When Reagan was gone, he lowered his voice, calm and confident, "We're going to do this together, okay? I'm going to walk you through it."

"Have you assimilated the other magic?"

"I'm ready to—on your go-ahead. This is the beginning of our dual-mage partnership. We have to learn to mix our magic together and work with unity."

"I thought I accepted yours." I closed my eyes and leaned into his body, feeling the raging storm of his magic and the ethereal, sparkling tidal wave of the foreign power.

"Good. Close your eyes. And breathe. Take in your surroundings. Open up to them. Listen to the nature around you. Feel it."

I did as he said, worried about all that power that wanted to suck me under and consume me. Afraid that if I completely gave in, I'd see light flares and rainbows forever.

"It'll all be okay, Penny," Emery said into my ear, helping me relax, pushing me toward a trance. "You can create a new normal, but first you have to accept that which feels different."

It almost sounded like he was reading it out of an ancient book. "Did you have to be coached like this?"

"No, but I've heard stories of people not being able to assimilate. Conrad and I prepared for it just in case it happened. I know the basics of what needs to be done, and I know you. Trust me, Penny. You'll be okay on the other side of this. And you won't be alone. I'll be right there with you, feeling the same things you do."

It was the last bit that finally tipped me over the edge. That reminded me that he was a man I trusted with not just my life, but with my very soul.

"Okay," I said, loosening up. Trying harder.

He started his coaching again, taking me into a trancelike state. To the edge of a cliff. All I needed to do was step off. Step off and fall into the absolutely enormous pool of magic waiting for me.

"I'm scared," I admitted.

"I know. But we'll jump together."

He took my hand, and though there wasn't an actual pit, I felt like he was readying us for one. Taking a deep breath, I kicked away my last safeguard. I mentally stepped forward.

And I fell.

# CHAPTER 21

Emery sucked in a breath as the gush of magic enveloped him, dragging him under. He held on to Penny for dear life. This wasn't what he'd expected—he'd thought there would be a momentary feeling of drowning, not this sensation of being dragged to the bottom of a vast ocean. It felt like the world should be in utter chaos to match what was happening to them.

"Breathe," he forced out as he was turned upside down and ripped from side to side, all without moving a muscle. "Breathe."

Her breath came in ragged pants, and he could tell Penny was clawing for air.

"Keep breathing," he said, forcing himself to do the same, crushing her to his chest.

Air went in, got stuck, and was then forced out. In, stuck, forced out.

"Almost there," he said, really hoping it was true. His legs weakened. His arms shook. He didn't know how much longer he could take it.

He didn't hear Penny breathing. Fear gnawed on his

nerves.

"Come on, baby. Stay with me. Keep breathing."

He heard a ragged breath. A stifled sob.

She was terrified. As a woman who was new to magic, and felt everything incredibly deeply, this had to be ten times worse for her. Given that he felt like he was going to drown…

"Almost there, baby," he said, rubbing her back. Pressure squeezed his chest.

He hadn't mentioned to her the risk that one of the partners, or both, couldn't assimilate. Such a failure would stunt the mages magically, maybe even kill them. He hadn't mentioned it because he hadn't thought it would be a problem. And it wouldn't have been, if not for the raging, all-encompassing magic she'd stolen from that goblin. Thank God they were forming a dual-mage pair, because if they hadn't, she would've eventually had to either assimilate the stolen magic or go crazy. And if she had been forced to face it alone, she might not have made it.

"Almost there," he said, his heart lodged in his throat as he listened to her ragged wheezing. "Almost. Don't fight it."

He felt her nod, and her nails dug into his sides. Slowly, painfully, the magic seeped into him. It expanded through his body and scratched down his bones.

Penny whimpered, but her chest rose and fell. She

held on.

"Almost…" Little by little, the fog started to clear. The intense pressure eased.

A sob ripped from her throat, and relief flooded him. If she had enough breath to cry, she had enough to live.

"We're there." His eyes misted as the pain drifted away, slowly but steadily. Magic still tore at them, whipping around and within them, but it was manageable.

Penny's breathing evened out. Her muscles loosened.

The strange flares of light—the splashes and splotches of rainbow—disappeared from his vision, and a new feeling welled up. Like their perfectly balanced bubble, this felt calming and blissful. Serene.

The feeling wasn't around them, though—it ran *through* them. Emery gasped as all the dark, painful places in his soul were filled with light and goodness. Her touch was soaring through him, sweet and lively and perfect.

He sighed and leaned back so he could look down on her face. Only a glimmer of light made it through the trees from the tent in the clearing, but even still, he could see her expression. Her beautiful smile took his breath away.

"We made it." She blinked as a drop of water landed

on her eyebrow. She shook her head to get the water off. "I was worried, but we did it. And this..." She snaked her hands up so she could wrap her arms around his neck. "This feels...like perfection. Utter perfection. And...magnificent. I feel like I am the holder of the universe. That sounds weird, but—"

"No." He kissed her, harder than he'd intended, and was relieved when her reciprocation was just as ferocious. "That magic you shoplifted is...incredible." And it was. It felt like it spanned space and time, limitlessly. Awesomely complex in a way that was mystifying, while still simple enough to be effectively used in their everyday magic. "Hanging out with Reagan has been good for you, Fast Fingers."

"I did not mean to steal it," she said in a grumpy voice. "Wait—I *didn't* steal it, I meant."

"Too late. You admitted it, klepto. Come on; we have a spell to finish." Feeling lighter and more jubilant than he had...maybe ever, he wrapped an arm around her shoulders and led her back to the clearing with the cauldron and the canopy.

His mood died quickly.

The other dual-mages and Penny's mom stood near the cauldron, looking down in confusion.

"What spell did they use?" Dizzy asked. He bent to look under the cauldron. "There's no fire."

"Well then, how is it bubbling?" Callie bent to check

what Dizzy just had.

Reagan was at the binder containing the spell. "Your potion didn't bubble when you did this spell?"

"Of course not. There's no fire." Callie stomped over to the spell stand. "But it's the same spell."

"Well, clearly they've gone off track, hon." Dizzy crossed his arms.

"Are we sure this Emery boy is playing for the right team?" Ms. Bristol stepped away and put her hands on her hips.

Dizzy turned to survey her. "You think he's gay?"

"No—that's not—" She dropped her hands, and Emery wondered where her shotgun was. "Is he really against the Guild? Would he have any reason to change the spell to something else?"

"Oh no, I don't think that's the case. That boy is smitten. No, but this wouldn't be the first time Penny altered a spell." Callie flicked through the pages. "Hey…what are these—"

"They are here," Darius said quickly, and he walked faster than was humanly possible to the spell stand to capture the binder.

"Just what are you hiding in there, vampire?" Callie centered her weight and lifted her chin. "We never did hear how you got Vlad and Roger to come on board. Maybe *you* don't play for the right team, huh?"

"It's the right spell," Penny said. Having slowed

when he did, she now strutted forward again. Unlike usual, she wasn't hunching under the combined stares of everyone in the tent. And when she glanced up at Emery, he knew why.

She had a teammate for life, an equal who'd agreed to stand in her corner, no matter what. Having always felt singular and solitary, different from the world around her, she could now feel the proof of her inclusion through their connection.

Likewise, he'd gained a more inclusive, consuming connection than he'd ever experienced. The dual-mage connection with his brother hadn't been this strong, and not nearly this balanced. He felt…at peace. Finally, for the first time in his life since his parents had died, he felt contented. Calm.

"It's the right spell." Penny put her hand out, and Darius filled it with the binder. "And the rest are spells Darius must've collected from the most advanced spell books in the world."

"I had them translated by the best," Darius said.

"Notice he never answered your questions," Ms. Bristol said to Callie.

Callie's eyes narrowed. "I did notice that, as a matter of fact."

"Mother, quit stirring up trouble," Penny said.

Ms. Bristol's stare swung around. "Young lady, just because you and that boy have come to an arrangement, doesn't mean you can sass your mother."

"Yes, Mother," she said, slinking up to the cauldron. Emery slunk along behind her like the coward he clearly was. Some things transcended confidence, it turned out, and Ms. Bristol was one of them.

"Clear out, everyone. Head to the house. The vampires can take over security." Reagan walked through the tent, waving her arms. "Looks like the danger has passed for the moment. Let's let them finish up."

"I still don't know if this is a good idea," Ms. Bristol muttered.

"Well, it's not a *bad* idea, you said so yourself." Reagan shooed everyone along.

"Yes, but we still haven't answered the question as to *why* it is boiling…" Dizzy checked to make sure there wasn't a fire again before allowing Reagan to move him along.

Darius lingered at the edge of the canopy, and Emery knew what was on his mind.

"You would not believe what she has been storing inside of her," he blurted out, unable to stop himself. "You wouldn't believe it."

Darius blinked, and a knowing gleam lit his eyes. Without a word, he turned and followed the others.

"You think he was right?" Penny asked, replacing the binder on the stand.

"I don't know if he was right about the godly power

thing or not, but I do know this added magic is going to give us an incredible edge over any other magical workers. Thievery becomes you, Turdswallop. Who would've thought?"

She scowled as she flicked the binder open. Her expression cleared as she leaned over the page. "We have to self-mutilate and then drop our blood into the suspiciously bubbling cauldron."

"Now who's going through the motions instead of sinking into the actual spell?" Emery took a deep breath before ducking to a duffel bag under a poncho in the corner. He extracted a case and took it to Penny. "I'd like to use this, if you don't mind."

She lowered her Swiss Army knife and waited while he opened the case. Gold and jewels glinted under the glare of the battery-powered lanterns. The six-inch blade was slightly curved, its length inscribed with intricate scrollwork.

"We found it among my parents' things," Emery explained as her eyes traveled the weapon. "My brother and I used it for our dual-mage spell, and I know he'd want me to use it for this. To keep my parents' memories alive...and his memory alive."

Tears glimmered in her eyes as she looked up at him, deep and soulful. "It's perfect."

They got into position, side by side and facing the cauldron. Ghosts of Emery's past soared around him, reminding him of when he'd done this last, of everything that had happened before and since. Underneath it all was the deep, throbbing peace that he now felt. The unity and oneness with Penny and the world around them. The past was there, and the hurt was there, but he wasn't afraid of it anymore. He didn't want to run from it.

He wanted to take her hand and embrace it.

"We can make the Mages' Guild something just and good," he said as he brought up the knife. "We will tear it down, but we can make sure it is rebuilt properly. With better checks and balances. With less power in the hands of a few, and more power in the hands of many."

She smiled at him, holding out her finger. "Yes."

He pricked her finger with the tip of the blade before doing his own. A crimson drop welled up. Meeting her gaze, he tipped his finger over the cauldron. She tipped hers.

"May we bind our strength, our power, our essence, and our magic. What is mine is yours, and what is yours I will cherish, until the sands of time call us home," he said, and waited for her to repeat the line.

But when she spoke, it wasn't the line from the spell.

"The Fates have brought us together, and in their image, I will cherish and honor you as my natural partner in this life and the next. With you, my life will truly begin. Our whole is more powerful than the sum of its parts."

The drops of blood hit the rolling waters. Black and white shot out of the cauldron before forming a re-splendent rainbow. Magic danced and rolled. A fizzy feeling crawled up his spine, making him gasp.

"And now it's complete," Emery said, taking her into his arms. "We're dual-mages."

"We don't have to drink it?"

He shook his head and smiled at her. "Counterin-tuitive, but no. This is one potion we don't have to drink."

Her smile was dazzling. "That's excellent. Now there's just one more thing to do, and we can finish out the rest of our lives in safety."

# CHAPTER 22

THE NEXT DAY I was sore, tired, and groggy. None of it had to do with cementing my dual-mage connection with Emery. It was all related to the private celebration we'd indulged in afterward.

I felt my face heat at the thought, but thankfully I was in the back seat. We'd taken one of the loaner cars, and Reagan was driving Emery and me down the winding road leading away from Darius's house in the woods. We were heading to a meeting with Roger. Emery sat in the front seat, going through some pictures Vlad's people had taken around town. He was trying to identify people he knew from the old days so the vampires could get a small idea of the power and experience they might expect in the coming showdown.

"How's Darius doing with the plans?" I asked, looking out at the sometimes-sunny day. Clouds drifted overhead, their color getting darker and more ominous the closer we got to the afternoon. A storm was gathering strength, gearing up to roll through.

Reagan shook her head as she turned the car down

the road leading to town. "He's frustrated. They can't get close to the Mages' Guild to check things out. Vlad is the master of cunning, his best people emulate him, and still he lost one of his people trying to get a peek of the front gates. They have spells all over the place."

"He won't accept our help," Emery said, stalling on a picture.

"Are you kidding? And risk the biggest assets in his arsenal? No way. I offered, too, if only to cut down the spells. But the Guild's security team is standing by in the wood near their compound, and their vampire allies patrol at night."

"Do they know the elder behind it?" I picked at my nail, anxiety plaguing me.

Reagan sniffed. "No. Ain't that a bitch? They've caught a couple of the vampires now. Vlad tortured one mercilessly, but the vampire couldn't talk."

Emery stilled in what he was doing and studied Reagan's face. "Magically silenced?"

"Seems like it. I couldn't get there in time to be sure. Vampires decay too fast after they're destroyed. Whoever is in league with the Guild is hiding their tracks well."

"So they don't have to be stuck on that side if they lose?" I asked.

"Maybe." Reagan shrugged, heading toward the freeway. "Or maybe they know how much they stand to lose if Vlad and Darius figure out who they are before they have the Mages' Guild locked down. Vampires tend to plan *years* in advance. Decades, sometimes. Elders are great at maneuvering. Whoever is doing this will have thought through all the pitfalls. The question is if Vlad or Darius can find any holes in their strategy, then exploit them."

I blew out a breath. "I don't know anything about Vlad, but Darius seems like a formidable nemesis."

"Vlad made Darius," Reagan said softly. "He taught Darius how to be Darius. I've learned that they maneuver around each other in a subtle dance. Sure, one would screw the other if they had no other option, but both of them would like to keep from burning that bridge, I think. And yes, they are formidable nemeses."

"We can't wait around forever." Emery resumed looking at the pictures. "We'll need to crash the Guild's party sooner or later."

"Sooner, obviously." Reagan chewed on her lip. "They've already attacked the shifters in town. They aren't waiting around for us to get our ducks in a row. We need to get going or we'll lose the upper hand. But we also need an angle with which to engage. Right now, I really don't think Darius is seeing it."

I tried to keep hopelessness from weighing me down. We'd be attempting this regardless, and negative thoughts wouldn't help the situation. Instead, I forced myself to focus on the problem, thinking through the spells I remembered from our attack on the compound and the ones the Guild had used on us in New Orleans. Maybe a pattern existed in the way they did magic.

"It'd be easier if I could get closer and just have a feel," I said without meaning to, thinking out loud.

"How far away do you have to be for that to happen?" Reagan asked.

"No." Emery shook his head. "They'll expect us to try and get a look. If we do, they'll be ready for us."

"With what, a color-in-the-lines natural and a bunch of mercenaries in leather capes?" Reagan looked back in the rearview at me, waiting for an answer.

"Watch the road." I pointed, because sometimes she seemed to forget which direction that actually meant. "And...I don't know. It depends on the power of the spells they've set up, I'd think."

"No." Emery stared at Reagan. "No. I can see that you're thinking about it. No! Two seconds ago you were explaining why Darius didn't want us anywhere near there—"

"I'm not Darius," she said.

"And it is a wonder how you're still alive. No."

"It's because I'm tough," Reagan said as I said, "It's because she's crazy."

"Anyway, we need to make sure the shifters are locked down." Emery went back to looking at the pictures. He wasn't having much luck, from what I could see.

Reagan nodded and glanced out the window. I pointed again.

"Roger is expecting us, right?" she asked. "Roger doesn't have a sense of humor when it comes to surprises."

Emery glanced at her. "Does Darius not talk to you about these things?"

"He does, but lately he's been forgetting to shield his thoughts, which are basically cyclical scenarios about how we can all get into the Mages' Guild unharmed. I have to tune him out or I'll go crazy."

"Roger knows, and I'm sure he passed it down. They have to be ready for the woman who chases shifters around the French Quarter with a snarl and a breadstick," Emery said, laughing.

"Why won't you guys let that go?" Reagan asked in exasperation.

"Besides," Emery said, "do you think Darius would trust Penny to go waltzing in there if the shifters didn't expect visitors?"

"She doesn't have any more control, huh?" Reagan asked.

"A dual-mage connection doesn't do anything to help the mages control their magic, it just increases their power level. And the"—he paused—"unity of using it."

"I heard your unity last night," Reagan said dryly. "So she's more dangerous?"

"I like to think of it as…more exciting." Emery turned back to me and winked.

"So we're just supposed to check in with their mages and make sure the shifters' wards and everything are up to speed?" I asked, looking out the window.

"I know this one." Emery waved a photo while shaking his head. He huffed. "He is as old… Still there, though, obviously. He's a real piece of work." Emery flung it onto the dash. "He's powerful, but he's—"

"Write it on the back of the photo. I won't be able to remember everything." Reagan grabbed a pen from the console and held it up for Emery.

A smile spread across Emery's face. "You have excellent memory from bonding the vampire. You can remember everything just fine."

"Right. Good catch." Reagan slammed on the gas as she pulled onto the freeway on-ramp. "Let me rephrase. Write it down, because it makes no difference to me. Strategy is Darius's department."

Emery laughed and continued going through the pictures. "Yes, Fast Fingers," he said, finally returning to my question. "Our mission is to make sure Roger's hideout is fortified. At least, that's why Roger finally relented and handed over the location of his hideout.

He thinks someone is getting through their mages' wards."

"Mages, plural?" I asked.

"Yes, he employs a group of them."

"And they aren't part of the pack?"

Reagan shook her head. "No. They have their own hierarchy and exist separately to the shifter hierarchy. But they answer to Roger as their boss. He relies on them to double-check each other's work, since he can't do it. Usually, that seems to work just fine. That I've heard, anyway. This is the first time I've heard him doubt."

I brushed the hair out of my eyes, feeling uneasy. "We're all working together, so why wouldn't Roger just come clean in the first place?"

"The shifters and the vampires view each other as the lesser of two evils," Reagan said. "They need each other in order to get rid of the Mages' Guild, but they don't trust each other. Just as soon as this is out of the way, the shifters will go back to hunting the vampires."

"That's kind of a misuse of power on the shifters' part." I loosened my seatbelt and checked in with the crazy magic rolling around my body. I'd been living with my natural magic for nearly twenty-five years. I was used to the feel of it. Now, suddenly, everything was different. I couldn't sit idle without noticing.

"Oh no, the vampires definitely deserve it." Reagan

nodded as she pulled off the freeway. "Vlad rarely asks people if they want to be vampires anymore. He makes them, then talks them around their panic. And he delights in doing it under the shifters' noses. He is a special kind of dick, that one."

"Uh-huh." I really needed to learn to stay out of it. Magical people had a collective screw loose.

"Penny." The way Emery said my name made tingles wash over my skin. Without another word, he handed back a picture.

I sucked in a breath. "Mary Bell." It was three-quarters of her face, as if she'd turned away as the photographer took the shot. Behind her was a line of buildings. Downtown Seattle.

"And..." Emery handed back another picture, and I already knew who it would be. Sure enough...

"John." I let the pictures fall to my lap, my stomach churning. "They really were recruited."

"They're both powerful, and they've met you personally," Reagan said. "They're desirable. I'm sure they are being treated like royalty. For now."

"They have no idea what kind of organization they've traded into," Emery said with an edge to his voice, reaching back for the pictures. "They might think things are fine now, but as soon as they aren't needed for intel, they'll have to pay their dues like everyone else. Considering how the Guild has changed, that could mean some pretty hair-raising things."

"Mary would be used to it," I said as I looked out the window, my heart falling. "She's sacrificed people in the past."

"Well then, she'll fit right in." I heard Emery shuffling through the remaining photographs.

I shook my head. "I thought she'd learned her lesson. And John…I wouldn't have believed him capable of that."

Emery's movements slowed down until he was very still. Reagan looked over at him with a grin.

"What?" I asked.

"She doesn't know," Reagan said to Emery. "Darius was trying to get your dander up by having his assistant hint that Penny had an attachment to John. He was trying to force out your true feelings. She wanted nothing to do with him. You know that, right?"

"He said what?" I leaned forward, trying to see their faces.

Emery gave Reagan a hard look before turning away. "Darius is good at manipulation."

Reagan laughed. "Very."

Silence stretched through the car, and I let it. I didn't feel like asking questions about whatever maneuvering Darius had done. I was still reeling from being wrong. Mary had packed up and headed to Seattle to join the Guild. John, too. They'd chosen to side with an organization that promised wealth and power at the expense of the innocent.

"They need to be taken down," I said, my resolve strengthening. "Hard."

Fifteen minutes later, we turned off a small road onto an even smaller one—a one-lane road with dense trees on either side. A wave of *mine!* rolled over me. I held out my hand to get Reagan to slow down, but Emery spoke before I could. "Stop."

He looked out the window.

"What are you doing, bird-watching?" Reagan asked.

Emery chuckled, but shook his head instead of commenting.

"It's like that thing vampires have," I told him. "The way they mark their territory."

"I know, yeah." He leaned forward and braced his forearms on his knees.

I clicked off my seatbelt so I could lean between the seats. "Do you sense something else?"

He leaned back and looked out the window again. "A premonition, but…" He shook his head. "I keep getting these warning premonitions. They're not about immediate danger. And, like now, it's not even helpful. All I saw was trees. Trees and shadows."

"Shadows…like…that druid?" I asked, pushing my magic out and trying to sense if there was any other magic nearby.

"No. The druid had a different feel about him. Something I didn't sense just now. I only felt…danger. A warning." Emery shook his head, clearly at a loss.

"Should we get out and walk up?" Reagan asked. "Maybe we should scout it out from down here?"

A horn blared behind us.

We all spun around in our seats. Even Reagan, who had three mirrors she could've used instead.

"Oh no," I said with a release of breath. "Why did you invite them?"

"I thought you did," Reagan said as Emery said, "I didn't."

"They've been following us. I just assumed you guys wanted them along for some reason." Reagan shrugged.

Moss's Lexus was behind us, with my mother and Callie in the front seats and Dizzy leaning forward from the back, waving.

"Well, this should be interesting," Emery said.

I didn't share his optimism.

# CHAPTER 23

"W̲HAT WERE WE going to do, stay behind, defenseless?" Callie asked as they met us between the cars.

"Defenseless? You're dual-mages, and the ward Emery and Penny constructed is unbreakable," Reagan said.

"Besides," my mother chimed in, holding out a deck of tarot cards, "I brought my tools. A change of location and influence might give me a different reading. Maybe I can get something that will help Darius."

This was clearly one of the times when she and Callie had decided to present a united front.

Reagan sighed. "Shifters aren't as abiding as vampires. They're a little more rough and tumble. Don't expect to get your way."

Callie and my mother both sniffed. Dizzy laughed good-naturedly, his version of sniffing. It was a bad sign.

"What do you think?" I asked Emery, stepping away from the others and joining him as he looked out into the trees.

"I get a bad feeling about these woods. About these shifters in general." He slipped his hands into his pockets. "It's almost as if there's a shadow lurking over us here. I don't like it."

I let the electricity in the air run through me, but whatever sense he was getting, I didn't share it. I felt alive out here. Happy and fulfilled. The lush landscape, unspoiled by people, was the perfect setting for me to roam.

"It has to be a premonition," I said, taking his hand. "Should we wander through the woods? Send the dead weight to the house ahead of us?" I barely kept from looking back at my mother and the Bankses to show who I meant.

He turned and gestured me ahead of him. "No. Let's meet with Roger and look at the ward first. We can go from there."

"House" was a small word for the shifters' shelter. It was a sprawling mansion, cutting into the hillside and nestled within the trees. The long, winding road up to it only had a few places where two cars could pass, with no walkways or sidewalks for pedestrians. Shifter magic pulsed from one side, then the other, as we drew closer—our progress had been noted and then watched.

The ward was more like a cobbled-together spell with odd seams and strange overlays, something Dr.

Frankenstein might have produced. It had a decent amount of power, but it could be exploited in so many different places that I couldn't do much more than shake my head.

"Nope. This won't work at all." Reagan took her foot off the brake and let the car roll slowly through the layer of magic. "And look, we can get in just fine. No biggie."

Emery was quiet as we parked in a gravel area with three rows of cars. Most of them were SUVs of some sort, the majority with big tires capable of off-roading.

"This is a different sort of lifestyle than the vampires," I said to myself as I stepped out of the car.

A large gray wolf stood up near the house, its nose twitching as it watched (and smelled) us.

"Where there is one wolf, there are bound to be at least three more," Reagan said in a low tone, her gaze sweeping the area. "Use your magic. Get an idea of how they're operating. All of this will be useful."

I did as she said, feeling four more wolves lurking in the trees, surrounding us. Another type of shifter, a prowling sort, was hidden to our left, moving in the opposite direction. "I can feel out pretty far now," I said to Emery.

"I can only feel close by. It looks like I got a taste of your add-on gift, but not the full potency." He looked at the sky as my mother and the dual-mages parked and got out of the Lexus. Frankenstein's ward swirled and glittered, thinner up top than on the sides. That spoke of an off-kilter spell. "We need to get them out of here."

"Who? My mother and the Bankses?"

"All of them." He turned and looked out at the trees. "Everyone."

The door to the mansion opened and out stepped Roger in faded blue jeans and a tight white shirt spreading across his broad chest. Despite his stacks of muscle, he moved with the grace of a predator in its prime. Shoulders back and head held high, he looked like someone who owned the world—and would fight for it tooth and nail if anyone tried to take it from him. His intense dual-colored gaze landed on us.

"Well, now, he is...*robust*," my mother said. I could practically hear the drool running out of her mouth.

"Mother!" I said through my teeth.

"What? I'm just appreciating the view. I'm old, not dead."

Oh my heavens, she was so embarrassing.

Roger stepped down from the porch and stalked toward us, his large arms swinging and his power slapping me in the face.

Emery turned around with fire in his eyes, his whole body flexing, reacting to feeling potent shifter magic for the first time. Roger saw it immediately and slowed, his muscles tightening under his snug clothing.

"Oh *my*," my mother said, and I nearly died.

"Whoa, whoa." Reagan stepped between them and put her hands out. "Hey, whoa."

"That is just normal shifter magic," I said to Emery. "He's a very powerful shifter. This is normal."

"They became a dual-mage pair last night," Reagan said to Roger. "Emery picked up a few new tricks that he clearly wasn't expecting." She dropped her hands and grinned. "Look at me, stopping a fight instead of starting one. Ha! It's like I'm growing up."

"Better you than me," Callie said, opening her satchel as she walked forward. "Let's get this show on the road. If I'm going to have people staring at me, I'd rather it be *people* and not animals hiding in the bushes."

"Sorry, bro." Emery stepped around Reagan and put out his hand. "Penny's magic is throwing me for a loop."

"No sweat." Roger's grip turned his knuckles white, and Emery's muscles started dancing too.

There was no way I was going to say what I was thinking and sound like my mother...

"Where do you want to start?" Roger asked, looking us over.

"The ward," Callie said. "Lead us to the trouble spots."

"I'll take the house." My mother stalked forward

like she owned the place. "I want to get a feel for—"

Roger gracefully stepped in her way, and a shock of power burst from his frame. Emery tensed and turned away, shaking his head. Apparently he could handle the dance of *Alpha*…until he was blasted in the face with it. He clearly wanted to retaliate.

Unfortunately, as a longtime matriarch and all around badass, so did my mother. "Penny, get my shotgun."

"Oh my God, *Mother*! This is his house. You can't just go wandering through. Clearly."

"They called us in to help," Callie said, strapping on her bulldog face and joining my mother's side. "Now we're here, and they keep us out?"

"They didn't call you. They called us." I didn't know whether to step in their path, or just run and let the shifters handle it. "You tagged along."

"Penny—" my mother started.

"I know, I know." I was unable to help sulking a little. "Don't sass."

"I'm not in the habit of letting non-pack affiliates in the house unattended," Roger said. "You are"—his eyes didn't flick around her person, but beat into her head like a dual-colored hammer—"the *Seer*, is that right? Penny Bristol's mother?"

She met his gaze without so much as sweating. I doubted many others could boast the same accomplishment. "That's right. And right now, I've been of very little use. I need more input. I need to be exposed to more magical influences. Which means I need access to your house. To your organization, or lack thereof."

He didn't flinch or even frown with the dig. Very self-assured, this shifter. "Of course." He glanced right, and a wolf went trotting away. "If you'll just wait here a moment, I'll have someone escort you around."

My mother shifted and her chin rose slightly. "If you're worried about me telling the vampires how you run things, there's no need. As far as they're concerned, I'm in the same boat you are."

He stared at her for a silent beat. She took the stare and gave it right back.

Finally he nodded. "Noted."

A few people came out of the house, two of them a couple of years younger than me and a guy about Roger's age, early thirties and with a resting dick-face that had me scooting backward into Emery. He was taller and leaner than Roger, but with the same grace and ease of movement. His hard brown eyes swept over everyone quickly before darting back to Emery, then Reagan, and then sticking on me. Wariness crossed his features, and I got the distinct impression that I made him uncomfortable. He'd clearly heard what I had done to Rex. As he got closer, I noticed a thin white scar running down the side of his face like a river, from his sharp cheekbone to his neck.

"Alder is the beta of the North American pack," Roger said, not shifting to the side as the scarred man came up behind him. "My second-in-command. He'll take you around the house, Miss...?"

My mother swayed in a disturbingly girlish manner. "Bristol. You can call me Karen."

Roger nodded sharply. "Karen." Finally, he stepped to the side with a tiny tilt of his head, a shallow representation of a vampire's bow. "Please don't give Alder a hard time, Karen."

She giggled—*giggled!*—before allowing Alder to lead her away without so much as a pistol.

Roger squared off again, blasting out another force of power, and I wondered if this was the shifter equivalent of elders shooting power at newbie vampires to make them cower. The younger guys behind him certainly seemed to feel it. One of them, a striking guy with dark brown hair, a square jaw, and a fetching cleft in his chin, turned a little brittle. The other, a shorter guy with a messy mop of light brown hair and a small hole in the shoulder seam of his T-shirt, took a step back and hunched.

Emery blew out a breath, now looking down at his feet with his hands in his pockets, his whole body tense. "This is going to take some getting used to."

"You can always blast him with power to get even,"

Reagan said with a grin and a manic light in her eyes. I knew that look.

"Don't do that." I patted Emery. "Whatever you do, don't do that."

"I wasn't expecting so many mages," Roger said conversationally, and his accusation rang loud and clear.

"Honestly, they followed us," I said, pointing at the Bankses. I wasn't going down with this ship.

Callie leaned toward me and, in a low tone, said, "Snitches get stitches, Penny."

"We thought we might lend a little experience," Dizzy said with a smile, opening his satchel. "Maybe even a little...levelheadedness. Things can be turbulent for a couple in the months after a dual-mage pairing. And as you've heard, Emery and Penny just paired last night. I'm sure you'd rather be safe than sorry."

Reagan started forward, flashing the two younger shifters a fiery gaze. "Who are your...associates?"

She'd wanted to say "underlings" to rile them up. I'd heard her do it before. That she'd refrained now meant she was on her best behavior.

Roger stared at her for a moment, probably sharing my thought wave. Unlike my mother, Reagan didn't just stare right back. She winked, grinned, and then flared her mighty magic. Only hers was a wave of beautiful complexity that I wanted to bask in before unraveling one subtle piece at a time.

Emery blinked at Reagan before shifting his haunted gaze toward me. "How do you stand this?"

"That"—I pointed at Reagan—"is new. The strength of that"—I made a circle with my finger around the shifters—"is new*ish*, and I haven't been coping all that well, actually. As you might've noticed from the meeting in Derry."

Roger waited until our exchange was finished (he didn't seem like a man who missed much) before half turning toward the two guys who stood behind him. "This is Devon, a sub-alpha residing in Northern California. He has great leadership abilities and is assigned to escorting—"

"Monitoring," Reagan interjected. In response to Roger's hard stare, she shrugged with a smile. "We're all friends here—why mince words?"

Roger's jaw clenched, but he didn't react. "He'll be escorting you around today, taking over should I be called elsewhere."

"What's a sub-alpha?" I asked Emery quietly.

"Roger overseas *all* the packs in this very large territory," Reagan said. "The overall pack is divided into smaller packs, each with a different overall status level depending on the kickassitude of the pack members. Each of those packs has an Alpha. If there are subgroups under that, each of *those* packs has an Alpha—"

"Reagan, honey, unless you have a pie chart handy, let's get moving," Callie said. "You're not doing anyone any favors."

"A pie chart?" Dizzy muttered as Roger started walking, his jaw clenched again.

"Reagan likes flirting with death," Emery said in an undertone as we followed Roger.

"This is honestly the first time you noticed? She bonded an elder vampire, for criminy's sake."

As a group, we headed directly for the tree line at the side of the driveway. I wondered where the mages that worked for Roger were. I'd thought we were supposed to chat with one of them while checking out their setup.

As if hearing my unspoken question, Devon, the shifter with the fetching cleft in his chin, glanced at the house. Roger hadn't had the patience to introduce the other shifter, which showed just how quickly Reagan could make a shifter reach a boiling point. When it came to rage, she could manipulate people just as easily as vampires. "Alpha," he said, "what about Patrick?"

"Go tell him to catch up. I'll speak to him about tardiness later." Roger stepped off the gravel driveway and onto a small path cutting through the trees. We could only go single file, so Emery put his hands on my shoulders and directed me in front of him.

Judging by the distance we walked, zigzagging

through the trees, the ward didn't cover the property in a dome. Instead, it clearly followed some other path. Just as we'd sensed on our way in, it was cobbled together in pieces and patches.

The path opened up gradually until we reached a small clearing. Roger stopped about ten feet from the ward and looked up, as though studying it. I hesitated beside him, wondering why he was pretending. Everyone knew only natural mages could see magic, and even then, they could only see wards when they were infused with a bunch of power and often spells.

"Don't bother sparing his feelings, Penny," Reagan said, tromping through the grass around the line of people in front of her with her sword out and her fanny pack open. "Get to the actual ward."

A blast of Roger's magic locked up Emery's body, his muscles flaring and his fingers curling into fists. The man clearly didn't deal with challenges well, whether directed at him or not.

Ignoring the tension, I neared the ward and studied the hodgepodge spell, which was weird and ill-fitting.

*Protect. Access. Barrier. Unseen.*

"The intent is conflicting." I crinkled my nose, closing my eyes to make sure I had it right. "This isn't solely a ward, but it isn't totally a spell, either. It feels like both, mashed together. Which I've done, so I guess it isn't crazy, but it doesn't work in this case."

Emery looked between me and the spell. "I can't feel the intent."

"Oh." I turned my frown upside down. "I guess sharing magic wasn't my add-on. This must be."

"No, I think we were right, but... We don't have time to figure this out right now."

Emery turned to face the ward, tracing his finger through the air, pointing out a strange seam that didn't seem to mesh with the overall construction. The freshly woven spell glittered on one side; on the other, I could only feel the spell's intent, not see its magic.

"They patched up the ward with a spell, it looks like," he murmured, clearly not wanting the shifters behind us to hear the assessment. I wasn't sure why. "That spell is practiced. I bet that ward isn't as much."

"Meaning..." Reagan had her sword up, with one hand beside it, trying to disguise her attempts to feel out the spell. "The ward is a newer creation they put up for the first time, but they've been using the spell all over the place?"

"That, or the ward was the collaborative effort of people not experienced in working together, and the spell is from one person with experience in this exact spell. There is no finesse to it, but its simple economy and uniform weaving speak of years of experience."

"The intent of this spell is to hide," I said, picking my nail as I analyzed it. "Maybe even to fool. Why would they patch up a weak spot in a ward with something like this?"

"Here." Callie and Dizzy stepped up together, herbs in Callie's hands and powder in Dizzy's. I watched in rapture as Callie crinkled the herbs just so before releasing them—or, more accurately, throwing them—in perfect timing with Dizzy's pinches and blows of powder. As they sprinkled the spell/ward with their efforts, it lit up like a Christmas tree, allowing us to see the finer intricacies.

"Oh!" I said as Emery said, "Huh."

"You don't need to teach *this* old dog new tricks." Callie surveyed her handiwork.

The spell spread farther along the sides and up, giving us a much larger picture of what was going on.

Suddenly, the patterns and patches all made perfect sense.

Shivers of fear coated my body. Emery grabbed my arm and stepped back before looking around warily. Without it needing to be said, I knew he was thinking about the warnings delivered through his premonitions. His anxiety when we'd first shown up. His constant wariness within the shifters' boundaries.

*We need to get them out of here.*

# CHAPTER 24

WITH THE WAY the original spell had been hacked into, then covered up, and the feel of the intent… There was no second-guessing. The situation was plain as day.

I blurted out the first thing that came to mind.

"Roger, you've got a traitor."

Devon reappeared on the path, walking behind a scrawny man with large black-rimmed glasses. Scrawny Man must've been a mage, because he was certainly no shifter—I didn't need my magic to tell me that.

Roger stepped closer to me, cutting off my line of sight. "What did you say?"

Reagan looked at the newcomer and put her hand on my shoulder, squeezing hard, silently telling me to zip the lip. There was no way to tell if the traitor was just one of the mages, or many, and where this new-comer fit in.

Her face had closed down, all humor sapped away. "What else do you need looked at, Roger?" she asked in a perfectly calm, steady voice. She'd picked up a trick or two from Darius.

"I did my part," Callie said, moving away from the ward/spell stiffly. "Roger, can one of these boys take me to Karen?"

Roger paused again, his gaze now beating into Callie. His focus wasn't there, though, I could tell. He was analyzing the sudden change in all of us.

"Andy," he said, his voice a whip crack.

"Yes, Alpha." The guy with the hole in the seam of his T-shirt scooted up and put out his arm.

"I'd break you, son. Just lead the way," Callie said.

I couldn't help my gaze dipping to the "Sweet Thang" written across the butt of her bright green sweatpants. The woman was colorful.

"Patrick, what do you think about this ward?" Roger asked.

"Well…" Patrick pushed his black-rimmed glasses up his nose and studied where the Bankses' *spell discovery* spell was now starting to wear away. "It seems a little mishmashed for sure. But you had, what, three mages erect the ward? That's to be expected. It has a good bit of power behind it. I'd have to check along the rest of the perimeter, but this looks good. We'll know if someone comes through or tries to tear it down."

"Who is this spell connected to?" Emery asked. "Who will get alerted if someone comes through?"

"Well…" Patrick adjusted his glasses. "It changes.

Generally it is whoever's on guard at the time. Whoever's overseeing magical security for the house."

"Who is…on guard right now?" Emery asked.

Patrick looked upward and sucked on his teeth. "I can't…remember exactly. I'd have to go look. It's not my turn yet, at any rate."

Roger studied Patrick, and I couldn't help but ask, "Is this how you run all of your operations, Roger?"

"It isn't," Reagan said, moving her fanny pack a little more toward her hip. It looked like an unconscious gesture. "Which makes me wonder why he would put up with it when the stakes are so high."

Roger blasted out his shifter magic, but he didn't so much as clench his jaw. "I've checked the schedule and had my people monitoring the effectiveness of our protections. So far, no one has been asleep on the job. The different mages have checked the work of their peers. As you've seen. Without understanding the magical side, there's not much more I can do. Except call for reinforcements."

Clearly he meant us, and I wondered if it was pride or something else that prevented him from saying it. It was also clear he not only thought someone might be getting through the ward, but was also worried about the loyalty and truthfulness of the mages he'd hired, who weren't totally under his control.

"Oh yeah, we've seen." Reagan shook her head.

"Where do you get these people, Roger? The street corner?"

Patrick squinted and pushed his glasses a little farther up his nose.

Emery took off walking, and I hurried to catch up. Reagan fell in behind me.

"Patrick, we're going with them," I heard a male say. It must've been Devon.

A phone chimed and Roger barked, "Yeah?" He didn't seem pleased with the way the day was unfolding.

*Tattle.*

I stepped over a spell snaking across the small path running alongside the ward. Reagan did the same, not needing me to point it out. She glanced back, and I could just see Roger stutter-step behind her before jumping over it at the last moment.

"Get Steve on it," Roger said as he turned around and pointed at the spot he clearly couldn't see, but had noticed us all avoiding. Devon grabbed the confused Patrick's shoulders and walked him around the area. Roger paused a moment, his gaze on Patrick, his eyes hard.

Patrick hadn't known the spell was there. That, or he'd forgotten. Either was bad, and clearly Roger had picked up on it.

"Steve," Reagan said, pushing me forward. "I wonder if that's the Steve we know."

The Steve we knew turned into an enormous lion, and had helped us out in New Orleans. He'd wanted to take a tumble in the sheets with Reagan before finding out she was already spoken for. He'd been mystified to discover who (and what) had spoken for her.

Emery had stopped on the path and was staring off to the right at a tiny clearing with a patch of trampled grass. The branches of the small bushes dotting the area looked like they'd taken a beating. No spell was currently stretched across the little clearing, but as I stood there, I felt a strange sort of echo. Almost like threads of magic, weak and wispy, fluttered across the space like broken spider webs.

*Hide. Fresh.*

Reagan had barely stopped beside me before following the path up to the trampled area. Roger didn't fall in behind her. Instead, with rumpled brow, he stared down at where the paths intersected.

"I'm going to just...use a casing...so as to...see if magic has been used here." Reagan dug into her fanny pack, coming out with an empty casing she then squeezed together. Her eyes flicked to Patrick before she ripped out her sword and applied the casing to it. I had no doubt her muttered "magical spell" was nothing more than a bunch of curse words. "Spell camouflage, I'd bet. The magic was strong, but not strong enough for the residual magic to last more than a day. I'd bet this happened last night."

"Residual magic?" I asked Emery quietly. "That's a thing?"

Emery turned away and started walking again. When I caught up, the two of us were a little removed from the others. "Yes," he said, "though not something I can usually make use of. The visible threads are usually gone in a couple hours. Could you feel anything?"

"A sort of echo of the spell's intent."

"Good." The word was barely more than a whisper, as though he was talking to himself. "That's another hole in our combined arsenal plugged up."

Fast footsteps approached, and I knew the others were catching up. We walked around two more trip-wires, clearly meant for whoever was using the path along the ward, before stopping at another mini-clearing. This one had older signs of disturbance, the area having nearly righted itself again.

Emery glanced at me, and I shook my head. I didn't feel any magic whatsoever.

"Devon," Roger barked, and the younger guy stepped up quickly, his hand still on Patrick's shoulder. He had been told nothing, but he still knew something was amiss, and that it probably had to do with Patrick. Smart guy. "Was this reported?"

"Yes, Alpha, three days ago. Beta checked it out personally but couldn't find any scents or tracks leading away. He assumed it was the magical workers."

"Patrick?" Roger said, not looking at them.

"Oh. Um…yes, sir? Alpha?" Patrick shifted and pushed up his glasses.

"You're wasting your time with him." Reagan shook her head and wandered through the clearing, a hand held low, feeling for magic without letting on what she was doing.

"Have your people been working on this area in the last couple of days?" Roger asked, rejecting Reagan's assessment of his hired help.

"Oh. Hmm." Patrick turned and looked in the direction of the ward before shifting his gaze low and tracing his finger through the air. He was using the plant life to find the bright, shifting magical patch over the ward, something that screamed *turnstile*, letting people in and out, undetected, like a doorway.

"Text your mother," Emery said, wrapping his fingers around my forearm. "She needs to get her task done and get out. Get them all out. Sooner the better."

"If they were going to attack, wouldn't they wait until nightfall so they could use their vampires?" I whispered, pulling out my phone with a shaking hand.

"I don't know. But I'd rather not leave it to chance." He started forward again. "Watch that ward. See how many more patches you can find."

The perimeter of the mansion was large, certainly

over a mile, maybe more than two. We didn't walk the whole thing, but then, we didn't need to. Every so often, another patch stood out, weakening the overall ward, allowing in anyone who held the right key.

"And what is the right key?" Emery said softly to himself, stopped at one of the areas and analyzing it.

Reagan joined us, her hands out now and feeling. Clearly she thought Patrick was too dumb to notice her lack of a fake spell.

"Is the house you're staying in locked down?" Roger asked me, watching the others. Devon stood with Patrick, a little removed. Patrick didn't seem overly interested in what was going on. There was a reason his peers had brought him on.

"The grounds aren't. Those are wide open with little tattletale spells intermittently set up. We want to see who's wandering around. The house is protected, though. We have a good ward set up. Unless you're on the preapproved list, you're not getting in there."

"Is anyone wandering around?"

"Only a couple of vampires, and they're giving the house plenty of space. Darius doesn't seem comfortable with the situation, but he hasn't moved us, so…"

"Picking on the one who doesn't know to keep secrets, huh?" Reagan rejoined us with a smirk.

"Was that supposed to be a secret?" Because what a stupid secret, if so.

"Do you need to look around some more?" Roger asked, silencing his phone. The thing rang constantly. He was a busy man.

"No. We've got...basically what we need," Reagan said. "We can head to the house now."

"Wait." Roger tapped the screen of his phone before putting it to his ear. He waited a beat before saying, "Send out Todd. We're in the west nine." He waited another beat before lowering the phone again. "The head mage is on his way."

I was about to ask why they'd sent Patrick to tag along with us rather than the head mage, but it was probably the same reason the kid had been brought on in the first place. Lack of attention to detail. You couldn't tattle on what you didn't notice.

A couple minutes later, the sounds of crunching grass and moving foliage interrupted a mostly uncomfortable silence. A bald, stocky man sauntered along the path, his gaze down and scanning. He was identifying the various plant-life markers of the spells, something I would expect of a head mage. A satchel draped across his body, open at his side, and his pushed-back shoulders and haughty movements screamed, *I'm the best mage in the world.*

Emery braced himself before going utterly loose, his usual stance right before Reagan ran at him. He swaggered toward me and wrapped an arm around me possessively. Reagan stepped toward the mage with her hand out to shake respectfully.

Both of those actions set off my alarm bells. Roger must've thought so, too, because another blast of shifter magic slammed into us, and his scrutinizing gaze landed on the head mage.

"Hi, I'm Reagan." Reagan pumped his hand.

"Todd, Roger's head mage."

"That right? Awesome. We were just admiring the ward. Did you put it up?"

Everything in me wanted to grab Emery's arm and drag him out of there. I didn't sense danger in any way, but Reagan's actions were so out of the ordinary that there could be nothing short of a world crisis on the horizon.

Puffed up from the compliment, Todd nodded and crossed through the group, glancing at a distinct bush at the side before stopping. "I orchestrated it, yes," he said, three feet from the actual ward. "I mixed a score of spells, then combined power with *lesser* mages in order to erect this particular ward." He looked at dead air, pretending to study his handiwork. He clearly didn't know who we were. "It's my best work."

"Oh yeah?" Reagan nodded, but didn't correct him on the location of the ward. I knew she wasn't too far away to feel it, which meant she was giving a subtle cue to Roger. She had faith that Roger had a good memory and sense of direction.

"How long have you worked here?" Emery asked.

Todd gave a "subtle" grin to Roger. "I'm afraid that's classified. But I've worked for Roger"—he looked up at the sky—"fifteen years, is that right?"

"You were hired before I assumed the role of Alpha," Roger said with his normal straight face.

"Right, yes." Todd laughed. "Of course." His chest puffed up a little more, if that was even possible. He thought he was more important than a guy who wouldn't blink twice about ripping his throat out if he proved to be the danger Reagan and Emery clearly thought he was.

"This is why the mage life is not for me," I mumbled. "All ego, no brains."

Emery huffed out laughter, turning away as he did so. Clearly he didn't realize I was as serious as a heart attack.

"Right." Reagan glanced around before giving Roger a pointed look, no flippancy or fire in her eyes. "Let's head back to the extremely nice house in the woods, shall we? Because despite the plain jeans and cheap T-shirt—which really works for you, Roger, don't get me wrong—you seem to love nice things. A little like the vampires in that way, I think…"

Another blast of shifter magic slammed into me, this one more potent.

"Tell her not to provoke him," Emery said through clenched teeth. "I'm not doing well at adjusting."

"Emery is cracking up, got it," Reagan said, back to her jubilant self.

That meant she thought a battle was coming.

"Todd," Emery said, distaste running across his face as he offered a slight bow. Roger pretending to be subordinate to Devon probably would've looked just as unnatural and painful. "You did great work here. I'd love to someday work on a team this powerful."

Todd curled his lip. "Experience will do wonders. I handpicked this team. For a job this big, you need the best."

"Yes." Emery motioned Todd ahead of him on the path. "And do you do much upkeep? The seams of a spell like this can fray, can't they?"

"Yes…" Todd glanced back with a mildly impressed expression. Then did a double take before continuing to walk. "Yes, that's right. We do have some. We also check it constantly to make sure everything looks right. I was hired to do a job, and as Roger can tell you, I take my responsibilities seriously."

"Yes. Patrick is proof of that," Reagan said from behind me.

I just barely saw Todd's reaction—a half-turn and an annoyed expression—before he got it together.

Emery slowed a bit and pulled me a little to the side,

motioning Reagan forward.

"Come on, Devon, up here with me." Reagan motioned to Devon, who was still shadowing Patrick. "You're too hot for a shifter. Ever think of becoming a vampire?"

A different blast of shifter magic surged forward, not quite as potent as Roger's, but not far off. It seemed there was a reason Roger was keeping the younger guy close. He clearly had potential. Except, just now, it wasn't good news. Emery and Roger tensed up at the same time, fire lighting in their eyes.

Emery ripped his gaze to the ground, jaw clenched again and fists balled. Roger, who was allowed to challenge any of his shifters, swung a fierce gaze Devon's way.

The younger guy caught the reaction and lowered his eyes, but his posture stayed poised and ready.

"Don't provoke him," Emery told Reagan.

"Oops. My bad." Reagan patted the younger shifter as he all but dragged Patrick forward. She followed behind, and I noticed the button clasp had been undone on the dagger sheath on her thigh, and the hilts of her three throwing knives stuck up out of her sock.

She was absolutely ready for battle.

"When did Todd get to work on the ward?" Emery asked as he fell back with Roger.

"He has overseen the security of this house for

years," Roger replied in a low tone, his expression flat. Something about the tightness in his eyes told me he was uncomfortable but doing a good job of hiding it. "I called him from Ireland as soon as I knew we'd be engaging the Guild. He started working on the ward then."

Emery shook his head, and I shook mine with him. He said what I was thinking. "This ward didn't just go up. It's old, with new patches. Some of those patches are *very* new. As in, the ward was broken through, and patched up, last night."

Roger stiffened and magic seeped from him, winding through my body and crawling up my back.

"In addition…" Emery scratched his cheek. "I'm not sure how much you know about me, but I get premonitions whenever Penny and I are in mortal danger. Moments before the kill strike occurs, I'll see it coming. It's saved our lives more times than I can count. In a few instances, I have also gotten blanket warnings. I don't totally know what they mean, but that mage"—Emery pointed up toward the others, who were now a good distance in front of us—"sets me off. He reeks of the feeling I get with those warning premonitions. This whole area"—he made a circle in the air with his pointer finger—"sets me off the wrong way. You've got a breach. After seeing the ward, that's as clear as day. But, at this point, I don't think it's a matter of finding and fixing the loose ends. I think you need to get your people out of here. If you stay and fight, you'll lose a lot of shifters before you even get to the Guild compound."

"They tried to thin your numbers at that shifter bar yesterday," I said. "If they know you're here, it's a no-brainer for them to run in with a bunch of magical spells, set them off, and get out. With your own magical guys against you, you'd be cooked before you knew what hit you."

Roger shook his head slowly, staring straight ahead. "My people are in and out of this place constantly. Nearly a hundred people are stationed here. Too many for me to uproot them on a hunch."

"I hear you loud and clear," Emery said. "And that's all I got. A hunch. But hunches like this have kept me alive for the last few years. They've helped me get out from under the Guild."

The people in front of us turned toward the house.

"I'll take it under advisement," Roger said. "I need to talk to a few of my—"

A shotgun blast rang through the air. My mother was in danger.

I was running before I had time to form a swear word.

# CHAPTER 25

A NOTHER SHOTGUN BLAST went off, followed by a deep rumbling. I crashed into the brush to get around the others, who had braced themselves but not put on the jets, when I felt the intent of a spell.

*Slash.*

I yanked at elements and wove them together as Todd turned. His hands up near his chest, full of leaves and herbs, he spouted off some Latin and shoved both arms forward. The spell, having already taken shape, just needed that push to be off. After it cut through Devon, it would be on to Reagan in a flash.

My own weave done, I threw it out as Reagan grabbed Devon and tossed him to the side. The spell just barely missed him and was speeding right for her face. She bent backward like someone in an action flick, her fingers spread wide to attack the spell.

Todd's spell unraveled as mine reached him, meant to blast him in the face and knock him unconscious so Roger could question him. I hadn't accounted for the dual-mage bond and the extra magic I'd *accepted* from the goblin.

My spell smashed into Todd, tearing off a layer of his skin before bursting. His head blew back…without his body attached.

"Finger-flinging leotards." My stomach churned and I burped fire. "I hope he was guilty."

"He tried to kill me. He was definitely fecking guilty." Reagan snatched her ringing phone out of its fanny pack and jammed it to her ear as we ran forward again. Shifter magic blasted out behind us, different than the challenging feeling we'd been hit with since we got here.

A glance behind confirmed that the shifters were changing. Roger into a burly gray wolf, larger even than his human body, Devon into a lean and lithe black wolf, just as tall at the shoulder as he was standing, and the third shifter, whom we'd largely forgotten about since he was behind everyone, became a decent-sized gray wolf. Patrick started before taking off through the trees. The smaller of the wolves chased him.

"There goes our hopes of a misunderstanding," I muttered as Emery grabbed my arm and pulled me closer.

"I'm a little busy—" Reagan cut off, running as fast as us even though she had a phone pressed to her ear.

"We need to get to the others and stay together," Emery said, confidence ringing in his tone.

"Stay in that house," Reagan yelled through the phone. "The ward will hold. Keep everyone in there until nightfall. I'll be in touch."

"What is it?" Emery asked. Roger caught up easily in animal form, falling in next to Reagan.

"Darius's house is under attack. Mages and mercenaries have it surrounded." She jammed her phone back into her fanny pack. "They're trying to break through the ward."

"They won't," Emery said confidently. "Not even if they bring in a couple of naturals and all their friends. That ward is too complex to tackle in an afternoon."

"What about the ward at Vlad's hideout?" I asked.

"I guess we'll find out."

Roger gave a small *yip* as he and the other wolves dashed by us, their lopes beautiful and graceful and way faster than I could run.

"Go get 'em, Lassie," Reagan called.

We rounded a bend and the house loomed ahead of us, the front door and surrounding wood blown out of it. Windows had been blown out, too, and glass glittered from the front lawn. Animals ran around or stood growling in furry chaos.

Magical intent bloomed over the house, heady and strong.

*Explode.*

"Get clear," I yelled as I ran, trying for a burst of

speed. "Oh God, Mother, please don't be in that house. Get everyone clear!"

"Penny, here." Emery ripped me sideways. Reagan had already turned.

My mother stood at the Lexus, the back opened up, feeding a magazine into some sort of machine-gun-looking weapon.

"Holy crap," Reagan said, running straight at her. "Ms. Bristol does not fuck around."

If there was one thing I knew about my mother when someone was attacking us, it was that no, she did not fuck around.

Callie and Dizzy stood in front of her, ingredients ready and in hand but mouths closed. They weren't doing spells yet. They saw us coming and relief crossed their faces.

"You're okay," Callie said on an exhale. "What took you so long?"

My mother glanced up, relief on her face as well. A moment later, determination crawled right back onto it. "Good, Penny, we need to get moving. We have to get out of here, bust Darius out of the house, pick up some sort of present, and then meet a different, incredibly attractive vampire so we can attack the Mages' Guild. We have a lot to do and a short window in which to get it all done."

"What—" I was about to ask what had happened

when her words sank in. "*What?*"

"I told you a change of scenery would be the best thing to shake loose more foretellings," Dizzy said. "Now maybe you'll listen to me more often."

The two older ladies huffed at the same time, but neither of them refuted him.

A shock of magic shot into the air before an explosion shook the house. A chunk of the far side of the house went flying, tumbling across the manicured lawn. An animal went with it, hitting the ground and not getting back up.

"They've got dirty mages," Callie yelled over the noise. "A lot of them. They have this place primed for attack. Karen saw it all. She was just blabbing everything she saw out loud. Which was fine at first, because that scarred one—Axel Rod or something—"

"Alder," Dizzy said.

"—was soaking it all up. But one of the mages overheard and tried to get off a spell. Then more joined in, the know-nothing hacks." She jerked her filled hands at the front of the house. "I had to blast us out of there. We barely got back to the car and the shotgun before they reached us."

"You must've missed," I said, glancing around and spying some blood splashed across the gravel. Another step brought me closer to the blood trails.

"Axel Rod dragged the bodies out of the way before

running back to the house to get their people organized," Callie said.

"It's Alder, hon," Dizzy said.

"Mages think with their spells, not with their heads," my mother said, cocking the gun and flicking a switch. "Bullets are much quicker than spells. No offense."

"None taken," Dizzy said, his face screwed up in concentration. "Reagan usually employs a similar philosophy."

*Explode.*

Another explosion sounded a moment later, debris flying up into the air from the back side of the house.

"Why are we standing here?" Emery yelled at Reagan. "Get the keys and let's go."

"No." My mother looked out at the driveway. "We can't get out that way. We've missed our window. They're coming. The enemy. The Guild, it must be, unless the shifters have another enemy that can attack in the daytime. My cards, my ball—even the tokens and trinkets—all painted the same picture. The Guild is coming after us before we're ready. But they have one huge, glaring issue. They don't realize we have chaos on our side, led by the power of three." She nodded at Reagan, Emery, and me. "Unpredictability. We need to counterstrike now, when they are occupied. We have to get out from under them. It is our absolute best bet.

And unlike the pizza situation"—my mother shot Callie a *look*—"I am nearly positive about this."

"My kinda plan," Reagan said.

"It's the worst kind of plan," I moaned.

"But there's a problem…" Reagan spun and struck out her hand, gripping her fingers in the air. A mage holding a fistful of green leaves sprouting magic ran around the corner and into an invisible wall. His nose spouted blood as he bounced off and fell onto his butt. The air condensed around him, squashing him.

I turned before seeing the completion of the gruesome display.

"Be more careful with your magic," Callie warned, her knees bent, ready to release a spell should anyone charge.

Wolves ran around from the far side of the house in a loose formation, Roger at the front. A lion roared somewhere in the trees, the sound rattling my bones.

"Mages will be pouring in through those magical doors they've been making in the ward," Dizzy said, his eyes aimed at the trees.

"They'll be easy prey for the shifters." Reagan patted her various weapons while shifting from side to side, clearly ready to go. "The shifters are in their element out there."

"Yes. We need to head off whatever comes up that driveway." My mother rolled her shoulders. "Roger had damned good timing, calling us when he did. Even still, they'll likely have numbers on their side. We need to run for it."

"If we can't take the car, how are we going to get out of here?" Reagan asked. "And what about the shifters? We can't just leave them behind."

"I didn't say we couldn't take the car, I said we'd missed our window. We have to stay and fight for a moment. As soon as the coast is clear, we'll get the shifters to follow us out." My mother's gaze didn't leave the driveway.

"How?" I yelled, feeling magic emanating from somewhere in the trees. Pressure rose and fell, vibrated and pulsed. There was no intent attached to it. No threads of magic rising up. I wasn't sure what it meant.

Emery's hand landed on my shoulder. "The warning. It's here again. Something is coming. Where's your power stone?"

He meant Mr. Happy-Go-Lucky, the stone that sent out a shock wave whenever an attack was imminent and our people were grossly outnumbered.

I ripped open the compartments of my utility belt. The other stones were all present and accounted for, but not that one. I dashed to the car and looked in the back, belatedly remembering I'd taken Mr. Happy-Go-Lucky and Emery's Plain Jane out because they were making sitting awkward.

"Stupid," I muttered to myself, ripping the door open and grabbing the stones.

Plain Jane pumped out a blast of power. Mr. Happy-Go-Lucky practically sang in happiness.

"Whatever is coming, it's coming right now," I said, stuffing the stones into their designated compartments.

Roger looked at us as the presence drew near, his dual-colored eyes intense and intelligent. A darker gray wolf with a scar walked up beside Roger, scrappy looking and dangerous. Axel Rod, as Callie kept calling him. A large bear lumbered out from the side and chuffed, joining the wolves, before various other animals did the same.

A few minutes ago, this scene had been chaos. Roger clearly knew how to lead, and he was damn good at it.

My heart hammered in my chest as silence descended over the scene. A cloud drifted over the sun, darkening the air. A whiff of coming rain rode the breeze.

"Is there a road at the back?" I whispered.

"No. One road in or out," Dizzy said, lifting his hand to wipe his forearm across his forehead. "Lots of woods all around. This is a shifters' stronghold. Roger chose well."

"The location, maybe, but not the people who were supposed to keep the location secret and safe." Reagan took two steps out, giving herself more space to work. I stayed right where I was, behind my crazy mother and beside my dual-mage partner. Safest place to be—and a good position to do plenty of damage. I was just fine with using magic and not a gun.

The whine of a small motor made me tilt my head. Another joined it, then one more, the chorus drifting toward us.

"Motorcycles," Emery said. "Dirt bikes, probably."

Another lion's roar made me grit my teeth, way too far away for me to feel any magic. A different roar—a bear—came from the opposite direction. The bikes' whines wobbled as the riders tried to get through the woods.

Roger stepped forward a few feet, and those behind him fanned out. Those not in the wolf pack stood to the side, waiting patiently.

Mr. Happy-Go-Lucky sent out a pulse of power. Like a wave, I saw it roll through the shifters, each animal flinching or bracing as they felt it.

"The mages on the inside were probably supposed to attack as the rest of them made their way in," Emery said quietly, anticipation in his voice.

Reagan's phone rang. "Really? *Now?*" She dug it out.

"They would've been sitting ducks, too distracted by the surprise attack to act." Emery rolled a ball of magic between his hands, and I saw immediately what he was going to create.

"Wait, add this." I started working as more whines

drifted out through the trees, all around us now.

"Two of Vlad's strongholds are under attack," Reagan reported. "They have a few combat-ready humans on hand to defend them. The third stronghold was left alone. Clearly the mages didn't find out about that one. That's the one he's in. Of course." She shook her head in annoyance, dropping her phone into her fanny pack. "That guy is just too good for his own…good."

"Or else the Guild didn't want to attack someone on their side," I muttered, my unease over Vlad having grown throughout all of this. There was never any one thing that made me nervous, but a lot of little things. Things it was getting harder to ignore.

The crunch of tires on dirt and gravel invaded the quiet afternoon. The glint of sunshine on metal announced the first car speeding up the small road. It slid around the bend toward the driveway.

"I have always wanted to do this," my mother said as she stalked forward.

"What?" I asked, my heart speeding up as more cars sped into sight.

She braced herself in the middle of the parking area entrance and lowered her gun. Brakes squealed as the drivers noticed. Tires locked up and skidded.

"This!" My mother aimed. "Say hello to my little friend!"

# CHAPTER 26

*KAK-KAK-KAK-KAK.*

The semiautomatic rifle spat bullets at the incoming cars. The first cranked the wheel. It just missed a tree and came flying into the parking lot.

Emery yanked me away as the next car dodged the gunfire, slamming into a tree trunk on the other side. Metal crunched as the car behind it didn't slam on its brakes in time to avoid a collision.

"There goes our way out." I gritted my teeth, finishing up Emery's spell as my mother continued to pepper the cars with bullets.

"The cars are in a single-file line because of the shape of the road. We'll just steal a few at the back," Reagan said, strapping on her own gun, which she'd previously stowed in the car. She didn't take it out, though. Instead, she ripped her sword out of its holster and checked her fanny pack.

"Ms. Bristol!" Emery shouted.

My mother raised the business end of the gun toward the sky, but she didn't step out of the way. Emery darted around her and released the spell. It hit the ground and expanded to his height, forming a perfect sphere. In a moment it started rolling toward the—now stuck—line of cars. Nearly there, it burst into blue flame, the heat so intense it blew back at us.

"Wow." Callie straightened up just a bit. "I had no idea naturals got *that* kind of boost when they formed a dual-mage pair."

The tires of the first car popped from the heat, the sound so loud they were nearly explosions. Paint peeled and shriveled as the magical ball of fire rolled over the vehicles.

"We've got special naturals. Come on." Reagan took off at a jog. "We gotta get out of here. I don't want to miss an opportunity to save my boyfriend. Again."

The shifters didn't follow. Instead, Roger looked at my mother, clearly waiting for her signal.

"Your mother has what it takes to be an Alpha," Emery said with a smile, waiting for me while I waited for my mother. I didn't want to run after Reagan until I was sure my mother was coming with us.

"Don't tell her that. You'll just encourage her."

"I heard that, Penny," my mother said, starting forward. The gathering pack of shifters started forward with her. "And Emery, acting the part of an Alpha is easy. You just have to know more than anybody else in the room, and not be afraid to stare the others down until you get your way."

"Roger wasn't even in that room." I flinched as another roar rose from way off in the trees.

"Roger clearly has sense and listened to his second-in-command. Now, enough talking. We need to get out of here before we lose too many of our people."

I jogged to her side. "What's the plan, here? Do I stay with you?"

"Penny Bristol, stop being so worried about plans! Your friend is taking on a line of mages by herself. Get down there and help her out."

A female mage broke from the tree line on the other side of the parked cars. She pinched something between her fingers.

*Tear.*

I didn't know what her spell would do, but I could see it somersaulting through the air. I pulled elements from the organized mass hovering above my head quickly, intuitively, the counter-spell already in my mind. As I weaved it together, still walking toward the line of cars, Emery's magic swished through me. He inserted some truly excellent embellishments into my weave, then took the whole thing from me and sent it off.

"Come on," he said, starting to jog.

Our spell tore through the coming spell without a problem, without even slowing down. It rocketed on, splitting into two. One half cut right through the middle of the mage I'd seen, and the other sliced into a mage I hadn't even noticed. All in a handful of seconds.

"Holy crap, that was a helluva upgrade," I said.

"Penelope Bristol, just because we are in a battle, does not mean swearing is suddenly okay," my mother berated.

"Yeah, okay, let's run," I said. If fighting an army of mages wasn't a good reason to get away from my mother, nothing was.

Drops of magical fire from our sphere burned on the dirt or blackened the metal of the cars. Papers, seat covers, and, probably, people still burned within them. We hadn't set the ball to track the people or cars, though, and certainly not the road. When it had reached a turn, it had kept on going, setting fire to a couple of trees and a swath of brush. Thankfully, Reagan had seen it and sucked the flame away, leaving only half of each tree a blackened mess.

"Oops," Emery said, noticing what I had. We ran around the first couple of cars. He touched one of the hoods before flinching away. "The metal is hot."

"Yes. It looks hot. Thank God for Reagan, or we would've set the whole place on fire."

Leftover flames crawled out of the windows of a Ford, reaching through the air in my direction. I swerved on the crackly, burned ground beside it, reaching the first bend in the narrow road. Intact cars lined the way until the next bend tucked them behind the trees and out of sight. Mages had left their cars and were hurrying toward Reagan, satchels open and ingredients in hand. She stood in the middle of five mages with her sword in one hand, and her handgun in the other.

"Hurry." Emery put on speed, rushing for her.

Two mages down the way slipped into the trees, and I knew they were going to cut through the woods to get to the house, avoiding us. No magic swirled around them, which would make them harder for the shifters to track.

"Roger's people can get those," I said, running right behind Emery.

A spell rose, shooting toward Reagan. With her left hand, she sliced her sword through it, unraveling it like a string on a sweater. With her right hand, she turned, aimed, and shot the mage who'd attacked her right in the middle.

"Crap, she's good," Emery said, and I could hear the competitiveness in his voice. If—no, when—we got through this, he'd probably train twice as hard to be better than her.

Feeling out the situation, I pulled down ingredients, weaved threads together, then braided them—what would have once seemed crazy complex felt freaking easy with the new magic at my disposal. I hop-stepped forward, turned, and ran my palms through the air, as though throwing a skipping rock across a calm lake.

The magic slid over the ground before it started rolling like rocks, picking up speed as it went. As I neared Reagan, I yanked my hands apart, still having control over the magic from a distance.

"Definitely a big upgrade," I muttered, watching as the spell busted the kneecaps of three mages, bringing them to the ground, before covering them like blankets. Their screaming cut off quickly.

Emery looked back with wide eyes. "This magic suits you."

"I feel your rage. Your wildness. It blends so perfectly with my magic that…I don't have to think. I just…go with it." I kept running forward as a fierce growl sounded somewhere to my right. A larger distance away, working toward us, another mighty roar shook my bones. Thank God the shifters were on our side!

"Scatter them so we can get by them," I heard from behind, my mother yelling directions.

*Kak-kak-kak-kak-kak.*

Bullets slapped the cars farther down the road on my right.

"Too dangerous, Mother! You might hit one of us."

"You do you. I'll do me," she yelled back.

I clenched my teeth and started another massive,

rolling fireball.

"I need fire, Penny," Reagan yelled, reading my mind.

I worked faster, knowing Reagan needed me to cover her using her magic.

"Now, Penny. Shoot it!" she said, jumping up onto a car, running across the hood, and then jumping down in attack mode, slashing her sword through a mage's shoulder. These mages had never trained with a moving target as animated and deadly as Reagan Somerset, and they were caught standing still.

"I don't know how to shoot fire—" I strained to grab more elements, bending them into my fireball so it would ignite and grow. Spark, heat, and a touch of destruction. For balance, I threaded in some of Reagan's icy magic, then something that gave me a feeling of glitter. Sparkly and fun and wonderfully explosive. "I might still be cracking up…"

I scrabbled up onto the trunk of a car, not able to jump as high as Reagan, and stomped onto the roof (not as graceful, either). Leaning on Emery's energy, I pulled strength up from my toes and shot off the spell.

Magic roared from my hands. For five feet, nothing happened, and I worried I'd just wasted all that energy. But then blue heat twisted to life, turning yellow and then orange before flaring. A stream of blistering fire spewed down the line of cars.

Emery dove out of the way. Reagan spun, her magic covering her in that complex symphony of ice and fire, blocking out my magic, and the mages in the way screamed and threw up their hands. Magical fire blasted them and continued onward, their bodies dropping like something had thrown them to the ground. The fire spread out the farther away it got, catching the reaching branches and setting fire to the trees.

Emery stood up slowly with wide eyes, watching the destruction for a moment before turning back to me with his mouth hanging open. Reagan had a huge grin on her face. She shook her head before waving her hand, and all the offshoots of my fire diminished to blackened char.

"I was just looking for cover. I didn't expect you to actually do it. Wow. You are the best kind of shocking, Penelope Bristol," she said. "The absolute best kind of shocking. What fun."

"She's nuts," I muttered, running after her. "She is fudge berries nuts."

A shape moved through the trees with us, a large black wolf guarding our flank, with leaner gray wolves following behind. It must've been Devon and his pack, pushed out of the larger group of shifters to babysit us.

"It's a wonder Roger didn't choose someone more experienced," I said, feeling magic ahead. Colorful threads waved through the trees.

The black wolf snarled before shooting forward with a burst of speed. He launched through the air, smacking a mage's chest with his front paws and latching on to the mage's throat.

"The experienced pack members probably know Reagan and found somewhere else to be." Emery's magic swished past me, darting through the trees to intersect the road. A mage cried out in surprise, then pain.

"This road goes on forever." Instead of sticking with it around the bend, I cut left to follow Emery's magic. "Shortcut."

The wolves sped up, getting ahead of us. Two branched out to the sides, their lopes graceful and effortless. Each brought down a running mage.

"They're starting to panic," I said, following Devon to the road. He peeled off as we got there, back to guarding our flank.

"That's good news for us."

Emerging onto the road, I saw two things. One was that the magical workers were scarce down here, having clearly seen all the fire and crazy through the trees and found different paths (not necessarily toward the battle). And two, we were nearing the end of the line of cars, the larger road out of this area not too far beyond that.

"Almost there." I shot my vermin zapper at a mage

standing next to a car in indecision.

Emery sent a wide blast of heat at a line of cars. It sliced through two mages whipping up a couple of humdingers. They sank down, spells unrealized.

"That's going to bother me," I heard Emery mutter. "How the hell—"

He was trying to make magical fire and couldn't. Point to me.

Reagan ran from around the bend, a deep score on her upper arm and blood dribbling down her skin. Her leather pants were torn, but the skin wasn't broken underneath.

"You okay?" I asked, catching movement in one of the cars near the end of the row.

Without warning, the whole thing erupted into fire before a huge, invisible pressure swatted down on top of it, crushing it to the ground. Reagan's magic surged, huge and strong and awe-inspiring. The car lifted into the air before being tossed, end over end, into the trees. Tree trunks snapped and wood squealed.

"My arm fucking hurts," she said through clenched teeth, continuing on.

"I don't think that's what Darius meant when he told you to keep a low profile," Emery said, chuckling.

"You guys got a were-donkey?" Reagan yelled into the trees.

The black wolf—Devon; I needed to remember they

were actually people—trotted closer.

"Because we need to get the old people down here in a hurry. We gotta go."

# CHAPTER 27

LESS THAN A half-hour later, Emery stood beside one of the Guild mages' extended cab trucks, waiting for the rest of the shifters to load up so they could move everyone out of the area. Penny stood at the SUV behind the truck, motioning for people to get in, and berating them when they took too long. Behind her, Ms. Bristol was doing the same thing, only a lot louder.

"What's taking them so long?" Reagan called from the SUV in front of him, a shiny Ford stuffed with furry bodies.

They were loading nearly a hundred shifters into all of the larger SUVs and trucks at the end of the line on the long road doubling as the driveway. The smaller cars had been driven or pushed into the trees and out of the way.

"They're trying to decide who will shift back into human form and who will stay in animal form." Only the more powerful could make multiple changes in a short period of time, each change taking a lot of power and energy. It really hindered quick getaways.

Emery checked the space under the camper shell before motioning another wolf in. "It'll be tight, but better than staying behind."

Roger stalked up the line of cars, in human form and nude. It only took a *look* from him and the shifters in animal form were speeding up, cramming in wherever they could fit. As he drew near, his intense power pounded at Emery in waves, setting him on edge.

"We're about done." He stepped around Emery and closed the hatch. He glanced at a wolf who'd been left out. The wolf knew better than to object—it went somewhere else to find a spot. "I'll take the SUV. Penny can go with you. We're headed to Durant, right?"

"Yeah. Just follow us."

Penny looked expectantly at Roger, having clearly thought she'd be driving. She flinched when he stopped close, then ripped her gaze to the sky and muttered, "It's like an eyesight landmine with shifters."

Emery chuckled and swung into the driver's seat before sticking his hand out the window and motioning for Reagan to get into the SUV.

"Who's leading?" she called.

"You are," Roger yelled as Penny hurried to Emery's passenger side.

"You'd think they could've thought ahead and brought some sweats or something." Penny glanced behind her at the three burly guys sitting nude in the extended cab, and the two marginally smaller women sitting on their laps. Beyond them, the bed of the truck was full of wolves and various other animals. "No offense."

"It would be nice to at least have a towel," one of the women in the back said, moving so her junk wasn't on the junk of the guy under her.

"I'm good without a towel," the guy under her said with a grin.

"And you're clearly good with a lot of fuzz. Ever hear of man-scaping, hairy balls?" the woman shot back.

The others laughed as Emery backed down to the larger road after the others. Once there, he waited for Reagan to get all the way out before slamming on the gas and following her. Nails scraped the truck bed and bodies bumped against the sides.

"We're going to save a damn vampire," one of the guys in the back seat said quietly. "Things you never thought you'd do…"

"You don't live in Seattle," the woman who was less concerned about hairy balls said. "It's been hell up here trying to pussyfoot around the Guild. If we have to pair up with vampires to take them down, then we'll pair up with vampires to take them down."

"Did you know James Cannes?" the guy on the far right asked.

Spicy shifter magic seeped into the cab, and Emery could feel a throb within it. He could see the spark that gave them the ability to change, like looking into an open chest cavity and spying a beating heart. He could also see how to disable it, much like Penny had disabled Rex's.

It was an incredible amount of power to have over the shifter species. Too much. In the wrong hands, it would be devastating. If not for Penny, who would never lose her way when it came to morality, he'd be eager to push the power to someone else. He didn't trust himself with the responsibility.

"Yeah," the woman said, her voice subdued. She directed her gaze out of the window.

"What happened to him?" Penny asked, turning in her seat to look behind her. She flinched and turned back around. "Lots of skin."

"Like what you see?" the guy in the middle asked. "I'll let you give me a tug."

A tight and prickly sensation squeezed Emery's chest. He connected eyes with the guy in the rearview mirror, changing his power to mimic their territorial vibe and pumping it into the cab. He wasn't a jealous man by nature, but he would not stand for another guy harassing his woman. Not in this lifetime.

Everyone in the back tensed, muscles going taut. The women both glanced at the guy in the middle before looking away again. They didn't plan to get involved.

"Not wise, bro," one of the guys on the end said in a low tone before averting his gaze. The one on the other side followed suit.

"We're drifting from the topic," Penny said in a low, husky voice. He knew that tone. She'd felt his possessive push of magic, his claiming of her, and liked it.

Preventing a smile, he upped the power, magic throbbing in the truck now, needing that guy in the back to look away before he did. Damned unfortunate timing, given that he was supposed to be driving a truck.

Those dark brown eyes flared with fire once before the challenge in them muted. The shifter tore his gaze downward.

Ms. Bristol had been right about what it took to get respected as an Alpha. Not that Emery had needed the lesson.

"He stood up to one of the members of the Mages' Guild," the woman said after Emery's magic receded. "Stopped him from picking on a teenage human male. It was James's job as a shifter, but also the right thing to do." Her voice dropped an octave. "That Guild member got a couple of his cronies together, found out where James lived, went to his house, and hacked him up. Hacked his girlfriend up, too, just for being in the wrong place at the wrong time." She swallowed. "Nothing we could do about it, either. The MLE office is in their pocket. No one wants to stand up to the Guild."

Penny nodded, staring straight out the window. Her magic rolled through the cab, hot and intense. "Until now."

"Fuckin'-A," the guy on the left side said.

They turned off the freeway as the sun lowered in the sky. They still had a couple hours before it would be dark enough for the vampires to go outside. He really hoped Ms. Bristol had gotten the time frame right.

"I hope my mother wasn't wrong," Penny said, echoing his thoughts.

"She's not wrong," the guy in the middle said. "I was there when she told the beta's fortune. She started getting into his personal life, and I thought he was going to smack her across the room to shut her up."

"That would not have been bright," Penny murmured.

Two of the guys in the back huffed out laughter. "Don't suppose it would've been, no," the one on the right said. "I was there, too, for most of it. I could feel the magic. She wasn't making it up. The way her voice and body and everything changed? No way. I saw Vlad's face in the crystal ball. It couldn't have been a picture or video, because vampires don't show up in video. That was legit."

"Yeah, that was whack, yo," the guy in the middle said with a toothy grin. "I didn't think crystal balls were real. Ain't never seen one. I'll never forget it."

"Everyone loves a fortune teller," Penny grumbled.

"Except for the frauds who try to get by on their looks and colorful rocks," Emery teased, earning a dark look.

They turned off the main road and onto a smaller one. He passed a bright pink sign and slammed on the brakes. Furry bodies slammed into the front of the truck bed.

"My bad," he said, catching another sign up the way. Instead of reversing, he pulled ahead to that one, realizing he was making the train of vehicles behind him stop as well.

"What's the matter?" Penny asked, magic rolling and boiling through the cab.

He pointed at the marked-up "garage sale" sign, studying the added red words and low slashes, hard to see on the pink paper. "I saw something like this outside the Bankses' house before the mages attacked. I never did get to piece together the code. The mages have been communicating with each other right under our noses."

"That's...a weird code," one of the women in the back said, leaning toward the window. "It looks more like punctuation than characters, doesn't it?"

Roger stepped out of the SUV behind them, still

completely naked, and a driver coming the other way slammed on her brakes. A woman in her twenties gawked out the window with stars in her eyes and a crooked smile. Roger didn't seem to notice.

"You've stopped because of the sign?" Penny asked. "That sign? The pink one?"

"What's the problem?" Roger asked at the window.

"We've got some sort of—"

"That's not code." Penny waved Emery on. "Don't be silly. That's just Veronica letting off steam. Go. Reagan will get there before us."

"But it's all marked up," the guy in the back said.

"She corrects the grammar on signs and things around the neighborhood. She's an editor." Penny pounded on the dash. "*Come on.* Let's go."

A honk sounded somewhere down the line. Roger stepped away from the car and stared down in that direction for a beat, and Emery had no doubt his nudity wouldn't detract from the sheer force of command he exuded. When no other honks came, he stepped back to the car.

"My God, he's terrifying," Penny mumbled, slouching in her seat.

"You're sure about the sign?" Roger asked her.

"Yeah." The woman from the back nodded and leaned back. "That fits."

"Oh sh—" The guy she was sitting on jumped and

shoved at her. "Woman, watch out where you put that bony butt. You're going to break my dick in half."

"Why is your dick hard in the first place?" she asked dryly.

"I'm straight, and I've got a naked woman sitting on me. You're under the impression I can control what my body does in this situation. I'm not trying to find a hole, so count yourself lucky."

"Ah, come on, man." The guy in the middle tried to scoot away from the one on the end.

"Enough." Roger's whip-crack command silenced the cab. His eyes bored into Penny. "You're sure?"

"Yes. Look"—Penny gestured at the window, accidentally flicking the glass with her fingers—"she put a command there, and added words to make that last bit a complete sentence. You guys, we're wasting time!"

Roger stepped away from the truck and headed back to his SUV. Emery pulled away, not gunning it, since they'd have to turn up the driveway soon, anyway.

"Your friend corrects grammar on other people's signs?" the guy in the middle asked.

"I'm glad someone said it," the one on the end said. "That's weird."

"It's not weird, it just ain't right," the one in the middle said. "She's basically walking around, calling people dumb."

"Well…if the shoe fits," one of the women said.

The other guy huffed out a laugh. "Maybe the sign makers will learn something."

"They ain't gonna learn shit," the guy in the middle said. "They probably won't even take the signs down."

"Well, I've learned something, and that's all that matters," the one on the end said.

"Yeah, you've learned that you can't get laid even with a naked woman on your lap," the unaffected naked woman said.

Everyone in the back busted up laughing, not at all tense or worried about the battle they were about to walk into. Their lack of fear indicated they were part of the select group of shifters Roger employed to keep magical people from outing themselves to humans in the Brink.

"There's Reagan's SUV," Penny said quietly, having ignored the banter in the back seat. She hunched in her seat and pointed off to the side where the vehicle was parked in a little turnoff.

Emery pulled in and parked, then got out and motioned for Roger to do the same. There was space for a couple more cars, and then they'd have to take up the road. Not that it mattered. Darius's residence was the only one up this way.

"What about the other locations for Darius's people?" Penny asked as they met up with Reagan. The shifters in human form let out those in animal form.

"They've been loaded into coffins and are on their way in." Reagan nodded a hello to Roger as he got out of his vehicle. "They'll be told where to meet us. He had them staying about an hour outside of town in a couple of newly acquired residences. They haven't heard a word from the Guild, and if it's because the Guild is already on their way there, they'll find empty houses to hide out in."

Emery remembered the number of hearses Darius had used the last time he'd needed to move around during the day. It wouldn't be enough for the numbers they needed. "Hearses?" he asked.

"No." Reagan motioned them toward the road. "Semitrucks. He has racks inside the trailers for the coffins, and humans to load them up. Darius might not totally possess Vlad's planning ability, but he's not far off."

"Well…I don't know." Penny slipped her hand into Emery's and looked around anxiously. "Vlad had two houses out of three ambushed, and Darius only had one. I would say he wins this round. Especially since…Vlad might not be entirely trustworthy."

"Vlad is not at all trustworthy, usually, but in this instance, it is probably only because of the distance," Reagan said, watching the shifters unload. Callie and Dizzy plucked ingredients out of their satchels as they made their way up the road. Ms. Bristol followed behind, her gun over her shoulder and a backpack in her hands.

"That counts. Clearly distance was a good idea." When Ms. Bristol neared, Penny asked, "What's in the backpack, Mother? You don't have bombs or anything, right?"

"Roger had one of his people gather up my tools," Ms. Bristol replied. "Very kind of him. I didn't mention that they weren't my best set. And no." She looked down at the backpack. "No bombs. Just a couple of grenades Roger had lying around, is all."

A grin broke through Reagan's face. "Great. Those will come in handy at the Mages' Guild. Now, what's our plan for ending the siege?"

"Since when do you use plans?" Penny asked.

Reagan nodded. "Good point. Let's make it up as we go along." She started walking.

"No, no. That's not what I meant!" Penny took a step toward her, then paused, looking out to the side with that same anxious expression.

"What is it—" In a moment, he knew exactly what she sensed. The danger of it. It was a feeling he'd never forget.

# CHAPTER 28

"I T'S HIM," I said softly, trying to pierce the shadows between the trees with my gaze. My heart was a terrified rabbit in my chest. "It's the druid. I feel him."

Shadows moved and shifted, dizzying my mind. A moment later, my stomach flipped and my magic settled down, stilling the fuzzy image. A familiar man stood in front of a tree by the road, now in plain sight, draped in shadows, a blank expression on his face and a line of red ink on his cheek.

"That's…helpful," Emery said in a hard voice next to me, clutching the back of my utility belt. He didn't want me to go running off. "The magic you stole from the goblin wipes out the shadow illusion. Mostly."

"It wipes out the brain fuzziness, not the shadow illusion. And he means us no harm."

"When did you become such an expert?" Reagan asked, sword in hand.

"I honestly have no idea." I wiped my face.

The druid took a step to the side and put out his hand. I sucked in a breath when Veronica stepped out from behind the tree and took it.

"What are you doing with her?" I asked, magic at my fingertips and an intense spell brewing.

"Oh thank God," Veronica said, rushing forward. Until she got to the road, that was. She stopped and looked both ways really quickly before running forward again. "Penny, the house is under siege! I went out to blow off some steam and police the neighborhood"—she held up her red Sharpie—"and when I was on my way back, I heard bangs and crackles." She put her hands up, made them into claws, and wiggled them. I squinted, trying to follow along. "I snuck a little closer to see what was going on, because, you know, it could've been you, but he"—she hooked a thumb over her shoulder at the druid—"stopped me and said it wasn't safe."

"You trusted a random stranger?" I asked, mystified.

Reagan, clearly sensing the threat had passed, since the druid hadn't hurt Veronica, moved off toward Roger, who was standing over my mother as she laid out a cloth on the tailgate of the nearest truck. The rest of the shifters were organizing, splitting into groups of various sizes. Their packs, I'd bet. Everyone was getting ready.

Veronica lowered her eyebrows. "Of course not! I tried to attack him. But I only had my pen, and that isn't much against a man his size."

A grin worked up Emery's face despite his hard eyes. "You got him," he said. "You marked his face."

"Yeah. I took him by surprise. My pen didn't do much good, though." Veronica's face fell. "Anyway, in the next moment, there was…this, like…red flash, but Cahal pulled me away from it. And then the guy who'd attacked me went flying, and…I don't know. It was really confusing. But then Cahal picked me up and ran me down here. He said we had to wait for you to come. That he was supposed to meet you here."

Leave it to Veronica to be on a first-name basis with an incredibly lethal and terrifying warrior-class assassin.

The druid—Cahal—stepped forward and handed me a little envelope inscribed with my name in a beautiful scrawl. Feeling a heavy weight in my stomach, I pulled a mauve card out of it and read the simple note.

*A gift.*

There was no signature.

I looked at Cahal for more, but his glacial stare gave me nothing to go on.

"Reagan," I called. She didn't so much as glance up, instead watching my mother with her tarot.

"Uh, Penny?" Veronica tapped my arm.

"Reagan," I called again, finally getting her attention.

"Penny?" Veronica repeated, whispering in a way

that tugged at my focus.

"What?" I asked, trying not to feel the press of time.

Reagan reluctantly tore her eyes away from my mother's work. She walked over, Roger in tow.

"Why are there a bunch of naked people gathered around?" Veronica asked in a shocked whisper. "I mean, don't get me wrong, *wow*. They have a perfect reason to show it all, but there are some dangerous people up near the house, and…well…that's not really a great way to go into battle, know what I mean?"

"Why the hell didn't anyone ever tell me how cool it is to watch your mother do her magic?" Reagan asked as she stopped next to me. "She even seems legit. Color me surprised."

Veronica's eyes went as big as the world as they slipped down Roger's body. Her face went beet red and she jerked her gaze skyward. "Sorry," she muttered.

I gave the note to Reagan. Roger leaned closer to see the two-word note as she quickly scanned the card. Her brow furrowed and she eyed Cahal. "Who sent you?"

As though for the first time, Roger noticed the large, incredibly lethal man standing a mere five feet away. The thick cords of muscle lining every inch of his frame went taut. A heavy gush of shifter magic boomed out and all the shifters waiting near the line of cars flinched and glanced up, their bodies tensing in anticipation of a fight.

Cahal didn't so much as bat an eye. He continued to look among us silently.

"If you don't tell us who sent you, we cannot accept you," Reagan said, thrusting the note at him.

"It is not for you to determine if I am accepted," Cahal said, ignoring the note. "I signed a blood contract to protect Penelope Bristol to the best of my ability. I have been instructed to take her away from the action if necessary."

"Well…" I snorted and shook my head. "There's no way that's going to—"

"Fine," Emery said, surprisingly, turning away. He glanced at the sky. "Is it possible to hurry your mother up, Penny? Time is ticking."

"No." I waved my finger at Cahal. "Nope."

"He got me out of the action, and I was glad for it," Veronica said, her gaze now shooting past me. "There are…wild animals. Oh my God"—she gasped—"don't tell me shifters are real! Are those shifters? Because there are vampires, and now shadow men, and…those *are* shifters, aren't they? Wow, they sure are built. I am on Team Shifter all the way."

"Not helping," I muttered out of the side of my mouth.

"Oops. Sorry. I'm just fan-girling a little." Veronica put her red pen into her pants pocket.

"You'd change your tune if you took a tumble in the

sheets with a vampire," Reagan said with a grin.

"Would you guys focus?" I demanded, a cold sweat covering my forehead. I was still unsure about the druid and the person who sent him. Surely someone of his stature had to be expensive. Who would have that kind of money?

"Could Darius have hired him, you think?" I asked.

"He would've said something," Reagan replied. "Even if he had kept the secret until today, once the house was surrounded, he would've instructed me on how to connect with the druid. No, it can't be him."

"Vlad?"

Reagan just shook her head. "Vlad would present him to you with a flourish. It's not like him to keep a gift of this magnitude under wraps. Not when you'd basically have to accept it because of the circumstances."

"Then who?"

"Whoever it was, Cahal seems extremely capable," Veronica said, stepping back to pat him on the arm. "He'll definitely help out. You should keep him."

My mother backed away from the tailgate, her hands on her hips. "Well, that's the shits."

My mother swearing tore my mind away from the situation. I couldn't help a little righteous indignation. All this hubbub about *me* swearing, and she goes off?

"What are your thoughts?" Alder asked, standing beside her.

Roger didn't take his eyes off Cahal to look.

"You'll need to leave me here. This is where my usefulness ends. After we secure Darius, I'll need to communicate with you through text." She blew out a breath. "I would've much preferred getting magic like Penny's so I could be part of the action."

"Did you get anything about the current situation?" Emery asked, stalking up the road a little on his own.

"Very little." My mother pulled over her crystal ball. "Charge them, basically. I got the idea that this group of mages is made up of cowards. Same as the group that tried to take on Roger. They won't stick around. The real meat of the magical world is waiting for you back at the Mages' Guild."

"And do you have anything that will be of use to us there?" Emery asked, clearly having taken charge. No one questioned it.

Alder held up a jagged piece of cardboard. "I catalogued the things she was saying, since she didn't have her tape recorder. It's not enough for a well-orchestrated plan, but..." He switched his weight to center mass, and it seemed like he wasn't thrilled with the next bit. "She says to let chaos be our guide."

Reagan raised her hand, then pointed at me. "We got chaos all day long."

I rolled my eyes. We'd spent a half-hour or so at the bottom of the road, not long enough to make it safe for

Darius and the other vampires to leave the house. "The sun doesn't seem to be complying with our window of opportunity."

"No. It doesn't," my mother said. "But that's the time frame we have. You need Darius. He is an important piece. I don't know anything about his entourage, but you definitely need him. Which is common sense. You didn't need me to tell you that."

"All right." Emery clapped once. "Let's get rolling. Roger, those of you who are in human form can probably sit this one out. We have plenty of power at our disposal, not to mention several booby traps that Penny and I can activate. Save the majority of your power for the next leg."

Callie and Dizzy hurried up the road toward Emery, clearly not wanting to be left out like my mother.

"Guard her until we can get her inside," I told Cahal, pointing at Veronica.

"You took the note. My contract has been initiated. I am only to guard you," he replied.

I gave him a flat stare. "I don't need you up there. But Veronica needs you down here."

He stared at me without comment.

"Hello?" Getting frustrated, I very nearly magically slapped him. "You essentially work for me, and I say you need to stay down here."

Blank stare.

While his eyes were certainly beautiful, I wasn't in the mood to sit and stare at them all day. "We're not going to get along, you and I."

"Penny," Reagan said, stalking toward Emery. "You're wasting your time with him. Contract killers—or defenders, in this case—do their job, and that's it."

I ground my teeth, wishing for a way around this.

"We'll watch her," Roger said. "My people have scouted out the area down here. We're safe at the moment, and should their people invade the area, we'll handle it." Roger shifted his gaze from Cahal for long enough to meet my eyes, his look full of assurance and confidence. She'd be fine.

I nodded. It would have to do. I was out of time.

"You are…very skilled, I can tell," Veronica said in a wispy voice. Her gaze started to dip.

I elbowed her. "Get a hold of yourself," I said through my teeth. She started and her face flared red again. "Stay safe. Let them protect you."

That handled (there was nothing I could do about Veronica's wandering eyes), I jogged up to join the others. Cahal kept pace effortlessly beside me.

"Here's what we're going to do," Emery said as I neared him. "Penny and I will take the left side of the house from the driveway. The Bankses will take the right. We'll hit them with some intense spells. Create fear. Shifters…" He stopped and waited for the animals to gather. Roger and a couple of the others walked up behind them, probably to make sure the plan was sound. "You cut through these woods here…" Emery pointed. "Go around to the back and come at them that way. We honestly have no idea if anyone warned this crew we'd be coming. Based on the fact that no one is watching this road—"

"I've taken out all the sentries," Cahal said, staring straight ahead.

Emery paused with his mouth open, possibly waiting for an explanation of some kind. When he didn't get it, he said, "Are you sure you got everyone?"

"Yes," Cahal answered. "I didn't want anything to impede my transaction with Penelope Bristol."

He kept saying "Penelope." It probably just reflected his devotion to the contract he'd signed. But I wondered…aside from my mother, who certainly would've told me had she hired an extremely scary magical creature to protect me, only vampires called me Penelope. From what I've heard, it was never *just* a gift when it came from a vampire.

Fear wormed through my stomach as Emery continued discussing his plan of attack with the shifters.

Vampires were crafty. They hedged their bets. And they didn't play fair. Anyone at all could have sent Cahal, including someone from the other side.

"How do I know you were actually sent to protect

me?" I asked him, stepping closer.

He turned a little, letting his gaze fall to me. "Because I told you so."

"I don't know you from Peter. How can I be sure you're not lying?"

"I am a druid."

I put out my hands. "That means nothing to me. I don't know anything about you."

"They can't lie," Reagan said, clearly eavesdropping.

"They can't, or they aren't supposed to?"

"Can't," she answered. "They take a blood oath when they're young."

"What if he didn't take the oath?"

Reagan scratched her nose. "Don't know."

"Then I would've died many lifetimes ago," he said. He didn't elaborate on that point. Before I could push for more, Emery glanced at me expectantly. I lifted my eyebrows, silently asking what he needed.

"Ready?" he asked.

I stared at Cahal for another moment, feeling a tight ball of anxiety sitting in the pit of my stomach.

"You cannot keep me from protecting you," he said in a low hum that spread a feeling of trust through my body. "Your safety is my duty."

"Stop emotionally manipulating me," I ground out, feeling the pressure of everyone waiting on me to get going.

A small smile curved his lips. "I cannot make a person feel. I can simply be who I am with conviction, and let them decide for themselves. Listen to your magic, Penelope Bristol. It will not lead you astray."

Frustration gnawed at me, but what could I do? Time was running out, and everything pointed to him being legit.

Then again, if he was legit, why was the person who'd sent him trying to keep it a mystery?

"Fine," I said through clenched teeth. "Let's go."

I turned and started walking, joined immediately by Emery.

"I don't like all the unknowns in this endeavor," I said, still feeling frustrated.

"No one does. The odds are stacked against us." He took my hand. "But it isn't the first time. If there is any certainty here, it is that we perform incredibly well under pressure."

The shifters took off, cutting through the woods so they could do their jobs and come around from behind. Cahal drifted up nearly to my side, staying a little apart and behind us.

We approached a curve in the road. Once we got around it, we'd be able to see the house. Expectation filled me, and we drifted toward the trees. A little farther and Emery let go of my hand and motioned for me to stay back.

"Let me check it out." He took cover behind a large tree at the last bend in the road before slowly looking around it. A moment later, he was back and everyone leaned in to hear what he'd seen. "They've got ten mages sitting out front, facing our way. Bored, by the look of them. I doubt they've seen any activity for as long as they've been here." He glanced at Cahal for any input, and got no response. "There are also groups gathered near the house. Most of them are working on the ward, and the rest are a bit removed, idle until needed. They're all in a stupor. If we go in hard and fast, we'll have the upper hand."

"What are the odds the mages at the Guild will be in the same stupor after waiting all this time?" Callie asked, digging through her satchel.

"Slim to none, I'd imagine. We caught them off guard last time. They won't let it happen again. These are likely the derelicts sent to thin us out, if possible. What happened at Roger's house showed us that."

"But it thins them out, too," I whispered. "It lessens their horde."

"Absolutely." Emery ran his hand down my arm, leaving a trail of lightning in its wake. "Ready, Turdswallop?"

"Yep. But you lead. I don't want to accidentally blow up another of Darius's houses."

He laughed and then took a moment to collect himself. Another moment passed before I realized that wasn't what he was doing at all. He was waiting for the older dual-mage pair to get all their ducks in a row. As soon as their hands were filled, Emery nodded.

"Give 'em hell."

# CHAPTER 29

E MERY PEELED OUT from around the tree and started at a fast run. I was with him a moment later, ready to help him take the brunt of the attack from the lookouts so Callie and Dizzy would have an easier *in*. Sprinting at the house, I immediately loosed a spell at the slouching mages out front. Emery followed it up with another.

Magic slammed into their bodies, catching them completely by surprise. Ingredients fell from their hands and littered the ground as they clutched their chests or immediately sank to the ground. Magic boiled through the air and the wind kicked up, pushing at me from behind. A spell from the dual-mages whirled past me, building strength as it went. It neared the house before it formed a full tornado, its funnel starting high and dropping down until it churned the dirt.

"Very cool," I said as it moved off to the right, toward more surprised mages. Some reached for their satchels, and others looked up in fright and started back-pedaling.

"Harder," Emery said. His next spell slithered across the ground before starting to roll, shooting out sparks and magical spikes. He was still trying to make fire.

"Nope." I stole from Reagan, who was running beside us with her sword out. Heat and ice wrapped around me, complex and beautiful. I mixed it with Emery's and my energy, with our magic, and then added in a dash of the goblin's *donated* magic and some silky darkness I realized was from the druid loping behind us.

My spell tore through the sky, zipping, pausing, spinning, and then rushing forward again, never in a straight line. It burst into flame as it met a group of mages who were speaking to life a spell. Turning solid, it knocked them back and kept going, sliding over the fallen mages and scraping half of their bodies away in the process.

"Oh yuck. I didn't mean for it to be so gruesome..." On it went to another group, slinking around a tree as it did so. That must've been the druid's influence. Fire flared again, mages were slapped through the air, and then the gross finale got an encore.

"That is...not at all the same spell as before," Reagan said. "That is..."

"Unique," Cahal said. "And rare, the ability to—"

"Shoplift," Reagan supplied.

"—use the magic of others," Cahal finished.

"Good ol' Fast Fingers." Emery shot off another spell. Like a blowtorch, magical fire surged through the side of the house before branching off in shoots, blowing through the trees. "She shared it with me. It's a much easier way to create fire."

"Ever think of asking first?" Reagan said, pulling the fire from the trees before the whole place went up. She dodged to the right and slashed with her sword. Someone screamed. Someone else went flying. When she rejoined us, she said, "It's kind of nice when everyone knows who I am. I don't have to hide as much."

"You should not hide at all," Cahal said, having done absolutely nothing to help us, beyond letting me crib some of his power. "Lucifer will find you regardless. You are hindering yourself by not reaching for your true potential."

"Easy for you to say," Reagan said. "You don't run the risk of being trapped in a job you don't want."

"I am already trapped," he said.

"Well, that blew up in my face," she muttered, before darting into the trees again.

"Trigger the surprises before the shifters get on scene," I said to Emery, meaning the little land mines we'd installed on our first night here.

On the outskirts of the house, I felt the magical detonators spark before magic bloomed out. I triggered mine, feeling the rush of energy as they struck out at whoever was around them.

That done, I started the weave for the giant rolling ball Emery had made up earlier. He noticed and helped me construct it, adding in a magical *seeking* property. Hopefully it would hunt the mages down before it ran out of steam.

"This will be a good one for the Mages' Guild compound," he said, shoving it off.

Someone ran out from the bushes, a spell ballooning up in front of them. The construction was straightforward, weave loose, and intent unoriginal.

*Kill.*

I countered it easily, washing it away before zapping the mage with my rodent zapper. It hit him dead center. He cried out as he fell backward.

Our magical ball rolled away before curving, the addition of the tracker doing its work. It took out two mages hiding in the thick trees before rolling away to the next group. Reagan crossed behind it before running down a mage trying to escape.

"They're running already," she said, jumping and kicking the mage in the back. She landed on her feet and put on a burst of speed, dodging a tree trunk and running through the reaching branches.

"How does Darius possibly keep that woman a secret?" Emery said as we reached the corner of the house and curved around.

Growls and hollers permeated the scene as shifters lunged or chased mages, having ambushed them out of nowhere. Regardless of Cahal not helping us with the actual attack, he'd done us a big favor by getting rid of all the Guild's lookouts. They hadn't seen us coming.

"Let's check on Callie and Dizzy," Emery said as Reagan caught up with us again.

"It's like the zoo opened its doors and said 'good riddance,'" Reagan said with a grin.

"Why you constantly torment them, I will never know." I shook my head.

"The Heir was born to rule," Cahal said, out for a leisurely jog by our side. "She will assert her dominance in many ways. This is but one."

"I don't think I like having him around," Reagan said.

Callie and Dizzy were walking along the side of the house, creating spells and firing them off with quick economy and obvious experience. Three trees were flattened, one was on fire, and a sort of magical dog had set upon a mage and was licking it with what looked like an electric tongue. It didn't seem pleasant.

"How's it going?" Emery said as Reagan darted into the trees again, probably to make sure everyone was gone. Or maybe to get away from Cahal.

"They tried to stand and fight for a little bit, but as soon as they saw the shifters, they took off," Dizzy said.

"It was a buzzkill." Callie put her unused ingredients back into her satchel.

"We'll have plenty to do later, hon. It's better this wasn't as intense as it could've been." Dizzy wiped his forehead.

Reagan sauntered back out of the trees. A wild boar and a panther followed her before moving off to the side. They stopped, looking at Emery for orders, since their Alpha was still down below.

"Make sure the grounds are clear," Emery commanded in a hard, clear voice. "Then hang tight. We need to get the vampires out. I don't want any surprises."

The shifters loped off in different directions.

"In your element, huh, Emery?" Reagan asked when she returned.

"He's a natural." Callie motioned at him. "He was born to lead."

"Well I guess that makes two of us, huh, Cahal?" Reagan stalked off to the house. "Let's see if Darius is in there fretting like a mortal."

He wasn't. Not even remotely. In fact, no one was even awake. The vampires were snug in their beds with the sunproof shades drawn or tucked into the basement in their bunks, getting a final burst of sleep before they had to head to battle.

Once they were all awake, they crowded into the

safe places in the house, two dozen hard-eyed vamps in sweats, knowing their fancy clothes wouldn't shift with them at the Guild.

Reagan stood at the edge of the living room with her hands on her hips and a grin on her face. She watched Darius stride toward her in slacks and a button-up shirt (he apparently wouldn't be caught dead in sweats, pun not intended) before shaking her head.

"Not a care in the world for your safety, huh?" she asked. "Or did you guys all run down to your beds as soon as you knew we were coming in?"

Darius slipped his hand around her waist, more open about his affection than usual around his vampire underlings. He looked down at her face. "This house is protected by the best mages in the world. It would take the Guild a month to break in, if they ever did."

"What about explosives?" she countered. "What if they blew the house up and exposed you to the light?"

"On the ground floor, I'd likely be covered in enough rubble to protect me, but if I'd thought they had physical explosives at their disposal, and not the incompetent magical explosion they tried, I would've simply headed down to the basement, which was turned into a bomb shelter years ago."

She stared at him for a moment. "This house has a bomb shelter?"

"Of course." He looked at her like she was mad.

"We're in hostile territory. It is important to be prepared. That's why I had us stay here even though the possibility of my informant leaking this house's location was strong."

Her eyebrows lowered. "It is a wonder that I am finding all this out for the first time, what with our pact to openly share information. Remember that pact? The one we've made several times?"

He ran his thumb across her lips, and her eyes softened. "I didn't think you'd be so dense as to miss the obvious, *mon coeur*. But please, let's soak in our last few moments of peace before we move on to the next thing. Vlad is mobilizing and the rest of my people are on their way to the meetup location. We have but a scant few minutes." He pulled her a little closer.

"I'll be careful," Reagan said quietly, and I knew he must've communicated with her through silent means. "But I can't stay home. You know that. This is my fight as much as it's Penny's, and even if it weren't, I protect those in my inner circle. She's my bra."

"Nope." I shook my head, kicked out of that nice little moment by her choice in words. Emery barked out laughter. "Not your bra. That's not the right term."

"No, I mean like, my bro, but a girl."

"Some people excel at creativity," Dizzy said somberly. "Sadly, you are not one of them. You should just stick with what you know."

Emery laughed harder as Reagan rolled her eyes. "Fine. My girl-bro."

"No. Friend," I said. "Friend works. Everyone will know you mean me."

"Penny is right," Dizzy said. "You have so few, we'll all get the relevance."

Emery was laughing in deep body chuckles.

"Let's all take a moment," Darius said as Emery calmed down. "Let's take a moment to appreciate the bonds we have formed. Soon we will draw heavily on those bonds, and rely heavily on our trust for one another."

Heavy raps sounded at the door. "Why is this locked?" my mother shouted through the wood. "Come on. We have to get a move on."

I heaved a sigh. "We really should've known that was coming. We really should've."

"At least your mother's strange antics are expected," Emery said quietly, pulling me tightly against his chest. "From now on, I have a bad feeling that nothing else will go as expected. They've had months to prepare for intruders. Months to watch us and make adjustments. We're going into the snake pit blind."

# CHAPTER 30

A S THE NIGHT stole the light from the sky, Reagan, Emery, Roger, and I stood in a thick grouping of trees, waiting for Darius and Vlad to leave their vehicle safe haven and join us. Darius had been prepared, only needing to call in the big work vans that would transport his people to the meeting site. His other people were already en route. The rest of us had climbed back into our stolen cars, adding to our fleet with the cars stationed at Darius's house.

I took a deep breath and tried to slow my racing heart. A dangerous presence poked at my awareness, and I remembered, for the umpteenth time, that Cahal stood with us as well. It was just hard to see him, given that he stood at a slight distance, swathed in shadow and perfectly still. He could teach the vampires a thing or two.

"They're coming," Reagan said, her voice subdued.

I rubbed my sweaty palms on my leather pants (Reagan had made me change at the house) before patting the compartments in my utility belt that held the power stones. Mr. Happy-Go-Lucky was strangely quiet, since we were not more than two miles from the Guild compound. This was as close as Darius and Vlad's people had been able to go without running into magical traps and tattletales.

"How is it you talk to Darius without words?" I asked to fill the silence.

Reagan grazed her finger along her temple. "Telepathically. Compliments of the bond."

"Huh." I glanced at Emery, his blue eyes hard and his stare vague. He was probably thinking through what was to come. We'd been to the compound before, and unless they'd change things just to mess with us, we knew the general layout. He had a better idea than most which areas were sure to be booby-trapped.

A soft vibration had Roger reaching into the pocket of his borrowed and very stylish cargo pants. Veronica had insisted the shifters should cover up, somewhat, to keep warm. I had the impression her primary motivation had been to cure her constantly red face and wandering eye. And while the vampires hadn't been pleased to share their clothes, in the end, they'd simply turned up their noses and pretended it wasn't happening.

They did not want the garments back.

"I hope Veronica and my mother are going to be okay," I said softly, shifting from one foot to the other.

"The ward at the house is strong, but who knows how long we'll take. Or if we'll even get out of here. The ward can be taken down eventually."

Cahal shifted his weight, drawing my notice to his presence again. He was extremely easy to forget, which was saying something for someone who was also so clearly lethal.

"You're going to make it out of here," Emery said, his voice fierce.

My chest tightened at the *you're*. "Don't you mean—"

"My people are all accounted for." Roger slipped his phone back into his stylish cargo pants.

"Everyone who's coming has been brought in?" Reagan asked.

"Yes. One hundred and seventeen shifters, including me. Most are in their animal forms, awaiting instruction. The rest will change as we move out."

"That's a good showing." Reagan nodded, giving him a steady gaze. "We're grateful you chose to join us."

His eyes sparkled just a little, even though his expression remained as hard as stone. "You're thanking me instead of ridiculing me? Hell must be freezing over."

Rather than tease him, which would be her normal reaction to such a statement, she looked away, troubled. "That would be the least of my worries."

"You cannot hide forever," Cahal said, his tone low and soothing.

"Yes, thank you, Mr. Broken Record." A flash of fire lit Reagan's eyes.

"Hide from what?" Roger asked.

"My reign as the ice queen. Cahal thinks I have the personality for it."

"He wouldn't be wrong," Emery said, a smile cracking through his stoic expression.

The vampires glided up out of the darkness, smooth and graceful. Mr. Crazy Handsome, Vlad, was dressed in a suit, of all things, with gleaming cufflinks somehow reflecting the dim moonlight. Darius wore his jeans and button-up, trying (and failing) to fit in with the shifter dress code.

"Mr. Nevin, how nice of you to come," Vlad said with his too-perfect smile.

"Vlad. Darius." Roger nodded, and magic seeped out and filled the air.

"Where are the vampires?" Reagan asked.

"Near the vehicles, for now." Vlad's eyes darted, picking up Cahal waiting amidst the trees. It had only taken him a matter of seconds to spot him, but for Vlad, it was probably a new record for obliviousness. "Well now…that is a surprise. Darius, you pulled out all the stops. But how, pray tell, did you get one of such magnitude? I am impressed."

"It is not my contract." Darius's jaw tightened. "It seems the Eliminator"—Vlad's eyes widened—"was given the option of two contracts, each of which invited him to name his price. One to terminate Penny, and one to protect her. Surprisingly…he chose the latter."

Vlad's eyes drifted to me, then back to Cahal. "That is surprising from the first to the last, yes. And who is bankrolling this happy turn of events?"

"Undisclosed. It is a mystery."

Vlad smiled, and I had to look away so as not to be awe-struck. "I doubt that you will leave it a mystery for long."

"No."

"Eliminator," Vlad said, a ruthless edge creeping into his tone. The varnish was pulled back, revealing the predator beneath. "Is this true, that you are here to protect Penny from harm?"

"I am to protect her from mortal wounding by any means necessary," Cahal said, his eyes not sliding toward the vampire.

"Any means necessary," Darius said quietly.

Vlad's eyes took on a vicious gleam. "And when does this contract expire?"

"Until the altercation with the Mages' Guild is finished, or after forty-eight hours, whichever comes first," Cahal replied.

"I see." Vlad turned and met Darius's eyes, something passing between them, before turning back to our circle of people. "Well, let's plan our entrance strategy—"

My phone vibrated in my utility belt. I flicked up the flap and pulled it out, conscious of everyone's eyes on me.

A text from my mother. I read it out loud. "'The window is closing. Beware the jungle.'" I read it a second time. "Yeah. Beware the jungle. What—"

"Textable fortunes. How convenient." Vlad glanced at Darius. "Look at all the fabulous talent you're collecting. I must take notes, lest you outstrip me."

"Ever heard of a sense of urgency?" Reagan said, shooting Vlad a scowl. "Ask her which jungle, Penny."

I hit send. "I was already doing that."

"What do you think is the best approach, given the changing circumstances?" Vlad asked Darius.

Darius looked out beyond me as though trying to pierce through the trees and see the compound in the valley below. "We need to play it by ear. Let the mages walk ahead of us and cut through any spells. It'll take the older dual-mages longer. Send shifters and vampires in with them. Reagan will lead a group, and Emery and Penny can take another."

"Three points around the compound?" Vlad asked.

"No." Roger's voice was gravelly compared to the vampires' velvety tones, but no less effective. Shivers crawled up my back and I found myself hanging on his every word. "We go down this side. It's a big compound. I've had a few people run it—"

"I'm sorry, *people* or…" Vlad's smile held a knife blade.

Roger's return stare held a grenade. Neither showed any fear of the other, only open and unbridled hostility. I took a step away.

"We can spread out once we get in, but if we divide ourselves into three groups around the entirety of the compound, we'll be at a severe disadvantage. We need to guard the prize." Roger's gaze swept over Emery and me, landing on Reagan. "We need to collect around the three of them, which means all of us going down this side. Let them be our guide. That's what my beta took from Penny's mom, and it makes sense. I saw what they could do at my forest estate. They know how best to fight the kind of magical attack we can expect down there. I know it's hard for a vampire to grasp, but we're *their* backup in this, not yours."

"Oh, *burn*," Reagan said, grinning.

Vlad and Darius stared at the shifter in silence, and thankfully my phone buzzed again.

I looked down at the screen. "'I can't duplicate that reading within the crystal ball,'" I read aloud. "'I would imagine it means the woods, but keep your eyes peeled in case that isn't it.'

"I mean…she probably would've said woods if she'd

meant woods," I said, reading the text again.

"It's not an exact science," Reagan said. "So let's just keep our eyes peeled."

"No, it is not," Vlad murmured, bringing up his own phone. "It is a wonder we are putting so much faith in it."

"If there is anyone who can make you a believer, it is Penny's mom." Emery took my hand. "The window is closing. Let's go."

"They're probably bringing people back from their failed attempts at sabotaging us," I said, pushing through the trees. If he had a path in mind other than down the slope, I couldn't tell.

"That, or the Guild has been alerted to us taking off, and they're preparing for us to show up here."

Another good point.

"Stop there, Emery. Penny." Roger held up a fist, holding his phone to his ear with the other hand.

"This will be a wonderful chance to see how they work in animal form." Vlad unbuttoned his coat jacket as he caught up with us. Apparently he'd be going in our group.

I did not miss Cahal stepping closer to me. He didn't trust Vlad.

"I've always wondered how they communicate with all those teeth." Vlad gave me a flawless smile, his face speckled with moonlight.

"Like you can talk," I said, and immediately regretted it when his smile spread. That smile wasn't rainbows and flowers.

Another set of shivers crawled up my spine.

I tucked a strand of hair behind my ear as the night moved. Shapes emerged from the shadows to my right to form a loose horde behind us, vampires all, in their monster forms, with long, sharp claws and gaping, fang-filled mouths. More shapes moved through the new night, slipping out from beneath bushes or around trees, barely making a sound.

The shivers zipping up my spine were starting to get frustrating. Still holding Emery's hand, because it kept me from jumping around like a lunatic and making a fool of myself, I flipped up the flap of the compartment holding Mr. Happy-Go-Lucky and brushed my fingertips across its surface. It was there, all right, happy to ride along.

Understanding punched me in the face.

This stone had always liked danger. It was happiest getting a ride with the most dangerous person in the group, largely because (I suspected) that person would likely draw the most fire and fury from enemies. It usually let out a pulse of power before a big attack, but once it was actually in battle, it just chugged along, waiting for the user to draw from it.

"It's started," I said, heart ricocheting around my

ribcage. "It's already started. The battle has begun."

Emery turned to me, but shadows draped his face and hid his expression. "I don't see any magic. The shifters and vampires would smell people if they were close."

I bit my lip, starting forward. Feeling the rightness of doing so. Feeling the pull to get moving. "It's just…"

When Emery didn't move with me, I loosened my hand to let go of him. He immediately followed me, his trust hopefully not misplaced.

Cahal wasn't far away, shadowing us. A moment later, I heard movement behind us. A backward glance revealed Vlad had changed into a white, swampy monster, his shifted form relaying his age and power. He was leading the rest of the vampires down with us.

The shifters hesitated, looking up the slope, probably for Roger's sign to go. My phone vibrated in my utility belt.

"It's a text from Reagan," I whispered, clicking off the screen. "She's tired of the slow approach. She's going to speed things up."

"You girls are…" Emery shook his head, and I just barely saw his grin. "Pairing you together was either sheer brilliance or the worst idea in history."

"Judging by how we work together during the bounty hunter gigs, I'd say the latter…"

# CHAPTER 31

A HUNDRED FEET or so down the hill, following animal trails, the shifters finally caught up to us, Roger in animal form and in the lead. No magic had marred our path, not even a tiny tripwire. I was about to comment on it when Cahal took two fast but somehow unhurried steps to my side and put his hand out, stopping me.

"Wh—"

He put his finger to his lips, cutting me off. Vlad crept closer, coming to a stop just behind Emery.

A twig snapped. Bushes rustled. Darkness draped across the wild landscape, creating deep pockets of shadow where anyone could be hiding.

*Seek.*

*Destroy.*

A colorful gleam of magic rained down from the sky, glittering as it filtered through the trees and sprinkled the ground. Three small strands of magic illuminated on the ground way down the path, probably tripwires with such little power that the strands were normally invisible to the eye, even for naturals.

Would I have felt those before running through them?

The searching spell dissipated, and the ensuing silence stretched through the thick trees.

"How'd you—"

Cahal slapped his hand across my mouth. He put his other hand, two fingers out, in front of his eyes, before turning it around and pointing just off to the right. He opened and closed his fist, held up a couple more fingers, and stared at me like his charades meant something.

Emery glanced over his shoulder at Vlad. Vlad nodded, not so attractive anymore, before turning and looking at another vampire.

The chain of command was in motion, and off shot the vampire who'd apparently been chosen as our lookout, eerily silent as she darted quickly through the brush and bushes. She disappeared out of sight before Cahal stepped back into the shadows.

Emery tugged me forward.

Everyone in this crew was *very* good at sneaking around, not to mention working together. I needed to up my game in the magic department so I wasn't dead weight.

A moment later, the lookout vampire loped back to us, falling in line easily. I hadn't even heard a scuffle.

She handed off a cell phone that she must've taken off the Guild sentry. Vlad handed it up and Emery put it into his back pocket.

Closing my eyes, I soaked in our surroundings as Emery led me along, feeling the calm flow of nature and the perfect balance of Emery and me. The magic *possibly stolen by accident* from the goblin beat within my chest, pure and powerful. Slowly I let in the magic around me, the heady, spicy power of the vampires, the deep earthiness of the shifters, and the slightly acidic yet strangely flowery essence of the druid. I funneled and weaved everything together, storing it in the collection of elements I always amassed above me when in pressurized situations.

When I opened my eyes, I saw a tiny strand of magic ten feet in front of us.

"Thanks," Emery whispered, the faint words riding his breath. He sent a counter-spell to easily knock out the spell in our path.

"What?"

"Organizing all of those elements for easy use."

I shrugged. If I'd realized he'd be able to feel it, too, I might have felt too much pressure to mess with it.

The second tripwire down, I felt a strange pulse to our left. Slowing, I closed my eyes again, much better at magical identification when I wasn't distracted by sight.

The feeling was so small and slight, but I narrowed

my focus on it…

Movement behind me. A shifter shot off through the trees, and I recognized the big black wolf, Devon.

It wasn't a person I'd felt, though. It was…something else. A flare, maybe?

"Do you feel that?" I asked Emery as we moved forward.

"No. What?"

"A mile," came a raspy voice, barely able to articulate the words. It had come from one of the vampires.

I nodded. It fit the feeling I'd picked up. "Yes, it's a magical mile marker. Huh. Why would they need a mile marker?"

"To coordinate their efforts, probably. Or"—Emery shot magic above us, unraveling a draping spell with the same searching intent that we'd encountered earlier—"to guide the sentries."

"Spellsh get den-sher now," Vlad said, his words wet and slurred. Clearly, talking through the distorted mouth and all those fangs got easier with age (or with practice), but it still wasn't perfect. "Dead-ly."

He was right. Powerful and more tightly woven spells glittered around us. Nothing surprising or challenging, though. Nothing we couldn't handle. It was like they were waving us in. Keeping away the non-magical riffraff, but inviting their kind closer.

"Why?" I asked, countering a tattletale spell. Another trap intended to lop off a foot. Still another, this one a badly executed booby trap capable of shooting magical spears.

"What?" Emery whispered, putting his hand out to stop my forward progress. Cahal stopped moving toward me. He didn't need to look back at Vlad or the shifters this time. One of each took off—one to the right, the other to the left—equally silent.

"They must know our power," I said, "but they're not doing too much to keep us out." Someone grunted to our right, followed by a quick shaking of the bushes. A mage lookout had been taken down.

Emery frowned at Vlad, whose vampire had not taken the enemy down quietly. Vlad stared back, not planning on apologizing.

"We have more power than they could've anticipated," Emery said, still waiting for a moment. He looked up, but no magic rained down, nor did I feel anything. "They have one, maybe two naturals. This is a lot of ground to cover for a natural. The spells in the compound will probably pose a problem."

"Or else this is a trap," I said, moving with Emery as he started forward again.

"Yes. Or this is a trap."

Two markers pulsed ahead, coming up on either side. "Five hundred feet," I said. "Probably."

"Yessh," Vlad said.

The dark shapes of trees loomed in front of us, but we'd come far enough for the end to be in sight. The ground leveled out up ahead, and beyond that, I knew the trees would be cleared leading up to the compound. Then, unless they'd changed it, came the huge ward. After that, we were inside.

If they chose to engage, there was no easy way to get out now. We couldn't just pull the plug on the whole thing, say *just kidding*, and head home. Not when we'd have to run two miles up a hill choked with trees and foliage, forced onto small paths.

Correction: *I* couldn't easily pull the plug. *I* couldn't run like death was chasing me, and hope to get away. But the vampires and the shifters probably could.

I blew out a slow breath. This was the time for absolute trust. If even one member of our team was on the wrong side (coughcough*Vlad*cough), things would get messy very quickly.

"Not to sound like a broken record, but where are all their people?" I flinched as Cahal moved in close to me again, and that felt like his answer. Either the enemy mages were very close, or he was wondering the same thing.

"You have to remember, Penny," Emery said, his knees bent and eyes constantly moving. The trees had thinned, allowing for moonlight to sprinkle down on him. On all of us. Soon we'd be visible to anyone looking. "The compound is large. They don't know where we're going to strike. They need to cover everything until they know for sure where we are. Then they'll pull their resources."

My phone vibrated.

Mr. Happy-Go-Lucky pulsed.

"Crap!" I said, no time for fancy swearing. I hopped from foot to foot as adrenaline flooded my body. My Temperamental Third Eye urged me to run to the right, then cut in toward the compound, magic flaring.

The text said, *Follow your gut.* My mother.

Another came in. Reagan this time. *Let's light up this bitch. Where are you?*

Yet another arrived, this one from Callie. *Campers! Campers!*

I didn't know what *campers* meant, but I knew what Reagan would be doing.

Giving us away.

"When in doubt…" And I took off running because I didn't have anything clever to say.

Surprisingly, it was Emery who caught up with me before anyone else, Cahal lagging behind. Welcome to randomly deciding things and just going with it.

I countered a spell blocking my path and caught a jumping shape out of the corner of my eye, magic suddenly curling from their hand. I pointed and said, "Maauuu," because that was all I could get out in time.

A shifter jumped in that direction, and I cut right.

Again, Emery was with me before anyone else. It didn't surprise me that he was the best at keeping up with quick, unpredictable pace and directional changes. He'd had experience.

A huge, throbbing spell shot up from somewhere in front of us. A *thrum* of vampire magic sailed in from behind us.

"Campers—she meant vampires!" I shouted. "It was auto-correct. We've got incoming vampires."

A shape darted out in front of us and an arrow took our would-be attacker down out of nowhere. Cahal reached back for another arrow, and I marveled at the fact that I had never once seen a bow strapped to his person. Or arrows, for that matter.

"I would've gotten him," I said to Cahal through harried breaths, trying to dodge a reaching tree branch and failing. It slapped me in the face.

"I've come to realize that participating in this skirmish at opportune moments will give me better odds of protecting you," Cahal replied.

"In other words"—Emery zipped off a spell at someone running at us from the side before countering a spell draped through the leaves and hanging down at head-height—"he didn't realize you're this unpredictable, and figures the skill set he's most comfortable with might help."

"It will," I said, feeling Mr. Happy-Go-Lucky pulse

again and I put on the brakes. Vlad slammed into my back, making me stagger forward, but Emery caught me and stopped my forward trajectory.

The vampire magic hit me like a wave. Emery spun as I did, and together we wove a spell that dropped unreal heat in a wall, far enough out not to get any of our people. Red flared in the night sky and the air was packed with inhuman squeals. The enemies trying to sneak up behind us were getting a bad surprise.

But some had made it through.

Fierce growls erupted, and our vampires rushed back to meet the attack. Soon I doubted I'd be able to tell who was who.

"Go," Vlad said, motioning Emery and I onward. "Take…down…warrrrrd."

My phone vibrated, barely felt, given how Mr. Happy-Go-Lucky had taken up a drumbeat of power in my utility belt. Maybe I'd been wrong before. Maybe it had simply been asleep. But now there was no denying that we were in the thick of it, and we didn't have much time to get that ward down before the whole place would be swarming, trapping us.

I yanked my phone out as we smashed through the trees and brush. Someone popped up sland slung a spell at us. I zapped him in the chest with my bug zapper and ignored the magic. It would shoot in a straight line behind us. Another popped up, her spell much nastier.

I curled some vampire magic into an ordinary slashing spell and sent it off, tearing down her spell—and her. Reagan had been right all those months ago. These mages were all cut from the same cloth. They were experienced, sure, and some of their spells packed a lot of power, but they were basic and easy to counter. It took hardly any brainpower. I never would've been the best had I gone the normal mage route, not considering how late I'd started. My power was in my unpredictability, my unique approach.

Stumbling into Emery's path, and then Reagan's, had been my lucky break.

My phone vibrated again, now jiggling in my vision as I ran.

The first said, *Stop thinking behind. Think in front.*

Already on it. Vlad had good instincts. Or lots of experience.

Second text: *Use the pyramid of power or all die an taken.*

Clearly my mother was working hard, because her grammar was slipping. If I got out of this mess, I'd tattle to Veronica.

"*When*, Penny," I said with clenched teeth, jumping to the side when another mage popped up along the path. She leaned forward to blow a spell at us. Cahal kicked her in the head. "*When* we get out of here." I ripped my gaze away from the druid and pumped my fists harder, my phone trapped in my palm.

"I feel that rock," Emery said as he pushed me left through thick bushes. Cahal rolled in after us and a thick stream of magic flew past. He rolled back, lifted to his knee, shot an arrow, jumped up, and followed us— all in one incredibly graceful motion.

"My god…Reagan's not even…that good," I said, my heart in my throat. "Pyramid." I was panting. "Pyramid of power. Need a…pyramid of power."

# CHAPTER 32

T HE TREES STOPPED just ahead, and three people waited beyond them, shifting from left to right and holding handfuls of ingredients. Magic wisps curled into the sky. Sounds of the shifter-vampire battle came from behind.

I wove a spell together as Emery shot one off. His spell hit an invisible wall, rebounding off it. A ward, fairly weak in power.

I altered my spell, and he enhanced it. I shoved it forward before sprinting after it.

Cahal's arm came into view, but he lowered it as the spell shattered the ward and continued its path of destruction, slapping against the mages. The remaining power wasn't enough to take them down. I jammed the heel of my palm into the nose of the one on the right before stepping back and kicking. Emery slammed into another, and Cahal gracefully went in for what looked like a hug before cracking the last one's neck.

"Wow. So pleasing to watch, but so incredibly ruth-less." I turned and braced myself, knowing what I would see.

Sure enough, a line of mages, spaced out, looked back at us. Slow to start, but fast once they got going, they ran toward us with spells curling in their hands. Something compelled me to glance the other way, and I'd never been more relieved to see a fireball. It blew through the air, swallowing a few mages, and then a swat of air squished them to the ground for good measure. Reagan had made it down and, without all the prying eyes, was using her full power in quick economy.

She waved at me to run with her, heading toward the huge ward that formed a sparkling dome around the whole Guild compound.

"I got this," Cahal said. He stepped away from Emery, raised his bow, and fired a stream of arrows faster than I could think. Draw, release, draw, release—the fletchings bloomed in chests and one in a neck.

"Thank you for choosing my side," I said as I took off for the ward. "Thank you, strange gift giver, whom I may or may not end up owing my soul to after this."

"Darius is going to call everyone to us," Reagan said as she met me. "The attacking vampire host wasn't as big as he feared, but they are at least middle tier and experienced. The elder in charge clearly wants the Guild to stay in control of this compound."

"I'm sure there are more; they just haven't worked around to this side of the compound yet." I looked through the shimmering ward, a collection of complex spells laced over that simpler ward that had protected the compound during our prior attack. My old friend, the watcher sitting up in the sky at the top of the ward, was still there. Its feet reached down through the ground, anchoring it. It hovered over everything, creating a hollow in the middle.

Now that I knew something about magic, I could put knowledge to my gut feelings. And the watcher emanated a feeling of deadness. Absence.

"Magic can't thrive in a place with no life," I said, losing the thread of the conversation, and my focus on the people around me and whatever was waiting on the other side of the ward. All I saw and felt was that big, looming beast, cutting the compound off from all the natural elements, and perpetrating the death and rot inside. "No wonder the mages are going crazy. They are magically suffocating. The lack of freshness, of magical wonder, is twisting their minds. They're shut up in there with no idea what they are doing to themselves in the name of defense."

"That's a poetic way of saying they screwed the pooch, and now they have to pay for their sins." Reagan put her palms up next to the ward, feeling. "Wow. This is a beast."

"Let's go," Emery said urgently.

I felt the shifter and vampire magic draw closer. I

also felt other spells rise, called into creation.

The phone in Emery's pocket chimed. He pulled it out and studied the screen.

"They are looking for a report," he said. "How could they not know we've already made it this far?"

"I'm sure they know." Reagan sidestepped, still feeling out the ward. Her magic wound through the air. "If nothing else, they know that we're some distance in. We killed everyone we came across. It's hard to check in when you're running for your life. Or when you have claws."

"Hopefully the mages inside think we're all fighting the vampires." I closed my eyes and sank into Reagan's magic before fitting it with the ability I hadn't intended to *blindly rob* from the goblin. Then I mixed in Emery's and mine, working at the pieces like a puzzle. The trick was in creating the right blend.

"What are you doing?" Emery asked me quietly.

"She's not working on this beast of a ward, that's what she's *not* doing," Reagan said.

"I'm trying to work all of our magic together to quickly erode this abomination and, if possible, point us to whoever masterminded it," I said. "I can't imagine a mage stupid enough to put it up without immediately realizing they needed to take it down again."

My phone vibrated in my hand. I sighed, momentarily distracted, before passing it on.

"Good shot, Cahal," Reagan said, clearly watching the show and not participating like she should. "Holy hooker stockings, Batman, you're a freaking machine."

"From your mother," Emery said. "Watch out."

"Oh good, yeah. Super helpful." I pushed away the sound of my phone vibrating again. Pushed everything away. It was just me and nature. The wind at my back. The packed earth at my feet. The soft moisture in the air, silkily petting my cheek and frizzing my hair.

I drew in a sweet breath, letting the life vibrate through me. Letting the magic I'd collected lead the way, moving within my energy.

Electricity singed my awareness, like a storm on the horizon. Emery.

Cold froze the air before swirling into flame. Reagan.

A calm breeze moving a single leaf across a still pond. Me.

The pyramid of power.

"Use the roots," Emery said at my ear. "Use the roots to anchor you."

I was already there, moving on to the next swirl of magic, solid and steadfast, ancient and fixed. A man trapped in a destiny he didn't choose. A magic that masked the obvious, but uncovered the hidden. Cahal. The druid.

I sucked in another breath as it all mixed together,

around and around, finding a way to mingle. To coexist.

I touched Reagan's shoulder, knowing her hands were feeling out that ward, that her magic was worming through the fabric, trying to find a way to break it down. Emery's rough hand took mine, giving me a greater zing of his magic.

"Why is everyone touching me?" Reagan said, trying to scoot away.

"The vampires and shifters are here," Cahal said, and then his hand was on my shoulder, his fingers curling around my bones and digging in.

"Hey, guy, I'm breakable," I said, wiggling my shoulder. I didn't think he was in touch with his own strength. Immediately, he loosened up.

I felt Reagan's power climbing upward along the dome. I branched it off and nudged it down to reach into the earth.

"Who's in charge here, me or you?" Reagan asked. It wasn't rhetorical; she honestly wanted to know.

"You. You're more experienced. Unless I see something, then I'll just take over."

"I miss working alone," Reagan said on a sigh.

A roar shook my bones and made me grit my teeth.

"Steve has a great roar," Reagan said, and I could hear the smile in her voice.

"Steve is such a mundane name for a roar that size," Emery said.

Reagan started laughing, and though her concentration seemed to waver, her magic spread out quicker, covering more ground and feeling out the spell in a way I hadn't realized was possible. It crawled along like a live thing, tracing the seams and digging into the holes. She was identifying all the weaknesses.

"Smart," I said, accidentally peeling an eye open as Cahal jerked me.

A vampire lashed at him, its jowls loose and hanging, fangs dripping blood.

Cahal didn't take his hand from me. He snatched a knife out of who knew where and slashed it across the vampire's throat. Another claw came up, and I couldn't help but react. Taking my hand from Reagan's shoulder, I sent out a pure pulse of dazzling white.

The magic hit the vampire center mass, knocking it back and opening it up. Black sludge oozed out of its middle as it hit the ground.

Emery fired off another shot behind us, and my phone buzzed in his hand. He glanced at it.

"'Hurry up,'" he read.

"That isn't very helpful, Mother," I said through clenched teeth, shooting off a complex though one-handed spell that ended up a bit cock-eyed but worked just fine.

Another vampire broke free, running at us. I called up magic, but before I could get it off, a massive lion (probably Steve) leapt forward from outside my line of sight. He slammed into the vamp, taking the scraggly, leanly muscular body to the ground. Steve's incredible jaws locked over the vampire's neck and he wrenched, taking off the head.

"Wow. That is freaking gross." I squeezed my eyes shut and turned back to Reagan.

"What happened?" Reagan asked, and I felt her jerk around to look. "Atta boy, Steve."

The magic was at the top of the dome now, inching toward that strange presence in the sky.

"No," I said, leaning into her and pushing the magic around it. "Don't touch it. Not yet. It has a…personality. It isn't just magic. It's more."

"Do not tell me that your weirdness is going to come in handy," Reagan said incredulously.

"Hurry, ladies," Cahal said. "We have mages approaching from the other side."

I snapped my eyes opened, looking at the approaching line of color as the higher-powered mages drifted through the compound toward us. They all had their hands up, and while they were too far away for me to make out details, I was sure they had ingredients in those hands.

"Dolittle's scapegoat. Go, Reagan. Hurry!"

# CHAPTER 33

"DO YOU NEED my hand?" Emery asked, his eyes widening as a vampire broke loose from the shifters and made a mad dash toward them. The enemy knew that Penny, Reagan, and he were the only way the group as a whole would get through the ward.

He shot off a spell, raking invisible nails down the vampire's middle, giving another shifter time to catch it before it healed.

The vampires were few and far between now. The first line of attack (or was it defense?) was just about exhausted.

"No, I have the feel of the magic," Penny said, under strain. He could feel her splinter some of Reagan's magic and use it as her own, shooting it deep down into the earth, looking for the root of the spell. The connecting threads. That technique shouldn't have been possible. But then again, they'd been doing the impossible together from the beginning.

Black fog clouded his vision. Magic zipped toward him from the side.

He turned immediately as his premonition faded away, spotting a mage who'd just run through the ward and fired off a spell. He met it with his own, easily counteracting it, and then took the mage down.

Cahal grunted as Penny shrugged off his hand. "Don't use all your arrows," she said. "We'll need them if we get through this ward."

Emery gritted his teeth. It wasn't time to pull the plug and drag her out of here. He wouldn't let himself give in to his fear.

Another mage ran through the ward. Two wolves broke off from the battle and ran at her. She dug through her bag with jerky movements, obviously not expecting the attack she was about to receive.

Emery turned, leaving them to it. She didn't have the wherewithal to get out of that.

A vampire, scraped and bleeding from many wounds, slashed through a shifter and jumped beyond another's reach. He sped at Reagan, whose back was totally exposed.

Emery braced himself, a spell at the ready, but didn't get a chance to attack.

Cahal took two unhurried, though extremely quick steps to cover the opening. Knees bent and body relaxed, he waited for the vampire to reach him in a dead sprint. The vampire jumped at him, claws out, mouth open, drool hanging from its fangs in a thick rope. Cahal stepped forward diagonally, bending gracefully to miss a claw, before reaching forward and grabbing the vamp by the neck and upper arm. He spun, using the vamp's momentum to redirect the creature, and flung him into the shifters running toward them in a herd.

Once done, Cahal straightened, took two steps backward, and resumed his position at Penny's back. He wasn't even winded, as though he handled upper-middle-level vampires on a daily basis.

Whoever had hired this druid had clearly paid out of the nose, and he had been worth every cent. Emery never would've defeated this guy if he'd accepted the other bid—the one to kill Penny—though he would have died trying.

"Fracken crackhead's pajamas, we have to break through this!" Penny yelled, sweat dripping down her face. He saw her glance up, then her body stiffened.

He followed her gaze…and almost emptied his stomach.

A seemingly endless number of mages walked toward them in horizontal lines, dressed in purple, red, and orange robes—high-powered magical workers, extremely capable, and sheriffs who were used to fighting under pressure. They'd increased their faction tenfold, obviously gearing up for this skirmish. Reagan, Penny, and he had a lot of power, but they were nothing compared to what was gathered within the dome. They wouldn't be able to compete.

"Just blow it up, Reagan," Penny said through clenched teeth. Her voice rose in pitch. "Just blow it up, or we'll need to move this operation elsewhere. Soon they'll be within striking range."

"I can't. That sucker up there is…trying to play footsie. What are you?" Reagan's voice was wispy, all her concentration on her task. "I haven't seen you before."

"It's a thing. It's a reflection of someone's personality," Penny said, still working on the root. She was closing in, Emery felt it, but they needed Reagan to crack the cusp of the spell. The watcher.

"But it's in the air," Reagan said. "It's just sitting on top of this ward. Or is it creating it?"

"You want her to live, yes?" Cahal asked Emery, his voice low and smooth. If he felt any pressure from the coming danger, he didn't show it.

"Yes—"

"Above all, you want her to live?"

"Yes."

Cahal's eyes flicked to the side. To the mass of power slowly walking their way, working on a monstrous spell, he had no doubt. They'd banded together to face a common threat. It would've been commendable if his people weren't the targets. "I will await your word to extract her. I would take her now, but—"

"No." Emery knew Penny was there. Knew Reagan was close. Knew that if he helped, he could push them over the edge. "Not yet."

"I will wait. I will rely on you for her survival." The druid's ice-blue stare burned into Emery's brain, and he felt the duty to protect Penny pass to him. Felt it slither in his blood and take root.

Emery nodded, accepting the responsibility he had already assumed, before moving to Reagan and gripping her hand. Magic ran between them, the feeling strange and surreal.

"That's unusual," she said with a furrowed brow.

"Penny needs you ready, and you're lagging. Show me." He closed his eyes like Penny always did, focusing on what Reagan felt with her magic. Unbelievably, an image lit the backside of his eyelids. The top of the sphere, incredibly high off the ground, the surface pocked and the seams weak. Reagan's magic had already eroded the weak points. But a glowing beacon sat in the middle, on the defensive, ready to react if foreign magic touched it.

"You said it has a personality, Penny?" Emery asked, going through his huge Rolodex of spells. Thinking of things he'd personally used, techniques he'd only heard about, and the Guild's unsavory practices.

"Yeah. Here. Quick!" Penny sucker-punched him with something hard.

He lost his breath, but captured the stone she'd thrust at him.

"Plain Jane," she said. "Your Plain Jane. It wants to be with you."

Emery didn't have time for power stones now, but he took it anyway, trusting her.

"They are advancing faster," Cahal said, voice still calm, body close to Penny. "They all hold something in their hands."

Emery felt the magic building, felt a wisp of deadly intent, which meant Penny had to be drowning in it.

"You've got thirty seconds," Penny yelled at him.

What sounded like a bear roared. Wolves growled. Air whipped behind Emery as if something had raced past him. A vampire, he'd bet.

Magic shot close to them. Emery felt the pull to leave Reagan so he could defend them.

"Let them handle it, Emery," Penny said in an urgent tone. "We need you here. Help her get that done."

Penny knew him incredibly well. It was almost eerie.

The stone throbbed in his hand. Reagan took a step back, her silent urge for him to take over. He kept his grasp of her hand. He couldn't properly use her magic without contact yet. He was slow to learn Penny's innate gifts.

"What do you do, pet dragons?" Reagan muttered.

The stone throbbing in Emery's hand stilled his thoughts. Power pumped through his body. Like a heartbeat.

"Blood magic," he said, spells running through his head from a book long since forgotten. Something he'd found in his surrogate father's room—a tome about circles and demons and bringing back the dead. He'd devoured it, fascinated by stuff straight out of bad horror flicks and gruesome tales told around the campfire. He'd even tried a spell or two before his brother had found out and ratted on him.

"They sacrificed someone for that spell—tore their soul from them so it could be used as the watcher, the keeper of the compound. Living flesh would've gone into the spell. The victim's screams. The blood of the lost." Emery racked his brain, trying desperately to remember if he'd ever heard about a counter-spell. Or something to peacefully set it off. "Peace," he said, ripping his eyes open.

He wished he hadn't.

The mages of the Guild had come to a stop on the other side of the ward. One of the three barons, dressed in a blood-red robe, stood out front, leading the spell they were calling into existence. It was hidden behind a shimmering, moving wall of magic, but Emery could see it rising.

"Shhhiii…" Emery gritted his teeth and squeezed his eyes shut again. "Get ready, Cahal."

"Don't you get ready, Cahal," Penny said. "Emery has this. He's right there. He has the answer. I feel it in him."

"Ra ra ra," Reagan said, shaking Emery's hand a little, whether cheerleading or telling him to hurry, he couldn't say.

"Peace for the tortured soul. Send the soul to its resting place." He braced himself and reached out, finding Penny's hand with the stone between it. Feeling a stronger force of serenity flow through him. Flow through Reagan. Sparkly white light danced behind his eyes. Deep black rolled through it. His grayish mutt met the two sides in the middle, and he held his breath. "Here goes nothing."

He took Penny's approach—rather than attack the spell, he embraced it with her serenity. With her care and beauty and love of all things natural.

"It's time," Cahal said, moving closer.

"I don't want to rush you, Emery, but *hurry*," Penny said, and for some reason, that was hilarious.

He laughed in deep belly chuckles as their combined magic surged around the watcher. The peaceful light infused the twisting and churning, anguished and decrepit spell. He wrapped it up snugly and sent the soul to its final resting place as Reagan stepped back into the ward and went to work, finding each crack and wresting it open. Lining the seams with fire or ice, depending on what was needed.

"*Now* blow it up, Penny," Reagan said, letting go of Emery's hand. "Then run like bloody hell."

# CHAPTER 34

I DIDN'T WAIT, and I didn't hang around. I shoved in a combination of Reagan's fire, my own blend of magical heat, and Emery's lightning, then I turned and sprinted.

"Wrong way." A large, strong hand gripped my upper arm and whipped me around. Cahal gave me a little shove. "Now run."

"Go, go, go, go," Reagan yelled as she sprinted back toward the trees.

The shifters and vampires, temporarily short on enemies as the large group behind the ward readied their spell, watched in clear confusion as we ran through them, away from the mages. Darius and Vlad were the first to follow. Roger led his lot after them.

"This way," Reagan said, turning left and running along the tree line.

*Seek and destroy.*

"We have a—"

Reagan whipped out her sword and stuck it up into the air, cutting through the spell filtering down.

"You got it," I finished.

"Where are we going?" Emery asked, keeping up with me as I barely made pace with Reagan. Cahal loped easily by our side, and his perpetual ease was starting to get on my nerves.

I wiped sweat from my face. "Following her."

Darius caught up to Reagan and looked at her.

"They took forever to get organized," Reagan said as an explosion of air, sound, and color blasted out at us, the ward and all the spells attached to it coming down in intense splendor. The force lifted me off my feet and threw me. Emery landed before I did, and I crashed into him. A wolf went rolling past. Then a warthog.

"It is really weird fighting with shifters." I pushed myself off the ground as Cahal swung up his legs and hopped from his back to his feet in a fluid motion. "Definitely starting to get annoying."

"We need to keep moving," Reagan said, pushing to her feet. "The ward is down, by the way. In case you missed it."

She turned and ran for the compound as an undertow of power shook my bones. The force of the intent fused my jaw shut and tensed every muscle in my body.

*STUN!*

I staggered, almost fell. Emery steadied me.

"Loo—" I pointed behind us. Shifters and vampires lingered back there, taking up the rear. They'd get hit first. "Nnnn!"

My mouth still not working properly, I dragged Reagan out of the trees and into the clearing as the magic thundered down on us.

"Fucking turdswallop!" she said, dropping her sword and shoving her hands out in front of her.

"Get behind us," Emery yelled at the vamps and shifters. "Hurry!"

A fog of thick, dense magic moved out from the compound, slow and strangely intelligent. It would track us, I knew. Sure enough, after a brief pause, it started drifting our way in no real hurry. No plans to dissipate until it met its mark.

"Fire," Reagan said, her eyes sparking. "Fire!"

"Your fire or my fire?" I asked, leeching some of her magic. Fusing it with mine. Spinning a weave.

Emery pushed in beside me, working with my efforts. Taking what I created and building it. Shaping it. Basically, bedazzling it.

"Anything," Reagan said. "Everything. It needs heat."

"And life," Emery said. "You were right, Penny. This organization is working with death. Decay. Magic works in opposites."

"So much for the theory that they'd only use spells from a book," I said, a trickle of sweat running down my back.

"This is from a book," Reagan said. "Everything they do is from a book. And I sure as hell hope we don't destroy the building it's housed in before I get to see the beast."

"Opposites," Emery said, his face screwed up in concentration, the artificial lighting of the compound barely reaching us. "Balancing spells makes them stronger. Harder to break. Clearly the originator of the spells they are using didn't know that rule. *I* didn't know that rule until I met you."

"I don't understand how. It's pure logic." I added another layer to the spell, feeling the beast bear down on us. Fire rolled between Reagan's fingers. She was going to use us as a cover to openly use her own magic.

"We can do it without that, Reagan," I said, knowing that the right people would know mages couldn't make fire like hers. Not even dual-mage naturals. Not even angel-touched dual-mage naturals.

"No, you can't," she said softly. "I made a choice to be here. So if my old man comes for me, you better back me up."

"Done," Emery said.

"How horrible is he?" I asked.

The beast of a spell had us in its sights, though I had no idea how it had identified us. The magical fog sped up, thundering toward us now, churning power and malevolence.

"Now!" Reagan yelled.

Emery and I shot off our spell, horribly small in comparison to the behemoth bearing down on us. It hit the mages' spell, turning and spinning within it. Fire erupted around it, a great flame that then reduced in height but not width, spreading across the underside of the spell like flame crawling along a ceiling. Little sputters and sparks shot out of it, licking up the sides. Thank goodness we had Reagan.

"In this, you have excelled," Cahal said.

"Not now, peanut gallery." Reagan made a circle in the air with her finger. "Let it work. Let's go."

"Wait, you don't—*we* don't need to stay and—"

Reagan cut me off by shoving me along. "Let's go. Let's circle around them while they think we're dying a horrible death."

As Reagan ran past the vampires, Vlad turned and watched her go, looking awestruck.

He clearly knew what she was, and he clearly wanted her.

I did not like that at all.

"Come on, Turdswallop, you can pick a fight with that elder later." Emery plucked at my sleeve to get me moving.

I had no idea how he'd read my thoughts.

Once again, we ran through the shifters and vampires, the numbers, thankfully, not terribly thinned by the latest assault. Just as thankfully, they hadn't become a disorganized horde—they waited for their respective leaders to start after us before filing in.

Reagan sprinted for the Guild compound, laid bare without that horrible spell suffocating the life from it. As we entered the compound, it felt as if it were taking a big breath.

Two mages ran from behind a corner of a building, harried and frantic, glancing over at us and staggering. One fell; the other regained her feet, turned, and ran the other way.

Emery zipped off a spell, catching the one trying to get away. It hit her in the back, making her arch and fall forward. Reagan was on the other, a knife in one hand, and a sword in the other.

"What's the plan?" I yelled, because any sense of direction was better than running around with our heads cut off.

The beast of a spell, now half the mass it had been, moved toward us still, stopping where we'd turned and slowly changing direction to follow us. The fire continued to eat it alive, defusing it a little at a time. Still, it wasn't gone yet, and the shifters at the back of our group knew it. They ran forward, spreading out around us, fur for miles.

Darius moved up with Reagan, looking at her. She shrugged and glanced back, their communication silent.

"Literally anything, you guys," I said, bouncing from one foot to the other. "Anything at all."

Emery, still holding Plain Jane, handed over my phone. A text message glowed on the screen.

I read it aloud. "'Cut off the head. Sweep out the legs. Reap what you sowed.'

"What the hell does that mean?" I yelled at the screen.

"Penelope Bristol, just because you are in a battle, does not mean you can start swearing," Reagan said in a terrible impersonation of my mother. "What'd she say?"

One of the wolves started to whine.

The intent of that beast of a spell throbbed into my back. "Yeah. We gotta move."

"Head—the High Chancellor," Emery said, grabbing my hand and pulling me along. "The feet must be the peons at the bottom. Though I'm not sure why that would be the case. Why wouldn't we go for the upper tier? The power players?"

"I'm sure they'll get hit in the crossfire." Reagan started a jog, moving right through the center of the compound.

"Split up," Emery said, motioning away our reinforcements. "Their forces need to be pulled apart. Fractured. Take away their—*Oh*. Cut off the head. Cut off their ability to think. We need to separate the horde from the mages who're orchestrating these big spells."

"Raise chaos," I said softly.

"On it." Reagan picked up speed, and I ran after her. There was one surefire way to turn everything on its ear—Reagan and I trying to work together.

Darius kept pace as well, but Vlad peeled off, joined by another vampire.

"I don't know that it's wise to let him roam around on his own," I murmured as we turned a corner.

"Now you're thinking like a true magical person," Reagan said, slamming on the jets. "Found some bad guys."

Ten mages stood facing the opposite direction. At Reagan's voice, they turned, all holding ingredients, magic billowing around them. Without warning, Reagan took off running, sprinting right at them. Darius was with her a moment later, claws out like Wolverine, mouth open.

I shot a spell ahead of them, felling three mages. Emery took out two more before I felt a tingling at my back. A haze clouded my vision, interrupted by a red spell headed straight toward me...but when I blinked, it evaporated.

Emery pushed me to the side and Cahal grabbed me around the waist and ran, bumping up against the wall and shielding me with his body. A mage popped out from around the corner of a building up the way, got a shot off, and ducked back down. It was the same color

I'd seen. The same event.

"He can feel traces of my ability to read intent, and I can see traces of his premonitions," I said, momentarily tingly inside. That lasted a nanosecond. I elbowed Cahal and pushed out of his grasp. "I was fine. Save it for when I'm actually in danger."

I darted out and zipped off a quick spell to down the last guy in Reagan and Darius's fight before catching up with Emery, who was running around the corner after the other mage. A shifter got there first, sneaking up behind the mage and launching at his neck.

A lion's roar seemed to shake the earth beneath our feet. Another deep-throated roar followed. Wolves took up the call from the other direction. That crazy warthog ran by, alone. If there wasn't more than one confused warthog, then Roger really needed to have a talk with that guy.

"Keep going," Emery said, running toward the records room that we'd broken into before.

Mages jumped out and spoke magic to life. Before they could get it realized, I countered their spell. Emery followed up with a spell to take them all down. From the other side, three more mages broke capsules and shot them at us. Reagan jumped in front and slashed with her sword, killing the spells before yanking out her gun and shooting the casters.

"I'm pretty sure that's cheating," I said, feeling

winded and knowing we still had a ways to go.

"Cheat to win." Reagan ran through the middle of the quad, and two vampires skirted in to join Darius. Marie and Moss, if I had to guess, though I was no expert at deciphering monster forms. Shifters filed in behind, in packs or alone, depending on the animal. One of them was limping.

Magic throbbed somewhere to my right.

*Obliterate!*

"They aren't trying to capture us anymore," I said, grabbing a hold of Reagan and pulling her back. "They've got another monster spell brewing."

"Unless they are making it while having a parade, this is a different group than the last," Reagan said, clearly better at directions than I was.

"Cut off the head," Emery said, marching forward with determination. "Swipe their feet. Ruin their concentration and careful planning with absolute chaos."

"Take them from behind," I said, adrenaline running hard through my body. Mr. Happy-Go-Lucky started to vibrate. Emery had tucked Plain Jane into his utility belt, but even though it wasn't on my person, I felt the deep drumbeat of its power pulse to life.

"This is where it gets hairy," Emery said. He grabbed my upper arms and stared down into my eyes. "If things look bleak, if you don't think we can make it through, you run, do you hear me? You let Cahal take you out of here."

"No."

He shook me a little, a deep pain moving in his eyes. "Please, Penny. For me. Get yourself clear. Get yourself safe. *Live*, Penny. I need you to live."

"You will be pampered. Looked after," Cahal said. At my hard stare, he did the first human thing I'd seen him do. He put his palm to his chest and, with wide eyes, said, "Not by me."

I barked out laughter. I couldn't help it. The super-old druid, who'd seen it all, did not want to be shackled to a nut case like me.

"Join the club," Reagan said, and I realized I'd said that out loud.

"Penny," Emery said again, pleading. Willing to sacrifice himself for me. Wanting me to live above all things.

My heart twisted in my chest. I held his gaze, everything in me breaking.

The world went silent for a moment, but my resolve only strengthened.

"No," I said, tired of other people telling me what to do. Tired of living a life someone else had chosen for me, and a path someone else had made me walk. Now I was carving out my own future, and I would choose the direction my feet walked. "You stay, I stay. We're a team. We'll finish this together."

He opened his mouth to argue, but a knowing gleam lit those beautiful Milky Way eyes. A grin tickled his lips. "Watch out, world, here comes Turdswallop."

"Why does everyone I know always ruin great moments?"

He grabbed my cheeks in his strong hands and smashed his lips to mine.

"Come on, Romeo and Juliet, we have a battle to start," Reagan said.

Emery pulled away, storm clouds raging in his eyes. Wildness rose in him, unruly and unchained. Electricity pooled between us before spinning higher and spreading out, joined by Reagan's complex and beautiful magic. Shifters had gathered, waiting for direction, and the hair on their backs stood on end. Vampires shifted in their monster form and clicked their claws in anticipation.

"Let's cut off some heads," Emery shouted, leading the charge.

# CHAPTER 35

"IT HAS TAKEN them this long to get this one spell in motion," Emery said, cutting right and running down the side of a building. The magic grew to our left. Had we kept going straight, we would've run right into the building *Obliterate* spell. "The team that already loosed their spell is probably regrouping with another. They'll do it in shifts. After we take this spell down, we need to cut out the leader. We have to do that for each of them."

"Get oder roup," Darius said through his mouth of fangs. He needed to practice more to speak as well as Vlad in his monster form.

"Get the other group," Emery said quietly as he turned to one of the shifters in the group. "Get people, doesn't matter who, on the first group of spell workers we encountered. Cut them down now, while they are rebuilding."

The wolf darted away, two reinforcements with him.

"Let's go around this way," Emery said, running

across a walkway and over dusty ground that might have once been grassy. I felt a pull to the next building. Confused, I glanced down, not sure what I was feeling or why. "Here we go."

I pushed the weird feeling away and refocused, slowing down with everyone else. My heart quickened as I once again sensed the magnitude of the spell that was brewing. *Obliterate.* Emery and Reagan were both looking at me.

"How close is it to being done?" Emery asked.

"Close," I whispered. "It's a monster, like the last one."

Reagan looked at Emery with a flat expression, then me. She winked.

"No, no, what are you—" She was already running around the corner with a sword in hand, and Darius took off after her. "Dang it, I hate when she does that."

I felt a familiar hand grab my arm. I sent a pulse of electricity through my body, through the hand, and into the stack of man attached.

Cahal flinched away and staggered.

Don't mess with a woman on a mission.

Emery and I followed Reagan at a fast run, moving straight toward the spell casters, and though I wanted to skid to a stop and about-face, I turned up the speed instead. There they were—another large group of mages, waiting in a line, staring up at nothing, hands full of ingredients and no feelings in their hearts. They were magical drones, attempting to let loose a spell they probably scarcely understood.

Even as we stood there, the spell rose and swelled, becoming a force unto itself. It puffed up and hovered above everyone, seeking its target.

A target that was among them.

I kicked the first guy, punched the second, and smashed three more with a thick weave that sliced right through them. Reagan hacked through their ranks with her sword, looking up with tight eyes, knowing that thing would drift right back down at any moment.

"Gun. This would be a good time for my mother and her gun." I speared someone with magic and barely dodged an attack by someone else—a rare mage who was thinking for herself. I knocked that woman out, because I didn't think she truly belonged here, not with a brain of her own, and magically slashed another.

It turned out I was excellent at close combat, magical style. *Thank you, Reagan, for those many horrible hours of training.*

Someone hollered as they flew over the crowd, and suddenly Cahal was by my side. The guy he'd thrown skimmed the spell above us. His holler turned into a garbled scream before cutting off. He fell down in a clump, the area that had been in the fog eaten away.

"We can't stick around under that," I said to Emery,

who grabbed a guy by the head, cracked his neck, and magically shot someone else.

"I know. Skirt the outside of the group. Keep them in the middle. They're tired and scared. Let them cower together."

A fierce snarl dragged my attention to the front of the line, where a single man stood opposite a very large lion. The mage, wearing a long, flowing robe and tall, silly hat, snatched a casing out of his satchel and fired it off.

Steve lurched forward, all teeth and claws and shifter magic, eating the spell or cutting through it, and slammed into the mage. A bear lumbered after him, opening its mouth wide and roaring at the mages at the front of the line.

"Penny!" Emery shouted.

I spun around, following the direction of Emery's pointed finger. The red fog, similar to the first monster spell, puffed out and swelled a little more. A few sparks flared from deep within it as it slowly started moving back toward the ground.

"Go, go, go." I turned and ran right into someone. Cahal stepped around me, grabbed the guy by the robe, and yanked him out of the way. The robe ripped and the guy barreled into a few other mages, three of them falling. Cahal pushed someone else out of the way and I ran in the newly created lane, Emery right behind me.

"Cut through," Emery yelled.

I pulled at the elements above me, wove them into something nasty, and shoved it out, ruthless in my desperation. Up ahead I could see Darius slashing and tearing his way to the front, all strength and viciousness. Reagan followed in his wake, letting him clear the way.

The fog continued to lower, just as unhurried as the last. Tripping over limbs, struggling through the panicking crowd, I shot another spell at the people continuing to file into my way. The fog was nearly close enough to singe. The wall to my left was unforgiving, and the crowd pushing at me from the other side blocking me in.

Emery yanked me back, pushing me behind him. As big as a linebacker and just as strong, he barreled up the line, shooting magic or just muscling people to the side. I followed closely with Cahal behind, his hands on my upper back, occasionally tugging upward when my foot caught on human debris. I didn't dare shrug him off, not with the spell drifting lower, trying to meet its target.

The bear up front swiped and someone went flying, half of her body grazing the fog. She screamed, but it soon cut off, and she fell in a boneless drop like the other mage. More people screamed at the back of the group, horrid, agonizing wails, as they were caught in the spell of their own making. When we were almost at the front and out, a throng of people pushed in our way, trying to escape the bear.

I caught sight of Reagan on the other side, her eyes widening. Cahal's hands tightened on my upper back. Emery started shoving, forcing people forward with pure brawn.

We wouldn't get out in time. That fog was right on us now, too big and dense for me to counter it in the half-minute we had left.

Without warning, a solid air wall slammed down in front of us. Emery ran into it face first, and I had to grab his hair and rip it down to keep him from popping straight up into the magical fog. People yelled and screamed in surprise as they were shoved by an unseen force, pushed back toward the bear. An alley had opened up, totally clear, but an invisible wall kept the mages out.

"Come on," Emery said, taking my hand to make sure I made it. Ducking as he ran through the opening.

This time Cahal's hands weren't helping keep me upright, they were pushing on my back to keep my head down—and to keep him stable as he all but crawled after me. Emery reached the end and rolled out. I dove, and Cahal rolled out after me.

The bear backed up, swiped at another person, forcing them back. The fog continued to lower, catching people within its choking grasp. Killing its creators.

"Find the next one," I shouted, panic still flooding my system. Tears—ashamedly—close to the surface.

That had been unbearably close. Terrifyingly close.

"We need to douse it in fire first," Reagan said to us as she jogged over, lines etching her face and worry tightening her eyes.

I danced out of the way so Steve could pounce on someone, fitting his massive jaw over their skull and shaking. I changed up the weave this time, remembering how the magic had worked with the last. Emery filled in easily. Reagan waited to add her bit.

"How many of these do you think they have?" she asked, traces of fatigue riding her words. She'd already poured so much of herself into the fight.

"Three barons." Emery pointed at a shoe that had flown off the foot of its wearer. "One." He pointed in another direction. "Two, if the shifters got that one."

"They did. Roger's teams have excellent follow-through. Ask Vlad and Darius. So one more, then." Reagan stepped out of the way as we threw out a spell. This time, it struck a little harder and sank in deeper before spinning to life and expanding, eating the spell away from the inside before spouting flame. Reagan's fire kindled a moment later, creating the illusion it was growing out of our spell, and ate across the outside of the fog.

"Maybe the High Chancellor," Emery said as we

started forward with a group of shifters and vampires in tow. The fog had already started drifting our way. Now it marginally sped up, in lazy, powerful pursuit.

We took off at a jog, joined by shifters and vampires. With the horde growing, we had an easy time picking off mages in twos and threes. A little farther, and I saw where Vlad had gone.

In a dirt patch that had probably once been grass, vampires tore through another gathered mass of mages, their ingredients scattered across the ground. Spells zipped or flared, but the vampires cut through them with their claws, working efficiently to take out the mages. Roger's team was gathered at the periphery, letting no one escape. Locking them all in with the vampires.

This mass of mages hadn't been able to get their huge spell off the ground.

"That Vlad is good," I said with grudging respect.

"Yeah. He didn't get where he is for nothing," Reagan said, turning. Darius stayed with her. "Right. That's group three. Either we have a High Chancellor getting another group ready… There's the fog coming. Let's change locations. It has another ten minutes before my—the fire can eat through it."

"Why would they make it move so slowly?" I asked, starting up a jog. My feet ached and my legs felt like jelly. I was running out of steam.

"If the three spells were drifting around at once, following you? The amount of effort and power it would take to bring even one of them down would've severely weakened…a normal mage. It would've kept you on the run. And then the many mages could have just slowly corralled you and blocked you in. You would've had to fight too many battles at once. But three things went wrong for them. They didn't get the spells all going in time, they weren't organized for the follow up, and they underestimated our power. It was a great plan, badly executed."

"The phone is buzzing again," Emery said, reaching for his pocket as a group of mages jogged into our line of sight. They stopped quickly, reached for their satchels, and…as one, they took off running back the way they'd come.

Reagan kicked up speed to follow them, the rest of us close behind. We ran around the corner, in hot pursuit, seeing them head for a building with an open door.

"We need to check the buildings," Emery said. "Flush them out."

As we hurried out into the middle of a collection of buildings, all the doors opened at once. Banged off the sides of walls. A veil of throbbing magic unrolled all at once between the buildings and dropped to the ground. Zips of magic flew high, spreading out and landing on top of the collection of buildings, securing the corners of the veil.

Each spell surged with power, each weave was tight and controlled, done by someone with a deft hand. Orchestrated perfectly.

Trapping our small host.

"They were saving their Natural," Emery said.

# CHAPTER 36

URPLE-CLAD MAGES FILED out and stretched out to the sides, creating a circle around us, satchels open at their sides and little round balls collected in their hands. Casings. They'd prepared all their spells ahead of time and could pose a rapid-fire attack for those they needed out of the way so they could trap Emery and I in. Another group of mages surged out, bedecked in red and orange, more than the first rush, filling in any holes in the circle or standing behind. Finally, a woman with a stern face, straight shoulders, and haunted eyes sauntered into our midst. The circle of mages opened a small gap that she could walk into, and the bright gold robe couldn't possibly overshadow the armor of confidence draped across her body.

The Natural. It had to be.

Reagan stood very still next to me. Emery was completely tense. Cahal had his hand on my shoulder. Mr. Happy-Go-Lucky throbbed with power and pleasure, in its element.

"I can probably break us out of here," Reagan said

quietly as movement flickered within one of the open windows.

"Probably?" Emery asked.

"It depends on how quickly they can fire off their spells." For the first time that I'd ever fought with her, she didn't sound sure.

Tendrils of panic wrapped around my chest.

Steve made a chuffing sound, his great lion form at our backs, his tail flicking lazily. I had no idea what any of it meant.

More mages showed up, gathering on the outside of the magical veil, waiting to battle the vampires and shifters who came to our aid.

"So many," Emery whispered, shaking his head slowly and looking around at the circle enclosing us. "They've collected so many."

"The promise of power is clearly alluring to a great many mages." Reagan's voice was filled with acid.

A phone vibrated as Darius pushed in close to Reagan.

"Keep thinking, Darius," Reagan said quietly. "Try to find the best approach."

"If you see an opening, Cahal, get her out," Emery said.

"Nope." My mind raced as I shrugged off Cahal's grip on my shoulder, looking at the mages' faces, the positioning of their bodies and hands. Taking a sampling of the—once again—stifling air. Something about their magic always cut off the natural element. "What do the colors of the robes mean?"

"Purple represents the highest tier of power in their hierarchy. They never, ever used to have this many." Emery paced in a circle, looking at the mages gathered around us. "Orange is the next highest, and red are the sheriffs. Some high, some maybe middle, but all excellent at fighting with magic. Thankfully, they only have one gold. I was worried they might've found another."

One, while surrounded by this mass of lesser power, was plenty.

"So we're surrounded by a collection of their absolute best fighters, equipped with pre-made spells," I summed up.

"Yep, that about sums it up." Reagan's voice held no humor.

"But why haven't they attacked yet?" I whispered.

"Because they want you alive."

"Well, well, well." A man wearing a long, shiny blue robe emerged from the doorway closest to us. With a withered face fraught with sagging skin, buoyed by a blue scarf, and knobby, gnarly fingers, he looked way up in his years and in need of a comfortable reading chair and a fire, not a magical battle in the middle of the night.

"The High Chancellor," Emery said, anger lacing his

voice.

"Here they said it couldn't be done." The man's voice sounded like old, crackly paper. "But alas, I have caught the famous Rogue Natural and his beautiful assistant."

"Ooh, Penny, I'd be pissed," Reagan said, throwing knife in hand. "By the by, that robe is an *extremely* loud shade of blue. Are you trying to compensate for something? Your equally *extreme* lack of youth, perhaps?"

"She's trying to rile him up," Emery whispered, his eyes roaming. "People do irrational things when they're angry or being badgered. Keep looking for an out."

"I must admit"—the man stopped just in front of the line of mages dressed in purple—"I did not think you'd get through the ward, much less escape my teams' spells. I barely approved the lengthy practice sessions required to prepare the mages to create those monstrosities. Overkill, I thought. And this last bit? Just a precaution. Yet…" He spread his hands, gesturing toward us. "Here we are. Miraculous. Can this all be contributed to two derelict naturals…or is it their silent partner who made the difference?" His eyes slid to Reagan.

"I just carry coffee for the vampire," she said with a steady voice. "He lets me tag along."

"Indeed." A thin-lipped smile spread across the High Chancellor's liver-spotted face. "Be that as it may,

I have a treasure trove here, don't I? Will you come quietly?"

"Dumb questions speak of an inadequate mind," Reagan said.

"Mouthy, for a vampire's slave." The High Chancellor looked off to the side as my phone vibrated again. The shifters' magic pooled around us, their hackles raised. The vampires stood stock-still, studying each movement and word.

"You realize that you have cornered a lot of very dangerous magical beings, right?" Reagan said, her body positioning selling a complete lack of worry. "I mean…" She pointed at me, and I slapped her hand away. I didn't need a spotlight on me. "Just cornering *her* results in some extreme situations. Almost as extreme as that hideous robe. But the Rogue Natural, an elder vampire, several powerful shifters, and the vampire's slave? You planned well, but this is probably your greatest mistake. Do your underlings realize how dull your mind has gotten with age?"

"Silence!" Spittle flew from the High Chancellor's mouth. Their natural shifted in her place. Reagan had clearly done this sort of taunting before. She knew the right buttons to hit.

"Oh." She threw up her hands, twirling her knife through her fingers as she did so. "And I didn't even mention the warrior druid you probably failed to notice. I won't point him out. It'll ruin the surprise."

"That is enough!" The High Chancellor took a step toward us, his face creased with anger.

The mages on the outside of the magic veil started moving—their hands working, their bodies ducking and shifting. Our reinforcements had arrived, only to confront a wall of mage and magic. They'd never get through in time.

The phone vibrated again. "Would someone check that?" I said through my teeth, the pressure a heavy weight on my shoulders. My magic boiling. The storm inside me brewing.

"See? Stage one of Wow, Did You Fuck Up." Reagan pointed at me again.

I slapped her hand away as Emery dug out my phone. "'Stay away from the cavern of buildings,'" he read.

"A little late for that," Reagan muttered.

"This is your final offer. Come quietly, and I will spare you the creative torture we have in store," the High Chancellor said as the people outside the veil moved faster. One of the mages jerked out of sight. A furry head appeared somewhere else, followed by a pair of paws, and someone else was dragged away.

The sound had been muted. We couldn't hear anything outside of our cage. Couldn't feel any new air. No whisperings of magic.

"I think I can counter that spell," Emery said, his eyes leaving the phone and shooting upward. "But it'll take me a minute."

"One minute, or a few minutes?" Reagan murmured without moving her lips.

"Resist, and I will destroy all you hold dear," the High Chancellor said.

"That was a helluva jump there, bub." Reagan hefted her throwing knife, and I held my breath, but she didn't throw it. She twirled it between her fingers again. "Not like we believe you anyway. You'll take Darius and ransom him off to the vampires, right? I mean, we both know he's worth a shitload—"

"Anything else from my mother?" I whispered while Reagan distracted the High Chancellor.

Emery handed over the phone, still looking at the ceiling. "'The easiest spell is above.' Which is no help."

I read the rest of the messages from my mother.

*Find your alleys.*

Alleys? When their formation splits, maybe?

*Reconnect.*

*Reap what you sowed.*

*Callie and Dizzy say they are with the others outside the stronghold. Didn't elaborate. Shifters and vamps clearing away people so they can work on spell. Far wall.*

"What the donkey spit does far wall mean, Mother?" I said, my fingers white-knuckled around the phone.

"Silence her!" The High Chancellor flung out his hand, pointing at Reagan.

"Here we go." Reagan hefted her throwing knife again before hurling it at their natural. Someone in purple dove in front of her, taking the blade and sinking to the ground.

Steve roared, guttural, powerful, and so loud that I accidentally screamed. The mages he faced visibly quailed, one of them dropping her casings and scrambling to pick them up. His muscles bunched and he leapt forward, crashing into a cluster of mages.

Cahal shifted behind me and an arrow was loosed. Red blossomed in the center of a mage's chest, and he looked down in surprise before he slumped. Cahal turned again, another arrow ready, his elbow bumping my arm.

My phone flew out of my hand and skittered across the cracked concrete. As I bent for it, a splash of red caught my eye. To my right, at the corner of one of the buildings encircling us, the veil of magic was discolored. The effect faded but then flared a brighter red and spread.

Callie and Dizzy. They were figuring out how to bust a hole in the spell, starting at the spot where it was likely anchored the weakest. Warmth filled my chest. Experience was a *huge* advantage.

"That wall." I pointed as Emery wove together a

complex spell. "The dual-mages are working on that wall. We need to combine our efforts."

The whisper of a sword leaving a sheath forced me to glance up. Cahal held a wickedly curved blade, black on black, the handle the same color as the steel. It glimmered in the light of the compound, promising death to anyone who dared trifle with him…or me.

A black haze interrupted my vision. Another premonition!

He jerked around, about to deal with a potent spell that had to have come from their natural, as I slammed up shields using Emery's and my survival magic. Ours was much more powerful, as we'd formed a dual-mage pair, and with the added might of the magic I *willingly accepted* from the goblin.

"Keep working," I told him as the spell hit my magical wall and warred with my magic. "We have to get out of here."

Reagan's ice magic poked holes in the walls as the mages encircling us took a step forward. They fired off spells so fast that I couldn't keep enough energy in my magical wall. Cahal moved and flowed like a peaceful stream, batting magic away with his (clearly magical) sword, working so fast that his movements blurred. But he couldn't get a second to charge. Or to throw a knife.

Darius hissed as he sliced through the center of one mage and threw another into a group of them. Shifters tore through people. One took a spell center mass. Another was hit in the rear.

Heart in my throat, I worked faster. Stinging sweat dripped into my eyes. "We're losing."

"We can do it," Emery said, desperation ringing in his voice. "We can do it. We always have before."

Through the roars, snarls, hisses, and screams, I heard rattling across the ground. My phone vibrating against the concrete.

The racket seemed to filter away as I glanced at it. Memories crystalized. Something whispered inside of me.

*Reap what you sowed.*

"The spells," I breathed, colors zipping around us. A vampire fell with black goo spreading out of her chest. "The spells," I said louder, looking around wildly. "When we were first here. My mother said to plant seeds, remember?"

Emery looked up at me with dawning understanding sparkling in his eyes. "Yes."

"Reap what you sowed!" I sank to my knees, putting my hands on the cement. Squeezing my eyes shut, blocking out absolutely everything around me, I opened up my magical senses. The whispers increased in volume, snaking through my blood, wholesome and pure. Nature cried out, begging for release. The magic Emery and I had planted pulsed somewhere deep within the earth, a time bomb.

"Grow," I said, *willing* those spells alive with everything I had. Connecting to the creations we'd made what seemed like so long ago, their imprint still heavily drilled down into the bedrock of the compound. I found a slice of myself stored in that once-barren soil. "Grow."

The ground trembled. Someone screamed. I glanced up to take in the situation. Ice poked more holes in the magical veil, cutting through the layers. The dual-mage pair peeled away the spell's anchor from the building, weakening it. Steve suffered a magical knife to the gut, pushing him back. Darius took a slash to his arm and dropped it to his side, clearly useless.

"Hurry," I begged, bleeding my energy into the spells Emery and I had created all those months ago. Sinking lower and drilling down one more time, hoping we'd done enough to crumble this crooked, corrupt establishment. That we would bring in new life. That a new organization would rise to replace the Guild, spread evenly across the country so no one grouping of power was too big for the area. I wanted to share my love of magic, and the pure bliss it was to be able to work it.

I wanted witches and mages to feel that bliss.

I wanted everyone to heal.

"Almost," Emery said as our survival magic wall dimmed. We didn't have enough energy to keep it going. Spells kept hitting it, further eroding it. "Almost." A whisper.

Eyes closed, heart open, I loosened everything up. I let go of my fear. And the magic poured out, a small stream that became a torrent, a gushing deluge.

The spells we'd planted so long ago burst into the compound. I felt them break through the ground, blasting their way out of the concrete. Taking chunks out of buildings. Fresh, natural beauty rushed up into the air. It spread across the ground and smashed into people. It insisted we pay attention.

I felt a tug on my middle, and warmth flooded my chest. A new feeling rose, welling from somewhere deep down, a chasm formerly untouched and unnoticed.

Emery put his hand to his sternum. "What is…"

"The gods are speaking through you," Cahal said, and his voice seemed to echo across a great chamber. "Let the angels use your voice…and sing."

The feeling rose, tingling hot. Like when I first *stol*—ingested the magic, rainbows painted across my vision, across all of the strife going on around me. The bloodshed.

The two images didn't fit together.

Still the feeling kept building, surging down to my limbs, reaching my neck. My heart started to beat faster. Icy fingers of panic wrapped around my chest.

"Give in to it, Penny," Emery said, crawling to me,

his eyes rooted to mine. "Give in to it. Like when you released that spell. Let it flow."

I swallowed. Fought my fear. And for the second time, held on to him for dear life as magic overcame me and sucked me under.

A shock wave of pure power exploded out from our centers, slicing through the open space. New life was given to the spells we'd seeded so long ago, fighting the decay that had infested the compound.

I could sense that those touched by this new hybrid spell were placed on giant scales, their worthiness weighed and measured. Their deeds were pored over, their hearts analyzed. Those who were found wanting…fell. They breathed one last breath and tumbled to the ground. I couldn't sense the parameters for the spell. I couldn't control who was affected.

Like a receding wave, the circle of magic, spanning a hundred yards or more, pulled back, settled down, and sank back down from whence it came, something I was absolutely sure I had no control over.

"What in the fu—" Emery breathed hard, pushing far enough away from me to look down at his torso. His wide eyes came back up to hit mine. "What just happened?"

"I don't know," I said, trembling. A current drifted by me. A whisper of sweet-smelling air from the wood.

Reality smacked me, and I spun, looking around.

Callie and Dizzy were still working at the spell, the hole they'd formed almost big enough to fit through. Reagan's magic had dimmed, her energy clearly sapped from taking on so many huge spells, and her progress on the magical veil was almost nonexistent. Our tattered party was mostly down, lying on the ground with blood seeping out around them. Of the few still standing, Reagan and Darius, one arm tucked against his side, fought back to back, standing in the middle of a cluster of mages rapid-firing spells.

Mage bodies littered the ground, some with wounds, some deceptively healthy looking. But many of them were still on the attack, their natural among them, now concentrating her force on Reagan. More mages waited outside, probably creating heavy losses for our reinforcements.

"But…that should've done it," I said, tears of frustration in my eyes, struggling to rejoin the fight. "That should've been it."

"It helped," Emery said, back to working on the spell locking us in. "Just a bit longer and we'll be out."

The mages, as a group, stepped forward. "We don't have a bit longer." I shook my head. My mother had never let me down when it really mattered. Never. What else had she said?

*Find your alleys. Reconnect.*

Vision shaky, I scanned the area for alleys. Then

looked around at the people who were still standing. Was her advice rhetorical? "Reconnect—"

My vision skittered across a face. Stopped. Swung back.

I widened my eyes and my stomach fell down through my feet.

"Mary Bell," I said, suddenly out of breath.

She smiled in a knowing way and stepped forward, putting out her hands for the others to cease fire. Her robe was purple. "Give in, Penelope."

"Yes, listen to your friend." I saw the High Chancellor stick his head out of the building door. He'd been hiding this whole time, the coward. How had he not been affected by the weighing spell?

I shook my head as Mary Bell pointedly looked to the side. The mages were slowing, easing up on their spells. Backing away a step.

Then I saw another familiar face and nearly threw up. Rage boiled through me. "John."

He glanced my way before narrowing his eyes at Emery. His robe was purple, too.

"You cannot escape," Mary Bell said, something moving in her eyes. A glint that I recognized. "You must put your hands behind your back, ask your friends to put down their weapons, and give in."

*Find your allies. Reconnect.*

"Fucking autocorrect," I blurted.

Mary Bell nodded, a tiny smile on her face. "Remember what I said." She paused, and her eyes implored me. "You are surrounded. You must give in...now."

That pause. As though she wanted to say *for* now.

*Find your allies. Reconnect.*

I remembered what Mary Bell had said in the bar in New Orleans: "The line between good versus evil is horribly blurred. Good people sometimes do horrible things. Bad people occasionally do good. So trust in the person who shows their good intentions. Do not listen to their words. Watch their intentions."

This was a huge leap of faith, but I wasn't sure I had much of a choice. The dual-mages weren't ready for us. Reagan's magic was so very dim. Her legs shook, and she was all out of snarky comments. Darius bowed just a bit, something he never did. He had to be tired. And that beautiful golden lion lay on the ground, panting shallowly, his tangled mane coated with blood.

"Okay." I dropped my hands and put them behind my back. "You win."

"Penny," Emery said urgently.

"You win," I said louder. "Let my friends go, though. Like Reagan said, Darius is worth money, and I bet you'd be rewarded for releasing Steve the lion, too. The druid has no real part in this. Let them all go. You can have me. I'll do whatever you want."

"No," Emery said, fierce possessiveness ringing through his voice. His magic welled up, sexy and wild, like the smell of rain in the air before a monsoon. He wrapped his arm around my upper body, capturing me to his side. "She will not go with you. You can have me. I have more experience anyway. The same power. She can't even function with normal mage training. She's useless. Take me."

"Now, now, Mr. Rogue Natural…" The High Chancellor stepped out of cover, which had to be the only reason he'd survived the weighing and measuring. "She is new to all this, isn't she? Exceptional, and still new. She can, of course, be trained. And you can be brought to heel. But we aren't barbaric. I ask only that we have some time to sit down and chat. About your futures."

Cold washed through me. Mary Bell glanced over at John, her eyes bright, and my doubt started to grow.

"I know how to work with her," Mary Bell said. John shifted, and something moved from his palm to his fingers. A casing.

"Yes, you were saying." The High Chancellor stepped farther forward and motioned at a burly guy. "Bind them."

John shifted and pinched. The spell slammed into their natural mage. She gasped in surprise. Magic rose within her hands to combat the spell.

Before she could, a throwing knife hilt blossomed

red in the center of her chest. Reagan had finally gotten her shot off.

Mary Bell turned, pinched her own casing, shot the High Chancellor, and swiveled, spraying those near her. The spell took hold, sending a clawing blackness across their bodies that then shrank down, cracking bones.

The High Chancellor wailed before sound cut off. He fell, hitting the ground as their natural sank to her knees.

Surprisingly, unlike him, it wasn't pain etched across her face. It was relief. She was happy this life was failing.

A chill washed over me, but I didn't have time to lament on the life she must've lived. On what Emery and my parents had certainly saved me from.

The mages hadn't even realized a traitor was in their midst before Mary Bell had another casing out, then another, hurrying forward and attacking the circle of mages surrounding us. On the other side, miraculously, John was doing the same thing, shooting the surviving mages, tearing them down with vile spells the left no room for error.

"Hurry, help them," I said, pulling everything I had left to join the barrage against the mages who'd now recovered enough from their shock to reach for their spells.

"We got them. You get that damned magical wall

down," Reagan said, resuming her fight with her sword.

Thank God she didn't need magic to take down an enemy. I yanked Emery toward the tear in the spell.

"What has taken you so long?" Callie demanded through the small hole she'd already created.

"Autocorrect." I worked as fast as my shaking hands would allow, Emery by my side. "Mary Bell is in there. And John—"

"Filthy ingrates," Dizzy said.

"No! They're turning traitor on the Guild. They're helping us!" I mingled our spell with that of the Bankses, enlarging it.

"I did always like John," Dizzy said, changing on a dime. "A good head for strategy, didn't I always say that? Very courageous."

I fanned their spell's power level as Emery added embellishments, our spell work clumsy with our fatigue. The edge peeled back farther, and the rest sizzled. Seams already weakened by Reagan's magic tore. Holes enlarged. Finally, a *pop*, and the whole thing dissipated into the air.

Dizzying relief washed through me. Tears prickled my eyes.

"We've got it," Callie yelled. "We're in!"

A large gray wolf, splattered with blood, one ear half gone, coat covered in blood, shocked me with his powerful dual-colored gaze before running past me to the dying fight within. Vampires, some limping, many splattered or burned, ran in after him, then more shifters.

"Okay, now we're talking," Dizzy said, hurrying in to join the fray.

Limbs trembling and barely able to stand, I still turned back to the fight, intent on giving it everything I had.

That was when the tears started to fall.

The chaotic movement had slowed, and this time, the few who were still standing were on our side. We'd done it. We'd taken on the largest magical organization in the Brink, and we'd won.

Sobs of relief washed through me as Mary Bell and John were backed to the wall, their hands up, cornered by two very large vampires.

"Wait—" I started.

Mary Bell's voice, confident and smooth, rose above the din. "You'll want the vampire behind all of this."

More people slowed, haggard and battle-beaten, and turned toward her. Mary Bell pointed at an open and empty door at the far end of the collection of buildings.

"The High Chancellor never outright mentioned him," Mary Bell said, her eyes gleaming again. And this time I recognized that gleam for what it was—the joy of reliving her youth. Of being in the thick of the action. "But some of the special powers he had, and the little tricks… I've been around a long time. I know a bonded mage when I see one."

Darius and Vlad zoomed forward at the same time, reaching the door at the exact instant another swampy white monster tried to surge out. They pinned him against the wall, their fangs dripping drool, the exhaustion momentarily sapped from their bodies.

The trapped vampire stilled, then relaxed. His skin fuzzed and changed, his body contorting, until a man form stood in its place. Darius and Vlad changed a moment later, still holding the other vampire captive.

"Isn't this a surprise," Vlad said with his light, musical tone. I stepped forward to get a better look, but my legs wobbled and gave out. I spilled onto the ground, my energy at rock bottom and my stomach growling with hunger.

"At least I made it to the end," I muttered, seeing Emery's hand reach down for me.

"We should get you home," he said.

"No, I'm good. I just need a minute—"

Two thick black boots spattered with all kinds of unsavory things hit the ground in front of me. No hand reached down. No command to get up issued forth. But expectation oozed from him.

Cahal stared down at me with a face full of storm clouds. "You made it impossible for me to do my job, Penelope Bristol."

Reagan, sagging against the wall to the right of me, started laughing.

"Why?" I took Emery's hand and let him pull me up. "I'm alive. You're alive. We're good. You fulfilled your duty."

Sparks flared in Cahal's eyes. "We're leaving. Now. I do not want to chance that anything else should arise from this situation."

Without another word, he grabbed me like a sack of potatoes and threw me over his shoulder.

# CHAPTER 37

N EAR DAWN, THE front door burst open and vampires in their human form, wearing rumpled clothing not all the way buttoned or zipped, rushed into the house and out of the failing night. They didn't glance my way or even nod, just turned for the hall without a word, getting to their safe haven.

"Hey," I said, pushing myself to my feet and groaning from the ache in my body.

Cahal stood by the window with his arms crossed, staring at me. His face was stony again, but his eyes told me he wasn't impressed with how the night had gone. The man didn't say much, but that didn't stop a person from knowing exactly what was on his mind.

A few more vampires ran in, these half-dressed, and turned toward the hall.

"What's the news?" I called after them.

Reagan staggered in next, circles under her eyes, her hair disheveled, and tears and burns marring her clothes. She took off her fanny pack and dropped it on the floor before walking past me like a zombie and falling onto the couch.

"I need a whiskey," she said.

Emery and Reagan hadn't done a thing to stop Cahal from dragging me out of the compound. I hadn't had enough energy to kick and scream, let alone zap him, but I had done an awful lot of threatening. When that failed to work, I'd resorted to purposefully annoying him, all the way back to the house in the car he'd chosen at random.

My mother had been intensely relieved to see me home, going so far as to hug Cahal for seeing me back safely. After hearing that our core group was okay, and that I had no other information because I'd been extracted too quickly, she trudged off to bed in exhaustion. Veronica, equally relieved, stayed up with me for a while, but exhaustion finally took her to bed.

I hadn't even tried to sleep. I'd been sitting in the same chair, in utter silence, waiting for the others to come back so I could get some news.

"What happened?" I asked, heading to the door. I stopped when I saw Emery stagger in, his shirt torn and splattered with blood, his face weary.

When he saw me, a smile lit up his face. "Hi, love." He spread his arms to put around me.

I half wanted to deck him for not stepping in when Cahal had ferreted me out of the battle zone, but he looked so happy and relieved. Instead, I fell into his arms and moved with him to the chair. He sank into it with a sigh before taking my hips and directing me onto his lap.

Darius walked in next, in his T-shirt and jeans, his hair styled just so, and only a small scratch on his neck to show that he'd been in a hairy battle near hours before.

"Do you always look perfect?" I demanded, because this was a little ridiculous.

"You should've seen Vlad leave." Reagan shook her head, watching as Darius picked up a remote and started pushing buttons.

Marie and Moss came in next, both stopping in the mouth of the living room and surveying me.

"Penelope, you look a mess," Marie said, and for once I could say, "Look who's talking. Is that a *man's* shirt?"

Her eyes narrowed.

"You fought well," Moss said, sounding like the sentiment had been dragged from his mouth word by word. He nodded, glanced at Darius, and then headed off to the safety of his room, Marie behind him.

Blackout curtains electronically slid across the windows as black shades fitting into the window frames rolled down behind them. Darius glanced at all of us, his eyes lingering on Reagan for a moment, before nodding and moving off toward the kitchen. I noticed his less-than-graceful walk, and his ever-so-slight limp. Even though his arm, which had been useless, was healed, he'd clearly taken a lot of damage if he still wasn't completely restored.

I started when Roger walked in, preceding Callie and Dizzy, who looked as tired as I felt. They nodded at me before sinking into the couch with dual groans.

I'd left the fight before people who were more than twice my age. I doubted I would ever live that down.

"Penny," Roger said, his sweatshirt tight against his muscled chest, his pants hugging too many things much too tightly. Veronica would have had a seizure. "How are you?"

Surprised, I touched my fingers to my chest. "Me?"

He shifted, uncomfortable, probably because he was in Darius's territory, and could feel it. Or, more probably, smell it.

"You were carried out so quickly..." Roger looked me over.

"Oh." I pointed at Cahal. "He was pissed. I didn't need to go. But...well, he's huge."

Roger's eyes swung around the room, belatedly picking Cahal out from the corner where he stood. A crease formed between his brows. "Of course."

"How are you guys?" I forced myself to ask, fear riding my words. Emery squeezed me.

"At last count, we lost forty-three," Roger said.

"Their wounds wouldn't heal…those that had them." He clasped his hands behind his back, pulling at the seams of his borrowed sweats. A troubled expression crossed his face. "Some of them didn't have wounds at all. I couldn't find any damage."

My heart sank. That was probably part of the reason my godly spell hadn't worked as well as I'd hoped. The great scales had taken out a lot of their people…but they'd also taken out some of ours. Sometimes the guys on the good team weren't always good guys.

"I'm sorry," I said. "Thank you, for helping us. Thank you, and their families, for sacrificing them."

His nod was slight. "I wanted to tell you that I have faith in you. I have faith that you"—he glanced at Emery—"and Emery can help build a better Mages' Guild. A fair organization that adheres to the magical rules we must all live by. Should you need my help, or someone to discuss…anything with, don't be afraid to contact me, at any time. I have declared you a pack friend. You are always welcome. And any of us will help you, should you need it."

Warmth infused my chest and tears came to my eyes. "Thank you," I said, touched he would offer me his friendship after losing so many people to the battle.

Roger offered me another curt nod, glanced down the way toward the kitchen, and turned toward the door.

"Roger," Reagan called out. He stopped near the corner, half his body out of sight, and looked at her, waiting. "Thanks," she said. "This wouldn't have been possible without you."

He walked on without a word.

"Did you do something to piss him off?" I asked, confused by his reaction.

"Just the usual." She shrugged. "I'm a pack friend too. He just pretends not to like me."

After Darius came back with drinks—Cahal drank brandy?—he settled down next to Reagan on the love seat, looping an arm around her shoulders. On the couch, Callie's chin slowly fell toward her chest, and Dizzy's head bobbed, his eyes half closed. They were beat.

"So what was the deal with the vampire?" I asked when no one volunteered the information.

Darius sipped his drink. "Marcus. An elder that has been around nearly as long as me. Not as many interests, though. Not as ambitious. For years, we thought he was headed toward a stupor. A sort of vacation from the world and our politics—like Ja before you re-energized her, Penny."

"Your fault, not mine," I said automatically.

"Indeed," Darius said as though something smelled. "It appears he has had his hands in the Mages' Guild for...decades. Now that we know the truth, it is all so clear. He formed an illegal connection with the High Chancellor, manipulated him, and set up a cash cow. Then he sat back with his hand out, watching the money roll in. He didn't have to be ambitious; he merely had to whisper a few suggestions into the ears of his ambitious puppets, goading them toward power, and he could stay idle."

"*Oohhh.*" The reason the High Chancellor had escaped the giant scales clicked. He wasn't in control—his deeds weren't his own. He hadn't been a match for an elder vampire. It also appeared the godly magic didn't affect vampires, because Marcus should've surely been thrown out with the bathwater.

"I am *amazed* you and Vlad missed Marcus's involvement," Reagan said, and I caught a glimmer in her eyes. She was going to rub that in. If Darius hadn't sort of deserved it, I might've felt bad.

"So why did he suddenly start taking a more active interest?" I asked.

"Because suddenly...there was a threat, and a vampire behind that threat," Darius said. "He, through the Guild, has been suffocating my territory, stunting my children's opportunities for growth. No one could stand up to the Guild's power, until you and Emery joined together. Being that you were connected to me..."

"He knew Darius would use you to tear down the Guild, which would allow Darius to expand his business in this area," Reagan finished for him.

I sank bank onto Emery, my mood turning dark.

Emery rubbed my back. "You have to always assume a vampire is using you for something, even if the deal is mutually beneficial."

"Don't feel bad, Penny," Reagan said. "They can't help it anymore. Darius tries to use me on a continual basis. That's why I have to keep him guessing by stealing his money and buying islands for no other purpose than to have them."

Darius froze in place. "What is this, now?"

She grinned mischievously.

"So Marcus launched back into action when he saw his empire being threatened," Reagan continued. "Which means, Penny, you basically woke up two vampires. You kicked them back into the vampires' political arena."

"I didn't. Darius started all of this," I said, sticking with blaming him.

"I knew that strategy couldn't have been the Guild's doing," Emery murmured, circling the bottom of his glass with the brown liquid. "It was too..."

"Good," Reagan said.

"Strategic." Darius curled a strand of Reagan's hair around a finger. "The Guild wasn't used to working at a higher level of strategy. Their timing was suspect."

"They didn't know their enemy," Reagan said.

"Now they do. We did a pretty good sweep, but there is always someone who escapes. Always someone who lives to tell the tale. You ousted yourself tonight, *mon ange*." Darius's voice turned hard. "Tomorrow we're leaving. I'm taking you to a remote location where you can hunt and fish and stay out of the public eye. You can work on your power."

"He means you'll need to lie low." Emery chuckled. "Again. Good luck with that, Darius."

"I can help you train."

I started at Cahal's voice. He was always so still and unimposing that I kept forgetting he was there.

Darius's eyes gleamed. He slowly sipped his cognac, not commenting.

Reagan's mouth curved downward as she surveyed the large, incredibly gifted druid. "That is just enough of a challenge to make me go for it."

"I have seen an Heir train with Lucifer," he said. "Briefly. In glimpses only. I was intrigued—*am* intrigued, I should say, with your power. More so now that I have seen how it complements Penelope's in such a natural way. I did not expect that."

"Penny's...or yours?" Darius asked smoothly, his eyes calculating. He was probably wondering how to tether another asset.

"The Godly Touch, vampire," Cahal said, his voice just as smooth, his eyes fierce. "Or the Angelic Touch, if that is your pleasure. It is one and the same." He paused, his eyes on Darius. "I know what you are thinking. You best be careful. If I hear you've tried to strip this dual-mage pair of their Touch, I will personally kill you, and sprinkle your ashes on the barren waste of an island you do not yet know you own."

"Wow, you're good." Reagan's eyes widened. "How did you know that's the kind of place I bought?"

"I had no desire of the kind," Darius said, completely at ease. Somehow. "But I am as intrigued as you."

"Let it stay that way." Cahal downed what was in his glass. He set it gently to the side. His gaze beat into Reagan next, and she was just as immune to its terror-raising effects as her bond-mate. "Let the vampire take you to a safe location. I will find you there."

With that, he walked out of the room and left the house.

"Okay…goodbye," I called after him. The door latched. "Thanks for helping… That was kind of rude."

"That is how they are," Darius said, unperturbed. "He has the same godly power you do, Penny, that was clear." He stared at nothing for a moment. "In all my many years, I have never seen as many myths and legends come to life as in the last few years. Something is building. Something big. And somehow, you are all a part of it."

Silence hung heavy in the room. Tingles walked

across my skin.

"Nah," Reagan said. "I don't buy it. Darius is just trying to start drama. Like arms dealers who try to start wars so they can make a profit." She looked at me. "Marcus greatly spread the Guild reach in anticipation of this fight. He'll be punished or killed for bonding without asking, but his network will help you. You'll have to turn everyone to a better, less power-hungry way of thinking, but at least you already have a network."

It was true. "Wait…what about Emery? And you? I can't build up a new Mages' Guild on my own. Or at all. I don't know the first thing about leadership."

Emery rubbed his thumb against my thigh. "Roger, Vlad, Darius, Reagan, and I all put it to a vote. This is your project. It will be in your control. Obviously, you'll need help. And you'll need to delegate. But you'll be in charge of bringing it about. You are the only person we would all agree upon, and Vlad just barely went with it."

"As if we would let *him* be in charge." Reagan rolled her eyes.

Adrenaline dumped into my body and all my limbs started trembling. I was unable to handle any more surprises. "Me? No! What do you mean you all voted and now I'm stuck with it? That's not how this is supposed to work!"

"When I first met you," Emery said quietly, "I was

only out to claim vengeance. A piece of me wanted the Guild to be better, but I was blind to the importance of changing it. It was you who calmed me. You who showed me the way. All this time, it has been you who has wanted to do the right thing, above all. To tear it down and build it up again. Your moral compass does not waver. Say what you want about your mom, but she kept you on a path of pure motives. Of inner peace and outward compassion. There is no one else any of us trusts implicitly to see this come about. It has to be you."

I couldn't breathe. My fingers curled into fists. "But...I..."

"Relax. Obviously you'll be guided. We're all going to help...and we're all going to keep an eye on one another. Especially Vlad."

"Nothing has to be decided right now." Darius finished his glass and stood, putting his hand out for Reagan. "Come."

She didn't balk at the command, taking his hand and allowing him to lead her farther into the house. In the back, a bedroom door shut softly.

I couldn't process what they'd just said. I couldn't think that far ahead. So I did what any self-respecting woman would do—I bundled it all up and dumped it into the *ignore* pile. It wasn't a list anymore, it was a whole pile.

"Shall we head to bed?" Emery asked, holding me tightly.

As I nodded, a soft knock sounded at the door. Looking through the peephole with Emery at my back, I felt nervous flutters fill my belly. Mary Bell and John stood on the stoop, tired and bedraggled, but still standing.

Letting out a deep breath, I opened the door. I'd be lying if I claimed not to be worried about an attack.

"Penny," Mary Bell said, that sparkle in her eye. "I won't ask to penetrate your ward. We'll be but a minute."

John looked at her in confusion before scanning the house.

"Um…okay…" I said.

"We're on our way to a hotel. One of Darius's children's," she said. "But we owe you an explanation before we lose sight of each other. I owe you my story."

I leaned against the doorframe, listening.

"We were both approached by the Guild, along with many others. Those not powerful enough—Well, you know what happened to them…"

I swallowed. They were sent to battle Emery, Reagan, and I, and they never made it home.

"John, I, and one other were invited back to Seattle. We were asked to join their fold, as it were. Both John and the other mage had reservations, but only John decided to take them up on it. Despite what he knew of their involvement with you, he was Bambi-eyed and feather-headed."

John shoved his hands in his pockets and shifted away, looking out at nothing. He didn't comment.

"I have been in John's place twice along my life's journey," she continued, leaning forward onto her cane. "I have been seduced by power, only to be left destitute in the fallout. I knew his fate would be the same. So I followed, knowing all along that I wouldn't be able to drag him back out when he realized what he'd gotten himself into—organizations feeding on power and the misfortune of others never let you come and go as you please. Death is often the only way to get out. I followed, knowing we were headed to battle, knowing they were collecting fighters for their side, against you." She held up a hand and smiled. "And knowing I had the experience to manipulate my way anywhere I needed to be. I may have come out disillusioned in the past, but I did learn a thing or two." Her smile faded. "My path was clear. The way to vindication for so many horrible decisions in my past." Her eyes misted. "I still hoped that I could help you, give you a fighting chance at freedom. So I followed John and stayed close, waited for him to suffer at the hands of power in the cold new world he had chosen. When he became disillusioned and wanted out, recruiting him to my cause was child's play. For all his age, he knows nothing of the world."

John let out a disgusted breath, but still he didn't say anything. How he couldn't be embarrassed, I didn't know. I was embarrassed for him.

"So you see, Penny Bristol, I never switched sides. I never doubted you, not even for a minute. I see great things for you. Big things. With the Rogue Natural by your side, helping protect you from the storms life throws at you, you will blaze like the sun." She wiped away a tear with a gnarled finger. "My time for fighting is done, sadly. I am too old. I very nearly didn't make it to the end of this battle. I had to sit down for half of it. But I will be watching you, and rooting for you. And should you need to hear of mistakes, so that you don't have to make them yourself, my door will always be open."

I wiped my tears with the back of my hand before stepping out and giving her a hug. "Thank you," I said. "You saved our lives."

Her smile was serene. "It feels better to be the hero than the villain."

I gave John a shove. "You're still on my poop list."

He frowned at me and rolled his eyes.

Mary Bell patted John's arm as she turned. "I think he has learned his lesson. I also think he'll sleep with one eye open for a very long time."

With that, she moved off to a black sedan Darius

had clearly supplied, John slouching in her wake.

"Okay, bye…" I waved. They didn't notice. "Is saying goodbye after a battle strangely forbidden or something?"

After I closed the door, Emery took me by the hand and led me to our room, leaving the exhausted dual-mages on the couch. "I wanted to ask you something," he said softly, closing the door and wrapping his arms around me.

"Anything." I closed my eyes against his hard chest, breathing in his smell, comfort and cotton.

"Will you visit my brother's grave with me? I want to pay my respects…and introduce you."

I smiled up at him sadly. "It would be my honor."

# EPILOGUE

MY SHOES CRUNCHED against the brittle ground. A white, crooked line stretched across the sky to my right, a scar on the blustery, gray day. My danger sensors blared, warning me that something hunkered in the distance, watching us.

"Don't worry about it," Emery said, looking around before glancing back down at the map in his hands. "It's harmless. We'll hear it coming before we smell it, and that'll be long before it's a real danger."

If he said so.

We'd just come out of the Realm, a magical place with an orange sky and gold dust floating around in the air. I was pretty sure I'd gawked at everything through wide-open eyes. Parts were achingly beautiful, rich with wild magic and twisted woods. Other parts had clearly been manufactured, apparently by elves, and wow, could they do better. They were horrible at mimicking nature. And still other parts were dark and treacherous, making Emery jittery as he tried to watch everything at once.

I'd felt the safest in those areas, though I had had no idea why. Probably insanity.

Three months had passed since we'd blown the Mages' Guild wide open. And I meant *wide* open, literally. The spells I had pulled from the ground had felt destructive, but I didn't understand the magnitude of the damage until I saw it again after the battle. Sides of buildings had blown apart. Sidewalks had crumbled. Debris thrown. The spell hadn't crawled across the ground like I'd felt—it had chewed it up, showing the earth below.

Just two days afterward, in each place I'd planted a spell, a tree had budded, reaching up through the destruction. Emery's buried spell had been similarly destructive, but instead of growing into a tree, it blossomed into a thorny sort of bush with black flowers. He wasn't pleased.

As my friends had threatened, I was placed in charge of the rebuild, though it helped that I had a budget from the Guild's huge coffers to see it done.

The first thing I did was level the place. Everything was taken out, including all the concrete. I had it hauled away to the dump, smoothed the earth over, and planted many more trees and flowers. It would become a sanctuary for all magical people, hosted and overseen by the mages. I wanted to develop a better rapport with other magical people. I wanted to create a community in Seattle that, hopefully, might carry over to other places.

Darius and Vlad called me naive. They called it an experiment. But with Emery at my side, defending my reasoning and my right to follow my vision, they let me go the untraditional route.

Next I'd need to fill the new Mages' Guild. I was still developing a system for that, putting together checks and balances. Applicants would, for now, go through a screening process run by people I trusted. And some I mostly trusted, like Mary Bell. Lastly, they would get to me, and I would do magic with them, using the magic the goblin had probably regretfully *handed over*. Like Cahal could, I could use those to suss out a person's inner qualities.

But that was getting ahead of myself. I wasn't there yet.

I was here, in No Man's Land with Emery, looking for the place his brother had been ambushed and left for dead.

"What would they be doing way out here?" I asked, covering my eyes with my hand to block out the sun. An outcropping of jagged rocks rose up about a hundred feet to our left. A strange creature crouched there, looking at us. I didn't know what he was, other than he'd followed us into the Brink from the Realm. The land stretched out before us, flat and barren, with a few cactuses standing in clusters amid a couple of scraggly bushes. Far to the right appeared to be a town of some sort, with small structures braced against the pale sky. "It looks like desert, almost."

"It is. My brother came through here on camel. I think." He shook his head, walking diagonally right. "As far as I know—and it isn't much, because the Guild tended to destroy evidence of the crimes they committed—he was headed this way to meet a magical prodigy. That's what he'd told me, anyway. Before he left."

I put my hand on his shoulder. He still had down periods, times when he just needed time to himself to reflect, but he'd climbed out of the depths of his despair. Now that things had calmed down for us, and he wasn't so anxious about the future, he laughed all the time. He joked and smiled. It was as though a weight had been lifted off him.

"What's…" He stopped next to a cactus and a circle of stones, looking down in confusion.

I joined him, immediately feeling the vibe of a sorrowful power stone, missing…something.

A stone about the size of my fist sat in the middle of the circle. While it had likely appeared as mundane and innocuous as Emery's Plain Jane, it now showed the effects of years spent in the desert sun. The effect was interesting, with unique color changes highlighting the little crags and flats.

"He..." Emery took a step back, his eyes glued to the rock. He glanced up and looked around before returning his attention to it. "He used to carry a stone about that size. Carried it everywhere. Like you do..." An incredulous expression drifted across his face as his beautiful eyes hit mine. "I didn't know much about power stones at the time, just that they existed and I could sap power from them, but he..." His voice cracked and he put a fist to his mouth. "He had a favorite. This... Was it this one? But how..."

The creature hiding among the rocks, a bent thing with horns on its head and out of the sides of its mouth, watched us.

"How long has that creature been following you around?" I asked, not pointing, lest it decide that I was inviting it to fight. I'd had a similar experience with a minotaur on the way through the Realm.

Emery straightened up and turned, his eyes going distant. They focused quickly, and a look of knowing came into his eyes. He glanced back down at the rock and shook his head. "Couldn't be..."

But his ragged sigh said he knew better.

"Years," he said softly.

That creature, whatever it was, clearly knew enough about Emery—and his brother—to know he'd want this power stone. A misunderstood guardian angel of sorts, he'd built a shrine for it.

"The stone is sad," I said quietly, looking at it. "It misses something. Or someone."

Emery nodded.

"You should take it with you. Your brother wouldn't want it left here. Not if it was his favorite. I'd hate for Red Beryl to be left on its own. Mr. Happy-Go-Lucky, however..."

He turned to me in a rush, putting his hand on the side of my face and tilting my head up. His lips met mine and lingered. Eventually he backed off just a bit so he could look down into my eyes. Then he sank to one knee in front of me.

"Penelope Bristol, will you marry me?" He took the ring box out of his pocket. "You can put the ring on your other hand and hide the engagement for as long as you want, but will you marry me?"

I smiled, elated. I sank down with him, throwing my arms around his neck. "Yes! And it'll go on the correct hand. My mother can just deal."

"That should make me happier, but..." He laughed, taking the ring out with shaking hands and slipping it onto my finger. This time, I let him slide it all the way down. It fit perfectly and vibrated against my skin pleasantly. "I love you. You are a gift that I don't deserve, but will gladly accept and cherish for the rest of my life."

He stood then, my hand clasped in his, and slowly

bent for the power stone. Gingerly, he picked it up and turned it over, studying every inch. A tear leaked down his cheek and he quickly wiped it away with the back of his hand.

"You lost your brother. It's okay to let go," I said softly. "I won't tell."

He laughed. "I don't care if you tell. I just know he would've made fun of me for it. Here."

"No." I didn't take the power stone from his hand. "You're—"

"I can't feel their personalities. I take power when I need it. I have no relationship with them. My brother wouldn't have wanted it left here, no, but he certainly wouldn't have wanted it in my hands. I got a thumping every time I snatched it and threw it in the yard. Or through a window. Or into a lake." He sucked in a breath, his eyes glittering and his smile beaming. "He gave me a black eye when I threw it into the lake. It wasn't even that far in…"

I took it from his hands, and my first impression was *what the hell?*

"It might need a moment to warm up to me," I said delicately, and moved things around so I could stuff it into the largest compartment of my utility belt. Even then, I couldn't close the flap. "This might need to go to Reagan. She'd have room in her fanny pack."

Emery smiled as he rubbed my back, looking down

at the circle of stones again before glancing behind him at the creature hiding in the rocky cropping. "I'd always thought it was waiting to kill me. I might've developed my keenest magic trying to get it off my trail."

"In a weird way, maybe it was your brother protecting you."

Emery barked out a laugh. "Yeah, seems about right. He was probably laughing down at me the whole time."

I rubbed his back and laid my hand on the stone within my compartment. It gave me a *get the hell away* pulse. "All right." I removed my hand.

Emery stepped away, his gaze going to my utility belt. "Of all the things I expected, that wasn't one of them." He sighed, looking down at the circle of stones, and his arm came around me again.

"Conrad…I wish you could've met Penny. The two of you are much more alike than you and I ever were. You two would have gotten along great, but I probably would have been the odd one out."

I hugged Emery tight. "He's lying. I'd be the odd one out. Luckily, I'm used to it…"

Emery chuckled and exhaled a trembling breath, and I knew he was saying goodbye.

Emotion surged through me, adding moisture to my eyes. Slowly, he turned us, sad peace infusing his eyes. "I've really missed him," he said, his voice quavering. "I'll miss him always."

"You have his memory. And now you have his moody power stone. You can guard those like treasures until you see him again."

Emery hugged me tightly and nodded, before slowly leading me back to the scar in the sky, our entrance to the Realm.

SOME AMOUNT OF time later, which was impossible to tell when using the various paths in that strange, magical place, we stepped out into the countryside. Not the Seattle countryside, where we'd been staying, working on my training, and trying to work on the new version of the Mages' Guild, but a foreign place with rolling hills covered in grapes and a dark sky dotted with pricks of light.

"Are we"—I hesitated to say "lost," since Emery didn't know that word unless someone else was leading—"taking a detour?"

"Just over here. I know I told you we'd go to a beach, but I thought maybe you'd like this place a little better." He led me up a lovely stone path through fragrant rosebushes. A little stone cottage overlooking vineyards sat on a small hill. He brought out a rustic bronze key and fit it into the lock before turning. The rusty handle clicked as it flipped over, opening into a somewhat musty dwelling. He put his hand on my back and escorted me inside while he flicked a switch.

Light showered the simple accommodations—the round wood table, brick-red floor tiles, and a couple pieces of overstuffed furniture.

Magic flowered, hot and stinging, and I noticed someone sitting at the kitchen table, delicate fingers tracking the stem of a glass of deep red wine.

"Hello," said Ja, the extreme elder vampire whom I'd accidentally roused from her stupor.

Emery shoved me behind him. "Watch our six," he instructed me. "What are you doing here, Ja?"

Her smile was shy and sexy and predatory all at the same time. "I come to pay homage to a great player in the game. Please, make yourselves at home." She gestured us toward the table, extremely hospitable even though it wasn't her dwelling.

Emery didn't step forward. "This is Darius's house. Why are you in it?"

Her smile grew. "I just told you. Please, grab a glass of wine. Darius keeps the very best collection. Did you know he has secreted his bond-mate away from the world? Isn't that strange? With a potent power such as hers, one would think he'd want to show her off."

"Reagan has no manners," I said, slipping around Emery and heading for the wine. I didn't know much about Ja, but I knew when she was dangerous to us in the moment. She was controlled and calculating, which meant the danger she posed was more of a long, slow burn. "Darius needed to give her a boot camp," I said, filling two glasses.

"I hope not. I found her crudeness rather charming. She embraced her barbarianism." Ja draped her arm over the back of her chair, looking relaxed. The opposite of Emery. "I rather enjoy the world of today. No false pretenses. No subtle charades. Industrialized nations put all their feelings on display. It takes so much less effort to read people. What a haze I'd been in these last…" She glanced at the sky. "I can scarcely count the years. Hundreds, it must be."

I sat gingerly at the table with my glass of wine. I put Emery's in front of the open chair, hoping he'd take the hint and sit down to it.

"I heard all about the attack on the Mages' Guild," she said, her smile demure. "My, how the men in this day and age will gush in response to the simplest flattery. It's almost boring. But the smell…" She wrinkled her nose. "I've never been one for animals."

Yikes.

I clasped my hands on the table, not commenting. What could I possibly say? She had an agenda, and I needed to let it play out. I'd met with Vlad a couple times. I now knew what most vampires were like. And also that Darius was way different than a normal elder. Why? No one would tell me, or else they didn't know.

"*Someone's* magic is extraordinary. Maybe more than one someone?" Sparks of fire danced in her dark eyes as she looked at me squarely. "You are a natural, you are a dual-mage, but…that isn't all, is it?"

Silence was key. No facial expression. No clenched jaw or clasped hands. That failing, I could steal Emery's approach and invite thunder clouds to roll across my face.

Her smile curved her lush lips. "Well. We all have secrets, after all. And Reagan most of all, I think. I had a suspicion. I now have a new one. Isn't magic fun? So many intrigues. So many surprises. I'm glad I took a break. I was so bored before. But not now."

"I would like to have a quiet night with my future wife, Ja. What is it you want?" Emery asked, and a sharp, heady burst of power filled the room.

Butterflies filled my stomach. Something about his assertive side unleashed his power. It danced with mine, spreading a tingling sensation through my body and dropping heat into my center.

"I apologize. Where are my manners?" She took a sip of her wine, closing her eyes to savor it. "Just this." Her beguiling gaze hit me. "I am in awe of you, Penelope Bristol. I had intended to gain a little favor by sending you the absolute best in the business. The very best. Someone highly sought after and extremely hard to get. After calling in a few favors, I procured him."

"Cahal," I said, fitting it all together. "You wanted to make sure I lived so you'd have a shot at controlling me."

"Oh no…" The predator in her flashed through her dark eyes. "Not controlling you, surely. Working *with* you. Helping you." I didn't believe her for a second. "But the druid refunded the deposit. Canceled the contract."

I frowned at her. "What now?"

Her smile stretched, a thinly veiled blade. She wasn't pleased. "You have an admirer, Penelope. Maybe a peer?" That was a probing question if ever there was one. She was asking about the magic the goblin had *inadvertently donated* to me.

"In fairness, I dragged him through situations that he wasn't really able to work in," I said. "We got trapped, and—"

"But you came out alive. He should have taken the funds. But he didn't." She took another sip of wine, then licked her lips. It curled my stomach. "He formed an attachment to you. Which I find interesting. He hasn't formed an attachment in years, I've heard. He's long since given up looking for his natural pair…his way out of his profession. And yet, suddenly, he finds a heart with you?"

"I have a natural pair." I pointed at Emery, still by the door. "I can't have two. Because of the word *pair.*

Which means *two*."

"Yes." Her eyes roamed over me. Seeing a riddle, I had no doubt. "Well." She finished her glass of wine, sat for a moment to appreciate it, and then removed her delicate fingers from its stem. "At any rate, I applaud you on your victory, Penelope. It is well earned."

She rose from her chair gracefully, nodded to me, half curtsied to Emery, and walked out the door.

He watched her as she disappeared into the darkness, and then closed the door and stared at the lock. He turned it, though vampires could open any locked door, and I could tell he was thinking about wards.

Yes, those would be going up.

"She sent him," I said as Emery sat opposite his glass of wine. His shoulders were still tight. "We might have guessed."

"Darius did," Emery said, his tone dark. "At first he thought it was Vlad, but Vlad's reaction didn't fit. So the only one left, in his mind, was Ja. She has an attachment to you."

"She thinks she owes me."

"Never cash in on that debt."

"Clearly she tried to force me to."

A smile curled Emery's lips. "Cahal must've known she would. He's been around too long not to know how vampires work. He gave you a nod with his refusal to take payment. He gave you an out."

"I owe him a great debt, not just for that, but for helping. We barely pulled through. Without everyone on our side…*everyone*, we wouldn't have."

He nodded and scooted his chair closer to me. "He didn't have to help for most of it. He wanted to. We'll send Reagan an expensive bottle of whiskey and put a note on it to say it's a thank-you gift for Cahal. She'll have to give it to him when he eventually shows up, if he does."

I laughed. "Perfect. And he will, because he said so, and they can't lie. So she'll have to sit and look at it."

He leaned back and his eyes took on a deep look. "Thank you. Again. For…my life. For…my return to reality. What you've given me is priceless."

I made him scoot closer so I could lean against his body. "You opened up my whole world. Let me find my feet, then helped me find my wings. Thank *you*."

He squeezed me tight. "Safe at last."

I closed my eyes to savor those words, my heart full of love and hope. "For now, at least, and that's what matters."